Praise for *This Time Next Year*

"A funny, pull-at-your-heartstrings read, this is the perfect companion for curling up with hot chocolate and a blanket. Unashamedly romantic and packed full of holiday sparkle, it's a hug in book form."
—Josie Silver, author of *One Day in December*

"[A] cute contemporary romantic comedy . . . The characters in this page-turning novel are richly drawn and transform substantially, especially Minnie, and all suggest that maybe happy ever after is up to us." —NPR Books

"If you make time for just one holiday read this year, make it Sophie Cousens's *This Time Next Year.*" —*PopSugar*

"With its distinctive British charm and New Year's Eve midnight magic, this swoony debut holiday love story is about two people whose paths have crossed numerous times." —*Parade*

"[A] touching debut . . . Flashbacks to New Year's past and subplots . . . add depth, while hilarious secondary characters inject levity in just the right places . . . Cousens's debut is ripe with both emotional vulnerability and zaniness." —*Publishers Weekly*

"A brilliantly written story about love, redemption, friendship, and self-empowerment . . . This book is an absolute delight . . . [and] a feel-good tale to cozy up with." —*San Francisco Book Review*

"*This Time Next Year* is a clever, offbeat romantic comedy . . . Cousens's colorful, quirky cast becomes embroiled in big, memorable scenes . . . Rom-com readers will revel in Cousens's wry, lively story, which probes themes of self-discovery, acceptance and forgiveness, and the abiding nature of friendship." —*Shelf Awareness*

Praise for *Just Haven't Met You Yet*

"Sweet [and] funny . . . It's just the story to offer a little romantic escapism during the holiday season." —CNN

"Hilarious moments, heartfelt charm, dynamic characters . . . this rom-com has it all!" —*Woman's World*

"Cousens creates a world full of lovable characters who are all trying their best to be happy despite life's many obstacles. Although all the characters are dealing with their own hardships, Cousens imbues the entire story with an uplifting sense of hope . . . The Jersey setting creates a cozy, windswept background to the deliciously slow-burn romance. A warm, witty, and absolutely charming seaside holiday that's perfect for fans of Sophie Kinsella." —*Kirkus Reviews* (starred review)

"Appealing . . . Humor and poignancy keep the pages turning. Fans of Sophie Kinsella and Josie Silver will find plenty to enjoy." —*Publishers Weekly*

"A wonderfully layered story of love and loss . . . This poignant romantic comedy follows the journey of an English woman discovering there's more to herself and her family history than she knew." —*Shelf Awareness*

"At times heartbreaking and incredibly hopeful, Cousens's delightful read is a sweet romance that gives Laura the freedom to grow as a character. Readers of Jill Mansell or Mhairi McFarlane will definitely enjoy." —*Library Journal*

"For the friend who loves curling up at home, pick up *Just Haven't Met You Yet*, a fun meld of drama and romance." —*Parents*

"Exactly the sort of fun, pacy, beautifully written romantic story I needed." —Lorraine Brown, author of *Uncoupling*

Before I Do

Also by Sophie Cousens

This Time Next Year

Just Haven't Met You Yet

Before I Do

A Novel

Sophie Cousens

G. P. PUTNAM'S SONS • NEW YORK

PUTNAM
— EST. 1838 —
G. P. Putnam's Sons
Publishers Since 1838
An imprint of Penguin Random House LLC
penguinrandomhouse.com

Library of Congress Cataloging-in-Publication Data

Names: Cousens, Sophie, author.
Title: Before I do / Sophie Cousens.
Description: New York : G. P. Putnam's Sons, [2022]
Identifiers: LCCN 2022027610 (print) | LCCN 2022027611 (ebook) |
ISBN 9780593539873 (trade paperback) | ISBN 9780593539880 (ebook)
Subjects: LCGFT: Novels.
Classification: LCC PR6103.O933 B44 2022 (print) |
LCC PR6103.O933 (ebook) | DDC 823/.92—dc23/eng/20220613
LC record available at https://lccn.loc.gov/2022027610
LC ebook record available at https://lccn.loc.gov/2022027611

Printed in the United States of America
1st Printing

Book design by Elke Sigal

For Tim

"Happiness in marriage is entirely a matter of chance."

—Jane Austen, *Pride and Prejudice*

Before I Do

Prologue

Audrey, barefoot and in shock, stumbled out of the church, alone. Gripping the hem of her white silk dress, she lifted it away from the damp paving stones of the porch. She had kicked off her shoes at the altar, unable to run in three-inch heels, but without them, the wedding gown was exactly three inches too long. Stepping into daylight, she was greeted by a brilliant flash. She blinked and then looked in confusion at the photographer's assistant, a gangly man in his early twenties with a slicked-down fringe. Why was he taking a photo now? Why was he even out here? The service wasn't due to end for another twenty minutes. Her heart pounded in her chest; she couldn't think clearly. *What would happen now?*

The photographer stood frozen to the spot, his Olympus camera held aloft. As they locked eyes, she shot him a questioning frown, then watched his expression change from concentration to concern as he took in her shoeless state, her smudged eye makeup, and finally the rising red lump on her left temple. Audrey followed his gaze down to her toes, protruding from beneath the dress. Her nails had been painted a rose hue called "Pinking of You." She'd found the name funny at the time.

"Audrey, why are you out here?" came a voice from behind her. She turned to see Paul, the best man and her close friend. He had followed her out of the church. "You should go back inside."

"I'm fine," she whispered hoarsely. She didn't want to be in the church.

Audrey could hear sirens. Blue lights flickered in the distance. Wedding guests started to spill from the church behind Audrey and Paul now. Her almost mother-in-law, Debbie, could still be heard wailing from within. Then the paramedics were at the gate.

"He's in there," Audrey said, needlessly pointing toward the church door.

Two men in green uniforms ran with a stretcher down the gravel path between the crooked gravestones. One gave her a sympathetic nod as he passed.

Paul was still in best-man mode, giving people instructions, ushering people out of their way. Noise and chatter and confusion filled the space that had been still and silent only moments before.

Audrey lifted a hand to her forehead, her head spinning. She felt the scene playing out at the wrong speed; one moment, everything looked slow, the air taking on a treacly quality, all motions labored and delayed. The next, everything zipped by, faces whipping around, voices rapid, like a tape on fast-forward. She saw her stepfather, Brian, walking toward her in slow motion. She couldn't talk to him. She couldn't talk to anyone. Her eyes darted from left to right as she looked for somewhere to go. She let the wind take her around the side of the church, the soft ground wetting her feet, her broken bouquet trailing from her hand.

Audrey found a small patch of woodland between the churchyard and the road that ran through the Millward estate. She sat down on the ground with her back against a tree, not caring about the damage it might do to her white gown. Now that she was alone and still, the pace of real life was restored, and Audrey finally had a moment to think. Had it been inevitable that it would end like this? Where had everything started to go wrong? Had it been at eight minutes past eight last night, at the rehearsal dinner? Or had today's events been set in motion many years before?

One Day Before I Do

ے۔

"*W*ho will be walking the bride down the aisle?" Reverend Daniels asked, looking between Audrey at the altar and her mother, Vivien, on the front pew. He seemed unsure whom he should be deferring to on the matter.

Josh reached out for Audrey's hand and gently squeezed it, a silent show of support.

"She will have two people walking her down the aisle, Reverend," Vivien announced, taking this as her cue to stand up and stage-manage the proceedings. "Her two stepfathers, Brian and Lawrence."

Brian and Lawrence were sitting at opposite ends of the front pew. They simultaneously raised a hand and then cautiously side-eyed each other. Vivien would have preferred her current husband, Lawrence, to be the one to escort the bride down the aisle, but Audrey had expressed a preference for Brian, who had played a prominent role in her life growing up. Audrey also wanted Vivien to know that the men she had dismissed from her life would not be so easily lost from her own.

"They'll take one arm each," Vivien told the reverend, glancing back to Audrey.

"Well, that is a lovely idea," said Reverend Daniels, tapping his fingertips together nervously. "But as you can see, the aisle at St. Nicholas's is rather on the narrow side. We've had problems in the past with, er . . . slightly larger family members being able to walk two abreast. I'm not sure we'd manage a three-way."

Josh let out a strangled-sounding cough, and Audrey pursed her lips to keep from laughing.

Vivien paced the width of the aisle, wringing her hands as she realized that the reverend was right. Though Vivien was petite, she walked with the confidence of someone used to commanding a stage and an audience. Her brown and caramel highlighted hair was pinned back into a bun and shone like a golden flame above her simple long-sleeved black dress. Her professionally plumped lips sported their trademark slash of red.

"Maybe a relay? Audrey could walk twice," Josh suggested. The note of sarcasm made her suspect he'd had a few pints at the ushers' lunch earlier.

"Then she'd end up at the wrong end," Lawrence pointed out, his white wispy eyebrows dancing in confusion.

"Josh." Audrey shot him a playful frown and shook her head. Luckily, Vivien hadn't heard him. Her focus was on the offending aisle, which was just sitting there, failing to be wide enough.

"I think the whole idea of being 'given away' is preposterous," said Hillary, who sat with his feet up on the pew in front of him, reading a copy of *Playbill* magazine. "Can't you just walk yourself down the aisle, Auds?"

"No, she can't. That would look negligent, as though we

have failed to come up with a respectable escort," Vivien shot back, her eyes darting disapprovingly to Hillary's shoes on the pew.

"I fear we'll have to move on from the entrance," Reverend Daniels suggested with a nervous laugh. "I have another family coming in at seven thirty to discuss a christening."

"Reverend, we can't move on until we get this right. I do wish I had been forewarned about the inadequacy of the aisle," asserted Vivien.

Audrey rubbed a fist against her chest, which had been feeling tight all day. This wedding was making her feel like a plate spinner, watching to see which plate was going to fall, then running to keep it turning. She wished her best friend, Clara, were here. Clara was good at keeping all the plates in the air.

"Maybe Brian could walk me the first half and Lawrence the second," Audrey suggested diplomatically.

Vivien nodded, satisfied with this solution, and Hillary muttered in a singsong voice, "Crisis averted."

"Excellent plan. So we'll position Dad Two on this pew here," said the reverend, scurrying down the aisle to mark the row with a red hassock, "and Dad One by the door." Audrey winced at his choice of language. She had always called her stepfathers by their first names, as she called her mother by hers. Vivien objected to the labels of "Mum" or "Mummy" on the grounds that they were ordinary and reductive.

"It's Brian and Lawrence," Brian said, gently correcting the reverend, and Audrey gave him a grateful nod. Not for the first time today, she felt wistful about her father's absence. What would he make of all this—the church, the wedding, the man she was about to marry?

"Most brides don't like to rush the entrance. The cadence

of your step should be: step, feet together, step, feet together," Reverend Daniels said while illustrating the rhythm of the walk to Audrey. "That way, your guests will have enough time to admire you from every angle."

Vivien started to imitate the desired step cadence.

"It reminds me of doing the cha-cha on *Strictly*," she said, and then started shimmying her hips and cha-cha-ing up the aisle. Vivien was always performing. She was the sort of person who narrated the stage directions of her life and would end arguments by saying, "And scene," before taking a small bow and leaving the room.

"Would you like to practice?" the reverend asked.

"I'm good," Audrey said briskly. "Step, feet together, step, feet together. Got it."

Josh reached out and started massaging her shoulders. She dipped her head to one side, leaning into his touch, his firm hands warm against her bare neck.

"Audrey can hardly walk in a straight line at the best of times. I'd make her practice if I were you," piped up Hillary, giving her a sly wink.

"Hillary has a point," said Vivien with a flourish of her hand. "What's the point in having a rehearsal if you don't rehearse? Come, come, it's your starring moment." She waved to Audrey and then snapped her fingers for Lawrence to sit in the marked pew, before beckoning Brian to take his position at the church doors.

"Life is not a dress rehearsal, until it is!" called Josh's mother, Debbie, from the back of the church. Debbie had been given the task of checking for drafts, moving herself around the pews, working out which seats would be most appropriate for elderly relatives to occupy. She was using an intricate color-coded system of stickers that the ushers would be briefed on later. A blue sticker meant "drafty, no one over seventy to sit here," white meant "adequate," and neon yellow meant "prime seating, little to no draft." Clearly the system was needlessly complex, but Debbie was having such fun "feeling useful" that it was kinder just to let her cover the beautiful church in hundreds of hideous stickers.

"First rule of show business, Auds, give the people what they want," Hillary said as Audrey shuffled past his pew and flicked his magazine. She thought he was enjoying his role as heckling audience member far too much. Hillary had been Audrey's nanny growing up. Her mother didn't believe in employing professional nannies—"predictable, dull people." Instead of qualified childcare, she had preferred to hire out-of-work actors to supervise young Audrey. Her logic was that actors would have more energy and enthusiasm for the task. Plus, people in the arts would have more interesting things to teach her child than "finger painting and 'Baa Baa Black Sheep.'"

While some of her earlier nactors (nanny actors) had been more competent than others, Hillary had been a great success and had become a permanent fixture in Audrey's life. Vivien held up their bond as a validation of her offbeat childcare choices. The fact that Audrey, to this day, still didn't know the words to a single nursery rhyme and had never once done a finger painting was beside the point.

"Where are the bridesmaids?" asked the reverend.

Audrey felt heat rising up her neck. *What kind of bride shows up to the rehearsal without any bridesmaids?*

"One of the two should be here any minute," she said.

"Reverend!" Debbie called from the back of the church. "This vent on the floor here is causing *such* a draft. I think we'll need to block it up somehow."

The reverend gave a resigned sigh, suddenly looking every

one of his seventy-six years, but he graciously put down his order of service and marched back up the aisle to inspect the offending vent. Josh's father, Michael, held his phone aloft and mouthed to Josh, "I'm just going to check the weather forecast," which everyone knew was code for "checking in on the test match."

Josh reached an arm around Audrey's waist. "Having fun yet? Hey, don't look so worried—it's all going to be fine."

Looking up into Josh's warm brown eyes, this face that she knew so well, she instantly felt more at ease. This was what this whole weekend was about—her and Josh, Josh and her; the rest was merely wrapping paper.

As if reading her mind, Josh said, "Imagine us here this time tomorrow." He dropped his eyes to her jeans and white blouse. "I like the dress. Red, bold move."

"You really think Vivien would have sanctioned a red wedding dress?" said Audrey, feeling herself smile.

Josh was dressed in his usual weekend attire of dark blue jeans and a well-ironed shirt in a pastel hue—today's choice was pink. He looked good in most clothes, with his broad shoulders and narrow waist, especially with the tan he'd picked up from his recent work trip to Singapore. Josh had been traveling a lot recently. In the three years they'd been together, his career had taken off almost as fast as Audrey's had stalled. He'd been in the same job since university, steadily promoted up the ladder, given more and more responsibility. Since dropping out of university seven years ago, Audrey had been employed by dozens of different places. Barista, waitress, photographer, receptionist, PA, dog walker—you name it, she'd done it. She was currently working at a theater box office, where the height of her responsibility was knowing the log-in for the online ticketing system and looking after the key for the cloakroom (which she'd currently misplaced).

"Well, you know I don't care what you wear," Josh said. "As long as you look like you—and you don't let your mother draw those frightening eyebrows on you." He gave a comical grimace and then bent down to kiss her lightly on the nose.

With the air vent inspected and a note made to find a mat to cover it before tomorrow, the reverend hurried back to reclaim his position at the front of the church.

The rehearsal seemed to go on and on. Though Audrey was a central part of it, at times she felt strangely removed. How many brides had stood in this exact spot in the life span of this fifteenth-century church? How many times had Mendelssohn's "Wedding March" been played? How many readings of Genesis, chapter two, verses eighteen to twenty-four? How much of this wedding was unique to Audrey and Josh at all?

It was her own fault. She'd been overwhelmed by the sheer number of decisions to make. Did she want wildflowers or roses? Church ceremony or civil? Band or DJ? What color would the bridesmaids wear? What food would they eat? Audrey knew she could be indecisive at the best of times, so she had ended up asking her mother for help. Vivien had been married five times, so was something of an expert when it came to weddings. But her strong opinions, coupled with Audrey's indecision, meant Audrey now had a wedding more aligned with her mother's tastes than her own.

Just as Audrey was reflecting on this, the side door of the church banged open and Clara burst through. Finally.

"Sorry I'm late. What have I missed?" Clara announced, dumping her handbag on one of the pews.

"Thank the Lord, finally someone interesting to talk to,"

said Hillary in such a charming, light manner that no one would take it as the insult it so clearly was.

"And this is . . . ?" the reverend asked Audrey.

"My maid of honor," Audrey said, feeling some tension dissipate as she watched Clara sprint up the aisle wearing a black and white striped jumpsuit with bright orange heels. She ran to give Audrey a hug, jumping up and down in excitement.

"Technically, matron of honor," Clara told the reverend, "but that makes me sound old and fierce, so I'm sticking with 'maid.' Sorry, I had a childcare crisis, but I'm here now, appendage free, and I'm even wearing a proper bra, which is pretty much the highlight of my year. Where do you want me?"

"Here," said Josh, pulling Clara in to kiss her on the cheek. "I'm glad you've arrived. Audrey couldn't relax without you; I could see her getting jumpy."

As he released Clara from the hug, there was a loud thud from the back of the church. Everyone turned to see where the noise had come from, and all eyes fell on a small black object now curled in the middle of the aisle.

"Heavens above, what was that?" Vivien cried, her voice pitched with panic.

Josh's paternal grandmother, Granny Parker, was sitting quietly on one of the back pews, absorbed in a Jilly Cooper novel. If the object had fallen just a foot to the left, it would have landed on her head. She calmly peered over her book at the shape on the floor beside her. As a hardy Yorkshire woman, Granny Parker was not easily rattled. A few years ago, so the story went, she had witnessed a mugging outside the Co-op in Huddersfield. She'd marched straight into the tussle and clunked the aggressor over the head with a plastic bag full of library books. Thanks to Granny Parker's preference for a chunky hardback, the mugger was rendered unconscious and later held accountable for his crimes.

"It's a bat," Granny Parker said, coolly inspecting the object beside her. "A dead bat."

The reverend clutched a hand to his chest.

Debbie started shrieking. "A bat? A dead bat? Where did that come from? We can't have dead bats raining down on guests tomorrow!"

"Oh dear, oh dear," said the reverend, shaking his head. "The bell tower does have a few in residence, but we've never seen them in the church, certainly not when people are in attendance."

"That's a bad omen if ever I saw one," announced Granny Parker as she looked across the church at Audrey. "A bad, bad omen."

"Granny Parker thinks everything is a bad omen," said Debbie briskly. "She thought the M25 Eastbound being closed was a bad omen. She thought this morning's rain was a bad omen."

"I know a bad omen when I see one," said Granny Parker darkly.

"Is it time to start drinking yet?" said Hillary, standing up and looking at his watch with a dramatic stretch of his arms.

The reverend nodded, no doubt keen to dismiss everyone so he could deal with the dead bat before his christening party arrived.

"Really, Reverend, this won't do," said Vivien, striding across the church to inspect the offending article herself. "Do you think it died of natural causes? Or are we to expect a whole colony of corpses tomorrow?"

"I'm not sure I'm qualified to do a postmortem," the reverend said with a smile.

"Can we fumigate the church tonight? Flush them out?" Debbie suggested.

"They're a protected species, I'm afraid. We can't interfere with them at all." The reverend bent down to inspect the bat more closely. "I can assure you, this has never happened before."

"Perhaps we need a new category of sticker to denote 'high risk of death by bat'?" Hillary suggested, biting his lip.

"A nasty, bad omen," repeated Granny Parker, slamming her novel shut with a thwack. "This would not happen in a Yorkshire church."

"Look, it's got gray whiskers, it probably died of old age," said Josh, who had now joined the bat-inspection party.

"I'm not sure that's going to fit in my dustpan," the reverend said nervously.

"Well, it certainly can't stay there!" cried Vivien.

"Don't get too close," Josh said, ushering everyone to stand back. "We don't know what diseases it could be carrying. Reverend, do you have any gloves, fire tongs? Anything we could use to safely dispose of it?"

"Josh to the rescue," Clara sang quietly to Audrey. They looked at each other and, without saying a word, communicated that this might be a good opportunity to exit via a side door and leave the bat-disposal project to those better equipped to handle such things.

2

One Day Before I Do

⤜⤝

*T*he air outside the church felt fresh and clean compared to the musty, stale air within.

"Well, I thought this wedding might be batshit crazy, but I didn't think there would be *actual* bat shit," Clara said as she and Audrey climbed into into the front of Clara's Škoda Karoq. "I love that Josh was straight in there ready to dispose of the body like CSI Batman. He thrives in a crisis, doesn't he?"

"What are these?" Audrey asked, looking back at the two bouquets of wildflowers currently strapped into the children's car seats.

"I bought them for you. Roses might be the official flowers decreed by Vivien, but I know you liked the wildflowers too, so I thought I'd cover all bases and get you these for your bridal suite."

Audrey felt a sting behind her eyes as the rising tide of relief at having Clara there threatened to spill out. She blinked away the feeling and leaned her head across the car, resting it on her friend's shoulder.

"Clara, that is so sweet of you, thank you."

"Are we waiting for the others, or shall we head straight to the pub?"

"Let's go. Josh is going to pick up his sister from the station, and the rest have enough cars between them." She paused. "I've missed you today."

"I know, I'm sorry, I had to park the kids with Mum, and she had a doctor's appointment this morning, and then I had to drive via Clapham to collect the wedding plate that everyone is going to sign. But I'm here now, child-free and entirely yours."

"Hallelujah," Audrey sang.

Clara let out one of her uninhibited laughs that reached every limb. Her short black bob was pinned back with bobby pins, and she wore only a dab of nude lip gloss on an otherwise makeup-free face. She had faultless skin and intelligent eyes, looks she'd inherited from her Chinese mother and Spanish father. But it was not just her looks that made her stand out, it was the way she held herself, the way she moved. Every gesture was larger than it needed to be—if she waved at you, she waved with her whole arm, not just a hand. If she smiled, it was a fully committed grin. Even watching her drive, there was an overblown quality to the movement of her hands on the wheel, the shift of her gaze to the rearview mirror; it was all larger than it needed to be. Since Clara had given birth to the twins, Audrey had noticed a new, slightly frazzled quality to her friend, a jumpiness, a tiredness around the eyes that would not be fixed by a single good night's sleep. But in essence she was the same girl who had befriended Audrey, age nine, in the school canteen when they both reached for the last chocolate éclair.

"So, how's the Monster of the Bride?" asked Clara.

"In her element, directing her first production," said Audrey.

"This must be a novelty for her. A wedding where she's not

actually marrying anyone." Clara gave Audrey a sly grin. "Can we play Vivien Wedding Bingo? We'll drink a shot every time she mentions one of her own weddings."

"No, we'd be under the table before the 'I dos.' How was it, leaving the girls? Is Jay going to cope without you?"

"He'll be fine, he has my mum to help. I'm here for you, no distractions. I don't want to be one of those shitty bridesmaids who spends the whole day checking in on their kids. Do you remember Katie Evans at mine?"

"She was the worst," said Audrey, smiling.

"I think she had her Bluetooth baby monitor on for half the service."

Audrey looked out of the car window and up at the gray, cloudy sky.

"Evenings are so light in June. Maybe we should have gone for a Christmas wedding, the stars would be out by now."

"And miss out on the perfect venue, with extensive grounds and on-site accommodation?" Clara asked, impersonating Vivien's clipped voice. They both smiled. "What is it you always say to me? The stars are always there, even if you can't see them."

"Did I tell you Josh bought me a new telescope as a wedding present?"

"Oh my God, I love him. He knows you so well."

Just as Audrey was beginning to feel herself relax in the warmth of Clara's company, her phone pinged, and she reached into her bag to check it. It was an e-mail, a generic newsletter from a London art gallery, but the headline jumped out at her. "Benedict Van Vuuren, one of the greatest sculptors of our age." It was a press release for a retrospective exhibition of his work. His name alone was enough to make Audrey bristle. Every cell of her body felt tense. She hadn't thought about him for months, and now his name jumped into her inbox the night before her wedding. She gave an involuntary shiver.

"Is that Jay?" Clara asked. "I told him I was driving most of the afternoon, so if there was an emergency, he should call you. Oh God, what's wrong, what's happened? Did one of them choke on a grape?"

Audrey shook her head, closing the newsletter, trying to keep her hands from shaking. If she started talking about Benedict, it would give him a presence at her wedding that he didn't deserve, take up headspace she couldn't afford.

"It's nothing, it's fine, just a boring e-mail."

She thrust the phone back into her bag. Her arms started to itch, faint red hives appearing on the delicate undersides of her forearms. She tried to scratch them, but the thick gel polish on her nails rendered them blunt and ineffective.

"Did you feel nervous, before your wedding?" she asked instead.

"Of course, the buildup is super stressful, there's so much to think about. Tomorrow all the tedious wedmin stress will be over, and you can relax and enjoy yourself. Then in two days' time you'll be in Ibiza, in that luxury hotel, with a honeymoon suite bigger than my apartment, and you and Josh will have plenty of time to make up for him being stuck in Singapore all month." Clara turned to raise an eyebrow at Audrey. "And I'll be sitting in London traffic, doing the nursery drop-off, my flat white from Pret the highlight of my morning." Clara reached out a hand to squeeze her friend's knee. "You're marrying Josh, how can it be anything but wonderful?"

Audrey mustered a smile, knitting her hands together in her lap and then turning to look out the window. Clara was right, a few prewedding jitters were entirely normal. She was missing her dad, she was intimidated by the size of the church and the sheer number of guests that were coming tomorrow, and now with Benedict's name jumping into her inbox, it was no wonder she felt a little on edge. As long as nothing else happened to freak her out, she would be fine.

⟜⟜

Audrey and Clara were first to arrive at the Red Lion pub. They found the private dining room already decorated and laid for dinner. The pub's red walls were covered in dark oil paintings depicting gory hunting scenes. Antique brass pint jugs hung from pegs along the low oak beams, and the dining chairs were lined with green and yellow tartan. Suffice to say, the décor of the pub didn't blend especially well with the pastel tones of the pink and lilac floral centerpiece and heart-shaped confetti that had been strewn across the table.

"Did the pub do this?" Clara asked.

"Debbie must have been here this afternoon," said Audrey, making a mental note to thank her mother-in-law-to-be for all the effort.

"Good old Debs." Clara sighed, picking up one of the lilac napkins with "A & J" embroidered in cursive writing. "It looks like Valentine's Day threw up in here. I think what we need is two strong gin and tonics."

"Vivien suggested a 'no spirits' rule tonight, and a firm no-seafood policy," Audrey said.

"Fuck Vivien." Clara laughed. "I'm baby-free for the first time in months—wine is not going to cut it. And I'm definitely drinking tonight, because I don't have to breastfeed for twenty-four hours."

"I think I'm going to save myself for tomorrow." Audrey agreed with her mother on this one. She knew it was easy to get carried away, especially when she was with Clara and Hillary.

It would be silly if she couldn't enjoy the day tomorrow because she had a hangover.

The rest of the wedding party soon arrived from the church. There wasn't space for people to stand around and chat, so everyone promptly took their seats. They were to be twelve in total, everyone from the church, plus Josh's sister, Miranda, and her date, whom Josh was collecting from the station.

"The London train was delayed," Debbie announced to the room as she passed around the bread basket. "Josh is on his way but said to go ahead and order or we'll miss our window with the kitchen. We must get our order in before that big group who've just arrived in the bar area. Does everyone know what they're having?"

No one knew what they were having. Everyone was too busy listening to Hillary tell an amusing story about the time he accidentally stole Michael Gambon's shoes. Audrey had heard this particular story numerous times before and noted it had gained several embellishments. Michael Gambon had not gone so far as to chase Hillary down Shaftesbury Avenue wearing only a towel last time.

"Sean Bean is from Yorkshire, you know," Granny Parker announced to the table.

"I think the story was about Michael Gambon, Mum," Josh's father said, patting his mother's arm.

"I know, and *my* story was about Sean Bean," Granny Parker said crossly, removing her arm from beneath his.

By the time everyone had gotten around to consulting the menus, of which there were only one between every two people, much to Vivien's chagrin, in walked Josh with the party from the train. At the exact moment they arrived, Audrey was coming back from the bathroom, and from the corridor, she was able to see the new arrivals standing by the door before they noticed her. The brass-rimmed clock on the wall told her it was eight minutes past eight when she felt her heart jump into her throat and her legs go soft beneath her. For there, standing beside Josh's sister, was a face she recognized. It was a face she had not seen in six years, and one she had thought she would never see again.

3

Seven Years Before I Do

༄

*A*udrey, waiting at the main exit of Baker Street tube station, checked her watch. Hillary was twenty minutes late. He had just started rehearsals on a new production, and Audrey suspected that if there was an opportunity to loiter and impress his new castmates, then loiter he would.

If he didn't show, she would spend the afternoon in the British Library. If she was serious about this new plan of hers, then she would need to study every chance she got. She didn't relish the prospect of changing university courses again, of what people would say, but the truth was, she had always wanted to study astronomy, she'd just never had the confidence to apply before.

The tube exit was getting busy, so she moved further inside the station to escape the throng of people. A photo booth stood in an overlooked corner of the tube station. The vintage-style machine had popped up a few weeks earlier. It had softly illuminated white walls, a mirror, and a single red panel with the words "4 PHOTOS, 3 MINUTES, 2 POUNDS" printed in a stylish square font. On the opposite side, an advert detailed how you could hire an old-fashioned analog booth like this for private events.

Away from the tide of people streaming from the ticket gates, Audrey paused to look at her reflection in the booth's paneled mirror. She was wearing black tights beneath denim cutoffs and a white tank top under an open lumberjack shirt. She smiled at her reflection, pleased with her new fringe. Did she look like someone who could be an astronomy student? What did an astronomy student look like? Mind wandering, Audrey noticed a strip of color photos sitting in the photo booth dispenser. She looked around, expecting to see someone waiting, but there was no one. She glanced beneath the blue curtain of the booth—it was empty.

After one more look around the station, she picked up the photos. The strip of four images showed a man, perhaps close to her age, twenty-one. He was blond, attractive, with an angular face and a slightly crooked smile. In the first photo, he was pointing to himself; in the next, he had pulled open his shirt and the word "WILL" was written on his bare chest in black ink. In the third picture, he held a heavy-handled magnifying glass up to one eye, miming searching for something. In the final picture, he pointed a finger directly at the lens; his face had been captured in an enormous smile. "I will find you," Audrey muttered.

Audrey stared at the photos; she was intrigued by both the message and the man. His fair hair was styled into a messy quiff on one side, his face was narrow, his jawline and cheekbones sharp. He had a light smattering of freckles across his nose and a small, straight scar at the top of his left cheek. His eyes were piercing green and looked directly at the lens in all but one of the photographs. Though logic told her otherwise, Audrey felt that the message in the photos was meant for her.

She scanned the station again. Surely, he must be nearby. Effort had gone into these, getting the timing right for each pose, to convey the message in four unstoppable flashes of light. They were not something to be left behind, discarded. She felt an illogical stab of desperation—she wanted to see this man in real life, to see if his eyes were really that extraordinary shade of green, or if it was simply a trick of the light, or a fault in the outdated inking process. Her curiosity felt so intensely piqued that she couldn't make herself walk away from the booth.

"Audrey!" A familiar voice cut across the station, pulling her out of her thoughts.

She looked up to see Hillary stepping off the escalator coming up from the Bakerloo line. He was dressed in a boxy white suit, a yellow cravat, and a black beret, an outfit that was garnering him looks of both approval and bewilderment from people he passed.

"I wasn't sure you'd still be here," he said, greeting her with a kiss on each cheek. "Sorry, I got waylaid by a beautiful busker at Oxford Circus."

"What are you dressed as?" Audrey asked.

"An art critic. What are you dressed as—an urchin farmer?" He raised an eyebrow as he eyed her outfit, then linked his arm through hers. "I suppose this is what geography students look like these days. I never ventured outside the arts faculty myself."

"Actually, I've decided geography is not for me. I think I'm going to switch courses."

"Again? Oh, thank goodness. What are we doing now?"

"Astronomy." Audrey bit her lip, her eyes growing wide as she waited to see his reaction.

"I thought you needed math for that." Hillary frowned.

"I do—I'm going to go back and take my math A level. Is this an insane plan?"

"Brilliantly insane," said Hillary, squeezing her arm. "You're still young. You can do anything you set your mind to, Audrey Lavery. Just don't ask me to help you study."

Audrey hugged his arm in hers, and after looking around one last time for the green-eyed man, she slipped the strip of photos into her handbag.

⁓⁓⁓

As soon as they were outside on Baker Street, Hillary announced that he needed to stop at the newsagent's to buy cigarettes. Still buzzing with confidence from his faith in her, Audrey latched on to the seed of an idea.

"I just need to nip back for something," she said. "Will you buy me some Chipstick crisps? I'll be back in two minutes."

"Crisps? You are such a heathen." Hillary shivered but then nodded and waved a hand to dismiss her.

The photo booth was still empty. Audrey pulled back the curtain and turned the swiveling stool until it was the right height for her. When she was satisfied that her eyeline was in the right place, she rummaged in her purse for two pound coins. She was going to leave a reply. She didn't know why, exactly; it was unlikely the man would come back for his photos now, but she would feel better about taking them if she left something in their place.

She pulled her notebook from her backpack and tore off a clean sheet of paper, writing a word on either side in blue pen, then retracing the lettering to make it as bold as she could. When she was satisfied with her handiwork, she pushed the coins into the slot with a satisfying clunk. For the first photo, she pointed to herself. *Flash.* Then she held up the sign she had drawn, with the word "AM" facing the camera. *Flash*. Next, she turned the paper over and displayed the second word, "HERE." *Flash*. For the fourth photo she posed in a kiss, her lips puckered, eyes closed, arms outstretched. *Flash*.

She didn't wait for the strip to develop—it would take several minutes, and Hillary was waiting. She heard the whirring of the machinery inside the booth and pressed her hand affectionately against the red panel. She was entrusting this machine with her message, with delivering it into a stranger's hand. Perhaps he would return, find her reply, and it would begin a conversation that went on for months, played out entirely in photo strips. They'd finally meet one day at this same booth and fall in love. Of course it was a silly fantasy, but the idea made her smile.

"There you are," said Hillary as she rejoined him outside the newsagent's. "What were you doing?"

Audrey shrugged. "Just answering the universe's call."

Hillary rolled his eyes as he tore open his packet of cigarettes. "Well, I'm sure the bathrooms at the gallery would be cleaner," he said, handing her a packet of salt-and-vinegar Chipsticks. "I thought if I had taught you anything growing up, it was a little refinement. We don't eat crisps, we don't use public lavatories, and we never, ever wear trainers unless we are exercising."

Audrey glanced down at her trainers and smiled.

As they walked down Baker Street, arms entwined, Audrey looked up at the sky and sent up a wish. She wished for the man in the photos to find her, as he'd promised.

4

One Day Before I Do

Audrey turned around and walked straight back to the Red Lion's loos. She couldn't go out there now, not until she'd had a moment to compose herself. How was he here? There were only two people invited to the wedding that Audrey hadn't met yet—one was a two-month-old baby—but what were the chances of the other one being Photo Booth Guy? If she'd been feeling an itch of doubt about the wedding, then this guy's showing up now felt like being showered in itching powder. She scratched again at the tight skin on her forearms just as there was a knock on the cubicle door.

"Auds, is that you? Let me in," came Clara's hushed voice.

Audrey opened the door, just wide enough to pull her friend inside. Then she bolted it shut again.

"Why are you hiding in here? Miranda just arrived."

Audrey felt the blood drain from her face. She gripped on to Clara's arm, as though she might convey the news physically, rather than having to say it out loud.

"Miranda's date—he's Photo Booth Guy."

Audrey sat back down on the closed toilet seat and dropped

her head between her knees. She felt suddenly dizzy, the walls of the cubicle closing in.

"No! Are you sure you're not seeing things?"

"It's him."

"You haven't met Miranda's boyfriend before?" Clara asked, slowly shaking her head. She looked uncharacteristically unnerved as she ruffled her neatly pinned hair, upsetting the sleek silhouette.

"He was a last-minute invite," Audrey explained, sitting upright and then squeezing over on the toilet lid to make room for Clara. "Miranda rang us last week saying she couldn't handle going to another wedding alone and could she bring a plus-one after all. She didn't even tell me his name."

"It can't be that serious, then, if he's so new on the scene," Clara mused.

"What difference does it make how serious they are?" Audrey asked wildly.

They heard the main door to the bathroom swing open. Both women held their breath as someone else—possibly Debbie, from the sound of the slightly shuffled, high-heeled footsteps—came in to use the bathroom. Audrey and Clara looked at each other in silence as the unknown person used the cubicle next to them and then washed their hands while humming a tune. The tone of the hum, and the choice of song, "Get Me to the Church on Time," confirmed the hummer's identity to be Debbie. Once the bathroom door had swung closed again, Audrey and Clara exhaled in unison.

"You don't still think about him, do you?" Clara asked. "That's all ancient history."

Audrey didn't need to answer. She didn't have to lie. Her face said it all.

"Shit," said Clara.

Audrey picked up her handbag, which was resting on the cistern. She pulled out her wallet, the metallic silver purse she'd been using for the last ten years and miraculously hadn't lost. Reaching inside the inner pocket, she pulled out the stack of photos she kept inside. There was the photo she'd taken of Josh at Covent Garden, then a photo of her and Josh together, laughing at a wedding, messing around with miniature paper parasols. There was a photo of her and Clara, aged eighteen, on their last day of school. Then there were the photos of him, of Photo Booth Guy. She had the original strip of photos she'd found at Baker Street all those years ago, and then the photos of them together. Six years had passed, and yet from what she had seen, he hadn't changed at all; he had the same angular features, sharp green eyes, and blond, disheveled hair.

"You keep these in your wallet? Audrey, why?" Clara reached out and took the photos from her. "What if Josh found them?"

Audrey studied her hands, feeling sheepish. "I don't know why I've kept them."

"Does Josh know the story?" Clara asked, holding up the photos.

"No," Audrey said, reaching to take the photos back and carefully returning them all to the folds of her wallet. It was complicated, the reason she'd kept them—a memento of one of the best weekends, but also one of the worst weekends, of her life, the weekend everything changed.

"Well, he'll recognize you as soon as you walk out there," said Clara. "What if he's been carrying photos of you around in *his* wallet for the last six years? What if he's been looking for you the same way you've been looking for him?"

The thought ignited some long-forgotten feeling in Audrey, a quiet flame she had been carrying for years.

"We have to go back out there, otherwise people are going to think you've got stomach problems," said Clara.

"I can't see him for the first time across a crowded dinner table. What if he does remember me? What if he recounts the story of how we met in front of everyone, what if—"

"What if you still feel like he's your soul mate and sparks fly across the table in full view of your fiancé and his mother?"

Audrey knew Clara was being facetious, but when Clara saw the look on her face, she must have realized this was too close to the mark to be funny.

"Okay, so how do we avoid this?" Clara tapped her fingertips against her chin. "You need to get him alone first, preempt his reaction. You'll just have to ask him not to mention that you know each other—explain it would be awkward for everyone involved. I'm sure he'll understand. It's your wedding!"

Audrey thought back on all the times she had looked for him in a crowd, imagined his face where it had not been. And now here he was, tonight of all nights. Could it be some strange serendipity? *No.* She tried to rein in her spiraling mind. It was simply an unfortunate coincidence. Like turning up to a party in the exact same dress as the host, or butt-dialing your soon-to-be mother-in-law during a particularly loud movie sex scene.

"You're right." Audrey clapped her hands. This was fixable. "We just need a plan."

"This is Maid of Honor 101," said Clara. "Remove angst, stress, and ex–love interests from the wedding."

"I didn't take that module. What do we do, set off a fire alarm? Create a diversion?"

"We just need to get him alone somehow." Clara pursed her lips as she thought.

Together, they came up with Operation Wedding Plate.

Clara would tell everyone that Audrey had nipped back to the church to fetch something. She would then ask the new arrivals to come outside one by one, to sign the wedding plate. This would allow Audrey a few minutes to talk to him, unobserved. It wasn't a great plan, but it was the best they could come up with from the confines of a badly ventilated pub toilet. Hopefully, the guy wouldn't even remember her, then Audrey could go back to worrying about regular wedding concerns, like aisle width, if the weather would hold, and the risk of falling bat corpses knocking out any of their guests tomorrow.

5

Six Years Before I Do

❧

*A*udrey was waiting on the opposite platform when she noticed him. It was definitely him, the man with the green eyes and the blond hair, Photo Booth Guy. How many times over the last six months had she imagined finding him? And now there he was, standing on the westbound platform at Notting Hill tube station. She knew the contours of his face like she knew the constellations.

For a moment it felt like Audrey couldn't breathe. Was this really happening? What was she going to do—run over there and tell him she'd stolen his photos from Baker Street months before? Explain that she felt some bizarre connection to him and had been looking out for him ever since? Clearly, he would think she was insane. Then he looked directly at her and called across the tracks, "I know you."

"Do you?" she replied, her voice breathy with adrenaline. She found herself smiling, which must have given Photo Booth Guy a clue that she knew what he was talking about. He smiled back, taking a step toward her, as though forgetting they were separated by the tube tracks.

"Will you wait? I'll come around," he called, then paused, waiting for her to acknowledge that she would.

It took him less than a minute to run round from the other platform. It felt like an eternity. If he recognized her face, he must have come back and found the photos she left for him. Would he think it odd that she'd done such a thing?

Finally, he was in front of her. He was taller than she'd imagined, at least six foot. He wore ripped jeans and a Van Halen T-shirt under a weathered black leather jacket. He was carrying a blue umbrella and a battered-looking backpack, with a camera case slung over one shoulder. His face looked so familiar, beyond recognizing it from the photo strip, Audrey felt as though she must have known him in another lifetime.

"Photo Booth Girl," he said, shaking his head, as though unsure of himself. "It is you, isn't it? I left behind a strip of photos in a booth at Baker Street, months ago. When I came back for them, your photos were there in their place. I think you left me a reply." He narrowed his eyes, as though looking for confirmation.

"I did," she said. A thousand questions leaped to her throat: What did the message mean? If he came back to the booth, how long did she miss him by? Had he kept her photos just as she had kept his? His face broke into an enormous smile. A dimple creased one cheek, and she noticed that one of his front teeth was slightly crooked, all of which only added to his subtle asymmetric charms.

"I have thought about you so much. Sorry that sounds . . ." He trailed off, looking at the floor. "I left you a reply the next day. I taped it to the booth."

Audrey shook her head. If he had left a message, she hadn't found it, and in those weeks after finding his photos, she had lingered by the booth more than she would care to admit.

"I didn't see it," she said, looking up at him, surprised her voice sounded so level when her insides felt like jumbled spaghetti.

"It was a long shot."

"What did it say, your message?"

"'Meet me here, Saturday, eight p.m.'"

She could smell his skin, mixed with the heat from his damp jacket, and she wanted to curl her face into his chest, to press her cheek against his worn T-shirt. "Plenty of people came," he said with wry smile, tilting his head to one side. "But none of them were you."

"I would have come, if I had seen the note," she said, jutting out her chin, feeling a thrill at her own unexpected confidence. They just stood grinning at each other, all coyness about this situation strangely absent. It was too special, too serendipitous. An invisible string had wound them together, something not to be dealt with flippantly but to be savored.

"Are you free now? Can I buy you a coffee?" His face looked serious, as though he was worried she might say no. Audrey nodded. She had been heading to the dentist's, then the library to take a mock exam, but there was no chance she was going to do either of those things now.

On the street, it was raining again, so he opened his umbrella and they both huddled beneath it, walking north toward Westbourne Grove. The patter of rain on his umbrella above them felt strangely intimate. Their pace slowed; they were in no rush to arrive anywhere.

"Who was it for, your 'I will find you' message? You're not a crazy stalker, are you?"

He laughed huskily. The depth of it made him sound older than he looked, like his laugh had been aged in oak barrels, worn with frequent use.

"Nothing like that. It was for a birthday card—my friend Toby's twenty-first. We all made photo messages to add to a collage. Toby always goes AWOL in clubs and I'm usually given the task of finding him." As he talked, he squeezed her arm with his, bringing her further beneath the umbrella, closer into his world.

"Why did you leave them behind?" Audrey asked.

"I was waiting for them to develop when I saw this woman fall by the escalator. She broke her shopping bag, and fruit rolled everywhere. I went to find her another bag. We rescued what we could, and then I helped her down to the platform. She was the kind of woman who will tell you her entire life story given half a chance. By the time I got back to the booth, my photos had gone and yours were in their place." He shook his head. "I'm embarrassed to say how much my friends have had to hear me go on about the mysterious Photo Booth Girl."

"Audrey, my name's Audrey."

He reached across a hand and gripped hers firmly.

"Hi, Audrey, I'm Fred."

6

One Day Before I Do

~~~

*A*udrey waited around the corner of the pub in case anyone saw her hovering through the front window of the dining room. She peered around the wall. What if Clara failed to lure him outside? What if Miranda insisted on coming out at the same time? Her heart was beating so fast, it felt as though it might be trying to break out of her chest.

She heard Clara's voice before she saw them.

"It's just that we want to get as many names on the plate before tomorrow as possible, so I'm rounding people up when I can, and since you were already standing . . ."

Audrey shouldn't have doubted her friend. Clara was impossible to say no to. It was why she was so good at her job. She was an image consultant in the music industry, which entailed persuading musicians to do, wear, and say things they might not otherwise want to.

"Sure, sure, no problem," she heard Fred say. His voice sounded the same, slightly lilting, with that gravelly edge.

Audrey pressed her back against the wall, her body tense. This had been a terrible idea, to meet him in the car park. It suddenly felt too covert, too underhand, as though she had something to hide. But there was no time to regret the decision further; he had turned the corner and was now standing in front of her.

"This is Audrey, by the way. I don't know if you've met. She's the one getting married," Clara said, her eyes flitting back and forth between the two of them.

He stood still, frozen midstep, and Clara took this as her cue to retreat toward the pub's front door.

"Audrey?" he said in almost a whisper, as though distrusting the word. The directness of his gaze sent a tingle down her arms, and she clenched her hands into fists at her sides.

"I saw it was you when you walked in and, um, I didn't want you to recognize me across a table full of people, in case you reacted like, well, like you're reacting now." Her words were rushed; she stumbled over them.

"Miranda only told me your name on the train. Whenever I hear the name Audrey, I always think of you."

"You agreed to come to the wedding of two people whose names you didn't even know?" Audrey asked, shaking her head and letting out a disbelieving laugh.

"Miranda asked me if I'd come to her brother's wedding, she didn't fill me in on the details." He eyed her with a calm, confident gaze. "You never called me."

"You didn't come, the day we agreed." She bit her lip. "And *you* never called *me*."

"Something happened the day we were supposed to meet. I did try to call, I tried to find you, I waited by our booth, so many times—"

"It doesn't matter now," she said, cutting him off. It wouldn't help her to hear his excuses. The fact that he remembered too, that he might have remembered it as she did, was only going to make his presence here more confusing. "It was all a long time ago."

"I can't believe it is really you." He smiled now, his shock dissipating. "Audrey the Astronomer, you haven't changed a bit."

He raked a hand through his hair, his eyes darting back to the pub door to check they were still alone, then he took a step toward her, erasing some of the space between them. "This is kind of . . . strange timing, right?" he said, his voice hushed.

She felt herself being pulled into some invisible web, his proximity scrambling her senses. She pressed her nails into her palms, reminding herself why she'd come out here, what it was she needed to say.

"I know. Look, I'd rather no one knew that we've met before." His eyes were drilling into her, beseeching her with silent questions. "That's the reason I came out here to talk to you. I don't want to tell everyone the story this weekend, it would be a distraction. It might make Josh feel uncomfortable, Miranda too."

"Sure," he said softly, a flash of disappointment in his eyes. "Of course, I understand."

"You won't say anything?"

"No." He shook his head, but his eyes stayed glued to hers. "I can't believe it is really you, or that you're getting married."

Thunder cracked in the distance. A storm was on the way.

"We should go back in," Audrey said. "My mother-in-law will be upset that we haven't ordered our food yet."

His mouth opened as though he had more to say, as though he knew if he didn't say it now, he would not get another chance. But Audrey didn't want to hear it. What could he say that would be helpful? What would it change if she heard his excuses—why he hadn't called, why he hadn't come? So she turned toward the back door before he could speak. He reached out a hand for her arm, and a current passed between them, like a burn. She flinched and then saw in his eyes that he had felt it too.

"I want to explain—I did look for you, Audrey, you disappeared . . ."

Audrey frowned. "*I* disappeared?" she said indignantly, then checked herself. "We need to go back in before we're missed, please."

Audrey shook her head and stalked purposefully back to the door, back to the rehearsal dinner, back to Josh, the man she was marrying tomorrow.

7

Four Years Before I Do

Audrey didn't remember the first time she met Josh; that's how much of an impression he'd made. In her mind, the first time they'd met was at a birthday party in a bar on Northcote Road, but Josh always claimed there was an earlier occasion. He said he had met her in the kitchen of her Tooting house share one evening. He'd come over to watch the rugby with her flatmate Paul. Audrey had been cooking, and he'd complimented her on the smell of her risotto as he fetched a beer from the fridge.

"What are you making?" he'd asked.

"Oh, I don't know yet, I usually just chuck in whatever I have in the cupboard, risotto à la leftovers."

"Well, it smells great," he'd said.

The conversation must have lasted less than thirty seconds, hardly the meet-cute great love stories are written about.

Audrey had been living with Paul and Clara for three months. This house was the first place Audrey had lived, other than her mother's house, that felt like a home. After dropping out of university, then failing to make the grade she needed to study astronomy, Audrey had traveled the world for a year. Her mother had offered to fund the trip—guilt money, perhaps. When she returned to London, it had taken Audrey a long time to get settled. She had moved from flat share to flat share in a series of disastrous arrangements. First there was Nelly, the evangelical Christian who wouldn't let Audrey watch or read anything containing a sex scene in the communal living space. Then there were Gary and Gilly, who turned out to be Southwark's most successful weed dealers, with a doorbell that rang around the clock. Just as she was contemplating the unappealing prospect of moving back in with Vivien and her latest husband, Clara announced that a room had become available in the Tooting house share where she was living.

Clara had found Paul through an advert on Craigslist. He worked in the city, had a double-barreled surname, and had studied politics at Cambridge. He wasn't the kind of person Clara and Audrey would necessarily have been friends with in real life, but he paid his bills on time, had no illegal or antisocial hobbies, and had a twenty percent–off membership card for the local wine shop. All in all, he was the perfect housemate.

It was Paul's twenty-sixth birthday party, at All Bar One, where Audrey *remembered* meeting Josh. Paul introduced his two flatmates to "the rugby lads," who all nodded in Clara and Audrey's direction. Of the group, it was one called Andrew who was the most forthcoming, whose eyes were the brightest, the one whose name locked in Audrey's mind. All she noticed about Josh that night was his badly fitting jeans. They were shapeless and baggy, the kind a teenage boy might have been bought by his mother and then continued to buy as an adult without thinking to explore other options. She thought he had a nice face, but then all of Paul's friends had nice faces—with their healthy skin, broad athletic frames, and teeth that suggested years of expensive orthodontic work.

These men were not Audrey's type. She liked skinny musicians, artists, creative types who had callings rather than careers. She liked lone wolves, not boys who played in packs.

Later that evening, she found herself queuing at the bar next to Bad Jeans Josh.

"Hey, Audrey, right?" he said, blushing slightly.

"Yeah," she said, returning his smile.

"I'm Josh, I was at Cambridge with Paul. We met briefly before."

She nodded, though she didn't remember.

"Paul said you were a photographer?" he said, wiping his top lip nervously.

Audrey suppressed an internal sigh. "What do you do?" was her least favorite question, but one everyone else seemed extremely attached to. Why did your job have to be your defining characteristic? She was currently working in a café while she tried to build her photography portfolio, often doing shoots for free, but she wasn't in the mood to explain all that now.

"Kind of," she said. "How about you?" She raised a hand to the bartender, keen to get his attention and go back to her friends.

"I work in the City, in reinsurance." Josh paused, and she blinked slowly. "It's a bit of a conversation killer, I know it sounds boring."

"Well, is it boring?" she asked.

"Not to me."

At that moment, the bartender came over to ask Josh what he wanted, and he politely deferred to Audrey, allowing her to order first.

"Thanks," she said, and noticed his cheeks turn ever so slightly pink again.

As she ordered her drinks, a tall brunette with a blunt-cut fringe muscled in at the bar next to Josh.

"I'm Harriet," she said to Audrey. "I'm in the Cambridge gang with Paul and Josh, I've known these boys *forever*. You must be the new flatmate."

Audrey recognized the flicker of something territorial in Harriet's arm around Josh. She wanted to say, "You can have him, love, I'm not interested in the slightest," but instead she nodded down to her drinks on the bar and said, "Well, it was nice to meet you both, I'd better get these to my thirsty friends." She thought she saw a flicker of disappointment cross Josh's face. He told her later he'd been racking his brain for something to say, that he'd kicked himself for making such a bad first impression. But in truth, he hadn't made much of an impression at all.

8

One Day Before I Do

∽

"There you are, Audrey! What in heaven's name can you have left in the church that was so vital? You didn't even tell us what food you wanted to order!" Debbie said the moment Audrey reappeared. "I can see your mother thinks we should have done a set menu." Debbie fiddled with the pearls around her neck as though they were worry beads. "We should have done a set menu, shouldn't we?"

Through the window, Audrey could see Clara in the car park getting Fred to sign the wedding plate. Josh stood up and pulled out the chair beside him, a look of concern creasing his face.

"Are you okay?" he asked quietly as Audrey slipped in beside him. "I didn't know where you'd gone." She nodded and gave his hand a reassuring squeeze. "I ordered you the chicken schnitzel," he told her. "Mum was fretting about getting the order in. You can swap with me if you'd rather have the lasagna."

"Schnitzel sounds perfect. Thanks for ordering, I couldn't decide what I wanted to eat anyway." She affected the most natural smile she could muster.

"This is Fred, by the way, Miranda's date," Josh said, introducing the newcomer who had reappeared through the other door to the dining room. Audrey felt her stomach drop as she dared to look across at him. It felt as though every eye in the room were on her reaction. Would someone see in her face that this man was not a stranger? But of course no one saw, no one was even looking—they were all too busy talking and enjoying the second-most expensive wine on the menu.

"Pleased to meet you," Fred said, reaching across the table to shake her hand.

She took it, but as soon as she pressed her palm to his, her face flushed pink and she pulled her hand back, just a fraction too fast.

"Thank you for inviting me," Fred said, addressing them both.

"Any friend of my sister's is a friend of ours," said Josh, furnishing Fred with a warm smile. "Where did Miranda go?"

Audrey could see her outside, signing the wedding plate. Clara was certainly thorough on following through with the cover story.

"You must order immediately," said Debbie, grabbing Fred's arm with such urgency that she nearly upended a wine bottle on the table in front of them. "We've ordered already, but you can go to the bar and add yours. Please tell them not to delay our food on account of the late addition. We simply can't miss our window with the kitchen. Vivien is getting impatient. It might be easiest if you and Miranda forgo starters, there's plenty of bread to fill up on."

When Clara and Miranda came back in through the door, Debbie gave them a strange look, as though she was aware that whatever they'd been up to, it was not on the preapproved, laminated wedding agenda.

"Hey, gorgeous," Miranda said, weaving her way around the table to give Audrey a hug. "Sorry we were late, train was packed. Josh told us all about the 'bad omen bat.'" She made a face. They both turned to look at Granny Parker, who was positioned near the far end of the table, polishing a spoon with her embroidered lilac napkin.

"Poor Granny Parker, it landed inches from her head," said Audrey.

"Have you met my gorgeous date?" Miranda said in a conspiratorial whisper. "You are going to love him. The second I met him, that was almost the first thought I had—*Audrey is going to love this guy.* I think your brains work the same way."

Audrey felt the blood drain from her face and the burn of rising bile in her throat. Miranda, of all people. Josh's sister. *Why did he have to be dating Miranda?* What if it became serious between them? What if they got married and Fred became her brother-in-law? The Parker family had a yearly meetup in Yorkshire; what if Fred got invited and she had to spend days, weeks, with him every year for the rest of her life, a constant reminder of what might have been? The thought sent a cold bead of sweat down the central curve of her back. *Would she make it to the bathroom if she was going to throw up?*

"I look forward to getting to know him," she managed to say, clearing her throat, before Debbie flapped her hands for everyone to sit down so that the waitress could distribute a round of drinks.

"Are you sure you're all right?" Josh whispered quietly in her ear. "You do look pale."

"Probably just hungry," Audrey said, reaching out to give his leg a reassuring pat.

"Not too overwhelmed?" Josh asked. "Were you upset

about the bat? You mustn't listen to anything Granny Parker says."

She shook her head and gave him the brightest smile she could muster. She just needed to get through dinner, act normally. It would only be a few hours, then she could go back to her room at Millward Hall and let out the silent scream she was swallowing. Still smiling, she glanced down at her forearms and saw the hives were growing redder. *Was it an allergy? Some kind of stress rash?* She quickly covered them with her napkin so that Josh wouldn't notice.

Once everyone's food had been ordered, Debbie stopped fretting and the atmosphere around the table became more jovial. Josh's father, Michael, inhaled his minestrone soup, then excused himself "to the loo." Audrey noticed that the television in the main bar was showing the cricket.

Fred was seated off to one side, so Audrey was able to avoid making conversation or eye contact with him. This didn't stop her from being acutely aware of him at all times—who he was talking to, whether he looked to be enjoying himself, how often he glanced down the table at her. She felt self-conscious at the idea he might be observing her facial expressions, her body language, the way she was with Josh.

"So, how did you and your chap meet, then?" she heard Brian ask Miranda. Josh was telling her something about boutonnieres for the groomsmen, and she strained to hear Miranda's reply through the layers of chatter around her.

"Oh, nothing too out of the ordinary," Miranda started to say. "It was—"

"Audrey?" Josh nudged her.

"What?" she said, a touch too sharply, as she tuned back in to what he was saying.

"I was just pointing out that this time tomorrow we'll be married." Josh's neck pushed back into the collar of his shirt, his eyebrows knitting into a wounded expression.

"Sorry," she said, biting her lip and then adding quietly, "Maybe I am a little overwhelmed. There's just so much to think about."

"Well, you shouldn't be anxious, your mum has everything in hand," Josh said, laying a hand on her arm. "Honestly, stop stressing."

"Stop telling me I look stressed and pale and crap, Josh," she hissed, removing her hand from beneath his.

"I didn't say you looked crap." Josh visibly blanched at her words.

Audrey picked up her butter knife, squeezing it tight before ripping a hunk of bread in two and aggressively buttering it. "Sorry, sorry," she said, "I don't know why I'm so on edge." *She did know why. She knew exactly why.*

Josh leaned over and put an arm around her. "It's supposed to be fun, remember? It's too late to change anything now anyway."

Strangely, Audrey didn't find these words reassuring. "'Til death do us part" suddenly felt like a *really* long time. It wasn't like in medieval days where you got married and then one of you would probably cut a finger chopping turnips and die of sepsis soon after. *Could the wonders of modern medicine be making a lifelong commitment more daunting?*

"I know. You're right, I'm being silly." Audrey tried to sound relaxed, to smile. The last thing she needed now was to be in a stupid fight with Josh, so she tried to stop having weird thoughts about sepsis and turnips, and to quell the small hysterical voice of panic beating furiously against the inside of her rib cage.

*O*nce the main course had been cleared away, Lawrence, who was seated at the far end of the table between Vivien and Granny Parker, stood up and tapped his glass. He was wearing a dark gray suit, impeccably tailored to disguise his increasingly portly build. He always wore a silk pocket square, which he pulled out to clean the lenses of his narrow rimless glasses. He looked overdressed for the balmy June evening; his already ruddy complexion had grown redder with the wine, and his gray hair was damp with sweat.

Just as the room fell silent, Michael returned from the bar, pocketing his phone. He tried to slip unnoticed back into his chair, but the untouched plate of scampi and chips in front of him betrayed the length of his absence and elicited a sharp look from Debbie.

"What's the score, Dad?" Josh whispered across the table.

"A hundred and eighty-five all out," Michael whispered back, and then flushed guiltily.

"Now, I know that tomorrow the role of speech maker has, unconventionally, been given to the nanny," Lawrence boomed, nodding his head toward Hillary. "Our resident Gary Poppins." Hillary laughed politely, as he always did whenever Lawrence recycled this particular joke. "So, I thought I'd take this evening as an opportunity to make my own little stepfather-of-the-bride speech. Though I am aware that is a position held by half the male population of England." He nodded toward Brian, who sportingly lifted his glass.

"We'll have none of that," said Vivien firmly, then pointed a stern finger at Hillary. "We'll have none of those comments tomorrow either, thank you, Hillary."

"Joking aside, as the current father figure in Audrey's life,

I'd like to say a few words on this auspicious evening, her last day as a maid."

Audrey heard Clara cough into her wineglass from the opposite side of the table. She looked across at Paul, who was trying to make a hat out of his napkin. She noticed the way Miranda was laughing at him; she'd always found Paul's silly antics amusing.

"Now, I know you and Josh have been living together for a while now," Lawrence went on, "so I'm sure you don't need me to explain the whys and wherefores of married life."

He winked at them both. Audrey cringed. She wished he'd sit down. There was something acutely awkward about having a toast made about you, especially by someone who didn't really know you. Josh reached an arm around her chair, kissing her shoulder lightly, just as she dared a glance down the table toward Fred. He was looking right at her. She dropped her eyes to her lap, the only safe place to look.

"But as someone who's been married twice, I do have a little wisdom to impart," Lawrence went on. "Marriage is a partnership, someone to share life's challenges and celebrations with." He smiled down at Vivien, who looked uncharacteristically tense. "Someone who will love you on the boring days as well as the interesting ones, and ideally have legs as good as Vivien's well into her sixties!" Lawrence gave a hearty laugh, and the others obliged with a polite titter. He lifted his glass in Audrey and Josh's direction. "I have had the honor of watching Audrey and Josh's relationship develop these last few years, and I can tell you, if anyone has what it takes to beat the divorce statistics, it's these two. And if I'm wrong, well, your mother has her divorce lawyer on speed dial, ha ha!"

Vivien's face tightened. Hillary howled with laughter. Everyone else at the table made politely amused sounds.

Audrey saw a look pass between Vivien and Brian across the table and imagined how awkward it must be for her mother to have one of her ex-husbands there.

"Now, as many of you know, I spent a large part of my early diplomatic career out in Me-hi-co," Lawrence went on. "Wonderful work, charming people, and I was lucky enough to attend a wedding or two while I was there—perk of the job as a visiting dignitary. They have a tradition in Me-hi-co where they lasso the couple together in the church." At this, he bent down to fetch something from behind his chair, pulling out a long garland made from rope and flowers. "It's supposed to symbolize unity. The lasso, or *el lazo*, is shaped into an infinity symbol, to signify how long the marriage will last." He held up the garland, twisting it into a figure of eight. "So, I thought this evening I would bind these two together."

A buzz of approval and anticipation went around the room. Vivien blew Lawrence an overenthusiastic kiss, then soundlessly clapped her hands together, soft as butterfly wings, before stealing a nervous glance back at Brian. Lawrence beckoned Audrey and Josh to make their way behind the chairs to come and stand beside him. The room was cramped, there was no room to move, but they obediently shuffled behind Debbie, Michael, and Granny Parker until they stood on either side of Lawrence's chair at the top of the table. Audrey let out a breath, then worried it had sounded too much like a sigh or even a stifled yelp of pain. A waiter hovered near the door, ready to take everyone's dessert orders, and Audrey could tell Debbie was worried that this unsanctioned lassoing ceremony might delay the pace of the next course.

Granny Parker held up her butter knife to Lawrence, tapping the inscription. "Stainless steel—also invented in Yorkshire."

"Excellent," he said, politely guiding Granny Parker's knifed hand back down toward the table. He picked up the garland in front of him. "I always thought I could have been a minister. It's the Catholic in me. If either of you want to confess anything before tomorrow, get something off your chest, I'm all ears."

Vivien laughed. Audrey clenched her teeth beneath her smile. She didn't dare look at anyone else, so she kept her eyes on Josh. He moved a finger over his top teeth, then pointed, ever so subtly, across at her. She frowned, then felt between her front teeth and removed the offending fleck of spinach. She cringed with embarrassment that everyone had seen this little back-and-forth between them.

"I might say a few words, while we're standing up here," said Josh, reaching out to take Audrey's hands. "Many of you know the story of how we got together. If you'd told Audrey four years ago that she would end up marrying Bad Jeans Josh, I'm not sure she would have been thrilled by the prospect." Audrey smiled at this, and she heard Miranda's laugh cut through all the other noise. "But from our very first date, part of me hoped one day we'd be here. Audrey makes me laugh every single day. She inspires me with how she sees the world, the universe, and she challenges me to be less uptight. She is always worrying about whether she's a good person, but honestly, Audrey, I've never known you to do anything worse than leave the flat in a mess. You're one of life's great people—from where I'm standing, the best person—and I can't wait to marry you tomorrow."

He leaned in to kiss her, while everyone around the table cheered. Audrey tensed. His speech, though lovely and sincere, only reminded her of what Josh didn't know. Would he still love her if he knew the unhappiness she had caused? She glanced across at her mother, whose eyes were intent on her wineglass. Perhaps it was Vivien who still knew her better than anyone.

Lawrence clapped to get everyone's attention, clearly irked at having his lasso ceremony highjacked by an impromptu speech from the groom.

"So, with the power vested in me by the Red Lion pub," Lawrence said, affecting a pompous voice, "it is my hope that you will be unified for eternity, in God's love and protection."

He reached up and put one half of the garland over Josh's head. In the cramped room, and with the end of the table and Lawrence between them, Audrey and Josh had to shuffle forward so that Lawrence could lift the other end of the loop over Audrey's head.

"The perfect fit," said Lawrence, looking between them both and holding out his arms. Clara and Brian both stood up to take photos on their phones.

Audrey's eyes connected with Josh's, and he mouthed, "I love you." She felt a weight shift from her shoulders, and her smile turned into one that was real. She loved this man, she did. Whatever had happened in the past needed to stay in the past—weddings were about the future.

"And now I have prepared a poem, a traditional blessing from Me-hi-co," said Lawrence.

Audrey moved a foot to steady herself, but her shoe caught on Lawrence's chair. She tripped backward, unable to catch herself, and the garland of rope yanked Josh, pulling him across the table, his arm falling onto dishes of half-finished food, hitting wineglasses, which smashed onto plates, spraying the table linen, the guests, and even the walls with streaks of red. Audrey felt a sharp pain down the side of her neck as the rope cut into her skin. She fell, pulling Josh down with her, and they landed in a sprawl on the floor, her arm slamming into Granny Parker's chair on the way down.

Beneath the sound of breaking glass, there was an audible intake of breath from the room, then a tense silence. Audrey blinked her eyes open.

"Jesus!" Josh cried, trying to free his neck from the noose. "Audrey, you nearly broke my neck!"

Audrey's arm hurt, her neck ached, and she felt the fire of rope burn on her skin.

"Oh dear, oh dear." Lawrence flailed about, pushed back his chair, picking up shards of glass from the table.

"Are you okay? Audrey? Audrey, talk to me!" came Vivien's panicked voice as she stood up to try to see what the damage might be.

When Audrey looked up from the floor, all she could see was Granny Parker's somber face, looming down from her chair. Then she said sternly, "Now, that is a bad omen, a very bad omen indeed."

9

Six Years Before I Do

$\backsim$

$\mathcal{F}$red shook off his umbrella before bringing it inside the café, a small gesture of thoughtfulness to the café owner's floor that Audrey noted with pleasure. There were only two seats left, in a booth at the back, so they squeezed in opposite each other. Audrey buzzed with anticipation. She immediately pulled out her wallet and showed him the photo strip she had tucked inside.

"I don't know why I took them. I thought they'd been forgotten. It was a silly idea to leave a reply. I didn't think you would come back, that it would ever get to you."

Fred pulled out his own wallet, took out the photo strip of Audrey, and pushed it across the table for her to see. This admission of having kept each other's photos felt so refreshingly candid; there was a thrill in jumping ahead toward intimacy.

She smiled down at the images of her, pleased with the sultry confidence of that final shot. Would she have left something that provocative if she'd seen the image first? Her hair was wild in the photos, wilder than she remembered, and the light shone through, giving a sort of haloed effect.

"I thought you might not be real," he said, shaking his head. "You look like an angel. I don't mean that to sound—" He blushed. "Just that there's something otherworldly, you know?" he said as a waitress came to take their order, then he reddened at her raised eyebrows and pen tapping against her notepad.

"Coffees, please," Audrey said, keen for the waitress to take their order and leave them alone again.

"Filter okay?" she asked, then turned to Fred. "Same for you?"

He nodded.

"Anything else?" The waitress looked disappointed. They were taking up valuable table space and clearly didn't plan on eating.

"You do those hot churros, don't you? With the cinnamon?" Fred asked.

The waitress nodded.

"Oh, I love those." Audrey clapped her hands.

"A plate of those, please." Fred gave the waitress a grin, and Audrey watched her soften, returning his smile before she walked away.

"Where were we?" he said, redirecting his attention to Audrey. "Right, I had just embarrassed myself, telling you I thought you were an angel."

She paused, biting her lip. He reached across the table to take back the strip of photos, as though worried she might take it away. His hand brushed hers as he reached for it, and she was keenly aware of the contact point. When he opened his wallet to put it back, she noticed he had more photo strips inside.

"What are those?" Audrey asked, suddenly worried she might be one of many women whose photos he'd collected. Fred paused before taking out another of the strips to show her.

"I've had a thing for photo booths since I was a kid," he

said. "The vintage ones, the proper analog machines. There are hardly any left; soon there won't be any." He held up the photo of her again. "I love that these photos don't exist anywhere but here. They can't be reproduced—this is all you have. It makes them more valuable." He held up another strip in his hand, looking at it before showing it to her. "My parents split when I was eight. On weekends with my dad, he'd take me to the arcade. I played video games, and he played the slots. If either one of us had any coins left over, we'd take a strip together at the booth on the way out."

They paused to thank the waitress, who had returned with their coffees and churros. Once she had gone, Fred passed the photos in his hand to Audrey. Faded, well-thumbed paper, bent in places, they showed a teenage Fred, perhaps fourteen, squatting in the booth next to his father, both pulling silly faces. In one, his father had taken off his porkpie hat and pressed it over Fred's face just before the flash went off. The father's face was caught midlaugh, a genuine moment of joy.

"These are my favorite pictures of Dad." Fred's eyebrows knitted, then he reached to take the photos back. "When I look at these, I can relive that exact moment with him, his energy. I can remember what he was like, full of life." Audrey knew precisely what he meant. She could conjure her father when she looked at the stars. She could hear his voice. Fred closed his eyes then, as though aware he'd navigated the conversation to darker terrain.

"You lost him?" Audrey asked, and he nodded. "I lost my dad too, when I was twelve."

"I'm sorry. Tell me about him," Fred said, his gaze intent on her face. She saw in his eyes a reflected understanding of how this particular grief felt.

Audrey inhaled slowly. "He was the first person to teach

me about the stars. He knew all the constellations, all the myths and legends. He'd tell me about Perseus rescuing Andromeda from the sea monster, then show me how to find her in the sky. I was always more interested in the science. I wanted to know what the stars were made of, what day of the year they would be clearest to the naked eye."

"You're an astronomer," said Fred, his eyes dancing with interest.

"An amateur one." She paused. "I plan to study it, though. I need to pass this exam I've got next week, then I can apply for a course in September."

"Wow, brains and beauty," he said, winking at her, and something in his easy manner made the words feel endearing rather than cheesy.

"The math doesn't come naturally to me, but I've been studying a lot. *A lot.*"

"Are your family supportive?" he asked.

"My mum is, but—" She let out a sigh. "I'm feeling the pressure, to get it right this time, and it's not the easiest atmosphere at home."

"How come?"

"My mum is marrying this guy I can't stand. It's creating a bit of tension."

She wasn't sure why she'd just shared this with him, except that he'd told her something personal about his family and this was weighing on her mind. There was something in the way Fred looked at her . . . she felt safe, like she could tell him anything.

"I'm sorry." He paused, and in his face, she saw that he meant it. "It changes your relationship with your parents, when they move on, doesn't it?"

"Yes, I miss how things used to be with my mother. We used to be really close."

He reached out and took both her hands in his. "You're going to nail this exam, then in a few years you'll discover a new planet, they'll call it Audrena, and you can send your mum's fella on the first recce mission. No fuel for a return journey."

"Ha, maybe," she said as Fred offered her the last churro. She took it, broke it in half, and handed a piece back to him. He accepted it and they shared a smile. Audrey felt energized by the sugar, the caffeine, and the conversation. *How could it be so easy to talk to someone she'd only just met, especially someone she'd fantasized about meeting for months?*

"I love that image, of you and your telescope, seeking out other worlds," he said with a far-off look on his face.

"It's a good hobby for an insomniac."

"You're kidding! Me too, I never sleep." He gesticulated wildly, as though he couldn't believe they had this in common. "I'm even writing a book about it—*The Insomniac's Almanac.*"

"Ooh, sounds interesting, tell me more," she said.

"I've been working on it for years. It's full of things to do alone after dark, ways to stop fighting with the night. I'll add a chapter on stargazing in your honor."

"That's exactly what it feels like, doesn't it? Fighting with the night. I don't trust people who sleep too well."

"Neither do I. My older brother sleeps so easily, and sometimes, when we share a room, I wonder what I would swap to be able to sleep like that. Like, would I give up a toe?"

"I'd give up a toe."

"Would you give up a foot?"

She paused, wondering. "Would I be guaranteed to sleep eight refreshing hours a night for the rest of my life?" He nodded. "If you asked me this question at three in the morning, I'd probably give you both feet."

"Not if you had my almanac. I'm going to dedicate it to you.

'For Audrey—so she can keep her feet.' You'll find it one day in a dusty bookshop and think of me."

"Is that your passion, then? Writing?"

"No. Photography is what I love," Fred said without missing a beat. He reached for his camera bag and pulled out a black Minolta camera with a large lens and a heavy leather strap. "Can I?" he asked, holding it up to take a photo of her.

She picked up her coffee cup and blushed. He snapped a photo and then looked at the screen.

"That came out better than I could have hoped."

She reached for it so she could see. It was an excellent photo; he'd captured her coy smile, half-hidden behind the cup, her hair softly curling around her cheeks, a flirtatious glint in her eye. She looked great.

"You're good," she said, then laughed as she handed it back. "You've made me look like someone else."

"The camera doesn't lie," he said, holding her gaze again, and Audrey felt the thrill of being looked at as though she was something precious, someone extraordinary.

"I've never owned a camera," she said, looking away, breaking the intensity.

"No?"

"I wouldn't know what to do with it."

"Well, that ends today," he said, standing up. "Come on."

"Where are we going?" She laughed.

"I'm going to teach you how to take a decent photo. Partly because I want to show you what I love about it, and partly because I want an excuse to spend more time with you, Audrey the Astronomer."

Audrey grinned. He didn't need an excuse.

10

One Day Before I Do

ᑎ

*A*udrey sat on the king-sized bed of the bridal suite at Millward Hall. She had a pack of frozen peas, kindly donated by the kitchen at the Red Lion, slung around her neck. Vivien kept reaching out a hand to lift the peas off so she could assess the damage beneath, as though the wound might have miraculously healed in the thirty seconds that had passed since she'd last examined it.

"That angry shade of red is going to look awful next to your white dress," Vivien said, her face creasing into a wince.

"Is garroted chic not in this year?" Audrey asked, rubbing the back of her neck with her spare hand. *This must be what whiplash felt like.*

After the *el lazo* disaster, Vivien, Clara, and Josh had all insisted on escorting Audrey back to her room. Vivien and Clara both had rooms at the hall. Josh was staying at the Red Lion with Paul so that he and Audrey would be less likely to run into each other tomorrow morning before the service, in keeping with tradition.

"Is it painful?" Josh asked, all creased brow and tender concern after shouting at her in front of the whole dinner table. He brushed a hand through his damp hair. They'd all been caught in the rain, running across the pub car park.

"It's not that bad, honestly. It was just the shock," Audrey said, waving away Vivien's hand. She just wanted them all to go. Her neck was throbbing, and she felt like crying, but that would only make everyone feel worse about the situation.

Lawrence had been keen to clear away the broken glass and go ahead with his reading, but Debbie had insisted Audrey would need to go and have a "nice lie-down" after such a fall. Audrey had never felt more grateful for Debbie's nerves. She'd waved a hand at the room, assured everyone she was fine, and said she looked forward to seeing them all at the wedding. She'd told herself to avoid glancing in Fred's direction, but it was impossible, and when she saw him, his eyes seemed to plead with her—to do what, she didn't know. What *could* she do?

"I think Lawrence should leave the *el lazo* ceremonies to the Mexicans," said Josh, still pacing up and down by the window.

The wind was now driving rain against the windowpane, the sound of a thousand tiny bullets trying to get in.

"It was a lovely sentiment. The space was too confined," said Vivien, giving Josh a sharp look before turning her attention back to Audrey. "You'll have a bath, release the tension in your shoulders, then you need to let that rope burn dry out. It must have a chance to scab, or you won't be able to cover it with concealer tomorrow." Vivien picked up her handbag from the bed, pausing as she noticed the hives and scratch marks on Audrey's arms. "What have you done to your arms, darling?"

"I don't know," Audrey said, crossing her arms to cover

them. "Some kind of allergy or irritation. It's fine, I'll take an antihistamine."

"Well, what in heaven's name are you allergic to? You didn't eat anything strange at dinner, did you? You aren't using any new products? I did warn you not to try anything new this month. Did you hear what happened to that costume designer's daughter? She did a cheap face mask the night before her wedding and came out in a beard of blisters. There was nothing anyone could do." Vivien frowned.

"Maybe she's allergic to weddings," Clara suggested unhelpfully.

"I'm sure I'll be fine in the morning," Audrey said firmly, rolling her eyes at Clara.

"Well, I shall leave you ladies to it, then," Vivien said, her hand reaching for the door handle. "The star of the show needs to be well rested for her opening night. Clara, can I trust you girls not to stay up too late?"

Clara nodded.

Vivien turned back to the door but then stopped and reached into her handbag. She pulled out a small tube of cream, which she handed to Audrey. "Depuffing gel, just a dab under each eye, works wonders if you leave it on overnight. I want that back, though, please, it's expensive."

"You just said not to put any new, untested cosmetics on my face," Audrey pointed out.

"Oh, so I did." Vivien bit her lip, looked briefly conflicted, then took back the tube. "Well, I'm sure you don't need it then."

Audrey squeezed her mother's hand. She appreciated the offer. Despite the pain in her neck, and her itching arms, despite wanting desperately to be alone, she still felt a pang that her mother was leaving, that even on her wedding night their relationship felt taut somehow. There had been a time when

Vivien might have stayed, might have curled up and slept the night beside her. She used to give Audrey these bear hugs, hugs she gave no one else. She would fold Audrey in her arms and squeeze, whispering, "Never grow up, be my baby forever," and Audrey would promise and squeeze her right back. But then she had grown up, in one weekend, and her mother had never hugged her that way again.

"You too, Joshua. Gorgeous as you are, you need your beauty sleep. No hijinks this evening. Don't let your grooms- men shave your eyebrows off or fake-tan your forehead. I know what you boys are like."

Josh smiled. "Don't worry, I'll sleep with one eye open."

Once Vivien had gone, Clara unzipped her suitcase and took out a dress bag, her outfit for tomorrow. She brushed it down and hung it up against the wardrobe.

"You should head off too, Josh," Clara said. "We might start ironing our underwear and doing some prewedding chanting, I'm not sure you want to be here for that."

"Sure," Josh said. "Do you mind if I have a private word with Audrey before I go?" His eyes were fixed on the dark clouds outside the window.

"Sure, I need to call Jay anyway, check he has the Screama- trons under control," said Clara, shooting Audrey a wide-eyed look before leaving the room.

As Josh walked across to her, Audrey worried about what he was going to say. Had he noticed the way Fred was staring at her during dinner? She swallowed the lump in her throat.

"I'm so sorry about your neck," he said, "and for shouting at you when you were hurt. It was a reflex, but I know that's no excuse."

Audrey shook her head. "It's okay, I'm sorry I took you down with me. How's your neck?"

Josh rolled his neck left and right, then reached out for Audrey's hand. "I'll live. Look, they say bad luck comes in threes, don't they? We've had a dead bat and mutual strangulation, so only one more disaster to befall us before 'I do.'"

"Don't say that," said Audrey, feeling goose bumps prickle her skin.

"I'm joking." Josh reached up to stroke Audrey's cheek with the back of his hand. "You don't seriously believe all Granny Parker's superstitious nonsense, do you?"

"Let's not tempt fate."

Audrey consciously tried to act normally, to compose her face in a neutral expression. This was Josh, whom she knew better than anyone. Josh, her best friend. So why did she suddenly feel so awkward, as though she were standing there with a stranger?

"You'd tell me if there was something else wrong, wouldn't you?" Josh lowered his eyes. "You've hardly cracked a smile since the church." He raked a hand through his hair again and let out a long, audible exhale. He looked so concerned, and Audrey hated that she had caused him to feel that way. She reached out for his hands.

"I was bracing myself for more dead bats," she said, affecting a goofy smile.

Josh's wounded look receded, and he wrapped his arms around her and leaned in for a kiss. "I'm sorry, I know it's been hectic, with me away so much, and our mothers both being so . . . heavily involved. But just think, by Sunday afternoon it will just be me, you, two sun loungers, and that salted fish they do down at Ses Boques." He reached up to push a curl behind her ear.

"I can't wait," Audrey said, leaning into him. "And I'm sorry I haven't been smiling enough. You know me, I get a bit lost in my own head when there are so many people around. I'm sure I'll be fine after a good night's sleep."

She definitely would not be fine after a good night's sleep.

"I don't mind if you don't smile, just as long as you're happy." Josh paused, waiting for her to say something. She nodded. "Okay, sleep well, and I'll see you in the church." Josh bent down to kiss her forehead. "I love you, Audrey, more than anything. Remember, this is just the beginning."

"I love you too," she said, and it was the truth.

Josh turned to go just as Clara came back through the door with another case from the car and a bunch of flowers under each arm. Josh hurried to help, taking the flowers from her and placing them on the dresser.

"I hope you have had these flowers before," Josh said, imitating Vivien's clipped, concerned voice. "We can't risk an allergy. Don't go rubbing pollen all over your face, now." He dipped his face into the flowers, and Audrey and Clara both laughed at his impression. Josh winked at Audrey. Then, already halfway out the door, he added, "By the way, what do we think of Miranda's new boyfriend?"

Clara dropped the suitcase she was still holding on her foot, let out a strange "Hhhmmwahh" sound, and then hopped around the room muttering expletives.

"Here, let me take that," Josh said, taking the case from her and lifting it onto the bed.

He put his arm around Clara, pulling her into a hug.

"Deep breaths," he said, taking a few himself. "You okay?"

"I'm fine. Won't be able to wear heels tomorrow, but I'm fine. What were you saying?" Clara grimaced.

"This Fred bloke. What do you think? Is he going to be the man to finally tame my sister?" Josh asked.

"I didn't get a chance to talk to him," said Audrey, feeling her cheeks grow warm.

"That's a shame, I think you'd like him," said Josh. "He's your sort of person."

"What makes you say that?" Audrey asked, affecting a breezy tone but feeling as though a swarm of wasps had just taken up residence in her throat.

"Just some of the stuff he was talking about in the car on the way from the station. He's a photographer, like you, loves all the old-fashioned technology. He collects photo booths and restores them or something. Make sure you get a chance to talk to him tomorrow."

"I'll try," said Audrey, her voice not sounding like her own.

"I can't see him being Miranda's type, though," Josh went on. "I always thought she went for posh boys, sporty wine buffs like Paul, not cool photography nerds."

"You went for a photography nerd," Audrey reminded him.

"Because you're sexy and smart, and I love everything about you." He leaned in to kiss her on the lips.

"Okay, get a room, guys," said Clara. "Oh wait, this is your room, but not until tomorrow." Josh let out a short laugh, then opened the door to go.

"I'm really going now." He paused, holding out his hand in the air, his smallest finger crooked out at an angle. "Pinkie swear not to stand each other up at the altar tomorrow?"

"Just go!" Clara said, laughing as she physically pushed him out into the corridor. Once he was gone, she locked the door so they wouldn't be disturbed again.

"Finally."

Audrey sat down on the bed and then flopped backward, flinging her arms out into a star shape. Clara jumped onto the bed next to her. "I've been dying to talk to you since dinner. He was watching you the whole time, you know."

"Who?" Audrey asked, her eyes still on the ceiling.

"Fred!" Clara said, reaching out to gently knock Audrey on the forehead. "Did you hit your head on the way down?" Audrey covered her face with her hands. "What did he say in the car park? Clearly he remembers you."

"He did. He said he looked for me, that he tried to call." Audrey said it dismissively, as though she didn't necessarily believe him, as though she didn't care.

"Did he tell you why he didn't show up that day, when you agreed to meet?"

"There wasn't time, he just said something came up. There's no point dredging up all the details now. I only wanted to make sure he didn't launch into the story of how we met in front of the whole table."

"Well, he was staring at you over dinner. Maybe he never got over you. Oh shit, what if he stands up in the church tomorrow!" Clara said, suddenly animated, jumping up onto her knees on the bed. "When the reverend asks if anyone objects. It will be like that scene in *The Graduate* where Dustin Hoffman beats on the glass window in the church, shouting, 'Elaine! Elaine! Elaine!' over and over again, and then she shouts, 'Ben!' and he runs down and starts whacking everyone out of the way with the cross from the altar."

"You know you have a habit of giving massive spoilers for classic films I haven't seen?"

Clara sighed. "Sorry. Such a great film. When they get on the bus together at the end, genius. Oh, or will it be like the scene in *Four Weddings* when the brother knocks on the pew and Hugh Grant gets punched by Duckface?"

"This isn't making me feel calmer, Clara."

"Okay, look, I'll be on Fred alert tomorrow, ready to tackle him to the ground if he so much as breathes too loud in the 'does anyone object' part."

It wasn't Fred she was worried about. "What if . . . What if it *is* a sign?" Audrey said, turning over on the bed to face her friend, testing the water.

"A sign of what?" Clara frowned in confusion.

"That Josh isn't the person I'm supposed to marry."

"Please! Of course you're supposed to marry Josh! What, you're going to run away with your what-if guy from years ago, just because he shows up at your wedding—with someone else?" Clara's tone was light, as though the idea was preposterous, but then she paused as she saw Audrey's serious expression. "Audrey, no!"

"No, no, of course I'm not," she said, purposefully rolling her eyes. "It's just thrown me for a bit of a loop, that's all. Fred always felt like an unfinished chapter, and now he shows up the night before I close the book on single life . . ." She trailed off.

"Classic cold feet. Completely normal." Clara jumped off the bed and then rummaged in her bag before pulling out a small bottle of vodka. "I was saving this for tomorrow night in case the wine was shit, but I think it might be best if we had a little snifter now, just to put a bit of warmth into those feet of yours."

"Seems sensible."

"You know, I can't think of one problem that vodka is not the answer to," said Clara as she poured two shots into water glasses. "Though, what with being pregnant and then breastfeeding, I haven't drunk much in the last year—I might have glorified the wonders of alcohol in my mind."

Audrey let out a laugh that turned into a sigh. "Maybe we should reconvene about the pros and cons tomorrow morning."

They clinked glasses.

Audrey took a sip and felt the warm sting of neat alcohol hit her throat. Seeing Fred again had opened a door into her old life. It was not a door she wanted to walk through just as she was about to get married. Perhaps breaking the "no spirits" rule would just take the edge off her mounting anxiety and help keep her focus on Josh.

11

Four Years Before I Do

⤜⤛

*A*bout a month after Paul's birthday at the pub, Audrey met Josh again. Audrey, Clara, and Paul were hosting a Halloween party at the Tooting house. Audrey was dressed as a cat, drunk on eyeball stew (punch full of maraschino cherries), and kissing one of her skinny musician types. On this occasion, the man was called Sage, and they were in the downstairs corridor while they waited in line for the bathroom.

Removing his tongue from her mouth, Sage grinned and pointed at the garden.

"You stay here, pussycat, I can't deal with this line, I'm gonna have a slash in the flower bed."

As he walked away, Audrey felt her head spin. She'd drunk too much, eaten too little, and feared the cat makeup on her face had been smeared by kissing. It had been a strange day. On her way home from the gallery, she'd walked past a bookshop and seen a title in the window that drew her eye, *The Insomniac's Almanac.* She'd run into the shop, dropping her bags of Halloween decorations; picked up the book; and gone straight to the dedication.

"*To Cathy—who always slept soundly beside me.*"

The crush of disappointment was so intense she hadn't been able to move for several minutes. Some optimistic instinct had told her that this was going to be the way she found Fred again, in a bookshop window, and it would start the next chapter of their story. But, glancing at the cover, she saw the book was not written by him, and so of course the dedication was not for her. As she took another swig of her eyeball stew to quiet the day's disappointments, a voice behind her in the line called her name.

"Hey, Audrey."

Turning around, she recognized one of Paul's friends, but his name escaped her. The only information she had logged was "bad jeans" and "boring job."

"Hey . . . ," she said tentatively. "James?"

"Close. It's Josh," he said, correcting her.

"I knew that," she said, raising a wobbly hand to his shoulder, finding it surprisingly firm as she staggered into him. "What have you come dressed as, Josh?" she said, enunciating his name. "Boring City guy?" He was wearing a suit, with a token-effort pumpkin mask pushed back on his head. He looked suitably embarrassed, and she laughed. "I'm joking!"

"I had to come straight from work."

"You did well. You're in the most terrifying outfit here." Audrey made a scared face. "The horror of the sixty-hour week."

He seemed to relax, and she remembered his nice smile. He was attractive, in a traditional, rugby-boy, wholesome sort of way, with his thick brown hair and his honey-colored eyes. But Audrey was drunk, and her thoughts were on Basil or Thyme or whatever his name was, the man who'd gone to urinate in the flower bed. He was a bass guitarist who wore a leather jacket that smelled of motorbike oil, late nights, and bad decisions.

"Is that your boyfriend?" Josh asked.

"Who, that guy?" Audrey pointed a thumb in the direction of the garden. Josh nodded. "No." She shook her head.

"Good, then you won't mind me saying I think he's a bit of a dick."

Audrey leaned back against the wall, tilting her head toward him, surprised that mild-mannered Bad Jeans Josh was showing any kind of strong opinion about someone.

"Why's that then?" she asked, amused.

"Because I saw him"—Josh paused, looking for the right word—"relieve himself in one of the wine bottles earlier, then put it back on the table."

"Oh, gross!" Audrey grimaced. They shared a smile, and in her punch-addled mind she noticed how much better he looked in a well-made suit than he had in bad jeans.

"How about you? Got your sights on anyone?" She swung around to look down the corridor at the heaving living room beyond. "What about Hot Witch over there?"

Josh brushed a hand through his hair and shook his head. "I'm not good at chatting people up at parties. People tend to assume I'm the boring City guy."

"Well, it might help dispel that assumption if you didn't wear a suit to parties."

Josh gave a wry nod of acknowledgment.

"So, humor me, if you were any good at chatting people up, what would you go for? Blonde, brunette? I bet you're a boobs guy—rugby guys are always boobs guys."

He stifled a smile, amused and embarrassed by her question. "I haven't played rugby since Cambridge, and I don't have a type, not based on looks anyway."

"Let me guess, girls with a 'good personality'?" She started making air quotes, but then wobbled on her feet and had to reach for the wall instead.

"I usually go for sarcastic girls who can't stand up straight, but you are making me think I should review my search criteria." This made her smile. "Do you want me to get you some water?" he asked, and she nodded, feeling suddenly dizzy. When he returned, she thanked him and took a swig from the paper cup he handed her as he muttered, "Ganymede at your service."

"What did you say?" she asked.

"Nothing." He shook his head.

"You said Ganymede, water bearer to the gods. I'm flattered."

Audrey only knew the reference because it was one of the star stories her father had told her. Ganymede was Zeus's cupbearer and, so the story goes, Zeus had honored him for his service by placing the constellation of Aquarius among the stars. Though Audrey had never ended up studying astronomy in a formal way, it didn't mean she'd given up her interest in the stars.

"You know your Greek mythology?" Josh said with raised eyebrows.

"I know my constellations."

Some inner, sober part of Audrey wanted to quiz him further, to ask him what other Greek mythology he knew, but she was unnerved by Josh's sober gaze, his unflinching eye contact. "Why are you looking at me like that, Ganymede?"

"I'm wondering what's so appealing about this guy you're kissing," he said, his face softening to something less challenging. "The one who urinates in wine bottles and has a back-to-front musical note tattooed on his neck."

Audrey shrugged. She had no idea. "He's a good kisser."

"You don't have to be a dick to be a good kisser," Josh said, dropping his eyes to her lips. They shared a moment then. Not a whole moment, she looked away before it could be, but it was the start of something, and it made Audrey's stomach do a backflip. Or maybe that was just her bladder putting pressure on her stomach. Josh was about to say something else when the queue moved, the bathroom was finally free, and Audrey darted in. When she came out, she nodded an awkward good-bye to Josh. Then she did a quick tour of the room, topping up other people's drinks before going to find her date, who was spraying beer at the neighbor's cat in the garden.

ঞ৯ৡৣৣ

*T*he fourth time she met Josh was on Oxford Street. Audrey was rushing to a meeting with an image library she was free-lancing for. He stopped her midstride as they crossed paths on the pavement.

"Audrey," he said with a huge white smile.

"Hey." She gave him a dazed look, unable to place him out of context.

"You don't remember me, do you?" he asked, his eyes sparking in amusement. All she could think of was Ganymede, but surely that wasn't his name.

"Yes, yes, sorry, my head was somewhere else. James, Paul's friend. How are you?"

"Josh," he said, shaking his head.

Josh! That was it, she knew it was a J. "I did know that," she said.

"We've only met three times, but you know, it's fine."

He said it lightly, but Audrey was immediately defensive. "We haven't met three times, and sorry if it takes me a second when I see you out of context while running to a meeting."

"Don't let me keep you," he said, holding up his hands and turning to go. Something about the hand gesture irritated Audrey: his tone and the implication of the type of person she was.

"Hey, you don't need to be a dick about it."

"I'm not trying to be." He laughed. "I just don't want to keep you from your important meeting. See you around, Audrey."

He walked on, and Audrey turned to chase after him.

"Hey, look, I'm not one of those people who never remembers people's names, okay? Honestly, I was just in another world, plus I think I was pretty wasted when we met before."

"I'm not having a go at you," he said, still walking, eyes ahead, but there was the hint of a smile on his lips again. "I'm completely irrelevant to your life, why would you remember me."

"Wow, with the attitude," said Audrey, falling into step beside him. "What makes you think you're so irrelevant to me?"

"I don't know. You make a point of never saying more than two words to me. And you do that thing where you look over my shoulder, checking whether there's someone more interesting to talk to."

"What, all of two times?" she said with growing indignation. "And I do not do that shoulder thing, I hate it when people do that shoulder thing. I needed the loo—I was probably looking to see if the bathroom was free." As she struggled to keep pace with him, she noticed how fresh-faced and healthy Josh looked, how warm and sparkling his eyes were.

"Until next time, Audrey," he said, giving her a wave and a nod as he turned to cross the street. She watched his broad back and his thick brown hair disappear into the crowd and felt herself inexplicably riled by the encounter.

She never forgot his name after that.

12

One Day Before I Do

࿇

"Look, it's just you and me now," said Clara as they sat drinking vodka on the bridal-suite bed. "I can't gauge if this is you having standard prewedding jitters, or if you are genuinely freaking out."

Audrey toyed with the idea of telling Clara the true extent of her fears. She had told Clara about her one amazing day with Fred, shared her frustration about his standing her up and then never calling. But she had not told Clara that she had fallen in love with Fred that day. That she had never felt so instantly seen and understood by another human being. That he had been her first love, short as their acquaintance had been. She was embarrassed—it sounded childish and naïve. Who believed in love at first sight? But Audrey had felt it, and her heart had not forgotten. Then she thought about the day he'd stood her up and realized her heart had not forgotten that part either, or what had come afterward—one of the best and worst weekends of her life.

"Do you ever think about Lucas?" Audrey asked, deflecting the question.

"Lucas? Ha." Clara exhaled a loud puff of air.

Lucas had been Clara's what-if guy. They'd dated for a month in their early twenties after meeting at a music festival. He was wild and spontaneous; he'd taken her skydiving on their first date. Clara had fallen completely in love with him and pretty much moved into his flat after three days. But when Lucas had inherited a farm in New Zealand and decided he wanted to move there, they'd broken up, and that was the end of it.

"You mean do I always wonder what might have happened if he hadn't moved away? Do I still Instagram-stalk him to see pictures of his ridiculously beautiful family sitting around on their farm in matching Fair Isle sweaters, shearing sheep like they're in some kind of sexy wool catalog? Do I still think about the fact that Lucas was probably the best sex I'll ever have and how I could've picked up my life and followed him, could've been Mrs. Wool Catalog?"

"Yes," Audrey said slowly, her eyes wide.

"Of course I do, but look—everyone has a Lucas, a fantasy of another life. Would our relationship have actually worked in the long term? Would his spontaneous 'hey, let's drop everything and go kayaking this morning' attitude to life have started to get annoying after a while? Probably. Would I have argued with him the same way I argue with Jay, about who forgot to pack Baa Baa and Bee Bee in the girls' overnight bag, who left the microwave plate covered in baked bean juice? Undoubtedly. Would I have been happy living in a sexy-wool-catalog aesthetic in New Zealand, away from all my friends, my family, and my job? Hell no! Look, it's human nature to wonder what might have been. It doesn't mean he's the person you were supposed to be with."

"Do you really Instagram-stalk Lucas?" Audrey asked.

"Yes. Don't tell Jay." Clara paused, watching her friend's face. "Look, if I had doubts about you and Josh as a couple, I would tell you." She paused. "Do you have any? Seriously."

Audrey thought for a moment, trying to picture Josh's face. She loved him. She knew she did. So why did she feel so guilty? Why did she feel as though the life she had built with Josh these last three years was as fragile as a line of dominoes, and in just one short conversation, Fred had pushed the first one down? "You told me once that you didn't believe in soul mates, that you think you end up with the person you love at the right time. But what if . . . what if there is such a thing, and Josh isn't mine?"

Clara rolled her eyes and reached for the vodka bottle, topping up Audrey's glass.

"Right, so this is not just prewedding jitters, then, this is an existential crisis about whether there's a higher power involved when it comes to who your life partner should be?" Clara shook her head and downed another shot. "The night before your wedding might not be the best time to be asking yourself these kinds of questions."

"And maybe I wouldn't be, if my first love, the person I was convinced might be my soul mate, hadn't just turned up and told me he still thinks about me too."

"First love?" Clara spluttered on her drink. "Audrey, you were obsessed with the *idea* of him. You didn't love him—you hardly knew him!"

"I know, I know, I know." Audrey stood up and paced back and forth in front of the window. "I'm being nuts. I know I am, it's just today, with everything going wrong." She pointed out the window. "There's this apocalyptic weather, and dead bats falling from the ceiling, and my Freddy Krueger neck, and my mum being . . ." She didn't finish that thought. "And now all these people are coming and it's too late, and I don't even deserve to marry someone as nice as Josh anyway." Audrey raised her hands to her head and pulled her hair into fists. "I never wanted a big wedding. You know I only went along with it because I wanted a big cake, and people said you couldn't have a big cake without having a big wedding. Then it snowballed, and now I'm part of this whole parade, and you're putting ideas in my head that there's going to be some kind of 'Elaine! Elaine! Elaine!' horror-movie moment during the service tomorrow, and I don't even know what that means because I haven't seen *The Graduate.*" She let out a sharp exhale, holding out her arms to show Clara her hives. "Plus, I think my body is allergic to weddings."

Clara walked across the room to pull her friend into a hug, stroking her hair with a hand.

"Shhhh," Clara said gently. "Okay, that is a lot to unpack, and I'm sorry I ever mentioned *The Graduate.*" She sighed. "Let me get this straight. The reasons you're stressed are: One, you think Fred might be your soul mate, not Josh." She counted the points off on her fingers. "Two, all these imaginary 'bad omens' are giving you the willies. Three, for some reason, you think you don't deserve to be with Josh. Four, you're scared about being the center of attention tomorrow, and five, Vivien being Vivien."

Audrey nodded mournfully.

"Well, if I know you, and I think I do, I suspect it might mainly be about the big wedding. You should have told me how much it was stressing you out, I would have forced your mother to dial it back a few hundred notches." She pulled Audrey over to the bed, and they sat down. "What can I do? Do you want me to try and scale back the church? We could make it close family only, everyone else just comes to the reception."

"No, it's too late to do that." Audrey bowed her head, closed her eyes.

"When clients of mine get stage fright, I tell them to focus on the material, the music itself, not the audience."

"I think I just need to get a grip."

Clara narrowed her eyes at Audrey, perhaps trying to work out what the cure for this flavor of stage fright might be.

"Let's watch an episode of *Friends* on my laptop to distract you while I fix this chipped nail you've picked off, then I'll run you a bath, and you'll have a good night's sleep in this delicious bed. Tomorrow you'll wake up and have the best day of your life, marrying the man you love. Does that sound like a plan?"

"Sounds like a plan." Audrey smiled. She could still feel the panic bubbling beneath the surface, but maybe if she squashed it down and pretended she was fine, then it would in fact be fine. *Fake it until you make it.* Thank God Clara was here to stop her from doing anything stupid.

13

Twenty-Two Years Before I Do

❧

Audrey first saw her mother kiss a man who wasn't her husband when she was six years old. Audrey's nactor at the time, Felicity, was in the garden running over a monologue for an audition. Audrey's questions about why dolphins weren't fish were proving a distraction, so she'd sent Audrey to play alone in the house. Audrey was making a den for her toy horses in the hall cupboard when her mother came in. For some reason, Audrey stayed silent; she did not call out a hello. Vivien looked through to the kitchen, up the stairs, but she did not look along the corridor to where the cupboard door was half ajar.

Audrey watched as her mother pulled a tall man who wasn't her father in through the front door. She pressed her lips against his, pushed him against the wall, and slid a hand between his legs while the man groaned. Audrey stayed silent. Then Vivien laughed, pushed the man back out of the door, wiped away her smudged lipstick, and hurried up the stairs. Audrey went back out to the garden and began to cry.

"What's wrong, hon?" Felicity asked her.

Audrey shook her head, pigtails bouncing back and forth. She didn't know.

"You want a snack? I've finished doing my lines," Felicity offered, holding out a hand to Audrey. They ate bread and butter with sprinkles, and Audrey forgot what it was that had upset her.

ೲೱೲೲ

Three days later, Audrey and her parents were eating roast chicken at the kitchen table. They had busy lives, but whether her mother was in a show or her father was writing all night, they always carved out time to have Sunday lunch as a family.

"Audrey, since the sun's out, shall we put the loungers out in the garden this afternoon?" Vivien suggested. "We'll get some buns from the bakers, make lemonade, set ourselves up for the day."

Audrey nodded enthusiastically. One of her favorite things to do was simply sit with her mother in the garden or in their den, and they'd make up stories together. "Our plays," Vivien called them. Audrey would invent characters and Vivien would put on their voices. It was a simple pleasure they could indulge in for hours.

"More scandal in Westminster," said Audrey's father, nodding toward the paper he was reading as he spooned herbed roast potatoes onto his plate. "How these politicians think they aren't going to get caught, kissing people in broad bloody daylight."

"Makes politics less tedious, though, doesn't it," said Vivien, patting his hand.

"Mummy kissed a tall man," said Audrey, emphasis on the word "tall," as though this was the most remarkable part of the story. Both her parents looked across the table at her, open-mouthed, which she took as a cue to tell them more.

"Mummy kissed the man with the big shiny shoes. She touched his privates in the hall. Mrs. Dunlop at school said we shouldn't do that. Mary Carter has three brothers, so she said she sees their privates all the time, but Mrs. Dunlop said brothers aren't the same as other boys."

Audrey watched her mother go completely white. Her father laid his newspaper down on the buttery potatoes and a greasy smudge started to seep through the gray paper.

That was the last Sunday lunch they ate together as a family.

14

One Day Before I Do

⁓

*A*udrey said good night to Clara, feeling so much better than she had an hour ago. The calm voice of a good friend and a few shots of vodka were the best antidote to panic. Once Audrey was out of the bath and alone, she put some cream on her neck and moisturized her entire body. She would wash her hair in the morning, but it was nice to go to bed feeling clean.

Before getting into bed, she walked over to the window. The apocalyptic rain had finally ceased and she could see the evening sky beyond the clouds. The moon was full, illuminating the garden below, and above was the familiar shape of the Big Dipper. Out of habit, her eye drew a line in the sky to find Polaris, the northern star. Looking up at the night sky usually helped her gain some perspective. In the greater context of time and space, what did her little wedding matter? Yet tonight, however much she tried to step outside herself, she couldn't find that perspective. It *did* matter to her, it mattered a great deal. Committing to someone for the rest of her life was a huge step. Promising not to screw up, forever, was undeniably daunting.

Looking out across the grounds behind the hall, she could see why this place was the most sought-after wedding venue in Somerset. She understood why Vivien had been so keen for them to secure the only available weekend in June. Behind the sixteenth-century manor house lay a well-manicured lawn, surrounded by neat box hedges. Beyond the lawn there was a range of horticultural curiosities: a walled vegetable garden, a hedge maze, an apple orchard, and a Victorian orangery. After the ceremony tomorrow, guests would have a chance to explore the grounds while being served canapés and champagne on the lawn. They just had to hope the storm would pass in the night, otherwise everything would have to be moved inside.

Audrey felt drawn to the dark garden. It looked so calm, wet blades of grass shining like jewels in the moonlight. Maybe a short walk in the night air would clear her head and help her sleep. She threw on jeans and a T-shirt and slipped on some sandals.

Outside, the night was cool and still, though she could hear the low roll of thunder somewhere far away. There was something about being out in nature, breathing in air that felt washed clean, that instantly calmed Audrey's anxiety. She heard an owl hoot in the distance and the low drone of crickets in the long grass beyond the box hedges. All the lights in the main building were off. She felt like the last person awake in the whole world. How late would Josh stay up? Would Paul persuade him to keep drinking in the bar? Had he broken Vivien's "no spirits" rule too?

Audrey wanted to call him, to hear his voice again, but it was too late. Besides, at three minutes past midnight, it was officially their wedding day, so it would be bad luck, and they didn't need any more of that. Instead, she strolled across the lawn into the vegetable garden and then peered through the darkness toward the hedge maze. She'd explored the maze before, in daylight. Now, with only the light of the moon to see by, it looked much more daunting.

Walking around the outside of the maze, Audrey brushed a hand against the beech hedge, following it around three sides of its square. As she turned the final corner, she saw a figure standing by the entrance. She nearly cried out in surprise to find another person out here in the middle of the night. The figure turned his head, and she saw who it was—Fred.

"I watched you come out here," he said softly. "I couldn't sleep, I was sitting on the window ledge, waiting for a break in the rain."

"How was the rest of dinner?" she asked, clinging to the life raft of small talk.

"Everyone left soon after you."

Audrey reached up a hand to rub her stiff neck, massaging it with the heel of her palm.

"How's your injury? That looked painful."

"I'm fine," she said, avoiding meeting his gaze.

"This is weird, right?" Fred said with an awkward laugh. "Me being here. I'm sorry if it's made you feel uncomfortable. I was trying to think how I would feel, if the situation was reversed and you were showing up at my wedding."

"Yeah, it's a little weird," she acknowledged with a smile.

"Shall we go in?" he asked, nodding toward the maze entrance.

"It's dark. What if we get lost?"

"You can't get lost in a maze. Just keep turning right and eventually you get out."

She took a step toward the entrance; it was as good a place to talk as any. Had she come out here subconsciously hoping she might run into him, knowing that he also struggled to sleep? Why did her whole body feel so alert to his presence, even in the dark?

"I used to love mazes as a kid," Audrey said, still running her hand along the hedge as she walked through the entrance. "I think my mum took me to Longleat once. They have a huge one there."

"When we talked outside the pub, you kind of caught me off guard," Fred said as he walked behind her. "I spent the whole of dinner playing out this conversation in my head, what I should have said. I want you to know, things with Miranda—they're not serious. We're not even dating; we're staying in a twin room. We met for the first time last week. I'm here because I lost a bet on a game of pool."

"You're here because you lost a game of pool?" Audrey asked, turning around with a playful frown.

"Yes. Miranda put up fifty quid for the winner, as long as the loser agreed to be her plus-one at this wedding."

"Wow. Okay."

"I'm only telling you that because I didn't want you to think I'd be coming on Parker family holidays or anything."

Hadn't that been her exact fear?

"You don't like Miranda? You don't think she might have the potential to be more than a sympathy date?" Audrey asked lightly, reaching a crossroads and turning left.

"It's not a sympathy date. I do like her, and I wasn't doing anything else this weekend . . ." He trailed off. "I can't help thinking it's strange, though. I've never agreed to go to a random wedding before, and then to end up at yours . . ." He reached for Audrey's arm to make her stop walking. She paused, and he gestured up to the starry sky. *Fate.*

Audrey held her breath, then slid her arm away and turned to keep walking, deeper into the maze.

"Why didn't you come, that day we agreed to meet?" she asked, her face safely hidden from view. She sounded far more measured than she felt.

"I was in an accident. A scooter ran me off my bike, and I cracked two ribs, hit my head. I was in the hospital for two days."

"I'm sorry," she said, feeling a nagging pull at the back of her mind that this might not be true.

"And I did call you—first chance I had, but you gave me the wrong number." *She had given him the right number. She definitely had.* "As soon as I was out of the hospital, I went back to our booth, stuck messages to it. I even posted a note with your photo on every noticeboard in every astronomy department I could find in London, in the hope you might see it."

Audrey didn't reply. The thought of him looking for her like that prompted an unexpected glow of affection. One of the worst things about him disappearing was the fear she might have imagined what she felt between them. Everything he was telling her now said she hadn't imagined a moment of it.

She increased her pace, taking a right turn, through a break in the hedge.

"You didn't call me either," he said.

"The number you wrote down smudged, I couldn't read it."

Audrey reached another fork in the maze and stopped, turning around to look at him again, inexplicably angry now. "What do you want me to say to all this? That I was gutted when you didn't show? I was. That I looked for you too? I did." Should she admit that she remembered every detail of their day together, that if only he'd been there, everything that followed might have been so very different? *What if, what if, what if.*

"I just wanted to explain. It is one of the biggest regrets of my life, that I wasn't there that day to meet you."

His face was earnest, imploring. The air smelled of dewy foliage, of summer evenings full of potential. The moon shone down on Fred's beautiful face, and she wondered if, in another life, this might have been the face she ended up knowing better than her own.

"I'm sorry, I know this is the last thing you need to be hearing right now. I don't want to upset you," he said.

Thunder cracked above them, and it started to rain once more, huge heavy droplets of water, like a shower turning on. The storm had returned.

"This way," he said, taking her hand and guiding her back the way they had come. Fred had to raise his voice over the sound of the rain, since he was facing away from her now. "I kept your photo. I still have it in my wallet."

He had kept her photo.

"I still have yours in mine. I don't know why." She blurted it out without thinking. As soon as she'd said it, it felt dangerous, disloyal.

He had led them back to the start of the maze. They looked at each other and laughed, both soaked to the skin. Audrey ran a hand through her wet hair, exhilarated. The rain wasn't cold, and there was no wind, so standing in it wasn't an unpleasant sensation.

"I really should go in," she said. "I need to get to bed."

"Of course. I'm sorry I kept you out here."

There was so much more she could say, but she didn't trust herself to stay, so she set off in a run across the lawn, raindrops slapping against her skin. Why the hell was rain so romantic? Especially rain in a moonlit garden; she really walked into that one.

As she got to the door of the hall, she looked back to see Fred still standing in the downpour, watching her. Audrey paused, holding his steady gaze for a moment, before turning to go. Inside, she slapped the wall in frustration. *What was she doing?* She knew she had the capacity to be changeable and indecisive in life, but not when it came to love. She wasn't the kind of person to get caught up in the words of a stranger. That was something Vivien did, and if there was one thing Audrey had promised herself from a young age, it was that when it came to love, she would not be anything like her mother.

15

Six Years Before I Do

❦

*A*s soon as Audrey heard Benedict's voice, she knew he would spell trouble.

Audrey had picked up the house phone and accidentally overheard her mother's conversation. Vivien always used the house phone. She didn't approve of mobiles, and reception was often patchy in some parts of the house.

". . . So will I see you when you're in London?" she heard Vivien say, in that sultry voice she used when she wanted something.

"I'm coming to see you, gorgeous, so I should hope so," said the man. He had an accent, maybe South African or Dutch. Accents weren't Audrey's strong point.

"We'll stay at my club next weekend . . . ," Vivien simpered girlishly.

Audrey slowly, ever so quietly, replaced the receiver. She felt a cold chill prickle her skin and a faint tapping sensation, chipping away at some foundation inside of her.

After splitting from Audrey's father, Richard, Vivien had married a fashionable French journalist, Jean-Luc. She had picked up their lives and moved them to Paris, enrolling seven-year-old Audrey in a school where she didn't speak the language. Audrey's main memory of that year was of having no friends and spending Sunday nights on the Eurostar, shuttling back and forth between her parents. She remembered a French nactor named Elise who would accompany her and who once let her try red wine on the train.

Neither Paris nor Jean-Luc turned out to be a good fit for Vivien. "That is the last time I marry a man who wears tighter trousers than me," was the only explanation Audrey was given for why they were moving back to Fulham less than a year after they'd left.

Brian appeared on the scene when Audrey was ten. He taught a Saturday-morning art class Vivien had signed up for. Audrey liked him immediately; he had a gentle manner and spoke to her like she was a grown-up. In Audrey's mind, Brian and Vivien had a wonderful relationship; they never argued, they were tactile with each other, they appreciated the same food and music. Plus, Brian took his role as a stepfather seriously. He knew the names of all Audrey's friends, picked her up from parties, even took an interest in her stargazing. She clearly remembered the week after her father died, when she'd been thirteen, sitting on her bed looking at her boxed-up telescope. Brian had gently asked if she would show him the night sky, to tell him about the constellations her father had taught her. He had made looking through that lens again possible.

Audrey pressed her forehead against the wall, willing her ears to unhear the conversation on the phone. Something in her mother's voice took her right back to being a seven-year-old girl who had to pack her life into a suitcase every other weekend.

A few days later, the man with the accent came to the house. Audrey recognized his voice straightaway. He was slightly older than Vivien, perhaps in his midfifties, with a broad frame and fine silver hair. He had thick pink lips that looked almost feminine, when everything else about him was staunchly masculine, with his bearlike gait and low growl of a voice.

"Audrey, this is a friend of mine, Benedict, he's a highly acclaimed sculptor. Benedict, my daughter."

Benedict reached out a hand and took Audrey's fingers, lowering his lips to kiss the back of her hand.

"I see good looks run in the family."

Audrey gave him a tight smile and quickly extracted her hand from his.

"Benedict is taking me to an exhibition. Would you like to come? Broaden your education?" Vivien asked. Audrey did not want to come. She needed to study, had a stack of statistics papers she needed to work her way through.

Vivien shouted good-bye to Brian, who was in the studio. Audrey noticed that when they were at the door, Benedict stroked his hand along the small of her mother's back.

When Audrey reflected on her parents' relationship, she could see that perhaps they had been too similar—they both had big egos, were jealous and fiery; they were north-seeking magnetic poles, too alike to connect. The dynamic with Jean-Luc had been similar. With Brian, Audrey felt her mother had found a perfect balance; he was her south-seeking magnet— calm and trusting, he softened her sharp edges. If balanced, temperate love could not last either, then what hope was there for anyone?

≈≈≈

The next evening, as they ate one of Brian's home-cooked toads-in-the-hole at the kitchen table, Vivien announced she intended to stay with her friend Sylvia in Margate that coming weekend. Audrey knew it was a lie before she'd even finished speaking.

"Will you send her my love?" said Brian. "I must buy her latest book; I did so enjoy her last one."

Once Brian had retreated to the studio and Vivien had stacked the plates by the dishwasher, Audrey broached the topic.

"I know you aren't seeing Sylvia this weekend."

Vivien's back tensed at the sink before she slowly spun around. "Hello, Little Miss Marple."

"How can you do this to Brian?" Audrey whispered.

Vivien sighed, tilting her head to a sympathetic angle. "Brian and I are excellent companions; I love him more than anyone, bar you." She paused, waiting for Audrey to meet her gaze. "But the lust part, you can't keep that—no one can. I didn't go looking for anything with Benedict, honestly I didn't, but I don't think I could have stopped it, it was beyond me." She blushed, biting back a smile, then said in a whisper, "It keeps me young, Audrey, I feel like a girl again." A silly grin lit up her face. "Do you remember when I played Blanche DuBois at the National, waking up to the reviews after press night, every one of them five stars? That is how he makes me feel, just being in his orbit. When you fall in love, you'll understand."

"Well, I don't like being your secret keeper," Audrey snapped.

"Then stop earwigging on things that don't concern you. I'm just embracing life before I get too old for anyone to love me." She pursed her lips. "He lives in New York; it can only be a short-lived thing."

"I think you're being selfish," Audrey said, "and the people who really love you won't stop just because you get old."

Vivien blinked furiously before turning away from Audrey to hide her face. "You're twenty-two, you have no idea."

Was Vivien right? Was she being naïve to think that when she met the right person, love could last a lifetime? Audrey had never been in love, not really. She'd had boyfriends she liked spending time with, but no one who made her grin the way Vivien had just now.

As she lay on her bed that night, she found herself taking the photo strip of the boy from Baker Street out of her wallet. She looked into his green eyes and imagined what he might be doing now. Then she wondered, not for the first time, who his "I will find you" message might have been for.

⁓

After their illicit weekend, Benedict went back to New York, and Audrey heard no more about him. She hoped that whatever it had been, that was the end of it. Three weeks later, she and Brian were in the kitchen, Brian emptying the dishwasher while she worked on a math problem at the kitchen table. She threw down her calculator in frustration. Maybe she'd been foolhardy to drop geography. Maybe a science subject was beyond her ability.

"This is impossible."

Brian came to rest a hand on her shoulder. "It is a lot, trying to cram a two-year math syllabus into five months."

"If I don't take the exam now, I won't be able to apply for a place in September. I'll waste another year."

"If it takes another year, it takes another year. The stars aren't going anywhere," Brian said, coming to sit down beside her. "You need a break. Come on, let's order Thai takeaway from that place your mother likes and watch the new BBC crime drama, take one night off."

Brian got up to wash his hands and asked Audrey to hand him the phone. As she picked up the handset from the counter, she noticed there wasn't a tone and instinctively pressed it to her ear. That's when she heard Vivien, talking in that sickening, simpering voice, then that unmistakable accent—Benedict. Audrey felt her hands tense around the phone.

"What's wrong?" Brian asked, sounding genuinely concerned as he took in her expression.

She should have slammed down the handset, made up an excuse, composed herself, but she just stood there with it clasped in her hand, feeling like a rabbit caught in the headlights of a huge truck.

Brian's eyes narrowed. He walked across the kitchen and took the handset out of her hand. She could have held on or made a sound to warn Vivien, but she did neither of these things. She just let the phone slip out of her palm into his. As Brian held it to his ear, she saw his face harden, his eyebrows draw into a frown. But he was frowning at Audrey, at her strange behavior.

"Why did you make that face, hearing your mother talk to her friend on the phone?" he asked, his voice breaking as he put the receiver back. Audrey shook her head.

"No reason," she said, her voice a whisper, and now they both knew she was lying.

"How long has it been going on between them?" Brian asked slowly. He looked so hurt, discovering her a conspirator.

"It's nothing to do with me," Audrey said. And then dramatically fled upstairs to her room, put some music on her headphones, and buried herself under the duvet.

⟡

*W*hen she ventured downstairs later that evening, she found her mother sitting at the kitchen table, red-eyed.

"He's gone, Brian's gone."

"What? Why?" Audrey asked, every limb feeling leaden with shame.

"He heard me talking to Benedict on the phone. We were only talking, we're friends. I don't know why he thought it was something else . . ." And then her words jumbled into tears.

Audrey sat down on the floor and gave her mother a hug, guilt cutting at her bones. She looked across at the kitchen table and had a distinct flash of déjà vu to a dimly remembered conversation sixteen years earlier over herbed roast potatoes. To the last time she'd ruined her mother's life by failing to keep her secrets.

ееее

Brian moved out and Vivien took to her bed. She canceled rehearsals for the play she was opening in a month's time. She saw no one, even when the frantic director came knocking. Audrey called Brian. "Won't you talk to her, please?"

"Audrey, you will always be a daughter to me, always, but don't involve yourself in this. There's history here."

This wasn't the first time. Did that make it better or worse?

Audrey hoped their separation might be temporary, but then, one Sunday Audrey opened the door to find Benedict, with a large suitcase in each hand.

"Hello?" she said, her face full of confusion. She was wearing a bed shirt with no bra, and Benedict's eyes fell briefly to her chest. She reached a hand up to her shoulder, covering herself with one arm. "What are you doing here?"

His eyes were now on her face, and she wondered if his eyeline had been accidental.

"Your mother needs me," he said, bringing his cases into the hall.

Audrey left him by the door, charging up the stairs and bursting into her mother's bedroom.

"Why is he here?" she hissed. Her mother was out of bed, doing her hair at the dressing table. It was the first time she had gotten dressed in days.

"Oh, has Benedict arrived?" she asked, pinning a stray piece of hair at the nape of her neck.

"With suitcases," Audrey said, in a way that made "suitcases" sound like a dirty word.

Vivien turned to her daughter, taking in her bewildered expression. "Brian isn't coming back. You know I'm no good on my own. Benedict is going to keep me company for a few weeks. I thought you'd be pleased, not having to babysit me anymore."

"It's not babysitting, I don't mind. I love it when it's just the two of us."

"I'm sorry, darling," said Vivien, looking anything but sorry.

"Well, you could have checked with me first. I live here too," Audrey said, pacing up and down the bedroom.

"It is my house," said Vivien sharply. "You're an adult now. You can go and live in the halls with all the other students if you don't like my arrangements."

"Why can't you just be on your own for a bit?" Audrey changed tack, pleading now.

"It's not how I'm built, Audrey. You know it's not how I'm built."

Audrey felt the weight of this settle in her chest. Falling in love seemed like a dangerous thing. Every time it happened to her mother, Audrey lost her family or her home. Love was not safe and warm, it was a wild wind that could rip your life apart.

16

Five Hours Before I Do

❦

*A*udrey woke up alone, sweating, her hair matted and damp against her forehead. It took her a moment to realize where she was. Picking up her phone, she saw it was nine thirty on the twenty-fifth of June. The date written on her marriage plate, on the invitations, and on the laminated wedding-day schedule. The date she would celebrate as her anniversary for years and decades to come.

Her mind felt like stewed soup, claggy with a cocktail of emotions and vodka. Vivien had been right about one thing: spirits were a bad idea. She could still taste the fuzz of alcohol on her tongue. She'd gone to sleep in a bad mood and the feeling hadn't dissipated. The shock of seeing Fred at the rehearsal dinner had passed, and now she just felt annoyed that he was here, saying all these things to her that she didn't need to know. It might have seemed charming in the moonlight and the rain, but in the sharp light of day it felt selfish and confusing for him to say anything—especially about posting a note for her in every astronomy department in London. There was something in this detail, that he had listened and remembered, that he had made such an effort to look for her . . . If she had only passed that exam, gotten into that course, would she have found one of his notes? *What if, what if, what if.*

There was a knock at the door, then Clara's voice.

"Hey, you awake, Auds? Breakfast stops serving at ten, but I can bring us up a tray if you don't want to go down?"

Audrey got out of bed and opened the door. She didn't want to stay in her sweaty sheets; she needed to get up, throw open the windows, slay the day. She'd never slayed a day before, but it sounded like the kind of thing she should be doing on her wedding day.

"You. I blame you for the vodka," she said, pointing a finger at Clara.

"Sorry. I'm a bad friend. What happened to your hair?" Clara asked. "It looks like you slept with it wet and now it's dried all weird."

"I'll wash it after breakfast, it's fine, you'll fix it with your magic curling iron."

"You're lucky you have a maid of honor who's a professional image consultant, because this image"—she waved a hand in front of Audrey's face—"currently needs a lot of consulting. By the way, Jay called this morning—he had a terrible night with the Screamatrons. Is it bad that I'm a tiny bit glad? Now he knows what it's like doing a night alone with them."

"Completely understandable. You want him to manage without you, but not too well."

"Exactly. I hope he remembers to pack their pacifiers for the wedding." Clara paused, catching herself, then clapped her hands briskly. "Not my responsibility today. You are my responsibility. Forget the girls, forget Jay, where you'd like to have breakfast is the only important question."

"You don't have to pretend you're not a mum this weekend

just because I'm getting married," Audrey said as she pulled out a blue wrap dress from her case.

"I know, I know, but you were such a great maid of honor to me and I—oh God, my boobs are killing me. I might have to pump after breakfast, do you mind? I'll be super quick."

"Of course I don't mind! I don't want you to explode. You can pump in the church for all I care. Come on, let's go down for breakfast, it smells of vodka and sweaty bedclothes in here."

"So you did sleep? No insomnia or anxiety?" Clara asked, observing her with wary concern.

"Like a baby," she lied. She'd decided not to tell Clara about her nocturnal meeting with Fred; it might make her worry.

"I don't know where that expression comes from, babies don't sleep. Hey, guess what? You're getting married today!" Clara said in a singsong voice, punching the air above her head.

"Yay me," Audrey said cheerfully. She waved her hands in the air, grabbed her phone, and followed her friend out into the hall.

∾≫≪∾

The breakfast room had a peaceful elegance to it, with two colossal bay windows looking out over the lawn and a back wall lined with bookcases. There was a long oak table at one side, laden with a beautiful spread of fruit salad, cereals, coffee, and pastries. As Audrey stepped into the room, heading straight toward the delicious breakfast options, she felt a snagging sensation, like a fly who had just been caught in a web. She sensed a breeze on her skin and a tug on her dress, and she looked down to see the front of her blue wrap dress hanging open. The tie of the dress had caught on the door handle and unraveled her like a badly made sweater.

"Here she is!" said Debbie with a wave, hand freezing in

midair as she saw Audrey's predicament. Josh's parents were sitting with Vivien, Lawrence, and Brian at the table nearest the door, and all their eyes were upon her. Audrey quickly spun back toward the door to try to wind herself back into her dress. Clara noticed what was happening and stepped smoothly in front of her to preserve her modesty.

"It's fine, nobody noticed," Clara assured her as Audrey grappled to unhook the dress from the door handle.

"I think people noticed," Audrey said through gritted teeth. Michael's face had turned a shade of beetroot at seeing Audrey's sheer pink bra.

"Well, you're just going to have to style it out, then, babes," Clara whispered. So Audrey did. She retied her dress, held her head high, then walked across the room as though she had not just flashed her breasts to her future father-in-law.

When she'd decided to come downstairs for breakfast, she'd been focused on seeing what pastries were on offer, whether they had any yummy homemade granola. She had not considered that everyone else staying at the venue would be having breakfast there too.

"The beautiful bride!" Debbie exclaimed, trying to cover everyone's blushes with conversation. Her face crumpled in concern when she saw Audrey's neck. "How are you feeling, dear? How's that abrasion?"

"Audrey, I hope we can expect a little more elegance in the church," Vivien said softly, rapidly blinking her eyes and giving her daughter a sympathetic head tilt.

Lawrence swung around in his chair. "So sorry again about the *el lazo*, Audrey, really bad luck that was. I've never seen that happen before. Quite, quite unfortunate."

Debbie was now by Audrey's side, inspecting the rope burn at close quarters. "No one will notice, dear. Everyone will be too busy looking at your gorgeous figure. I mean your dress, not your figure. Your figure *in* your dress. Hopefully your veil will cover the worst of it." Debbie squeezed Audrey's arm, but Audrey could see from the look on her face that Debbie did think people would notice. "You can always airbrush it out in the photos, they can airbrush anything these days, can't they?"

Audrey wished she could airbrush herself out of this conversation.

"We saved you a place," Hillary called across the room. He was staring at her with wide, unblinking eyes, presumably trying to convey how unsatisfactory he felt his current breakfast companions, Miranda and Fred, to be. There were two free seats at his table, one opposite Fred, the other beside him. Audrey *really* should have thought through this "coming down for breakfast" plan.

"How did you sleep?" Fred asked as she took the seat beside him.

"Fine," she said, her eyes firmly on the table in front of her. "The rain kept me awake for a while."

"Rain sometimes clears the air," Fred said.

"Fred went out in it!" Miranda said, laughing, reaching for the pot of tea in the middle of the table. "I woke in the night and nearly screamed when I saw this sodden figure at the end of my bed." Miranda sniffed the air. "Who's wearing Purple Haze?"

"I am," said Clara. "Incredible."

Miranda was a professional perfumer. She could identify almost any perfume or scent in a room, including the washing detergent people had used on their clothes.

Vivien approached their table and handed Audrey a mug of steaming liquid. She was dressed immaculately in a lemon twinset, with her hair pinned back and a simple powdered face.

Unlike Audrey, her mother would never be seen in public without some form of hair and makeup in place.

"Vivien is wearing Chanel No. 5," said Miranda, closing her eyes, "and a bergamot and mint hand cream."

"I am," Vivien said, looking impressed, then turned to Audrey. "Hot lemon, it's what my voice coach always recommends before curtain. You shouldn't have coffee, it will make you jumpy. Now, I know you said you were going to do your own hair, but you know Debbie and I both have appointments at the salon in the village this morning and I penciled you a slot, just in case you changed your mind." Vivien reached out to touch her daughter's hair. "This is a little wild."

"She's channeling Russell Brand," Hillary said, giving Audrey a wink.

"The salon's called Curl Up and Dye," Debbie called from across the room. "Isn't that so amusing?"

Audrey pulled her hair back into a ponytail with an elastic from her wrist. She could not think of anything more stress inducing than having her hair done by someone she didn't know, while sitting between Debbie and her mother.

"I haven't washed it yet, that's why it's a mess. Clara's going to do it, she's great at hair."

"I thought you styled bands, not brides?" said Vivien.

"I was thinking we'd dye it green and then do a sort of punk updo," Clara said seriously, coming back from the buffet bar with two coffees and putting one down in front of Audrey.

Vivien's face fell for a moment, until she realized Clara was joking. She intercepted the coffee in front of Audrey.

"I don't have the constitution for jokes this morning, Clara. You know how my nerves are before an opening night, you mustn't test me." Her eyes darted back to the large windows and the gray rain, which was showing no sign of stopping.

"Will it ever end? We don't have enough pink and lilac umbrellas to go around—the guests will be soaked. Nothing worse than a damp audience. Hopefully, some people will have the good sense to bring their own."

Watching Vivien talk about umbrellas, Audrey had a sudden flash of memory, of meeting her mother after a show at a stage door behind Shaftesbury Avenue. It had been pouring, and Audrey had brought a flimsy umbrella not up to the task. Vivien had scanned the crowd of well-wishers and autograph hunters, and when she'd seen Audrey, she'd walked straight through the crowd, pushed her broken umbrella aside, and enveloped her in a huge hug. They'd run off into Soho, giggling like children, their heels getting soaked in the puddles. There was a lighter side to Vivien, which sat alongside her more austere, diva-ish façade. Only those closest to her were ever allowed to see it, and in the last few years it had been ever more closely guarded. Had it gone, or was it just that Audrey was no longer allowed to see?

"Were the ushers briefed about escorting people between the church and the house?" Vivien asked, pulling Audrey back to the present. "You know, when Lawrence and I got married, we hired professional ushers from the theater. They were so efficient."

Clara caught Audrey's eye as she mimed doing a shot.

"I can make sure the ushers know," Fred said, and Vivien pressed a hand on his shoulder in gratitude.

"That's very helpful of you, Frederick." She had a habit of lengthening people's names, whether that was what they were called or not.

"Don't let the weather rain on your parade," called Brian cheerfully from the table by the door. "Remember our wedding, Viv? Rained cats and dogs the whole afternoon, but we still had a ball, didn't we?"

Vivien looked flushed by Brian's words and muttered, "Well," before walking toward the window to more closely inspect the sky.

"Audrey, I'd better get a chance to talk to you today," said Hillary, gently kicking her beneath the table. "You're not going to be all boring and bridal and too busy to speak to me, are you? I mean, yes, I can carry on being completely adorable to all your friends, but really I am only here to see you."

"No one gets quality time with the bride on her wedding day," said Clara, sitting back down and hugging her arms against her chest. "Everyone knows that."

Audrey's head was beginning to spin with all this attention, all these questions. Why hadn't she stayed in her room? Why had she come to breakfast with her hair a mess? Why hadn't she tied her dress up properly? Crucially, why wasn't she allowed coffee?

"I bet you wish you'd gone for room service," Fred said, leaning toward her, reading her mind. She looked sideways at him and instantly regretted it. His green eyes cut through all the noise. There was something about Fred's face. She pushed back her chair and stood up.

"You'll have to excuse me, I have a . . . a thing," she announced to the table. Then she walked over to the breakfast bar, picked up two croissants and a pot of coffee, and walked purposefully back toward the door.

Except she didn't want to go back to her room. People could find her there. The laminated timetable of hair and makeup and "getting-ready photos" would begin, and then there wouldn't be a minute left to be alone, to think. So instead of going upstairs, she kept going, down a small corridor that led through the bowels of the old house. She needed a quiet room, somewhere no one would look for her, just for twenty minutes. After opening several old wooden doors, she found what she was looking for: a small, cozy-looking cleaning cupboard, full of linen and towels, a vacuum cleaner, a mop bucket, huge bags of toilet paper, and boxes of miniature soap and shampoo. No one would find her here. She pulled the dangling light switch, made a seat for herself out of a pile of towels, and tugged the cupboard door closed.

"Focus, Audrey, focus," she told herself. Sometimes, when emotions started to overwhelm her, they could escalate into a panic attack. She didn't want that to happen on her wedding day. She needed to get ahead of it, to pull herself out of whatever tailspin she was in. Seeing Fred had flung open a door, and she needed to work out how she was going to close it, for good.

17

Six Years Before I Do

❧

As Fred held the door open and Audrey stepped outside the café, she saw with surprise that the rain had stopped. Fred suggested they walk down to Hyde Park.

"Where were you headed, before you spotted me on the platform?" he asked.

"The dentist, and then the library," she said, grimacing. "I should call to reschedule, but I don't have a phone right now. I managed to put mine through the wash yesterday—it's currently sitting in a bag of rice."

"I don't know if that trick works after a whole spin cycle."

"I have faith." She grinned. "The rice trick hasn't failed me yet."

"Do you want to use mine?" he asked. She shook her head. "I'll feel responsible if your dentist blacklists you and all your teeth fall out."

"Well, you can feed me puréed churros if they do."

"Deal."

When they got to the park, there was a brass band playing on the bandstand. It was an upbeat, joyous tune, and Fred started to swing his hips, dancing his way along the path just as the sun came out from behind a cloud. He was a good dancer with natural rhythm, as though the music were pulling him in time with the notes. Audrey usually only liked to dance in the anonymity of a dark nightclub, but Fred took her hand and swung her around, encouraging her to move with him.

The conductor must have seen them dancing on the grass, because the music changed, and the band started to play "Singin' in the Rain." Fred threw down his bags in delight and pulled Audrey into an up-tempo waltz around the bandstand. His hands were firm and confident, clasping her waist and hand. It was exhilarating, and for a moment, she felt as though she were flying.

What was she doing here? Dancing around the park with a stranger? This was not how Audrey had predicted her Saturday would go. She'd thought she'd be getting a filling replaced, followed by several hours of linear algebra, not being transported into some 1950s musical theater fantasy. Fred began singing, making up the words, and Audrey felt a swell of delight, his enthusiasm infectious.

"Did you arrange this?" she asked, slightly breathless, as he spun her around and around on the grass in broad daylight.

"Yes, I called ahead. I like to have a full brass band on standby whenever I have a date with a beautiful girl."

"This is a date, is it?" she asked, unable to hide her smile.

"A fortuitous meeting," he said with exaggerated grandeur.

When the music came to an end, the band put down their instruments to applaud their dancing. Audrey and Fred both bowed and clapped for the band in return. A few onlookers cheered, and an elderly man with a shock of white hair came over to tell them that seeing them dance like that had made his day. Unlike her mother, Audrey had never been much of an exhibitionist, but for some reason, today she didn't mind being the center of attention.

They left the bandstand and walked further into the park.

"You know, you're just what I imagined you'd be like," Fred said, looking across at her with a dimpled grin. "Sexy and smart."

"So are you," she said, then blushed. "You have this infectious energy, like you're hungry to live every moment all at once."

"I do want to live every moment," he agreed. "I don't want to wake up in fifty years with any regrets. I think as soon as you stop wanting to learn, explore, change things, that's when you get old." Fred looked out across the park, then reached down and firmly clasped her hand. The intimacy of it made her stomach feel deliciously molten. "If this was our first date, what would you want to do?"

"Something unforgettable," she said breathlessly.

He grinned and started pulling her along faster and faster until they were both running through the park.

Further south, beside the Serpentine, was a fairground. Fred led her straight to the Ferris wheel, where they queued for a ticket. They bought warm nuts, which smelled of hot sugar and cold days, to eat in the queue.

"A Ferris wheel? Nice, but it's not exactly *original* first-date territory," she teased.

Fred turned around to the queue of people behind them and said loudly, "She's a harsh critic, ladies and gentlemen."

"Shhhh," Audrey said, pulling him back around to face the front.

He leaned forward and whispered in her ear. "We're not just riding it. We're going to jump off it."

She rolled her eyes, assuming he was joking. "Why would we do that?"

"Because it's the best way to get to know someone."

Fred left his umbrella at the ticket kiosk, stuffed his camera bag into his rucksack, and then strapped it to his front. They climbed into one of the red plastic bucket seats and pulled the chain across their laps. "Sometimes life feels like a hamster wheel. You get caught up in the practicalities of existence and all the joy gets pushed aside in favor of necessity. Sometimes you just need to jump off the wheel." With this, he unhooked the chain across their seat, and for the first time, Audrey realized he might not have been joking about jumping. He stood up and reached out for the bar above them, launching himself out of the seat so that it swung, alarmingly, back and forth, and she had to hold on to the sides to keep her balance.

"What are you doing? You're going to fall!" Audrey said, panic in her voice.

"When you get off the wheel, you see everything in a whole new way, and the ride you're on—you stop taking it for granted."

There was shouting from below, people yelling at him to sit back in his seat. Then he reached out a hand to her, holding his whole weight with only one hand.

"Come on. You'll be fine, I promise. We're at the top of the wheel now, I'm going to hold on to this bar for a few minutes, and then when we're closer to the ground, I'll jump. Do it with me."

He was insane; there was no way she was getting out of the chair.

"Don't you remember being a kid, being fearless, wanting to climb and jump and play? Why do we stop doing that? Look, we're not far from the ground now; you won't need to hold on for long."

Audrey saw something in his eyes then, a calm confidence, like she needed to trust him, and she found herself standing up, reaching out for the bar too. More shouting from below; she didn't dare look down. She grabbed hold of the bar, pushing off from the seat, letting her legs dangle beside his. She wouldn't be able to get herself back into the chair now; she would have to hang like this until they were low enough to drop.

"I'm going to slip," she cried, her breath catching in her throat.

"No, you're not," he said, and as she glanced down she saw a crowd gathering, a security guard approaching the ticket kiosk, people pointing up at them.

Her heart pounded, her arms ached, her palms were sticky with sweat, she would break a leg if she fell now, they were still twenty feet in the air. Why had she done something so reckless? She should have been in the library, reviewing Newton's second law of motion, not testing it out. Would she be able to take her math exam next week if she had a broken arm?

The wheel had almost come full circle, but it was still a six-foot drop.

"Now copy me, just swing and jump," he told her.

"I can't!" she cried, her voice breathless.

"You can. Do it now. Jump straight after me, bend your knees when you hit the deck, then we run, fast, okay?" He turned to face her. "I'm not running without you."

"Okay."

He swung back and forth, launching himself over the edge of the balustrade, landing with a thud on the metal platform. He turned around, calling "jump" to her, and she saw she would have to face the angry ride owner if she stayed where she was, so she swung her legs to gain momentum and leaped, landing with a loud slam on the metal floor. She didn't have a moment to pause for breath because Fred was calling for her to jump again, over the railing of the ride, down onto the grass, away from the security guard who was heading toward her.

She followed Fred, somehow clearing the railing. She saw him start to run, her legs throbbed, and she didn't think she could catch up. She turned to see two men in safety jackets chasing after them, shouting, and her heart surged in her chest as she saw Fred stop to wait for her. He held out his hand, she reached out and clasped it, and they ran together. It was reckless and dangerous, and completely out of character.

Audrey had never felt more alive.

18

Four Hours Before I Do

❧

$\mathcal{I}$t was calm and peaceful in the cupboard. There was something comforting about the close walls, the dim light, and the quiet, the blissful quiet. Audrey only wished she'd stretched to a plate and a cup for her breakfast-to-go. When she'd picked up the coffeepot and the croissants, she'd envisaged going back upstairs, where there were cups and saucers as part of the in-room tea-making facilities. Now she was getting crumbs on clean linen and had to make do with drinking her coffee from a dusty water glass she'd found at the back of a shelf.

How long could she stay in here before someone came looking for her? What would happen if she never came out? Even when people finally tracked her down, what if she just refused to open the door, claimed she was sick? She couldn't walk up an aisle if she were sick. She looked around the cupboard at all the cleaning products and wondered how much bathroom cleaner she'd have to drink to make herself just sick enough to postpone the wedding. Not sick enough to do any real, long-lasting harm, just ill enough to get a few days' reprieve. Audrey covered her face with her hands—was she really thinking about drinking bathroom cleaner? She suspected these weren't thoughts a bride should be having on her wedding day.

Audrey occasionally had these strange, intrusive thoughts, things she wouldn't admit to anyone. Her mind sometimes ventured down a dark avenue without permission, and it scared her. It was like standing on a roof terrace, looking over the edge and wondering if the fall would be high enough to kill you. She wasn't considering jumping, but still, she stepped back from the edge, just in case. Clara had once told her this was not abnormal; it even had a name—"high place phenomenon." Your brain sees a dangerous situation, like the edge of a building, and it reacts by stepping back, but you interpret the action as the suppression of a desire to jump, as though there is a part of yourself you don't trust not to do it. The French called it *l'appel du vide*, the call of the void.

In her early twenties, after everything that happened with Benedict, Audrey had developed some unhealthy, self-destructive tendencies. She always chose the bad boys to kiss at parties, men who were not kind or caring. She always drank a little bit too much, was the last to leave a party when she knew she should go home. She hadn't looked after herself. That part of her life was over now. Since choosing lovely, decent, kind Josh, she had said good-bye to her darker, self-destructive side. He had saved her from herself. But what if that side wasn't gone? What if she was still there, in that cupboard, about to answer the call of the void and ruin her wedding?

There was a sharp knock on the door of the linen cupboard, which made Audrey spill hot coffee down her dress.

"Shit!"

"Audrey?" Hillary's voice came through the door.

"I'm not here," she said pathetically, but Hillary opened the door anyway. "Seriously? Do you have me microchipped or something?"

Hillary peered into the cupboard and sighed. "This is the location of choice for your wedding-morning freak-out?" He moved a few towels aside and made a seat for himself on a box full of miniature shampoo bottles. He'd brought an espresso cup of black coffee with him.

"How did you know I was here?"

"You had that look in your eye at breakfast, like someone pulled the pin out of a hand grenade and passed it to you. There are only four potential hiding places on the ground floor, and this was the second one I knocked on."

"Why did you think I'd be freaking out? I'm not freaking out, I just wanted to have breakfast in peace. A quiet moment of reflection before, you know, committing myself to someone forever and ever and ever and ever. And ever." Audrey started hyperventilating. With Hillary now stealing half the air, there wasn't enough oxygen in the cupboard.

Hillary leaned toward her and laid a hand on each shoulder before pulling her into a hug.

"Don't you worry. Hillary's here. We'll sort it all out." The kindness in his voice, the unexpected earnestness, broke her. Audrey let out a single sob.

He held her for a moment before asking, "So, is this 'croissants in the cupboard' routine a genuine cry for help, or are you furnishing me with material for my speech later?" He let her go and rooted around in his jacket pocket before pulling out some nicotine gum.

Despite his acerbic manner, Hillary could be sensible and serious when he needed to be. He was the kind of person who, if you asked him for a drink when he'd just sat down, would call you a lazy cow and declare he wasn't getting up again for love nor money. But if you phoned him at two in the morning and said you needed rescuing from a nightclub, he would cross London to get you, no questions asked.

"Do you remember me telling you about Photo Booth Guy?" Audrey said, shuffling on her own chair of towels to get more comfortable. "The guy I had that one amazing afternoon with, who never showed up for our date the next day?"

"No," Hillary said. "Wait, is this the guy with the tattoo who you got obsessed with, who inspired you to get that horrible smudge on your shoulder?"

"I can't believe you don't remember this, Hillary! It was about six years ago—"

"There is a distant bell ringing," Hillary said, waving a hand at her. "*Qu'est-que le relevance?*"

"He's here. He's Miranda's date, Fred."

"That pale boy?" Hillary said, his voice rising an octave.

"Yes, him." Audrey frowned. "Do you think it means something, him showing up this weekend?"

Hillary paused, popped a second piece of gum into his mouth, then stood up a mop that had fallen across his lap.

"I think there was always going to be something that threw you off today. If it wasn't some specter from your past showing up with good hair and beautiful cheekbones, it would have been something else." He fixed her with an unblinking gaze. "Do you think maybe you're depressed, Auds?"

"You always think everything boils down to people being depressed!" Audrey cried. "I'm not depressed, this is the happiest day of my life." Then they looked at each other and both started snorting with laughter. That was the problem with Hillary, you could only have a serious conversation with him for so long, and then he would inevitably make you laugh. "I'm serious, Hillary. Help me. What am I supposed to do? Do you think him being here is a sign that I'm making a mistake?"

Hillary looked contemplative for a moment and made a "hmmm" sound. Audrey held out her palms, inviting him to elaborate.

"Did you ever hear the fairy tale about the princess who got everything she ever wanted?"

"No," Audrey said, rolling her eyes.

"The girl who marries Prince Charming, gets a golden carriage, and moves into a lovely castle with four turrets and room for a day spa. In the twenty-first-century version, she also gets a fulfilling job as a girl boss at a FTSE One Hundred company. She's emotionally balanced and normal, and together they go on to have a great life. You haven't heard this one?"

"No, I haven't," Audrey said impatiently.

"Do you know why you haven't heard it? Because it's a shit story. No one wants to read about the princess who got everything she ever wanted—she's tedious and dull and irritatingly smug." Hillary gently shifted his shoulders around so he was looking her in the eye. "We both know perfectly well you're not actually going to run off with Mr. Cheekbones today. No one does that in real life. You'd get as far as the motorway service station and then turn around and come back again—it would all be painfully embarrassing. Plus, no one else is ever going to let me do a best-man-of-the-bride speech at their wedding, so don't fuck this up for me. This is the happiest day of my life."

Audrey started to laugh, and then cry, and then both at once. Hillary pulled her head onto his shoulder and kissed it.

"Just remember what today is all about—you and Josh. You know he's not my type, but I'll concede he's a pretty remarkable man, and he loves you to distraction." Hillary stretched out his legs. "Can we get out of this cupboard now? I really can't abide spaces this small. They take me back to the green room at the Donmar Warehouse, and I feel like I'm about to be thrust on-stage in an inadequately sized loincloth." He gave a theatrical shiver.

"Yes." She nodded. "We can get out of the cupboard now."

Hillary was right. Of course he was right. Audrey had lost sight of something in the maze last night. She'd lost sight of Josh.

19

Four Years Before I Do

❧

"*W*hy don't you invite Josh?" Audrey found herself saying next time she, Paul, and Clara were planning one of their infamous Tooting dinner parties.

"Really?" Paul said in surprise. "I didn't think you'd ever said two words to Josh."

"I haven't, but he seems like a nice guy. It would be good to mix up the guest list."

Paul shrugged and exchanged a look with Clara.

"What's that look?"

"Nothing," Paul said. "Josh thinks you don't like him, that's all."

"Why would he think that?" Audrey said indignantly.

"Because you didn't remember his name when you ran into him in Soho," said Paul.

"Did he tell you that?" Audrey felt her cheeks grow warm.

Paul looked down at the piece of paper where they'd scribbled a list of names to invite to Saturday's Sausage Fandango dinner. It was a tradition Clara had initiated, bucking against the trend of elaborate three-course meals. At the Sausage

121

Fandangos, guests were asked to bring their own chair, their own bowl, and at least two bottles of red wine. Clara cooked her now-infamous Sausage Fandango Stew, which consisted of sausages, tinned tomatoes, mixed beans, and enough spice mix to make it taste of something. They would set up a trestle table along the kitchen and out into the corridor, then pack in twenty dinner guests. Anyone who ever came left wondering why everyone didn't do dinner parties this way.

Paul shook his head but added Josh's name to the list.

"Fine, we'll invite Josh, but we'll have to invite his girlfriend too."

"Okay," Audrey said with a purposeful shrug of indifference.

"Kelly," Paul continued. "She's a Canadian underwear model. Ridiculously tall. I don't know if she'll be down with the Sausage Fandango vibe."

"Well, we don't need to invite them, it was just an idea," said Audrey, but Paul had already added them to the list.

"If we're inviting Josh, I'll get him to ask his sister too. She's just moved to London. I think someone said she was hot."

"That's settled, we'll invite them all," said Clara, giving Audrey a knowing look, though Audrey wasn't sure what it was Clara thought she knew.

*When the dinner party came around the following Saturday, Audrey made more of an effort than usual. She styled her hair, put on red lipstick and even a dress. Every time the doorbell rang, she rushed to answer it. The fourth time she answered the door, she found Josh standing alone on the doorstep. His hair had been brushed neatly to one side, and he wore a soft cotton maroon T-shirt with the bad jeans she'd noted before.

He smiled down at her with a coy friendliness, perhaps re-membering the terse tone of their last conversation in the street.

"Hey, um—James, right?" she teased, biting her lip as she looked up at him.

"Hi, Amy," he said, deadpan, leaning in to kiss her cheek. The smell of his aftershave, all cedar and soap, then the light touch of his lips ignited her with an unexpected thrill.

"Are you on your own?" she asked casually, glancing out onto the dark street.

"Kelly's meeting me here," he said, following her into the hall and handing her two bottles of red wine. The embossed labels made her suspect they were half-decent, not the six-pound plonk everyone else brought.

They stood watching each other in the narrow hallway for a moment. How had she failed to notice how good-looking Josh was, with his warm smile and sparkling, intelligent eyes? Had he changed something about his hair or was it just that he smelled so good tonight? Something was definitely throwing her off, because he certainly wasn't the type of guy she was usually attracted to. Audrey tapped the wine bottle in her hand.

"I guess your girlfriend isn't the sort to urinate in the wine bottles then," she said, but the perplexed look on Josh's face told her he didn't remember the conversation they'd had last time he was here.

"I hope not," he said, his forehead knitting into a confused frown.

"Oh no, of course not, I only said that because . . . well, the Halloween party, do you remember the guy I was . . . ?" *Why had she mentioned anyone peeing in wine bottles?* "I didn't think your girlfriend was actually likely to pee in a wine bottle." Audrey glanced at the pinewood floor, willing it to swallow her. When she looked up, she noticed a woman had appeared on the doorstep holding a camping chair and two helium balloons with "Happy Birthday" written on the front.

"I can pee in a wine bottle," the stranger said cheerfully. "I had to at a festival once, I've got a surprisingly precise stream."

The woman was pretty, with long red hair, a freckled face, and a warm, open smile, not at all what Audrey had imagined Josh's girlfriend would look like.

"This is Miranda, my sister," said Josh, an amused look on his face. "And I definitely didn't need to know that about the precision of your stream," he added, grimacing.

"Hi, I'm Audrey. Whose birthday is it?"

Miranda looked in confusion at the balloons she was holding, then her eyes grew wide in horror.

"Shit! Back in a sec!" Miranda yelled, dropping the camping chair on the doorstep and running off down the street, balloons flailing behind her.

Audrey and Josh looked at each other and laughed. As they stood side by side in the hallway, waiting to see if Miranda and her balloons would return, their eyes lingered on each other for slightly longer than might have been appropriate.

"Well, I'm glad to see you're not wearing a suit today," she said. *Oh jeez, why was she being weird with Bad Jeans Josh? Just because she'd noticed he had nice eyes and great hair and smelled really, really, really good?*

"I took it off especially for you. I usually sleep in it," he said, a glint of mischief in his eyes.

"Oh, James, you're such a kidder." She sighed.

They heard the tap of heels running up the street, and Miranda reappeared on the doorstep.

"Sorry," she said, bending over to catch her breath, "I told this woman in the corner shop I'd hold her balloons while she went to the bathroom and then I just clean walked off with them. She was pretty pissed off."

Audrey had a feeling she was going to like Miranda.

ettee

 s they were sitting down to eat, Kelly arrived and squeezed in next to Josh. She was nearly six foot tall and had luminous skin and chestnut-colored hair with incredible volume. It didn't even go flat over the course of the evening; in Audrey's experience, even the biggest hair always went flat by the end of the night. Josh looked genuinely relaxed in her company, his body language confident and self-assured. He was thoughtful, getting her drinks, introducing her to everyone, keeping her included in the conversation. Audrey had purposely seated herself at the other end of the table from them but kept finding her gaze drawn in their direction. She noticed Kelly didn't eat the Sausage Fandango—she'd brought an edamame salad in her bag.

Audrey was sitting between Jay and some guitarist friend of Clara's. She heard herself laughing louder than usual at everything Jay said, then glancing to see if anyone at the other end of the table had noticed what a great time she was having. They all looked too busy having their own great time to notice. She couldn't stop herself from having this performative "good time" and hated herself for being such a loser. *Why was she acting like this?*

When she saw Kelly stand up to go outside for a cigarette, Audrey leaped up to follow her.

"Hey, Kelly, right?" she asked, joining her in the garden, pulling a jacket around her shoulders against the cold November evening.

"Yeah, you're Audrey? Thanks for inviting me. Cute party."

She pronounced it "par-dee," and Audrey couldn't keep herself from staring. Kelly was beautiful in a way you didn't often see outside an Instagram filter.

"You're here with Josh, then?" Audrey asked, as though she couldn't quite remember.

Kelly grinned like someone newly in love. "Yeah, he's so great. In Canada, we have this idea of what your classic English gentleman is like, your Kit Haringtons or your Eddie Redmaynes. I didn't think guys like Josh existed in real life." Kelly laughed to herself and lifted a thin menthol cigarette to her lips before offering one to Audrey.

"In what way?" Audrey asked, taking one on a whim.

"I don't know, he's old-fashioned, so polite and proper." Kelly said "proper" in a poor attempt at an English accent. "He has manners, he's kind."

Kind. Audrey had not been attracted to anyone she would describe as kind before. Had Fred been kind? Maybe, but she didn't know if you could tell that about someone from one afternoon. The back door opened, and Josh appeared on the garden steps. He was carrying a thick gray woolen coat, which he draped around Kelly's shoulders.

"I thought you might be cold," he said.

"What did I just say?" Kelly laughed and leaned in to kiss him on the cheek.

"Are you talking about me?" he asked, and Audrey noticed the timbre of his voice, how deep and delicious it was.

"Apparently, you're a very good boyfriend, James," she said, tilting her head and taking a drag of her cigarette. She'd stopped smoking years ago, and it tasted stale and unpleasant in her mouth. Kelly looked confused.

"Why do you call him James?"

"Oh, I'm sorry. You City guys all look the same," Audrey said.

"A little joke we have, Audrey never remembers my name," Josh explained.

Why hadn't she noticed how hot Josh was at Paul's birthday, or at the Halloween party? He had liked her then, she could tell.

"That pear tree isn't going to thrive there," Josh said unexpectedly, pointing to a small tree at the back of the garden. "There's too much shade from those cedars next door. You should move it over here by the fence, where there's more light."

"Josh knows all about trees," said Kelly proudly. "He spends every weekend planting them all over London."

"Really?" Audrey asked, and Josh looked down at his shoes.

"He's set himself a goal to plant a thousand trees in his lifetime." Kelly leaned over to kiss him again. "Isn't that the cutest thing?"

"I help out sometimes with a reforestation project," Josh explained.

"It's a charity that plants trees in the city and cultivates new woodland," Kelly added.

Oh great, so now he was some kind of sexy lumberjack environmental crusader too. Audrey didn't need any more fuel to feed this ridiculous crush she was developing. An image of Josh shirtless with a huge spade, digging holes in the earth, single-handedly reforesting Britain, had forced its way to the forefront of her mind. His modesty about volunteering only made it more endearing. Why couldn't he have some unappealing hobby, like foxhunting or Morris dancing?

"It's how we met," Kelly went on. "I'm doing a PhD in biodiversity economics."

Audrey swallowed. "I thought you were a model."

Kelly smiled. "I only do that on the side, to help pay for my tuition."

Audrey felt a wave of inadequacy wash over her.

"Audrey's a student of astronomy," Josh told Kelly, and Audrey shot him a grateful look. She was surprised he'd remembered.

"An amateur student," she said. "It's just a hobby."

Kelly and Josh both looked up at the clear, star-studded night sky.

"What can you show me?" Kelly asked, giving Audrey a smile of encouragement.

"Well, the easiest thing to point out is the Big Dipper," she said, pointing upward. "You see there's a line of five bright stars. If you imagine they're a slightly crooked pan handle, and just below, on the right, that's the pan."

"I think I see it," said Kelly, but she was looking in completely the wrong direction. Audrey moved to stand behind her, lifting her arm to guide it to the right spot in the sky. "Oh yes!" Kelly bounced excitedly.

"That star there is called Dubhe, it's about three hundred times brighter than our sun," Audrey said, shifting Kelly's finger. "If you can find that, and then Merak below, together they're known as the pointer stars. They'll guide you to Polaris there, the North Star."

"And that will always show you north?" Josh asked.

"Polaris is the center of it all. All the other stars appear to be in perpetual motion, revolving around the night sky; you can't pin them down. Polaris is a fixed point, so you can use it to navigate. You draw the shortest line from the star to the horizon, and that's north. She's our celestial compass."

Kelly and Josh were quiet, and Audrey let go of Kelly's arm, conscious she had gotten carried away and that other people might not be as interested in the night sky as she was.

"It's amazing you know all that," said Josh, looking at her with wide, curious eyes.

"Yeah, wow, Audrey, that's pretty cool," said Kelly brightly. "If I ever get lost in space, I'm calling you."

⟿⟿⟿

As the evening went on, Audrey drank more, trying to distract herself from the stab of jealousy she felt every time she looked in Josh and Kelly's direction. Somehow, the fact that she quite liked Kelly made it worse. Everyone around the table appeared to have coupled up. Paul was flirting with Josh's sister, Miranda, doing his usual party trick of impersonating various Bond villains but giving them regional accents. Miranda had tears streaming down her cheeks at his Brummie Blofeld. Clara was chatting animatedly with her fiancé, Jay. The guitarist was flirting with Clara's friend Billy, and Audrey, as ever, was alone. Suddenly worried she might be the drunkest person in the room, she picked up two bottles of wine and walked around the table topping up everyone else's glass.

At the end of the night, she found herself in the living room, kissing a man called Hamish. He was Jay's flatmate, a performance poet who wore a porkpie hat. He had tried to kiss Audrey in the past, but she had never been keen. Clearly a cocktail of wine, jealousy, and loneliness caused her to make bad decisions.

"Bye, Audrey," she heard Kelly say behind her, and pulled her lips away from Hamish's to see Kelly and Josh, holding hands in the doorway.

"Sorry to interrupt," said Josh. "We were just leaving."

"Thanks for having us, we had a blast," added Kelly.

Audrey thought she noticed Josh eyeing Hamish with the same air of disapproval he had given Sage at the Halloween party.

"Nice to see you!" Audrey shouted, a little too loudly.

"Shall we go somewhere quieter?" Hamish whispered into her neck as the door closed behind them, and she tried to nudge him away. Her head was full of smoke, cheap red wine, and a creeping sense of self-loathing that she knew would hit her with full force in the morning.

"I'm going to bed," she said, abruptly standing up. "Good night."

"Can I come?" Hamish asked hopefully.

"No, no you can't."

⁓⁓⁓

The next morning, as the three flatmates cleared up the aftermath of dinner, Clara said, "Did you notice how Kelly's hair didn't get flat even by the end of the evening?"

"Yes, I noticed that!" Audrey cried, and then had to sit down because she was too hungover for such animated exclamations.

"Who knew someone that spectacular looking could be so normal *and* be doing a PhD," said Paul as he stacked the dishwasher. "Josh is such a dark horse."

"What do you mean?" Audrey asked, getting up slowly to put the kettle on and make them all coffee.

"Well, I don't know where he meets these women. Fit girls always love Josh. I don't think he's any better-looking than the rest of us."

"Audrey clearly thinks he is," called Clara from the living room, where she was now sprawled on the couch, apparently too hungover to help. "And I saw you and Miranda, Paul. You can't complain you never get the girl."

"I don't think anything about Josh," Audrey said, scowling in Clara's direction.

"Did you know Miranda's a perfumer? She's got the most incredible nose," Paul said wistfully.

"And lips?" shouted Clara.

"You'd better start showering then, Paul," said Audrey.

"Hang on, I get it now," Paul said, tapping a finger against his chin. "Josh was slightly mean to you because you didn't remember his name, and now he's unavailable." Paul cupped his chin between thumb and forefinger. "That's really strange, I've never known Audrey to go for guys who are unavailable and slightly mean to her. Have you, Clara?"

They both laughed, and Audrey felt her cheeks burn. The observation was so perceptive that it felt like a small, sharp skewer, piercing a chink in her armor.

"You're both idiots," she said. "I couldn't be less interested in Bad Jeans Josh."

"You do know that as soon as you started dating someone like that, you'd lose interest," Clara said, finally emerging from the living room with her arms full of discarded wine bottles. "He's too straight for you."

"I don't want to date him, but what makes you say that? Why is he too straight?" Audrey asked, propping a hand against her hip.

"Because he's a nice guy and he'd treat you right. He wouldn't mess you about, so you'd assume there must be something wrong with him," said Clara.

"You'd ditch him in favor of some arty wanker who never calls you back," Paul said.

"Weren't you kissing Hamish last night?" Clara added, as though suddenly remembering.

"Handsy Hamish, no!" said Paul, putting a fist into his mouth.

Audrey was never drinking again.

Clara and Paul both collapsed into fits of laughter. Once they'd composed themselves, Paul reached out to give Audrey's shoulder an affectionate squeeze.

Usually, she would laugh along. The three of them teased one another like this constantly, and Audrey often gave as good as she got. But this morning, something about the accuracy of what they were saying, coupled with a hideous hangover and her regret over Handsy Hamish, made her have to bite down hard on the inside of her cheek to stop herself from bursting into tears.

20

Three and a Half Hours Before I Do

ादॅ

*S*ometimes tears were cathartic. Even though nothing had been resolved in the cleaning cupboard, Audrey came out of it feeling lighter. She concluded that the shock of seeing Fred again was all tangled up in her anxiety about having a big wedding. None of that changed how she felt about Josh. Perhaps this compulsion to run out on the wedding was merely the call of the void again—just because she leaned over the edge, it didn't mean she *actually* wanted to jump.

Outside the cupboard, as they walked back along the corridor, she and Hillary passed the open doors of the Grand Suite, the ornate ballroom that was being set up for the reception that afternoon. There were twenty round tables spread out across the floor, each covered with a starched linen tablecloth and laid with shining silver cutlery. Catering staff were polishing glassware, and the florist was positioning centerpieces of white and pink roses on glass plinths of differing heights to give a "waterfall of flowers" effect. A shaft of sunlight—a break from the rain—streamed in through the window, illuminating the elegant scene. All of this, for her and Josh.

"I think we're reaching saturation point on the pink," said Hillary. She could tell he hated it. He'd already told her that if he were to ever get married, there wouldn't be a jot of color, everything would be black and white. Before he could expand on his thoughts about the room's décor, Hillary's phone began to ring. Seeing the caller ID, he frowned, told Audrey he would catch up with her later, and then darted off to take the call in private.

Audrey wandered between the tables, looking at name tags tied to small jars of pink and lilac sugared almonds. She thanked the florist for the care she was taking over each arrangement, then chatted to some of the waiting staff, who had moved on to folding linen napkins. At the top end of the hall, Corrine from Corrine's Cakes was constructing their five-tiered vanilla sponge. It was truly a work of art—smooth white icing decorated with a canopy of intricate edible white flowers and petals. It must have taken hours to create. Audrey gave a satisfied sigh. One thing she knew for sure—she loved the cake.

"This looks incredible, Corrine," Audrey said, staring in wonder at it.

"What are you doing here, hon? Shouldn't you be getting ready?" Corrine asked, stepping forward to give Audrey a hug. They'd only met once, at a cake tasting in London several months before. They had sampled a dozen flavors but ultimately opted for a vanilla sponge. Vivien had insisted it was the least controversial option. Audrey had been drawn to the Mocha Surprise, a deep chocolate with a coffee fondant layer, but she couldn't decide between that and the vanilla, they were both so delicious. Josh had sought a compromise, wondering if they could have a variety of flavors, a different one for each layer, but Vivien had advised against it—it would be much more expensive, and besides, everyone *loved* vanilla. Audrey found herself smiling as she looked at the cake. It was truly spectacular.

"Just taking it all in, the calm before the storm," Audrey said.

As she stepped away from Corrine and turned back toward the cake, something fell from the top and landed at Audrey's feet. The women both paused, silent for a moment as they looked to see what it could be. The bride figurine was lying on the floor. Corrine quickly bent down to retrieve it, checking the figure for damage.

"She's okay," she said with a sigh of relief, clutching the figurine to her chest. "I hadn't secured the bride and groom properly yet; she must have jiggled to the edge when I turned the top tier. Don't worry, she isn't damaged. It's always the last thing I do, once all the layers are angled correctly."

Was this bad omen number three? Audrey looked back at the figurine of the groom, standing alone on the cake. Something about his face looked sad, as though he knew his bride had just tried to escape.

"Maybe she jumped," said Audrey, more to herself than to anyone else. Corrine laughed as she placed the bride back next to the groom.

"There we go. I'll glue her on with a dab of icing. Then she won't be able to go anywhere."

Audrey looked down at her own feet, feeling for a moment that Corrine was talking about her. She wondered, if she tried to move, whether she would find herself glued to the floor.

21

Three Years Before I Do

❧

*A*udrey felt stuck. Everyone else was going places, and she was going nowhere. Clara had just been promoted at work and was planning her wedding. Paul had a new job at an American bank. He was working longer hours and spending all his spare time at Miranda's. Audrey was working three jobs and spending her free time mindlessly bingeing box sets.

She had grown tired of all the early starts working in the café, so she'd gotten herself a job as a receptionist in an art gallery. She'd also signed up for few weekend shifts at the local pub, then fit her freelance photography gigs around the edges. Friends sometimes asked her when she was going to "get a proper job," but she had no idea what kind of "proper job" she might do. Her CV felt like a catalog of false starts. After school, she'd done a year of anthropology, changed to geography, dropped out, failed to get onto the astronomy course, and had then given up the idea of a degree altogether. Some days she loved the variety of her life—she was in no rush to be settled and didn't feel the need to commit to any one thing. But on other days she felt as though everyone else was on this life train that she'd forgotten to buy a ticket for.

One Saturday in February, Audrey was in Covent Garden, taking photos of cobbled streets for a stock image company. She moved her lens up from the ground, and there, in the viewfinder, she found Josh. She hadn't seen him since the Sausage Fandango dinner several months before.

"Amy," he said, and she looked up.

"James," she replied, grinning.

He was wearing a pale blue shirt and jeans, his brown hair ruffled, as though he'd just gotten out of bed. He had a day of stubble on his chin and a slight tan, both of which suited him. As he walked toward her, she was reminded just how tall he was, how broad his shoulders were, how nice it might feel to be wrapped in those firm arms. *These were inappropriate thoughts to be having about Bad Jeans Josh.*

"Are you working?" He indicated her camera. The smile in his eyes told her he was pleased to see her.

"Taking arty photos of cobbles and fire hydrants—living the dream," she said, raising her lens to snap a photograph of him.

"Have you—" He paused, dropping his gaze to the ground. "Have you got time to help me with something? Just for ten minutes, and I'll buy you a coffee."

Her heart leaped in her chest. Why was the image of him shirtless, digging holes to plant trees in, so fresh and vivid in her internal fantasy image library? She shrugged, trying to hide this giddy feeling with nonchalance.

"Sure," she said, and they fell into step walking down Long Acre.

"Paul once told me you had this nickname for me," he said.

Audrey frowned in an overblown show of confusion. "Bad Jeans Josh." He narrowed his eyes at her, but there was a spark of mischief in his tone. Audrey opened her mouth to deny it but then found she could not, so she laughed instead.

"That was mean of him. They really aren't that bad—"

"No, you've put it out there now, you can't take it back," Josh said, a smile playing at the corner of his mouth. "It's not just you, Kelly mentioned my wardrobe could do with an update. I'm supposed to be here clothes shopping, and then I run into you and . . ."

Audrey felt slightly annoyed with Kelly for trying to change Josh; she had grown fond of his dorky jeans.

"Sure." Audrey smiled. "Though I'm sorry I ever said that."

"I forgive you. The nickname I used to have for you was far worse."

"Oh really. What was that?"

"You won't like it. It's not complimentary," he said, swinging his arms as he walked.

"Well, I won't help you unless you tell me."

"Fine. Up Herself Audrey." He said it with a sigh, glancing at her sideways. "Sorry."

"Up Herself Audrey, wow, that *is* worse than Bad Jeans Josh. What made you think I was so up myself?"

"I don't know," he said as they walked, avoiding other pedestrians on the pavement. "You always acted like you didn't want to talk to me, like I was too irrelevant even to remember."

"I can't think what gave you that idea, James."

"It was my issue. I liked you back then, and you wouldn't give me the time of day . . ." He trailed off but then turned his head and made a face, as though to illustrate this was a funny story from the past, rather than anything still relevant today.

"I would have given you the time of day," Audrey said, the giddy feeling building inside her. "Though I do have a strict policy on the number of new names I will remember per day. I think I'd hit my daily quota when we met."

He tilted his head, biting his lip, an acknowledgment that he liked her joke. "If you're going to be nice to me, I'll have to think of a new name for you."

"And if we're going to buy you new jeans, I'll have to think of something else to call you."

"Then we'll just have to be Amy and James."

"Which one will I be?" Audrey asked, and Josh let out a loud, unfiltered laugh, which sent a satisfied glow right down to the soles of Audrey's feet.

*Audrey led them to a fashionable store on Bow Street. Josh followed her around the shop as she started scouring the shelves full of jeans in every shade of blue, black, and gray.

"What size are you?"

He shrugged. "Maybe a thirty-six long?"

She pulled five or six different designs from the units, and a shop assistant guided them to a large changing room with a red velvet chaise longue positioned outside it.

"Promise to be brutally honest," Josh called from behind the curtain. "Don't spare my feelings."

"Have I ever been known to do that?" Audrey jumped up to try to fix her fringe in a shop mirror while he was changing. She quickly added some nude gloss to her lips and rubbed some smudged mascara from beneath her eyes.

When Josh pulled back the curtain, he was wearing a pair of fitted dark blue jeans. They looked amazing on him, but his oversized shirt hung loose over the waistband.

"You need to tuck your shirt in, I can't see the fit properly. Maybe try them on with a T-shirt."

The eager shop assistant handed Josh a T-shirt from the shop floor, and Audrey watched as he unbuttoned his shirt in front of her, momentarily revealing his bare chest before pulling the T-shirt over his head. *Okay, wow. Look away, Audrey.* She found herself searching the ceiling, suddenly conscious she didn't want to be caught staring at his washboard stomach. *Why was it called a washboard stomach anyway? Was it because it looked hard and firm, and you could scrub clothes clean on it? She would definitely take off her clothes and scrub—*

"Audrey?"

Audrey blinked, pulling her gaze back to his face.

"Yeah, good. They look really good." She swallowed. "Wait, turn around. Yes, um, no, I think you could go an inch tighter; they're slightly baggy on the butt."

He gave a single clap, appearing pleased with her rigorous feedback, then drew the curtain across to change into the next pair. She was sorry not to see him take off his shirt this time.

Twenty minutes later, they walked out of the shop with three new pairs of jeans and the T-shirt. They found a coffee shop around the corner called Bean Here Before.

"Have you been here before?" he asked.

"Nope. False advertising," she said.

He ordered himself a black coffee and asked Audrey what she wanted.

"Let's try a Very Berry Latte," she said, looking up at the menu.

"You like those? It sounds revolting."

"I don't know, I've never had one before." She shrugged,

then observed his confused expression. "Let me guess, you're the guy who orders the same thing every time."

Josh laughed. "Yes, I always order black coffee, I know I like it."

"So you're just going to drink black coffee for the rest of your life? Think of all the other hot beverages you could be missing out on."

They took their coffees over to a secluded window seat. Audrey looked down at her coffee, piled high with cream and pink sprinkles.

"You want to try it?"

Josh looked amused. "Are you working for the Very Berry Latte marketing board or something?"

"No, I can just see you're curious now."

He rolled his eyes and reached for her cup. He took a sip, then pretended to gag. "It's no black coffee, but it's actually not bad."

"Well, now you know what it tastes like," Audrey said, reaching for it back. "So, Josh, tell me what someone who works in reinsurance does. Do you insure things that have already been insured? Would it be like me working in re-photography, where I take photos of existing photographs? Or a chef who recooks food, like a microwave chef?"

"Not quite," he said, suppressing a smile. "We insure the insurers, help spread the risk of huge projects. I specialize in sustainable energy, wind farms, tidal power, billion-dollar investments. We help make these projects possible, that's the simplest way I can describe it."

"That does sound interesting."

"It is. Though I'm stuck on a tedious project right now. There's an innovative new tidal project I'd love to be a part of, but I don't have the hours."

"Why don't you ask if you can move? Give the boring project to someone else."

Josh smiled. "It doesn't really work like that."

"If you don't ask, you don't get." Audrey shrugged. "They might not know you're so interested in this new one. Is the tree planting related to your work?"

Josh shook his head, gazing out the window at the street. "No, that's just a side project I do on my own time." He paused. "I read somewhere that if everyone on the planet planted a hundred and sixty trees, we'd be able to cancel out a decade of CO_2 emissions. I was aiming to do just that, but I reached that number last year, so I set myself a new goal."

"You're making me feel bad I haven't planted any; I can't even keep a houseplant alive."

"Well, I'll plant one for you next time I go," he said, running a hand through his hair.

"Can you call it Cuthbert?"

"You don't usually get to name it," he said, his eyes dancing with amusement. "Though I do sometimes write my initials on the support stake. I'll put your name and Cuthbert's on the next one I plant." He paused, tapping a finger against his coffee cup. "Tell me more about you, Audrey. What do you get up to when you're not charting the wonders of the solar system?"

She ruffled her hair, letting it fall in front of her face. "I don't think I've found my calling in life yet. I've jumped around a lot. I'm currently working in a gallery and a bar, plus I do a bit of freelance photography work. I guess it's like trying on jeans, I haven't found my perfect fit yet." She paused. "Hillary used to call me the Weather Girl because I'm so changeable." Josh was listening to her with rapt attention. "Kelly must be pretty driven, if she's doing a PhD at her age."

"She is." Josh nodded. "She's a couple of years older than me, though."

"Things are going well with you two, then?"

"She remembers my name most days, so that's something." Josh's teasing eyes lingered on hers, and Audrey gently nudged his foot beneath the table.

"Jean shopping today, ring shopping tomorrow?" She said it in a light voice but then regretted it immediately. Asking about his girlfriend felt like picking a scab she knew she should leave well alone.

To his credit, Josh didn't flinch or look horrified, as most men their age would have. He simply said, "Not quite yet."

"But you want that? Marriage, kids, a semidetached with a patio on the commuter belt?"

"Of course," he said thoughtfully. "I would love to have a family one day, a home of my own."

The simplicity of his reply wrong-footed her. She was used to men who ran a mile at any suggestion of settling down. All the drummers and poets and performance artists who railed against conformity, who wouldn't be pinned down to a third date, let alone a committed relationship.

"How about you, are you seeing anyone? How about that guy from the Sausage Fandango?" Josh asked, his eyes back on his coffee spoon.

"Oh, no." Audrey let out a sharp laugh. "Too busy with my PhD in cleaning beer glasses. I'm doing my dissertation on anti-streaking techniques." He frowned slightly, as though reluctant to join in with her self-effacing joke. "I don't think I'd ever have the guts to get married," she said, as much to herself as to him.

"Why do you say that?"

"How can you ever be *sure* it's the right person? My mum is on her fifth marriage, and every time she falls in love, she's *so* sure." Audrey paused. "'Til death do us part' just feels like a lot, you know?"

"We can just stick to 'til the end of our coffee do us part' then, if you like," he said, and she bit back a grin.

"Seriously, though, why would anyone get married in this day and age?"

Josh paused for a moment, properly contemplating the question. "Because it's the biggest commitment you can make to one another. It's a declaration to the world that this is your person, the one you love, body and soul. It's saying that no matter what life throws at you both, you are going to be there, holding each other's hand every step of the way." Josh's eyes flickered with some inner fire. "In this cynical world, isn't there something wonderful about the pure, unbridled optimism of marriage? To stand up and say, 'Screw the odds, I'm pinning my colors to the mast, bright and bold,' because if you're going to commit to anything in this life, shouldn't it be love?"

Wow. She had not expected such an earnest answer. Audrey couldn't look Josh in the eye as her entire body pulsed with some new feeling she was struggling to identify.

"Well, you've sold me. I'm more than happy to commit to another cup of coffee now, maybe even a slice of cake. But if we fight over it, we'll have to get a lawyer to split it down the middle." He laughed at this. "And you have to be daring and order something that's not black coffee this time. Deal?"

"Fine." He smiled, and the tone of their conversation lightened again.

They talked for hours. Audrey lost track of time. Talking to Josh felt like experiencing a catalog of emotions all at once—he was fun and teasing but also serious and insightful. He appeared genuinely interested in everything she had to say. There was a clear edge of flirtation, but never so much as to be inappropriate. Audrey felt the beam of his attention like a heat lamp on a cold day. When he eventually said he had to go, it felt like the lamp going out, a cold draft blowing in.

In the street, as they said good-bye, it felt suddenly awkward between them. Part of her felt like it would be normal to swap numbers, to be able to text him later and ask how the jeans were received, but another part of her didn't think it'd be appropriate. *Would it feel like overstepping if there weren't this fizz between them? Did he feel it too?*

"Good luck," she said instead, handing him the bag of jeans, which had been sitting beneath her feet at the table. "They really do look great on you."

"Thank you, Audrey," he replied, his gaze lingering on her face for just a moment too long before he disappeared into the flow of pedestrians walking toward Covent Garden tube. That extra second of eye contact told her he did. He felt the fizz too.

Three Hours Before I Do

∽

"*D*o you feel that?" asked Clara as Audrey came through the door of the bedroom. "It's like the whole house is creaking in the wind. It feels like the end of the world out there." Clara was sitting on the window seat, looking out at the rain, which had started again in earnest. "I've never seen anything like it. Maybe you should be getting married in an ark."

"Or a swimsuit," said Audrey.

"What happened to you at breakfast? You disappeared," Clara said, turning away from the window to face her.

"I just needed a few minutes of quiet," she explained. "I went to see them setting up the tables downstairs, and the miniature bride jumped off the top of the cake, right in front of me."

Clara narrowed her eyes at Audrey, tilting her head in concern. "There were too many people at breakfast, weren't there? Did Fred say something to you?"

Audrey shook her head. "No, I'm fine. I'm going to go shower and wash my hair. We'll get dressed. It will all be wonderful."

Telling people that she'd seen the bride figurine make a suicidal leap off the wedding cake was not going to help anything. She'd let Granny Parker's omen talk get inside her head. *This had to stop.*

In the bathroom, Audrey ran the shower and sat down on the closed toilet seat. She pulled out her phone and was confronted with the article about Benedict again. If anything felt like a bad omen, it was this. She found herself googling his name, something she hadn't done in years. His website announced an upcoming exhibition at the Tate Modern. There were photos of pieces of his work she recognized, sculptures he had shown her years ago in his gallery. *Why did she do this to herself?* She knew why, though. His last words to her loomed large, like the curse of an evil wizard in a fairy tale: "I hope one day you love someone, maybe even plan to marry them, and someone comes along and takes it from you."

Audrey shook her head. Why was she endowing his words with some kind of prophetic significance? She needed to focus on happier things. She scrolled to one of her favorite photos, saved on her phone. It was her, aged ten, at her mother's wedding to Brian. She was holding both their hands; Brian was looking at Vivien, but Vivien's eyes were on Audrey, and she looked besotted. Audrey's arms began to itch again. She turned off her phone and tossed it down onto the bath mat. No more scrolling today. She loved Josh, she wanted to marry Josh; everything else was just messing with her head.

She had a shower and washed her hair, the soapy water stinging the rope burn on her neck. Emerging from the steamy bathroom, Audrey found Clara sitting on the bed attached to a double breast pump.

"Wow," Audrey said, "that is . . . loud."

"Sorry, sorry, I know, baby stuff, ugh. I'm only feeding them a couple of times a night, so I hoped my boobs wouldn't notice, but apparently, they have. I'll just drain them now and then I'll be all yours."

"Thank you for being here, Clara," said Audrey, sitting down next to her friend and marveling at the strange machine currently sucking milk into two small bottles with a strange *voom, voom, voom* sound. "I know it hasn't been easy for you to get away."

Audrey noticed the lines beneath her friend's eyes, the stray grays in her hair that had not been colored in, the lines on her forehead that remained even when her face was not in motion.

"It looks hard, this mothering thing," she said gently.

Clara stifled a sob. "Don't! You'll set me off. My hormones mean I'm on the edge of crying whenever I pump."

"You had twins, seven months ago," Audrey said. "I wouldn't have held it against you if you'd said no to being my maid of honor."

"*I* would have held it against me," Clara said, running a finger beneath each eye to stop her mascara from smudging. "You don't have babies and then bail on your friends when they need you. I'm not going to be that person." She shook her head. "Besides, you're making out like it's a chore to be here—I got an uninterrupted night of sleep last night, I'm living the dream." And then she burst into tears. "I miss them so much." And then she laughed through the tears. "I'm sorry, I didn't know I was going to miss them like this. When I'm with them, they need me constantly, it makes me feel like I've lost who I am. Then, when I'm without them, it's like a part of me is missing. I can't even think about going back to work in a few months. How am I going to do the job I used to do, going to gigs all night? I just can't see how it's going to work."

"I think it's probably normal to feel that way, and you are doing an amazing job." Audrey rubbed her friend's shoulder. "Maybe work will let you evolve your role, go to less gigs?"

"You know what these musicians are like, they expect you to be available all hours."

Audrey felt for her. She knew it was not going to be easy for Clara to do her job nine to five, and Clara loved her job—it was her identity, or at least, it had been.

"I know what will cheer you up. Shall I get the dress out?"

"Yes, yes, yes!" Clara said, clapping her hands, her face brightening.

Audrey walked over to the heavy-duty white dry-cleaning bag hanging on the back of the closet door and carefully pulled the zipper. Inside, the dress was wrapped in cream tissue paper; just the sound of the paper made Audrey feel like a child on Christmas Day. It was one of her mother's dresses, the one she'd worn to marry Audrey's father.

"Wow," said Clara. "You're lucky your mum kept it so well."

Clara detached herself from the milking machine and screwed tops onto the plastic milk bottles. Then she pulled up her blouse and helped Audrey take the dress from its paper-and-plastic tomb. It was a cream silk fitted gown with a cowl neckline and a low back, with tiny silk buttons all the way to the floor. Audrey had deliberated over hundreds of different dresses. In the face of such overwhelming choice, she'd opted for one that meant something. This dress had a connection to both her parents, on a day when only one of them could be here.

They laid the dress on the bed. Clara pulled up a prede-signed wedding-day playlist on her phone, then she set about drying and styling Audrey's hair in front of the dressing-table mirror. As she tonged pieces into loose curls and sang along to

"Wedding Bell Blues" by Laura Nyro, Audrey felt a wave of gratitude. Her friend, who had been through the toughest year of her life, who was clearly exhausted and emotional and worried about the future, had still found time to make her a wedding playlist, to pick up the wedding plate, to buy her wildflowers. Maybe all this debate about soul mates missed the real love story, the one she had been lucky enough to have for nearly twenty years now.

"Why are you looking at me like that?" Clara asked, narrowing her eyes at Audrey in the mirror.

"Just thinking how grateful I am to have you. How much I love you."

"Did you inhale my milk hormones when I was pumping? You're getting all soppy on me," Clara said, before kissing her lightly on the head.

⁓⁓⁓

$\mathcal{H}$alfway through the tonging process, after a brief knock on the door, in swept Hillary, with a deep-set angry brow and pursed lips.

"You can't be in here now, Hillary," said Clara. "Bridesmaids only."

"I'm the bride's best man, that's basically a bridesmaid. She doesn't mind. You don't mind, do you, Audrey?"

Audrey shook her head. "What's wrong?"

"I just got off the phone with my agent." Hillary sighed, then pressed a fist against his lips. "I didn't get that part I auditioned for. The director thinks I look 'too young.'" Hillary slumped down on the bed. "I'm forty-five now, when am I going to stop being discriminated against for my youthful appearance?"

"Most people would be happy to be told they look young," Clara pointed out.

"I'm tired of playing pretty-boy parts, they're always the dullest roles. I'm due a career renaissance like Hugh Grant or Matthew McConaughey, where their craggy wrinkles and receding hairline give them a new depth of expression. As a man, do you know how many more interesting roles you get offered when you lose your looks?"

"I wouldn't say either of those men have lost their looks," said Audrey.

"You need to look like the weight of the world has pummeled your face, that's when the Tony Award nominations come rolling in. I have been cursed with a full head of hair, perfectly taut skin, and eyes that convey a youthful vigor."

Audrey stood up and walked over to the bed, pulling him into a hug.

"I promise you—you will look old and gnarled one day."

"I've done my time as Marius, I'm ready to be Jean Valjean," Hillary said dejectedly as he rested his head on Audrey's shoulder.

Seeing Hillary so disappointed, and Clara so hormonal and emotional, Audrey realized both her support columns were wobbly. If she wobbled too, the whole roof might come down.

"Not to be insensitive about all this, but Audrey does need to walk up the aisle in a few hours, and you are kind of messing up her hair," Clara said, attempting to disentangle Hillary's arms.

Clara tucked Hillary into Audrey's bed and made him a cup of chamomile tea. He claimed, only a little overdramatically, that he couldn't be alone right now. Clara made him promise not to get in the way or make any unhelpful comments about Audrey's wedding look. Then she instructed Audrey to put on the dress before she did her makeup. Audrey raised her hands above her head so that Clara could carefully lift the dress over her. The feel of the silk against her skin gave Audrey a strangely sensuous thrill.

"Virginal white?" asked Hillary, peering over the edge of his teacup and raising one eyebrow.

"Didn't we just say no running commentary?" said Audrey.

Hillary pinched his lips closed and hugged his chamomile tea. Then, as Clara pulled the dress down over Audrey's hips, all three of them heard a terrible ripping sound. Both women locked eyes with each other. Clara darted around to look at Audrey's backside.

"Oh shit, oh shit!"

"What is it?" Audrey squealed.

"The whole back seam, it's ripped wide open."

Hillary let out a high-pitched squeak before clapping a hand firmly across his mouth and spilling his entire cup of tea over the bed.

23

Six Years Before I Do

⌒⌒

*O*nce Benedict moved in, Audrey tried to get out of the house as much as possible, but there was only a certain number of hours she could spend in the library or in Clara's dorm room.

"No boyfriend on the scene, then?" Benedict asked her one morning over breakfast.

Audrey pulled her arms up inside her T-shirt awkwardly. She'd taken to wearing baggy clothes around the house.

"Audrey's saving herself for Brad Pitt," Vivien said when it became clear Audrey didn't intend to answer his question.

"Ew, Brad Pitt's in his fifties," Audrey said, eyeing Benedict with loaded disapproval.

"If I could only have my time again." Benedict sighed, leaning back in his chair and spreading his legs out in front of him so they nudged Audrey's. "Never was a truer adage uttered than that youth is wasted on the young."

"I agree." Vivien sighed. "Books can wait, darling, you should be out there enjoying yourself."

Audrey bit back all the comments she wanted to make, about her mother's having had enough fun for both of them.

Instead, she hid behind her copy of *New Scientist*, missing Brian with a fierceness she found hard to control.

On the plus side, Vivien seemed happy again—she was back in rehearsals for a new play, not drinking so much in the evenings, going to Pilates, and seeing her therapist. Plus, Audrey had to concede that Benedict genuinely appeared to care for her mother. He bought Vivien tickets to concerts he thought she would like, he read *New Yorker* articles aloud to her in the evenings, and she often heard them laughing together. He was gregarious in a way Brian had never been, and Vivien was clearly smitten. She walked with a new lightness about the house. Objectively, if Audrey took herself and Brian, and the desecration of a marriage, out of the equation, she could see they were a good match. So she decided to endure his presence in their lives. She comforted herself with the knowledge that this couldn't be a permanent arrangement. Benedict lived in New York—he had an apartment there, a teenage son, a life. This was a rebound arrangement. Surely, he would have to go home soon.

But not soon enough. One Sunday morning, Vivien was out having her hair done and Audrey was taking a shower in her en suite. When she stepped out to dry herself, she looked up to see Benedict standing in the open doorway of her bedroom, staring at her naked body.

"Jesus!" she screamed, kicking the door closed with a slam.

"Sorry, I was just . . . I came to see if you needed any laundry done," he stammered through the closed door. When had he *ever* done her laundry?

"Don't come into my room!" she screamed, mortified. Had she left the door open like that? She hadn't thought anyone was home, but still, she was sure she'd pulled it closed. How long had he been standing there, watching her shower? "Go away!" she yelled.

Benedict apologized as soon as she came downstairs, blustering that he'd popped in to look for some whites to put in a wash with his shirts and found the door to her bathroom wide open. He did appear embarrassed, with his red cheeks and sweaty brow. Audrey decided to give him the benefit of the doubt, though her skin crawled when she pictured the look on his face as he stood there, staring at her. She didn't mention the shower incident to Vivien. But she went to buy a lock for her bedroom door.

⸺⸺

A week after ShowerGate, Vivien and Benedict came back from dinner at the Ivy. When she heard the key in the lock, Audrey tried to sneak upstairs so she wouldn't have to endure a drunken conversation with them. She wasn't quick enough, though, and they were through the door when Audrey was still only halfway up the stairs.

"Audrey," her mother cried in delight, thrusting her hand out to show off a huge sapphire ring, surrounded by a circle of diamonds. "You'll never guess—we're engaged!"

"Isn't it marvelous?" Benedict asked, standing behind her, leaning forward to kiss Vivien's neck, and she laughed as they stumbled into the hallway.

"You can't be engaged. You're not even divorced yet," Audrey said flatly, feeling her throat constrict as she watched her mother's face fall.

"I hoped you'd be happy for us," Vivien said, her voice breaking like a chastised child's.

"Well, it's hard to keep the enthusiasm levels up when you getting engaged is such a common occurrence." Audrey turned to walk up the stairs. She knew she was being cruel, but she couldn't help it—the fire of disappointment that this was to be their lives, that he was here to stay, was too much. Worse was the knowledge that she had done it, she had given Brian the phone. If only she'd hung up straightaway.

She heard her mother's drunken footsteps in the kitchen, the sniff of overdramatic tears. Vivien's emotions were always precariously close to the surface when she was drunk. Audrey continued upstairs; she would apologize in the morning. But as she stepped onto the landing, she heard the stomp of heavy footsteps behind her and then felt a hand reach out and grab her wrist.

"Don't disrespect your mother like that," Benedict barked, pulling her back to face him.

"Let go," Audrey spat, but her voice shook as she looked down at him on the stairs.

The index finger of his other hand pointed in her face as he growled. "You are the worst kind of entitled little brat, you know that? You've been allowed to do as you please, with no respect for anyone."

He was so angry. She could feel the heat coming off him. Though he was standing a few steps below her, his bearlike build meant his eyes were at her level.

"I love your mother and I will not have anyone upset her—do you hear?"

Audrey didn't reply, her breath caught in her throat.

"I said, do. You. Hear?" Benedict repeated sternly.

"Yes," she nearly whimpered.

Benedict stepped up onto the landing in front of her, blocking the path to her bedroom. "You might have had Brian wrapped around your little finger, but not me. You need to grow up. While you live under your mother's roof, you will show her some respect." Audrey nodded, shocked into submission. "Now, go downstairs and congratulate her. I won't have you ruining this evening for Vivien."

Audrey wanted to flee to her room, then leave this house as soon as she could.

"I'll apologize tomorrow," she said quietly.

"You will apologize now," he said, and he put a hand around her upper arm and guided her back down the stairs. Audrey bit back tears; she had never been treated like this by anyone, and every cell in her body burned with the shame of it, the indignity of being manhandled.

Benedict steered her into the kitchen, where her mother's face looked pale and haunted. Presumably she had heard every word of their little exchange on the stairs.

"Congratulations, Mum," she said, the "Mum" in itself a covert rebellion. "If you're happy, I'm happy for you."

Benedict nodded his approval and then marched out into the garden to smoke a cigar. Vivien looked at Audrey like a wounded deer.

"I am happy, honestly, Audrey. I've never felt this way about anyone. And I know you think it's quick and you feel for Brian, but honestly, darling, this is . . ." Vivien smiled. "I didn't think I believed in soul mates before, but, Audrey—he's the part of me that I didn't know was missing."

Audrey saw in Vivien's face that she meant it. So she swallowed everything she was feeling, hugged her mother, and whispered in her ear, "I'm sorry."

"Let me have this, please. Don't fight with him, I can't stand it."

As she looked over Vivien's shoulder at the tall, overbearing figure in the garden, she promised herself that for her mother's sake, she would try.

24

Two Hours Before I Do

 ❧

"*W*hat have you done?" Vivien asked, shaking her head in slow horror as she inspected the back of Audrey's dress.

"The seam split," said Clara. "We literally just pulled it over her head incredibly carefully."

"I wish you'd bought a new dress, darling. This is thirty years old, the thread is probably rotted."

"I thought you'd want me to wear it," Audrey said, her voice cracking. "This dress is part of our family history."

"I never said I wanted you to wear it." Vivien's face creased; she looked genuinely confused. "I would have rather you'd gone for a more structured style; you have to be so very thin to pull off this unforgiving material."

"She is thin," said Clara fiercely.

"Of course she is, Clara, but not catwalk thin, plus she's shorter than I am." Vivien sighed, and Audrey saw Clara purse her lips, as though biting back some further opinion. Audrey was still reeling from the revelation that wearing her mother's dress meant nothing to Vivien, even though clothes meant everything to her.

One Saturday as a teenager, Vivien had taken Audrey to a vintage store to choose a dress for her sixteenth birthday. They'd spent hours trying things on, speculating on who might have owned these clothes before, making up stories about them. Her mother always spoke so passionately about buying clothes with a history, clothes that had meant something to someone. "You don't find the dress, the dress finds you," she'd said. They had ended up buying matching minidresses and wearing them home. It was one of Audrey's favorite memories, her mother laughing at the looks they got as they strutted down Carnaby Street, arm in arm, like sisters.

"Take it off, and I'll see what I can do. I brought an emergency needle and thread, but this fabric will need something incredibly delicate. Clara, could you nip down and ask the florist, the caterers, see if anyone has something finer?"

Clara duly disappeared on this errand, and Vivien helped lift the dress off over Audrey's head. She was left standing in her underpants and bra while her mother inspected the torn seam.

"How long ago was your last fitting, have you put on weight? Most brides get too thin in the weeks before their wedding. With all the stress and last-minute arrangements, they forget to eat."

"Two weeks ago, and no," Audrey fumed. "I think it's just a dodgy seam." She clenched her jaw, still feeling offended that Vivien seemed so indifferent to her wearing this dress.

"I saw it happen, it was like a horror movie," Hillary piped up from the bed. Vivien gave a start; clearly, she had not noticed that Hillary was there.

"Why is Hillary here? You can't have a man watching you get dressed."

"It's Hillary, he doesn't count," said Audrey.

"I definitely don't count," Hillary said. He had the breast pump on his lap and was fiddling with the wires.

"What are you doing with that breast pump?" Vivien asked.

Hillary removed his hands from the machine and grimaced. "I thought it was a travel coffee machine."

"A travel coffee machine?" said Audrey. "That's not even a thing."

"This won't do." Vivien clapped her hands at Hillary. "Make yourself useful, please. Half the groomsmen have no idea how to tie a cravat, and guests will start arriving soon. There's no time for lounging about."

Hillary reluctantly climbed out of bed. He came to give Audrey a gentle kiss on each cheek, looked her straight in the eye, then, putting a hand on either side of her head, said, "It will be okay. No one's going to be looking at your ass, and if they do, well—you have a fucking great ass."

He swung his jacket over his shoulder and waved his hand in the air. Vivien looked back and forth between Audrey and the door.

"I don't think that is appropriate," she said once he had gone. "You two have such an unconventional relationship."

"I don't think so," Audrey said. She couldn't believe her mother, of all people, was commenting on the nature of anyone else's "unconventionality."

Vivien went to stand in front of the long mirror and held the dress up in front of her. She let out a sigh.

"I did love this dress. Wedding dresses do suit me, you know."

"Don't get any ideas," Audrey said, with a smile, despite herself.

"'Oh, in my youth I excited some admiration. But look at me now! Would you think it possible that I was once considered to be attractive?'" Vivien said, adopting an American accent.

"You know you're still attractive."

"That was Blanche DuBois," Vivien said, still with the accent. "'I don't want realism, I want magic. Yes, yes, magic!'" She paused. "She was my greatest role, wasn't she? Everyone said so, that I was born to play her."

"You'll have plenty more great roles," Audrey said, and she watched her mother put on a smile.

"Today, the star of the show is Audrey Lavery." She held a hairbrush up to Audrey, as though it were a microphone. "Audrey, tell the audience how you feel."

Vivien was being playful with her, like she used to be, but Audrey didn't feel like playing. She sat down on the window seat.

"Can I ask you something? Are you happy?" she said seriously, watching Vivien carefully.

"Goodness, whatever makes you ask that?" Vivien frowned in confusion.

"Do you ever think about Benedict?"

Vivien shook her head, not as an answer but as an indicator she didn't want to talk about him.

"I see he's getting an exhibition at the Tate Modern," Audrey went on. "It flashed up on my phone this morning."

Her mother froze; then, with her eyes downcast, she said, "Oh." Her hands reached to smooth the seam of the dress, a small muscle pulsing in her jaw. "Well, I'm sorry if that upset you."

"Are you in touch with him? Have you spoken to him . . . since?" Audrey asked, her eyes intent on her mother's face.

"No, of course not."

"You once told me you thought he was your soul mate," Audrey said.

"Did I?" Vivien looked incredibly sad all of a sudden, her taut expression sagging, the shutter to the emotions behind her eyes closing.

"Yes, and you'd be married to him now if it wasn't for me."

Vivien stood up straight, marched over to the bathroom door, picked up a dressing gown from the hook, and handed it to her daughter, who was still standing in her underpants and bra. Audrey felt a sting at the fact that her own mother felt offended somehow by the sight of her half-naked body.

"Why are you bringing all this up today? You don't want to think about all that unpleasantness when you're about to get married." Vivien walked over to the window and looked out. "When will this rain end? We should have waited until August. Rain in August is rarely so unrelenting."

"What if Josh isn't my soul mate?" Audrey said, refusing to be distracted by talk of the weather. Vivien turned her head sharply from the window.

"Where's all this coming from?"

"I just want to talk to you properly for once, like we used to." Audrey closed her eyes in frustration. When she opened them, Vivien was waiting, listening. "Everyone says if you have doubts, you should listen to them. What if Josh is my Brian?"

Vivien stood, holding on to the curtain, looking out at the rain. "If he's your Brian, then you're in luck. Brian is"—she sighed—"one of the best men I've ever known, and he was the most wonderful husband." Vivien looked up at the sky, where the sun was glowing white behind a gray cloud. "I was Icarus, tempted to fly too close to the sun."

"But now you have Lawrence . . . ," Audrey said, willing her mother's story toward a happy ending.

"Lawrence is a kind man, a lovely companion. You know I

am no good on my own. But it's not what I had with Brian, or even with your father."

This wasn't making Audrey feel any better.

"What about Kosmo or Jean-Luc? What about Benedict?"

"Love changes us, there's a metamorphosis. Everyone I've loved has changed the shape of my heart." There was a weariness behind Vivien's eyes.

"So, who was the love of your life, then?" Audrey pushed. "Who do you think you were supposed to be with?"

Before Vivien could answer, Clara burst through the door with a sewing box. "We're in luck. The florist had a whole sewing kit with all sorts of needles and threads."

Vivien pulled her shoulders back and wiped at the corner of her eye as she went to inspect the needle options.

"Right, let's get on with this, shall we?" She turned to Audrey. "Let's not allow a few unfortunate events to put us off our stride."

The image of her mother's shape-shifting heart stuck in Audrey's mind. She thought of the photo she'd seen of Vivien marrying Kosmo on a Greek island, at the age of twenty-two. She'd worn a white sundress and a flower in her hair. None of her friends or family had been in attendance. Vivien described her first wedding as the "fanciful finale to a holiday romance"— one her parents had forced her to annul as soon as they found out. Audrey remembered the photo of Vivien clasping Kosmo's hand. She looked so happy, but then she looked happy in all her wedding photos. In every one, had she thought it would last? Was this romantic streak her mother's fatal flaw? Forever chasing that feeling of immortality you get when the right man's hand is clasped in yours?

25

Six Years Before I Do

⤳

*A*udrey clasped Fred's hand in hers as they ran across the park. After jumping off the Ferris wheel, Audrey and Fred managed to outrun the fastest of the security guards. They made it to the busy intersection at Marble Arch, where they were safe among the bustle of people all queuing to cross the road. They looked at each other and laughed. Every inch of Audrey's body fired with adrenaline.

"You're insane," she said, still trying to catch her breath from running and laughing at the same time.

"Maybe," he said, the whites of his eyes luminous and wide. "I'm impressed you jumped."

"Shouldn't I have?" she asked.

"No, we could have broken our legs." He grinned, and his face was so full of energy, Audrey felt fueled just by looking at him.

"I take it we're not going back for your umbrella?"

"No, let's hope it never rains again." He laughed.

They crossed the road and turned right, down Oxford Street.

"What's next on this date of near-death experiences, then?" Audrey asked.

"Food, I think. I'm hungry. You?" Fred darted into a Tesco Express, and she followed.

He strolled down the aisle, picking things up and putting them down. Audrey's eyes were drawn back to his hips; he had this swagger, this confidence in his gait. There was something highly sexual about him, even the way he moved through a supermarket. She watched a teenage girl pause in the aisle to look at him. So Audrey wasn't the only one who noticed.

"What meal is this you're buying?" she asked.

Fred had put a bottle of prosecco, her favorite salt-and-vinegar crisps, and two tins of peaches into his basket.

"Bus snacks," he said, then, as though remembering he hadn't filled her in on this plan, added, "Have you been on the open-top tourist bus before? They drive you around and tell you the history of the city." Audrey shook her head. "Want to ride around and learn something new?"

"Sounds fun. I'm in."

Outside the store, Fred took her hand again as they walked to the bus stop. On board, they took a seat in the back row of the almost empty top deck. Fred pulled the lid from the peach can, speared a peach with a disposable fork, and handed it to her. "I bet you don't remember how good canned peaches taste."

He watched her, waiting for her reaction as she took a bite. The peach was soft and juicy and bursting with sweet flavor.

"Oh wow, you're right, they're phenomenal. Why do I never eat these?"

"Canned fruit is criminally underrated."

Fred popped open the bottle of fizz. No one objected to their drinking on the bus. They didn't have glasses so took turns taking swigs. The sweet peaches went perfectly with the bubbles, and Audrey felt a strange intimacy in sharing the bottle with him, his lips pressed against the glass rim moments before hers. There was a slightly manic energy to Fred; he buzzed with an enthusiasm that was impossible not to get caught up in.

They ate and drank and listened to the bus guide, talked and laughed about everything and nothing. Audrey looked out at the city, at all the people going on with their lives, oblivious to the fact that she was spending the day with Photo Booth Guy, and he was *wonderful*.

"This city has been inhabited for millennia," the buoyant voice of the guide crackled over the PA system. "New versions built on top of the old. Beneath us sits Roman London, Shakespeare's London, medieval London—it's all there, beneath our feet."

"It's crazy, isn't it? Think of all the people who have lived in this city before us. How different their lives would have been from ours," Audrey mused.

"In all the past versions of London, do you think there's ever been an Audrey the Astronomer and a Fred the Photographer who sat on a bus together eating peaches?" Fred asked, his cheek creasing into a dimpled grin.

"Definitely not. We're entirely unique."

As they talked, flirted, drank each other in, they flitted from topic to topic with seamless ease. To anyone listening, it might have sounded like a disjointed stream of consciousness, but to Audrey, it felt like talking to a new, exciting version of herself. She felt this strange sense of recognition, as though nothing she said would surprise him because he already knew it, because he *was* her. They were like two versions of historic

London. In one sense they were completely different cities, but in essence, they were the same place.

At one point, Fred pulled out his notebook and showed Audrey his notes for *The Insomniac's Almanac*. She paused on a list of countries.

"What's this?" she asked.

"Places that look better at night than they do in the day. I'm going to visit them all when I've saved up enough money. All these adventures are waiting, and I feel like I'm wasting time staying in the same place."

"Today hasn't been wasted," she said.

"No, today I've met the person who is going to come with me. You'll bring your telescope, I'll bring my camera, we'll explore every inch of land and sky."

He sucked her in with his words and his wild green eyes. He was probably joking, but it didn't feel like he was. He reached for her hand again and squeezed it tight. It was like finding the jigsaw puzzle you fit into, when this morning she hadn't even known she was a jigsaw piece. Audrey squeezed back—a silent message that she felt this too. This was everything she'd imagined meeting the right person would feel like.

⁎

*T*hey got off the bus near Regent's Park to check out an art installation about the solar system that Audrey wanted to see. A sculpture of the sun stood in the middle of the park, and you had to find the planets hidden around the city.

"I think Uranus and Neptune are halfway across London, but Mercury, Venus, Earth, and Mars are all somewhere near here," she said as they strolled along a tree-lined avenue.

They sat down on a patch of grass and Fred showed her

how to use his camera, how to change the shutter speed and the aperture size. She picked it up easily.

"It's basically a telescope, only you can't see as far," she teased him.

"Maybe I don't need to see that far," he countered, "when there's so much to look at right here."

Wandering further into the park, they found Mars, a huge red orb of dappled marble that spun on its axis. They lay down on the ground and took turns spinning it with their feet. Audrey took a photo of their shoes against the red planet, and when she showed Fred the result, they both laughed at the blur of trainers.

"I like this one," she said.

"I like it too," he said, taking the camera back from her and snapping a photo of her lying next to him. "But I like the ones with you in better."

She looked at the screen he was holding out for her to see. It was obvious in her eyes how much she liked the man on the other side of the lens. She turned her gaze to the sky.

"I read somewhere that our universe has two hundred and eighty-five galaxies for every single human on earth, and more stars than there are grains of sand. I can never get my head around that."

"Tell me more cool space facts, Audrey the Astronomer," Fred said, turning on his side and propping his head up on his elbow.

"On Pluto, the snow is red; on Mars, the sunset is blue." She paused, wondering what else to tell him. She had an encyclopedic knowledge of facts about space at her fingertips.

She knew what was interesting to her but not necessarily what would interest other people. "Did you know there are rogue floating planets out there, not in orbit around a star—they're just alone, drifting through the universe?"

"Could we live on them?" he asked.

"No. All life needs a sun," she said as Fred started spinning Mars with his feet again. "I read this theory about the multiverse—that there could be an infinite number of universes, all with their own stars and galaxies. Logically, it would mean a planet exactly like Earth would repeat itself over and over. We'd have doppelgängers out there, leading variations of our lives. Anything that can possibly happen *will* happen an infinite number of times."

"Ideas like that make my brain melt," said Fred, stopping Mars from spinning and pushing it so that it spun the other way.

"You just made all the Martians very dizzy," Audrey said, helping spin the planet faster and faster with her feet.

"I often wonder how humans can be so clever, making houses, cars, phones, pasta." He smiled. "And yet we'll never know the answers to these big questions. We don't even know what we're doing here, on this tiny rock among the stars."

"Would you want to know, even if it made your brain explode two seconds later?" she asked, turning onto her side and putting her feet back down on the grass next to him.

Fred contemplated this for a moment.

"Now, or later in my life when I've lived more?"

"Now," she said, watching his face move, his expressive eyebrows, his features in perpetual motion.

"I don't know. I think, before my brain exploded with the vastness of the multiverse, I'd want to kiss you," he said. Then he rolled away from her and stood up. Audrey felt her blood pump loud around her veins in deafening anticipation. He reached out and took her hand, helping her to her feet.

As they stood facing each other, Fred leaned forward and gently kissed her on the lips, then drew back and smiled that crooked smile of his. She felt something awaken inside her, and she had to reach for his hand to anchor herself to the ground. She had never felt this kind of crackle before, this magnetic draw to another human.

"This is crazy," he whispered.

"I know," she said.

They strolled hand in hand through the park and found the sculpture of Earth, but the crowds were busier there and they couldn't get close. As they meandered back toward the bus stop, he put his arm around her and kissed her shoulder in the most tender way. It was such an intimate gesture, anyone observing them might have imagined they'd known each other far longer than a few hours. On the bus, Audrey desperately wanted to kiss him properly, but it was busy, and it felt too public.

When they pulled into Baker Street, Audrey said, "We're back where we began, at the photo booth."

As they got off the bus, his arm was still around her shoulder, and her skin tingled at the prospect of where this was going and how. They got to the booth and climbed in, both giddy with laughter, drawing the curtain behind them. Fred found change in his pocket and she sat on his lap. As the flash went off, she kissed him, a proper full kiss, his lips soft and hot, his tongue meeting hers, the flash of light from the photo booth scorching the feeling onto her lips. The flashes stopped, but the kiss continued, hungry and urgent, and she felt the tinderbox of tension between them explode. She had never been kissed like this, never felt a kiss in every atom of her body. They heard the whirl of the booth, and the photos hit the slot.

"Did you feel that?" he asked, breathless, his pupils wide.

"Yes," she said.

"I think this booth might be magic."

Outside, they collected the photos and huddled together to see. In the first three photos, most of her face was obscured by his, but in the final image you could see their lips meet, and Audrey blushed at the rawness of the image.

"You keep them," he said.

"You don't want them?" she asked, challenging him with her eyes. She hadn't even asked where he lived, she knew so little about him, and yet she felt she already knew everything important.

He looked at her and then started, as though suddenly remembering something,

"Shit. What time is it?" He pulled out his phone and looked at the blank screen. "I'm out of battery. Fuck, I have to be somewhere. You just pulled me into a different space-time continuum, Audrey. I completely forgot where I was supposed to be today."

"Go, if you need to." She couldn't hide her disappointment. *How could he leave now?*

"I don't want to go anywhere." He frowned, glancing at the large clock on the opposite wall. "But it's my mum's birthday, we're throwing her a surprise dinner, and she's going to be there in . . . fifteen minutes."

"Go, go." Audrey laughed, satisfied with his excuse. "Of course you must go."

She carefully tore the strip of photos in two and handed him the top two. "Write your number on the back," she commanded, a newfound confidence in her stance and tone.

He pulled a fountain pen from his bag and wrote his number on the back of her half. Then she wrote her number on his. She gave him her home number, in Fulham; it was safer than the broken mobile currently drying in a bag of rice.

"I don't want to wait to call you," he said. "I'm not going to be cool about this."

She smiled, her cheeks aching with pleasure. "Let's not wait, then. Let's meet here tomorrow."

His eyes lit up at the idea. "Okay, here, at our booth, first thing. I'll bring breakfast," he said.

Audrey blinked, remembering she couldn't make tomorrow morning. "I have to meet my mum's fiancé in the morning, a peacekeeping mission. Can we say one o'clock?"

"I'll be here," he said, reaching up to brush a strand of hair behind her ear. "Don't make any plans for the rest of the day, or for the rest of your life." He said the last part lightly, as though he wasn't serious, but something in his eyes told her he might be.

"Go, go, you're going to be late for your mum!" She laughed, pushing him toward the tube.

He leaned in to take her arms now, looking down into her eyes. "I found you. I found you."

She nodded. "You found me."

He kissed her again, and Audrey wanted to follow him, to say she would walk him to his dinner, anything to spend another minute by his side, but he squeezed her arm and said, "Tomorrow," and then disappeared into the crowd.

She did not see him again for another six years.

26

Ninety Minutes Before I Do

ᑭᑭ

*V*ivien fixed the dress. You could tell close up that the material didn't hang smoothly, but crucially, Audrey wasn't going to show the whole congregation her underwear. In the mirror, Audrey saw a real bride. She looked elegant, poised, strangely ethereal. She'd had these recurring dreams over the last few months where she was a bride without a face, just a blur beneath a veil. But now here she was, in a dress, with a face—this was real. As she stood in front of the mirror, her mother came up behind her.

"You look exquisite, darling. Consider my reservations dispelled, you *can* pull off this fabric."

"Thank you." Audrey reached out a hand to touch her mother's arm.

When Clara went into the bathroom to do her own makeup, Vivien took the opportunity to revive the conversation she and Audrey had been having earlier.

"Now, you mustn't have doubts about Joshua. There's nothing to doubt," Vivien said, leaning in and putting a hand on

Audrey's shoulder. "You complement each other so well. He's so sensible, so grounded."

"You didn't answer my question, about who the love of your life was."

"I think, if you're lucky, you get more than one. Or maybe you're luckier if one lasts you a lifetime, I don't know." Vivien gave a childish shrug.

"Did you have doubts before any of your weddings?"

"Every time!" Vivien cried. "Getting married is like sky-diving. There's always a moment before you jump out of the plane where you think, What am I doing? I'm jumping out of a plane—I must be mad! But then you jump and you're glad you did. Unless you forgot to pack a parachute."

"What's the parachute in this analogy?"

Vivien paused for a moment. "Mutual kindness. Don't marry a man you wouldn't want to be divorced from, that's what my aunt always told me. If a man isn't kind to strangers, or at least respectful to his enemies, know that one day you might be a stranger to him, you might be his enemy. Joshua is definitely the sort of man you could be divorced from. That's the highest compliment I can give him."

"The wisdom of Vivien Wey," Audrey said with a grin.

"You get married enough times and you learn a thing or two." Vivien gave her daughter a wry smile. "Goodness, that reminds me, I have something for you." She turned away, going to her handbag on the bed and leafing through some papers inside. "I didn't know when to give this to you. It was supposed to be last night, but then with your injury . . . well. I never know with these things."

Vivien handed a creased envelope to Audrey.

"What is it?"

"It's from your father. A letter for me to give you on your

wedding day. He wrote it once he knew he wouldn't live long enough to see it."

Audrey felt herself welling up and put a hand across her mouth to stop herself from sobbing.

"Don't cry. You'll smudge your makeup. It's a happy letter, I'm sure, wishing you luck." Vivien reached out and wiped a finger beneath her daughter's eyes, but Audrey noticed that there were tears in her mother's eyes as well.

27

Seventeen Years Before I Do

ᴄ✦ᴏ

"Do you remember the story of Andromeda?" her father asked as he and Audrey lay side by side on the tartan blanket, looking up at the night sky over Hampstead Heath.

"Was she the one whose parents tied her to a rock as some sacrifice to a sea monster?" Audrey asked.

"That's the one."

"I guess they hadn't heard of social services in ancient Greece."

"Very good," he said, gently elbowing her in the ribs. "Look, you can see her tonight." He pointed out the constellation in the sky, moving his arm slowly between a line of stars. "See her arms pinned out at right angles?"

"I don't think that looks anything like a woman." Audrey sighed, referring to the constellation map, then trying to identify the formation in the sky above her.

"You have to use your imagination, it's not a dot-to-dot."

He sat up, rearranged his woolly hat, then opened his leather drawstring backpack and pulled out a thermos. He was wearing so many layers, yet Audrey noticed he still looked desperately thin. He slowly unscrewed the lid and poured the steaming hot chocolate into two tin mugs.

On clear nights, Audrey and her father had taken to coming up here, sometimes with the telescope, other times making do with just their eyes. She stayed at her dad's place one night a week and was always glad when the weather allowed them to go out. Audrey didn't dislike his new wife, Carmel, but she tended to dominate conversations. Time with her father was so precious, Audrey didn't want it diluted.

Clasping the hot chocolate in her own gloved hands, Audrey shivered, and her father wrapped an arm around her.

"You cold? Want to go?" he asked.

"No, I'm fine." She'd sit here until her toes froze as long as he was happy to stay.

"Good, because we're meeting this nice sea monster here in a bit, and I promised him dinner."

Audrey humored him with a smile, then they sat in contented silence.

"So, your mother's getting married again," he said, and she felt his arm around her tense. "You like Brian, don't you?"

"I do," she said. "He's nice."

"Good. I'm glad. I like him too." His arm around her relaxed, and he took a long, deep breath. "You know what I find interesting about the constellations?" he said. "Ancient civilizations that didn't exist in the same time period, or even on the same continent, chose the same stars to connect in the sky, even made up similar stories. What does that tell us? That our eyes pick out the same dots of light from the thousands that are up there. When you think of human history, of all the war and conflict, isn't there something heartening in such commonality? We have always looked to the stars for answers, used stories and mythology to help make sense of what is beyond our reach."

"I don't know if I'm trying to make sense of anything when I look up. I just like knowing what I'm looking at," said Audrey, and her dad reached his hand up to ruffle her hair.

"You are a better scientist than me, then. Perhaps it is the writer in me who sees the stars like chapters in a book, thrown across the sky in no clear order or chronology. If only I could rearrange them in a more orderly way, in a shape that made sense to me, then I would understand the story better. Yet logic tells me those stars are millions of light-years apart, they care not a jot that they share space in our sky. Are we fools to look for meaning?"

"Are you okay, Dad?" Audrey looked across at him. She was not used to hearing him talk in such a serious, meandering way. It sounded as though he was asking himself these questions, rather than her.

"I'm fine." He sighed, and clasped both hands back around his cup. Then he said more brightly, "Did you know that a star's light can still be seen long after it's gone?"

"That's one of the first things you taught me."

"Some of the stars we're looking at now, they don't exist anymore. Yet we can still see their light traveling toward us." He tapped the side of his head. "As long as someone is here to see the light they created, then they are not gone."

Audrey shifted her body toward his, suddenly concerned.

"You're not sick again, are you, Dad?" she asked, her voice trembling.

His eyes darted away, unable to meet hers.

28

Seventy Minutes Before I Do

ᏜᎾ

There was a knock on the door of the bridal suite, and Miranda's long red hair, now curled into tight ringlets, appeared around it. She was dressed in the same lilac floor-length bridesmaid dress that Clara was wearing.

Audrey gave a single nod to her mother, a thank-you for the letter, and then she quickly stowed it in her white clutch. She would open it when she had a moment alone.

"Oh wow, look at you! I'm going to cry!" Miranda said, coming in and waving both hands in front of her face.

"Miranda came to the hairdressers with us," Vivien said, pressing a hand gently against her hair-sprayed updo. "Doesn't she look fabulous?" Miranda pulled self-consciously at the rigid ringlets. "Right, I'll leave you girls to it. Nothing worse than a crowded green room. I have to speak to the violinists about their positioning in the church and help Debbie stow the confetti somewhere dry. Can you believe we didn't have a wet-weather confetti plan? Utter madness!"

Clara emerged from the bathroom, and she and Miranda

177

both complimented each other on how good they looked in the same dress.

"You both look lovely," said Vivien, seeing Clara and turning back from the door. "Now, I know you two missed the rehearsal last night, but has Audrey filled you in on the entrances and exits?"

"I'm sorry, I've been the worst bridesmaid," said Miranda. "I couldn't get yesterday off work for the rehearsal, and then this morning the hairdresser took forever."

"It's fine." Audrey waved a hand in the air.

Vivien coughed, keen to be heard. "You'll follow Audrey down the aisle and then walk out with a groomsman. Clara, if you could walk with Mark, the tall chap, and then Miranda, you'll walk down the aisle with the best man, Paul."

Miranda's eyes suddenly took on a pained expression and her chin began to wobble. Though she and Paul had broken up over a year ago, Audrey knew it had been a significant relationship for them both and there might still have been feelings there.

Audrey caught Clara's eye. "Maybe the other way around."

"Yes, Miranda's taller than me, it might look better if she walks with Mark," Clara added.

"Fine, fine, work it out among yourselves." Then Vivien turned back to Audrey, reached for her arm, and said, "You have the parachute, I know you do. Now all you need to do is jump."

As soon as Vivien left the room, Miranda's face crumpled.

"Sorry, that was tactless of her." Audrey winced, putting an arm around Miranda.

"Sorry." Miranda wiped at her cheeks, and Clara ran to get her a tissue. "This is your day, and I'm your bridesmaid. I shouldn't be making it about me." But as she said "me," she erupted into tears and it came out "meeeeeeee."

"I don't own the day," said Audrey, feeling surprisingly stoical suddenly. What with Clara and Hillary having wobbles about motherhood and their careers, what was one more life crisis thrown into the mix? "Is it awkward, with you and Paul?"

"Not especially. We were getting on really well at dinner last night. It's just, I've been a bridesmaid eight times, and today I remembered that saying. You know, 'Always a bridesmaid, never a . . . a bride,' and, and, I'm probably never going to get married." Her voice escalated in pitch as she spoke, until it was a tiny squeak.

"That's not true," said Clara, putting an arm around her. "You look completely fabulous. You have your shit together, this Fred guy you're with is superhot." Clara gave Audrey an apologetic look for bringing Fred into this. "And you know getting married isn't the only end goal, right?"

"Only married people say that," Miranda said, blowing her nose loudly on another tissue. "And I don't look fabulous, I look like some insane children's book character with these stupid ringlets." She tugged again at her hair. "And Fred isn't even really my boyfriend, he's a random guy I roped into coming with me at the last minute because I couldn't face going to my brother's wedding alone, especially with Paul here." She looked up at Audrey. "Sorry, I know I shouldn't have brought some random guy to your wedding."

Miranda looked so dejected and full of misery that Audrey's heart ached for her. "Don't worry about that, you could bring fifty random guys if you wanted to. This is my fault. I shouldn't have asked you to be a bridesmaid. I know you've been asked by so many other friends, I just—"

"No, no, this is *my* issue, I'm so honored you asked me."

Clara stood up and retrieved something from her bag. It was a box of chocolate letters that spelled out "Just Married."

"I bought these for Audrey, but I think you might need them more." Clara opened the box and tactfully jumbled up the letters before handing them to Miranda. As she popped a chocolate M into her mouth, Miranda seemed to calm down.

"Everyone tells you it will work out, your person will turn up, trust that fate has a plan. But what if it doesn't? I have friends in their forties who waited, who held out for the perfect guy, and now they're too old to have kids and they're alone, and you know, that's fine if that's what you chose, but some of them didn't choose that. Some of them bought into the notion that there's someone perfect out there for everyone, and maybe if they'd settled for that guy who was fine, they'd be married now with two lovely kids, not alone with three cats in a one-bedroom flat in Roehampton." Miranda had three cats and lived in a flat in Roehampton.

Audrey looked at Clara as Miranda stuffed both a chocolate J and S into her mouth at once. She'd had no idea Miranda felt like this.

"And the worst part is, talking to Paul at the rehearsal dinner, I . . . I just don't know what went wrong there. He's so great and funny, and he smells so inoffensive. You know how I have issues with dating because of my highly attuned nose. Most men smell dreadful." She sniffed. "Paul might have been olfactory perfection, and I screwed it up."

"You still like Paul?" Audrey asked.

"I don't know. Yes." Miranda sighed and closed her eyes.

"I know weddings can be stressful, they can raise a lot of feelings." Audrey reached for Miranda's hand. "You don't need to walk down the aisle with me if you don't want to. You don't even need to wear the bridesmaid dress if you'd prefer not to."

"Thank you, thank you, I just, I think I might vomit or cry, or cry-vomit, and then I'd ruin your day. Not that I'd be vomiting about your wedding. I just look at what you and Josh have, and you and Jay, Clara—you're like this model dream couple. Why can't I have that?"

Chocolatey dribble escaped from Miranda's mouth, and Audrey reached out to dab it with a tissue.

"I'm sure it's out there for you," said Clara, catching Audrey's eye and giving her a concerned look. "But you know, nothing is perfect, everything is a bit of a compromise. Jay and I are definitely not a 'model dream couple.'" Clara paused, biting her lip. "We haven't had sex in over a year."

"What?" Audrey turned to her friend. Why hadn't she said anything about this before now?

"Everything's just been so full-on with the girls. No one sleeps, and we snipe at each other all day, and, well, sometimes I just can't stand the sight of him by the time I climb into bed at night. I can't even lie facing him in case I open my eyes and see his big stupid round face, and it makes me so angry I can't sleep. But you know what, that's fine. I love him, we'll get it back. All my married friends have troughs; sometimes you just need to live in the trough and roll around in the shit for a while."

Audrey couldn't believe what she was hearing. Before they'd had the twins, Clara and Jay had been the kind of couple who snuck off in restaurants for a quickie in the bathroom. They were insatiable, completely besotted with each other, and she rarely saw them argue. Yes, they'd both found it hard becoming parents, but they were still Clara and Jay.

"Why didn't you tell me?" Audrey asked.

"Last week, Jay went into the cupboard to get some paracetamol for Lily, and he said, 'Why is our medicine cabinet so messy?' Why? *Why?* We wouldn't even *have* a medicine cabinet if it wasn't for me. You think he's *ever* bought medicine? Do you think he even knows the difference between paracetamol and ibuprofen?"

Miranda had stopped sobbing now and was staring at Clara with a strange, slightly scared expression.

"And when Lily and Bea were six months old, *six months*, he said he thought we shouldn't use disposable nappies anymore, that we needed to do our part to save the environment and we should switch to washable ones. Can you believe it? I mean, he changes about ten percent of the nappies, at best. Can you imagine he's going to wash and dry the sodding things too?" Clara's face had gone red. "Sometimes he walks into a room now, doesn't even say anything, but just the way he's breathing makes me want to kill him. Last week he came home from work, and I was washing up bottles for the fiftieth time that day, and he was talking on the phone, laughing his stupid fake laugh he does with this coffee supplier, and I just wanted to pick up the saucepan that was drying by the sink and smash it into his skull until he stopped laughing." Clara noticed Audrey's worried expression and waved a hand dismissively. "But I love him. We'll be fine. It's just being a parent, lack of sleep. Everyone feels like this when they have kids."

Miranda looked entirely composed now.

"I can walk down the aisle with you, Audrey, it's fine." Then she patted Clara's shoulder and offered her the chocolates. Clara took one, biting down on it with a sharp crack.

"Can you fix my horrible ringlet hair?" Miranda asked cautiously. Clara nodded.

Audrey swallowed a new wave of panic. If any couple was "meant to be," it was Clara and Jay. Anyone could see it—in the way they sat on a chair together, limbs entwined, the way they spoke in their own short-form, coded language, the fact that they looked for each other first in any room and their eyes lit up at the same things. If marriage and children had broken them, what hope was there for anyone?

29

Three Years Before I Do

∽

*N*ow that their friend group's average age was twenty-five, "the wedding years" had begun in earnest. It felt like there was a wedding almost every other weekend. This Saturday, it was Ben and Dee, friends of Paul's from Cambridge. They'd gotten to know Clara and Audrey through various social events at the Tooting house, so all the housemates, plus Jay, had been invited.

Audrey clocked Josh in the church immediately, sitting just a few pews ahead of her. She recognized his broad back and polite manner as he stood up to allow other people past. She couldn't see Kelly with him.

"Did some other halves not get invited?" she whispered to Clara, who was sitting next to her.

Clara shrugged. "Not that I know of. It feels like everyone got invited."

"I would have happily not come," said Jay, who was sitting on the other side of Clara. "You know I'm missing Latitude for this?"

"Oh shush. You'd rather be here with me than at a festival

without me," Clara whispered, running a hand down his thigh. "We're going to dance all night, then have a lazy hotel breakfast tomorrow."

"You're right, I'm happiest wherever you are," Jay said, leaning across to kiss her neck and making an inappropriate "grrrr" sound.

"Guys, we're in a church! Do I need to sit between you?" Audrey asked in her best schoolmarm voice.

Fortunately, the swell of the organ put an end to their inappropriate display of affection, and the congregation all stood to sing "All Things Bright and Beautiful."

"What wedding present did you get them in the end?" Clara whispered to Audrey.

"I mapped them a binary star," Audrey replied.

She was currently earning close to minimum wage, so she was having to get creative with gifts. Audrey's job at the art gallery had not lasted long. She didn't like having to wear smart clothes every day or deal with stuffy customers. It may also have been that the exhibition space reminded her of Benedict, but she had not dared let herself dwell on that factor. She'd served her notice and signed up to a local dog-walking agency. It paid less, but she was getting fit and had more time in the day for photography work.

"What's a binary star?" Clara asked.

"Two stars gravitationally bound to one another. From a distance they look like one, but close up you can see they are two individuals, orbiting around one another. It's the closest thing in the cosmos to a committed relationship. I made Dee and Ben a chart mapping where they can find their binary star with a little index of everything I know about it."

"Audrey, you bitch, that's such a great gift. I got them fucking pillowcases."

Audrey stifled a snort. "Well, I give everyone the same binary star, but they'll never know, will they?"

"Well, Jay and I want our own," Clara whispered. "I'm not having their mucky cosmic seconds."

Audrey thought for a moment. "It might sound like a romantic idea, two stars drawn into each other's orbit, but most close binaries end up destroying each other. Don't worry, I'll pay up and get you a proper gift. Do you want salad tongs?"

During the service, as Ben and Dee made their vows, Audrey's eyes were drawn to Josh, and she remembered what he'd said about marriage: *"If you're going to commit to anything in this life, shouldn't it be love?"* She wasn't usually moved by weddings; they felt like productions, where people recited a script to audition for the role of "married person." But with Josh's words in her mind, she found herself welling up as she watched Dee say, "I do."

At the lawn reception, she saw Josh laughing with some of his Cambridge friends. He had a tan and was dressed in a perfectly fitted morning suit. She would not seek him out, she would wait for him to come and say hi to her. But she found she couldn't stop her eyes from being drawn in his direction. When the time came to sit down for dinner, Audrey's heart tripped in her chest when she saw the seating plan. She could have kissed Dee—she'd put her at a table with Josh. She walked through the tent to find her seat and found him already at the table, pulling out the empty chair beside him.

"Hello, Amy," he said, leaning in to kiss her on both cheeks, placing a hand gently on her waist. She felt a tingle of electricity. He smelled of cedar or pine, freshly ironed cotton, and something earthy and male. "Lovely to see you."

"Hi, James," she said with a purposeful air of casual detachment.

Over dinner, Audrey tried to be on her best behavior. She drank slowly, adopted the tone of someone who was civilized and mature. She wanted to wipe clean any image Josh might have had of her drunkenly kissing Hamishes or men named after herbs.

"How many trees are you up to?" she asked.

"Two hundred and nine," he said. "Plus, one for you."

"You remembered," she said with a smile.

"Of course. I even made him a tag. 'Audrey's tree—Cuthbert.'"

"I'm impressed you didn't forget about Cuthbert," she said, her eyes meeting his.

"Of course not," he said, and the fizz was right there, just where they'd left it several months before.

"How's work going? Have you solved the energy crisis yet?"

"Not yet, but I need to thank you. I did what you suggested, I told my bosses I wanted to move on to the tidal projects, and unbelievably, they let me."

"See, didn't I say, it's always worth asking. If you're good, they want to keep you happy."

A smile played at Josh's lips. "You always make things sound so simple, Amy."

"I try. So, how are things with Kelly?"

Josh shifted his gaze to the table. He picked up a jug of water, then busied himself filling everyone's glasses. "Kelly and I broke up."

Yes! "Oh no, how come?" Audrey asked, feigning concern. *Why hadn't Paul told her?*

"She finished her PhD placement and went back to Montreal. It wasn't going to work long-distance."

"Oh, well. I'm sorry." Audrey didn't trust herself to say more. She had tried not to dwell on Josh over the last few months, but now, sitting beside him, it was like seeing a familiar view that you'd forgotten how much you liked.

"How about you, are you seeing anyone at the moment?" Josh asked. He blinked, brushed a hand through his hair, straightened the fork in front of him; that adorable shyness was back, the shyness she'd seen at Paul's birthday last year.

"You know me . . . ," she said with an evasive smile.

"I don't, actually." He paused, then tilted his head to one side. "Though, whenever we meet, I think how much I'd like to."

Audrey's belly swirled with pleasure.

"Well, what can I tell you?" She tapped a finger against her chin. "I like my coffee strong and my tea weak."

"Tell me something your barista wouldn't know," he said, his voice low, his eyes fixed on her in a way that made her want to tell him everything all at once.

"My favorite type of eclipse is an annular eclipse, where the sun becomes a ring around the moon. I love risotto, there's something about the texture. I nearly said no to this wedding, and now I'm glad I said yes." She dropped her eyes back to Josh and saw she could lose herself in his honey-brown eyes. "Tell me something you love," she asked.

His face softened. "Okay." He thought for a moment. "I love the smell of the cobbler's. My dad used to take me to one in London where he got his shoes reheeled. I liked watching the machine they used, the smell of the glue." The image of a young Josh, being thrilled by reheeling shoes, melted something inside Audrey. Now she wanted to know everything that had ever made him happy. "And I'm glad you said yes to this wedding too."

Audrey fizzed with pleasure, but just as she was about to say something else, the woman sitting on Josh's left turned and stole him away.

"Hi, I'm Susanna, Ben's cousin on his mum's side. Are you friends with the bride or the groom?"

Though Audrey knew nothing about Susanna, she hated her instantly. She went on to monopolize Josh for the duration of the beef bourguignon. Audrey turned her attention to the right, to a married man called Gareth. He engaged her in conversation about the rising property prices in Clapham, the benefits of a loft conversion over a basement build, and the importance of taking control of your pension in your twenties. Audrey didn't have the inclination to steer the discussion to a topic of her choosing, so she nodded along politely.

"And what do you do?" Gareth asked, eventually switching from transmit. She poured herself another glass of wine, numbing herself to Gareth's inane question.

"Currently, I'm a dog walker and I do a bit of photography."

"Best marry someone rich, then." Gareth guffawed. "I can't imagine you earn enough doing that to keep yourself in nice frocks."

Audrey imagined smashing her wineglass into Gareth's round, arrogant face, but instead she said calmly, "I enjoy it. I get lots of fresh air, I love dogs—except this one Pekingese called Bruno, who's a complete asshole—and I can make the hours work around my photography gigs."

"You must come from money, then," Gareth said with a knowing nostril flare.

"I never ask my family for help financially. I earn enough to support myself."

"That's not the point. If you're from money, you can doss about doing pottery or acting or dog walking or whatever, because you know you're not going to starve in a ditch when you're old. You know one day you'll inherit a house in Putney or Chelsea."

"Fulham," she said, and Gareth snorted appreciatively.

Audrey picked up her glass of wine and excused herself from the table. She wasn't going to be able to remain civil if she stayed. She went to sit on the toilet with her glass of wine. Gareth was right. He'd put into words something that she'd always known at the back of her mind. She'd been allowed to flit from course to course, from job to job, because she'd always had the safety net of her parents' money to fall back on. Her friends were saving for houses or paying mortgages, and she'd never even considered that expense. The fact that she'd had every advantage in life somehow made her current state of mediocrity feel worse.

When she returned to the table, she noticed Susanna was leaning in, placing her ample cleavage right on Josh's side plate. Gareth looked keen to continue telling her what an entitled failure she was, so Audrey took back the reins of the conversation.

"Why do people get married, Gareth? Why did you get married?"

He paused, contemplating her question. "It's better for the kids, isn't it, once you have them. Plus, there are the tax breaks. Crissy gave me a two-year deadline when we started dating." He nodded across the table toward Crissy. "Said she was, and excuse my French, 'tired of fucking about.'"

"And they say romance is dead."

Gareth gave her a slightly leering grin. "You're funny. How come you're single then?"

"I'm holding out for the right tax breaks," she said, and Gareth roared with laughter. "Susanna, what have you managed to find out about Josh here?" Audrey asked, turning back to her left.

Josh's lip twitched into a smile. God, she wanted him. Maybe it was the wine or the new threat of Susanna's clear interest, or Gareth's recent swipe at her self-esteem, but right now, Josh appeared a beacon of everything that was good in the world. She wanted to win, she wanted to be the person he talked to, the person he kissed tonight.

"I've learned plenty." Susanna grinned. "Josh here claims to be a dog and a cat person, which you can't be. He also says his favorite place in the world is the top of a Scottish mountain. I've never climbed a mountain in my life, I can never find the right sports bra," she giggled, "but maybe Josh could get me up one." She leaned forward in another blatant cleavage parade, a peacock unfurling its feathers. Audrey saw a flicker in Josh's eye. *Surely this wasn't working. Was it?*

Audrey put an arm across her own modest chest and reached to refill her wineglass.

"Is all that walking how you got these huge thigh muscles, Josh?" Susanna asked.

Josh suddenly pushed back his chair. "If you'll excuse me, I'm just going to use the bathroom before dessert arrives." He stood up, then leaned down to say to Audrey, "If the waitress comes, can you please tell her I'd like the cheese board?"

"Sure," she said, feeling a small fizz of victory that he had asked *her* to order his dessert and not Susanna. Then she did an internal eye-roll at the fact that this ridiculous crush on Josh had turned her into such a vapid bonehead.

While Josh was away from the table, the bride and groom started to circulate among the tables, and to Audrey's annoyance, Dee sat down in Josh's empty chair to chat to Susanna. Josh did not come back for his cheese board, and when she looked around the room, she saw he'd been intercepted by the groom at the bar. Audrey listened quietly to the conversation going on around her and reached for the bottle of dessert wine.

"Audrey, I assume it's Hepburn you're named after? Tough bar to live up to there—one of the most beautiful women in the world," said Gareth, smirking.

"Oh, do fuck off, Gareth," she said.

*W*hen the dancing started, Audrey stepped out of the tent to get some air. She found Josh helping the father of the bride move some chairs that were getting wet in the drizzle.

"Here you are. You neglected your cheese," she said, and he grinned at her then.

"Audrey Lavery, if I'm not mistaken, I think you might have missed me."

"No, I just don't like seeing good cheese go to waste."

"You came looking for me. You're not having fun at this wedding without me."

"I didn't, and I'm having plenty of fun, thank you."

He held her gaze, unblinking, and a wave of desire coursed through her. She didn't want to play this game, she was drunk—her verbal sparring capacity was impeded.

"Come with me, I want to show you something," she said, reaching out for his hand.

She pulled him around the side of the tent, out into the dark, drizzly night.

"Where are we going?" he asked, hesitating slightly.

Once they were out of view of the party, Audrey turned and planted her lips firmly on his. She could tell that he hadn't expected it, but then she felt the surprise turn to want and he kissed her back, his arms folding around her, his lips soft but urgent. Something inside Audrey melted into air.

"We're doing this, are we?" he murmured, his breath hot on her cheek, when there was a pause in the kissing.

"Looks like it," she said, holding on to his shirt collar, feeling her whole body respond to his lips.

"I can't work you out, Amy," he said, pulling his head away from hers but still holding her in his arms. "I thought you hated men who climb the corporate ladder, who aren't in a band, who order the same cup of coffee every damn time."

"I do, generally. It doesn't mean I don't want to kiss you tonight."

He frowned. "So, I'm just tonight's entertainment, am I?"

"No," Audrey said, leaning in to kiss him again, but he leaned back.

"Audrey, I don't want to do this, not like this."

"It doesn't feel like you don't want to do this," she said, arching an eyebrow at him.

He smiled kindly. "Of course I want to, you're insanely beautiful, and funny, and an infuriating enigma. I just . . . I don't want to be one of your drunken flings."

Audrey blanched. "Because I do this all the time?"

"No. I don't know." He raked a hand through his hair, looking up to the sky, searching for the words. "I like you, I really like you. I want to take you out on a proper date. As much as it pains me to stop this, I don't want this to be an end-of-night kiss that you regret or don't remember in the morning."

"I'm not that drunk, Jesus!" Audrey rolled her eyes. "It's a wedding, I've had a few glasses of wine." She knew she'd had a few more than that. She pushed his hand away from her waist, embarrassed. Turning to leave, she felt her cheeks burn red with shame. "Whatever, Josh, maybe I just wanted to kiss someone tonight. It doesn't have to be you."

He reached out to stop her and pulled her back toward

him, his face inches from hers as he said softly, "I'm sorry you feel that way, Amy, because for me, it does have to be you. I moved the whole table's seating cards around so I could sit next to you. I have thought about kissing you, a lot, and I definitely want to kiss you again, but I'd prefer you to be able to stand up straight when I do. I want you to remember every second, like I know I will."

She staggered backward slightly, which wasn't helping her cause. She felt admonished, but also that there might be something quite romantic in what he was saying.

"So, you'll give me your number and I'll call you tomorrow, and I'll ask you out properly," he said calmly. "I'm hoping you will say yes."

He stayed where he was, his face inches from hers. How was he showing this level of self-control? She averted her gaze; she wanted to kiss him again so badly. His lips felt so good, his neck smelled so wonderful. She was not used to this, to a man saying no.

"Have it your way, but I might have lost interest by tomorrow," she said, steadying herself and then letting him take her arm to guide her back to the tent.

"What if I promise to plant you another tree?" he asked quietly.

"Well, then we'll see," she said, dropping her head onto his shoulder. "But it has to be a good tree, not a crappy spindly one that all the other trees pick on, or one that's got tree disease or something."

Josh pulled out a pretend notepad and mimed writing, "Take back crappy spindly tree with tree disease."

Inside, Audrey ordered a soft drink at the bar. Josh picked up a paper drink parasol and put it into her glass. She re-

sponded by taking another one, opening it, and tucking it behind his ear. It was a silly thing to do, and they both laughed.
The wedding photographer captured the moment. It was the
first photo taken of the two of them together. It would be Audrey's favorite.

30

Sixty Minutes Before I Do

❧

The photographer, Sian, was late. She and her assistant were supposed to arrive two hours ago to take photos of the bridal party getting ready, but they'd been caught in traffic on the A303.

"Half your guests will be stuck in it if they're driving down from London," Sian said. "It's always terrible around Stonehenge. Probably the worst thing that can happen on your wedding day—no guests."

Audrey didn't have space in her brain for any more crises. All she wanted was a moment alone to read the letter from her father. Then she wanted to walk up the aisle, in a dress that covered her ass, with bridesmaids who weren't crying; marry Josh; and silence the call of the void that was telling her to jump off the cake.

"Can you take the dress off, so I can take a photo of it hanging up on the closet?" Sian asked, adjusting the curtains to allow more natural light in.

"No," Clara said, a little too forcefully. "We practically had to sew her into it. She can't take it off. Besides, she's done her makeup now, it would come off on the silk."

Everyone looked at Audrey, to see what she wanted to do.

"Let's just take some photos like this, with Miranda and Clara."

As they posed for photos, Hillary poked his head around the door.

"Let's get one with Hillary too," said Clara, beckoning him over. "He's basically a bonus bridesmaid."

"Sorry to interrupt, but Granny Parker wants a quick word with you, Auds," Hillary said with a grimace, knowing how little Audrey would want to go and have a "quick word" with Granny Parker. "She's in the morning room. Do you want me to tell her you're too busy?"

Audrey exhaled. If she went to see Granny Parker, she might be able to find a quiet place to read her father's letter on the way. There was an hour before the service, she still had time. She took a step toward the door.

"You can't go out there in your dress!" cried Clara. "People will see you."

"Help me take it off then," Audrey said.

"Okay, wait," said Clara, holding up a palm. Then she quickly pulled a pillowcase off one of the pillows on the bed. "Put this on your head, just to protect the silk from any makeup," she said, plonking the pillowcase over Audrey. "Then we just need to shimmy it off, being careful of the weak seam."

Audrey stood, with a pillowcase on her head, while Audrey and Miranda carefully lifted the silk gown back up over her head. Clara shouted, "Shimmy! Shimmy!" the whole time, as though Audrey knew what "shimmy" meant or how she was supposed to do it. She heard several clicks of a camera.

"These are not really the kind of getting-ready photos I want, Sian," she said, her voice muffled by the pillowcase. "Me in my underpants with a pillowcase on my head."

"These are brilliant," said Sian. "You'll look back and laugh about this moment one day."

"Will I?" Audrey said through gritted teeth. When the dress was finally off, Miranda pulled the pillowcase from Audrey's head while Clara returned the dress to its hanger. Audrey threw on the clothes she had been wearing earlier, then picked up her white clutch and headed for the door.

Walking along the corridor, she found an empty flight of stairs and sat down to open the letter from her father. She felt her heart in her throat as she pulled the piece of paper from the envelope. New words. She had read almost every word he had written, that he would ever write, and here in front of her were new ones. Her eyes nearly stumbled with eagerness.

> *Darling,*
>   *I cannot stop thinking about you, about last weekend. Please don't think I am ignoring you, but I dare not call or e-mail you after last time. I cannot do anything until after the wedding, I can't risk ruining the day for Audrey with dramas of my own. Meet me at the club on Monday at twelve and we can work out what to do. I miss you . . .*
>   *All my love,*
>   *V*

What?

This was not a letter from her father, this was . . .

Audrey reread the piece of paper in her hand. Her mother's writing. Had Vivien handed her the wrong envelope from her bag? Rage boiled inside her. It was never-ending, her mother's addiction to having something shiny and new. Who was this letter even for? Which unsuspecting man had become Vivien's latest obsession? Audrey tore up the letter and stuffed the pieces back into her clutch. She couldn't get involved in one of her mother's toxic affairs right now.

She stood up, picked up her clutch, and thundered down the stairs to find Granny Parker. Whatever the woman wanted to say, it had better not be about more harbingers of doom.

31

Six Years Before I Do

୧୬

*A*udrey arrived at Benedict's gallery walking on air. After the life-changing afternoon spent with Fred the day before and the promise of seeing him again this afternoon, nothing could dampen her mood, not even a morning with Benedict. She only had three hours to wait until she would see Fred again, at their photo booth. She had taken care with her appearance. She was wearing black jeans, a plain blue blouse, and a little makeup, and her hair was styled in loose curls. She felt attractive, rapturous about life. Today was the beginning of everything.

Benedict had made an effort to be nice to her since the night of the engagement. He bought her favorite caramel macchiatos from the coffee place on the corner, asked her questions about her upcoming exam, and had taken to smiling at her in a strange, avuncular way. She tried her best to avoid him. She'd even started looking for somewhere else to live, but it wasn't easy. Now that she'd dropped out of her course, she wasn't eligible for student accommodation. She needed to pass her math A level and apply for astronomy; then she could request to live in the university halls. *What would happen if she didn't pass the exam? That wasn't something she liked to think about.*

On Thursday, Benedict had cornered her in the hall, hold-ing out yet another white flag of caramel-flavored coffee.

"Look, Audrey," he'd said, "I think we might have gotten off on the wrong foot. I know how much it would mean to Vivien if you and I rubbed along together a little better." He paused, still holding out the cup. Grudgingly, she took it. "Would you let me take you out, to an exhibition or something, just the two of us? I think if you got to know me, you might not think me such a bad egg."

Her instinct was to shoot back a hard no. But then she took a breath and thought of her mother, and the wounded look on her face that night in the kitchen. Whether she lived here or not, Benedict was now a necessary irritation in her life, like mosquitos on a Mediterranean holiday. So she agreed. She could endure an hour of walking around a gallery with him, in the name of diplomacy.

Now, as she peered through the locked doors of the gallery, she regretted agreeing to meet at his exhibition; it wasn't neu-tral ground. Besides, the place seemed closed; there was no one else there. She turned to look down the street and recognized Benedict's bearlike gait before his face came into view.

"It's closed," she called with a theatrical shrug.

Benedict just grinned and waved a bunch of keys. "It isn't open to the public on Sundays, but I have the keys."

Audrey's stomach tensed. She would never have agreed to a private viewing, just the two of them; it was far too . . . too what? What was she worried about? She couldn't name it, but the idea made her uncomfortable. Maybe it was the memory of him standing in the doorway of her bathroom, his eyes on her body that moment too long.

"I thought we were going to an open gallery, with other people." She frowned.

"Better to see the art this way. No distractions," he said, holding open the door for her.

He was so confident and smiley in that moment, it would have been hard to say no without causing offense, and she was here to make peace.

Inside, once he'd turned the lights on and Audrey took in the sculptures dotted around the gallery floor, her anxiety slowly began to ebb away. There were giant abstracts of the female form, finished in gold, bronze, and pewter. Magnificent pieces, emanating femininity and strength, all soft, fluid lines in hard metal. Each piece was huge, twice the size of a real person, yet there was a lightness to each of them, as though the figures were about to burst forth into motion. She had seen images of Benedict's work in brochures he left around the house, but seeing them in real life was an entirely different experience. She walked up close to one, marveling.

"They're so much bigger than I imagined they would be. These are all yours?"

"My life's work," he said proudly. "In the next room are some pieces from my protégés, but these are all mine."

He walked her around, telling her about each one. Hearing him talk about his work, the impression she had of Benedict began to change. When he discussed art, his passion was infectious. He was clearly incredibly talented, and she felt oddly privileged that he was taking the time to tell her about each sculpture in so much detail.

As they stood in front of a piece named *Emergence*, Benedict pointed out an abstract shoulder bone. In one sense it was just an angle of golden metal, but in another it clearly read as a female shoulder—it was captivating.

"I love this one," she said, almost to herself.

"You do?" he said, sounding pleased.

She didn't imagine an artist of his standing would care a fig what a twenty-two-year-old girl like her thought.

"This is one of my favorites. What do you like about it, Audrey?"

She thought for a moment, contemplating the piece. "I like how feminine it feels, even though it looks nothing like a woman. These mounds here." She felt herself blush. "Even though they aren't . . . you know, they still read as something womanly."

"Goodness, girl, you can't even say the word 'breast' to me. You really are repressed." Benedict laughed, a genuine, chesty laugh.

"I'm not repressed," Audrey said, her forehead furrowing into a frown, her cheeks glowing red.

"You're the most repressed girl I've ever met." He smiled, amused by her blushes. "When's the last time you had sex?"

"I don't think that's an appropriate question."

Benedict let out a bellowing laugh. "You don't need to tell me. I can tell from the way you hold yourself, your spikiness, all that pent-up frustration." She frowned, but he seemed to find her discomfort amusing. "Don't be so British, we're all adults here. That's what you want, isn't it, to be treated as an equal, the same as the grown-ups?" Benedict moved back toward a sculpture on their left. "This piece is called *Bloom*. It depicts the unfurling of a girl into womanhood. You see these petals of the flower; do you see what they are?"

Audrey saw the flower was not a flower at all; every petal had nipples. She found herself smiling despite herself.

"Breasts."

Then they were both laughing. He looked at her for a moment, then back at the artwork, before taking her hand. "Let me show you something."

Benedict guided her through to the second room, away from the daylight coming in from the street, away from the outside world. She didn't like him holding her hand, but she thought it would be rude to snatch it away. He led her over to a mirror and positioned her in front of it. Audrey averted her eyes, instantly feeling tense in the windowless room.

"Please indulge me. Is it such a chore for you to look at your own face?" She stood still as he leaned over to a large panel of switches on the wall next to the mirror. He turned off the gallery lights, leaving only a single spotlight above the mirror shining down on her. She shivered, uncomfortable under such an intense spotlight, in an otherwise dark room with Benedict so close behind her.

"Look, here," he said. He took her handbag from her shoulder and placed it on the floor, then pointed over her shoulder at her clavicle bone. "You have a very pronounced bone here, so elegant, just like your mother's. Have you noticed?"

She froze. "I don't want to do this." She tried to turn away, but he held her arms in place by her sides, pinning her there with no effort at all.

"You should look. You're a beautiful girl, Audrey, but you lack the posture and the confidence of a woman. You slouch when you walk, you hide your chest. The way you hold yourself, it's like watching a Ferrari being driven by a learner, it genuinely hurts my eyes."

She must have rolled her eyes, because he clicked his tongue at her.

"That too. You have the mannerisms of a twelve-year-old. If you want to own your femininity, you need to stop making these childish facial expressions."

Withered by his words, she stood frozen, unsure of what to do. He reached around and lifted her chin, his eyes on her reflection the entire time. Then he pushed his hand gently into the base of her spine, forcing her hips down and her breasts out. She didn't want his hands on her, but she was paralyzed, her inner voice muffled and mute. She found herself clay beneath a sculptor's hands, being molded to his purpose.

"There, look. So much better," he said, proudly inspecting his adjustments in the mirror. As she looked, part of her conceded he was right, she did look more grown-up, more assured, in her body at least. She momentarily forgot Benedict's presence behind her until she felt his hand skim her neck and heard the smallest sigh of appreciation. She flinched.

"Please don't do that," she said, her voice high and childlike in her throat.

He waved a hand dismissively. "Audrey, I see women as angles of bone and skin; it is my job. You mustn't always make things so personal."

"I am more than bones and skin, and I'd like to go now," she said, reaching out for the panel of lights to escape this intense spotlight, but as she pressed the panel, she only managed to turn the spotlight off, plunging them into darkness. He laughed at her mistake, and she felt adrenaline and fear course through her veins. She was a rabbit, cornered by a fox in its den.

"Wrong switch, I think," he said, his tone light and cheerful. "Let me get it for you." Then he reached up his hand, and she felt it brush against her breast, pausing just a moment before continuing up to find the light switch. She didn't even move from under his hand, she just let it sit there, her body entirely disconnected from what her head was telling it to do. Could it have been an accident, a mistake in the dark? A chill spread across every inch of her skin. Before she could process what had happened, all the lights were back on and Benedict's jolly smile suggested nothing untoward had taken place.

"Well then," he said. "Thank you for letting me show you my work." He sauntered toward the gallery door, and Audrey followed him, in a daze. "I can see you have an artist's eye. I knew you would understand me and my foibles a little better if you saw my pieces."

Audrey stared at him in bemusement.

"Oh, your bag?" he said. "You left it in the other room."

It was back by the mirror. She swallowed, not daring to show externally the panic she felt inside. Light on her feet, she ran, lifting her bag hastily from the floor, spilling the tin of peaches she had at the top, the ones she had bought on her way to the gallery as a gift for Fred. She watched the tin roll across the floor into a dark corner. Glancing back over her shoulder, she saw Benedict had followed her in here. In her mind's eye, she saw herself bending down to retrieve the peaches, his hands reaching for her hips as she crouched. She abandoned the can, swinging quickly back around with her bag and running past him, back to the safety of daylight and the gallery door.

"In such a hurry. Are you sure you have everything?" Benedict asked, his voice all friendly confusion.

She nodded, mute, her heart pounding against her chest, telling her to go, to get out, to escape. "I have certainly enjoyed our little chat," he said, reaching out to adjust the bag strap on her shoulder. She wanted to slap him away, but she didn't. "And remember to walk a little taller, shoulders back, chin up, my little Ferrari." And then he made a growling sound, like an engine revving.

She thanked him. *She thanked him.* Then marveled at the fact that her manners were so deeply ingrained. In the street, as soon as she was far enough away, she stopped, leaned against a lamppost, and gasped for air.

32

Forty-Five Minutes Before I Do

Audrey hurried along the corridor to the morning room, avoiding eye contact with everyone she passed. She found Granny Parker sitting in a wing-backed chair, reading a different Jilly Cooper novel from the one she'd been reading last night. She looked slightly like a Bond villain plotting some dastardly plan for world domination.

"Ah, Audrey," she said.

"I must be quick, Granny, it's not long until the service. Is everything okay?"

Granny Parker shut her book. "I didn't get to talk to you last night, after that debacle at dinner. I wanted a word before the wedding." She patted her book in her lap. "You'll be the first in six generations of Mrs. Parkers who hasn't been a Yorkshire lass, you know."

Audrey nodded, humoring her. "Well, it's good to shake up the bloodlines now and again, isn't it?"

"Parkers are as Yorkshire as tea and cake, as Yorkshire as the Dales."

"Are you saying you disapprove of me because I'm too southern?" Audrey asked in a friendly tone. She was used to Granny Parker's eccentricities.

"I don't disapprove, I just see what I see." Granny Parker paused, drumming her fingers against the spine of her book. Audrey watched the woman's face, the crease lines around the edges of her lips like they were a well-played concertina. Her face looked as though every emotion had lived there at some stage or another, but beneath the wrinkled folds of skin, the older woman's eyes were sharp and clear. "Omens are the universe's way of telling us something isn't right."

Audrey blanched at this. She could see Granny Parker truly believed what she was saying.

"Well, I don't agree," she said tightly. "People see what they want to see."

Granny Parker reached out a hand and squeezed Audrey's arm. "I've got a sense for these things, I always have done, I feel it in my knuckles." She tutted. "Your soul's too heavy for one so young. You're carrying something around with you, and you need to put it down. Don't bring it into your life with Josh, it wouldn't be fair." She paused and let out a slow sigh. "But I suppose we are where we are. I make my peace with it today, for Josh's sake." She pulled out a small blue purse and handed it to Audrey. "I wanted to give you this before the service. Something borrowed, something blue, something Yorkshire, through and through."

The woman looked so sincere as she handed her the purse, Audrey tried to swallow the previous insult about her having a heavy soul.

"What is this?"

"Soil, from the farm I grew up on." She peered at Audrey,

her eyes now soft and kind. "Every Parker woman had a piece of Yorkshire in her, and so I'm giving you a piece of it for you and yours. Even though Josh has turned into a right prissy southerner."

Audrey smiled at this. "Thank you."

"Do you think he'll ever get back to farming? You could leave London, the two of you. He used to love helping with the cows when he was younger. I don't like to see him getting soft behind a desk."

"He's not soft, Granny. He goes to the gym, he plants trees most weekends—it's physically demanding, trust me."

"Ah, he's soft. My husband could pick up a cow, he could."

Audrey smiled. "Well, there's not much demand for cow lifting in London."

"I also wanted to give you this," said Granny Parker, taking a well-thumbed copy of *Riders* by Jilly Cooper from her bag and handing it to Audrey. "Three things you need in a marriage—trust, humor, and a little bedroom inspiration from Jilly Cooper."

"Thank you," said Audrey, wishing the planet had chosen this moment to spontaneously combust and erase this conversation from the solar system. "I'd better go. I'll try and work on lightening my soul." She squeezed Granny Parker's hand as she stood up. "Can I ask, what was it about Grandpa Joe that made you know you wanted to marry him?"

Granny Parker looked thoughtful for a moment.

"It was the way he looked after his animals. He had such care for every one. I remember he had this heifer recovering from a twisted stomach, and he slept two nights in the barn with her, talking to her, rubbing her belly. He canceled tea with me to sit with her. That's when I knew he was the one." Audrey smiled at this. "You follow your gut when it comes to love, or the cow's gut, in my case." Granny Parker gave her a serious, searching look, but then returned to the book she was reading.

"Thank you. I'll see you in the church, then."

"I hope so, Audrey, I hope so." Then she gave a little cough, which sounded to Audrey like her cue to leave.

33

Three Years Before I Do

◦⁓◦

*J*osh called. Just as he said he would, the morning after Ben and Dee's wedding. Not a text or a WhatsApp; he picked up the phone and called her, and they arranged to have dinner the following Saturday. Josh took her to an Italian restaurant in Soho. He wore the jeans she had picked out for him all those months before and a perfectly ironed blue shirt.

"So, Audrey, tell me more about yourself, your work, your family," Josh said, putting down the menu. There was none of the playful banter or confident control he'd shown at the wedding—he looked nervous.

"What is this, a job interview?" Audrey teased him. "Shall I tell you my strengths and weaknesses, an example of how I respond under pressure?"

Josh dipped his head and then she saw a red flush escape from his shirt and run up his neck.

"I'm joking, Josh, sorry. I thought you were down with the teasing."

"No, I am, I . . . I just want to know more about you. Sorry if that sounded like a job interview."

"I like interviews, I've been to enough of them," she said brightly, worrying she might have been too harsh, that she was too prickly with people. "I think it's a sensitive topic for me, because I've moved around a lot, I haven't stuck to anything. Now I feel about five years behind everyone else in terms of having my life sorted."

"I don't think anyone's as sorted as you might think," Josh said, refilling her water glass. "And you've stuck to photography, haven't you? What started your love of cameras?"

As she looked across the table at Josh, an image of Fred came unbidden into her mind. She hadn't thought about Fred for months, and yet now, in this restaurant, she had a perfect image of him: his scruffy clothes; his wild, gesticulating manner; his enthusiasm about the camera slung around his neck. Josh was calm, reserved almost—an entirely different kind of man.

"Someone I knew was into it. They showed me what they loved about it, and it inspired me to buy a camera. When I went traveling a couple of years ago, I took it with me and taught myself how to use it. I've found it hard to make a living out of it, though. Maybe I just haven't found my niche."

"Well, I think it's amazing that you're working all these other jobs so you can do what you love."

Was that what she was doing? Was photography really what she loved?

The waiter interrupted her thoughts, and Josh engaged him in conversation. After they ordered food, she asked, "So, what did you study?" She felt keen to deflect the conversation away from the topic of her career.

"Politics and economics," he said.

"Of course you did. Dr. Sensible, with the degree from Cambridge and the proper job." Audrey was teasing him again, but something about his expression made her feel he didn't want to be teased about this.

"You say that like it's a bad thing."

"It's not a bad thing."

"My parents didn't have a lot of money when I was growing up," he said. "My dad's a 'self-made man.'" Audrey noted the air quotes. "He invests in risky ventures. It's highs and lows, and when my sister and I were little, there was a run of lows. We lost the farm that had been in our family for generations."

"That must have been difficult."

Josh gave a single nod. "I remember being ten, needing new shoes because my feet were growing so fast. We went to the shoe shop, and my mum's card didn't work. She was so embarrassed, bustled my sister and me out of the shop, saying we'd have to make do. She cut out the toes of my old shoes and covered them with black masking tape, saying it was 'just until Dad gets the cards sorted.' I wore those shoes for a whole term. You can imagine how the other kids reacted. I swore to myself then that when I grew up, I'd get a well-paid, reliable job, whatever that was, so that my kids would always have shoes that fit them."

"Oh, Josh, that's heartbreaking," Audrey said, leaning over to put her hand over his on the table.

"Sorry, I didn't mean that to sound like such a sob story."

"Do you tell that story on every date to make women fall a little bit in love with you?" She gave him a sly grin. Neither of them moved their hands from the table.

"Yeah, it's not even true. I made it up so you would sleep with me. I find painting a picture of a pathetic little ten-year-old kid who had the shit kicked out of him at school is a real turn-on for most women," he said, rolling his jaw.

"Works for me, every time," said Audrey, and Josh laughed.

"Okay, tell me about your traumatic life events. Or better yet, tell me why all the men I've ever seen you kissing, I've felt an unexplainable urge to punch."

"I have terrible taste in men."

"But you like me."

"You're not my usual type." Audrey smiled. "And who says I like you?"

"Well, I told you the shoe story," he said, lifting his gaze to meet hers. "Your heart's mine now, Lavery."

Though she knew he was joking, Audrey felt her heart beat harder in her chest as though it had heard his words.

They talked until the restaurant closed. Audrey discovered Josh was not the man she had pegged him to be. He was not from the same privileged background as most of Paul's Cambridge friends. He'd been to a grammar school, then gone to university on a rugby scholarship. He talked about his education as something he was grateful for. People who took their privilege for granted didn't do that. He had this attentive way of listening when she spoke, as though he was storing every word. When she couldn't decide between two dishes on the menu, he said he would order her second choice and they could swap if she preferred the look of his. At the end of the night, he walked her all the way to her front door.

"Can I kiss you?" he asked.

Audrey had never been asked that by a man before. She didn't think most men would think to ask.

"I don't know, can you?" she flirted. "You told me off last time I tried to kiss you."

He smiled at that, leaning in to the challenge, and she inhaled the intoxicating smell of him, the warmth of his breath the moment before his lips made contact with hers. His kiss was firm and confident, like the kiss at the wedding, but slower, less urgent. As his tongue probed beyond her lips, Audrey felt light-headed; she didn't want to be out on the cold doorstep, she wanted to be inside, in her warm bed.

"Come in," she whispered, gently biting his lower lip.

"Not tonight," he said, and she felt a sharp stab of rejection in her chest. Why wouldn't he come up, when tonight had gone so well? "Can I see you tomorrow?"

"Tomorrow?" She looked at her watch. "It's already to-morrow," she said, tugging his shirt collar. He shook his head, though he seemed torn.

"I'll text you later today, then. Thank you for tonight, Audrey, I had a wonderful evening."

Then he leaned in to kiss her one more time before turning to walk back toward the tube station. Audrey was left rather bemused, the taste of him still on her lips, her body tingling with unrequited desire.

Inside, Paul was still up, watching a documentary about wine production.

"How was your date with Jooosh?" he asked.

"Good," she said, but her face must have shown confusion. "What?"

"Well, he just came halfway across London to walk me home, but then he didn't want to come in."

Paul laughed. "Not every guy wants to get laid on the first date, Auds."

"Don't they?" she asked, still confused.

"Well, clearly most men do. Josh might be the exception to the rule. He doesn't sleep with women until he's in a commit-ted relationship."

"What? Paul, you could have told me that! I've just come across as a complete floozy trying to get him to come in!"

"You are a complete floozy."

"That's not the point."

Audrey started as Miranda walked in behind her, wearing Paul's pajamas and carrying two cups of tea.

"Hey, sorry, I didn't know you were here," Audrey said, hoping Miranda hadn't heard that conversation about her brother.

"Sorry my brother isn't as slutty as I am." Miranda laughed.

"Thanks for telling me she was here, Paul." Audrey covered her face with her hand.

"Oh, don't worry about it," Miranda said, putting a hand on Audrey's shoulder as she walked past.

Paul switched off the TV, and Miranda cuddled in beside him on the sofa.

"She likes him, I can tell, and Audrey never likes anyone," Paul said, then turned back to Audrey. "I can see you guys together, you know. He needs someone fun like you, and you need someone solid and decent, well-endowed in the trouser department." Paul hugged a sofa cushion in his lap and gave her a devilish grin.

"Okay, I definitely don't need to have that image in my mind," said Miranda with a grimace. Audrey picked up a cushion and threw it at Paul, then turned to go upstairs.

"We played rugby together, I promise Josh is worth waiting for," Paul called after her, ignoring Miranda's squeals of disgust.

Could Audrey see herself dating Josh? She hadn't thought that far ahead. Until tonight, she'd just pegged him as some illogical crush she'd developed. Sure, she fancied him, she enjoyed his company, but she hadn't imagined being in a *relationship* with him. Josh was sensible, conservative, old-fashioned somehow; he had a very clear idea of what he wanted out of life. She was none of those things. They were certainly not the same soul, split in two, inhabiting different bodies. He wasn't anything like—well, like Fred.

Her mind danced straight back to that name, and she shook her head in irritation. It had been three years. Was she still hoping that some cosmic thread was going to bring him back into her life somehow? Or was Fred just the excuse her mind always made to stop her heart from making itself vulnerable again?

As she lay awake in bed that night, staring at the ceiling, she realized that her date with Josh was the first date she'd had in years that she genuinely hadn't wanted to end. She'd wanted to talk more, listen more, kiss more, feel more of that molten desire. She also knew that the more you let yourself feel things, the more power you gave someone else to crush you. These were the feelings that destabilized everything.

34

Thirty Minutes Before I Do

꿍

"*A*udrey! Why aren't you dressed?" cried Vivien, intercepting her in the corridor. Audrey clenched her jaw. If Vivien had given her the letter meant for her lover, it meant either she still had the letter from her father, or she had mixed up the envelopes and given hers to whichever man at the wedding she was currently sleeping with.

"Granny Parker wanted to talk to me," Audrey said, feeling her arms itch with a new ferocity.

"That old troublemaker is probably *trying* to make you late. If I have to hear about one more thing that was invented in Yorkshire . . ." She shook her head and clapped her hands. "Hurry, hurry, we can't keep people waiting in a cold church, a cold audience is never as receptive as a warm one. And *please* don't scratch, Audrey."

Audrey couldn't bring up the letter now. She didn't want to know about her mother's new affair. It might be the tipping point that broke her resolve not to go hide in the cleaning cupboard for the rest of the day. Back in the bedroom, Clara helped her into the dress for the third time.

"Shall we get a photo with the mother of the bride?" Sian suggested.

Audrey gave a tight smile and held out an arm. Vivien marched over and immediately positioned herself in her "red carpet pose"—one foot in front of the other, body side-on to the camera, chin tilted down. Audrey tried to smile. She knew she would want a photo with her mother to look back on, but all she could think about was the letter, torn up in her bag.

Clara's phone pinged again. "Jay's in the church. I've told him to take the girls out if they cry. There's nothing worse than babies screaming through a service, is there? Especially when there are hardly any other babies coming, so everyone will know they're mine."

"I won't mind if they cry during the service, they're only babies." Of all the things Audrey was worried about, babies crying during the service was not one of them.

"I hope he brought their jackets," Clara said to herself, then shook her head. "But I am focused on you. Where's your bolero?"

Eventually, they made their way down to the lobby, where Brian and Lawrence were waiting to drive them up to the church. St. Nicholas's was only five hundred meters away, but in this rain, it felt safer to drive.

"What a vision!" Lawrence said.

"You look beautiful, Audrey," said Brian. "I'm so proud of you."

"Thank you," Audrey said, and for the first time today she felt excited, confident even.

The dress was fixed, everyone who was going to cry had cried, she hadn't had a Fred-related freak-out in at least an hour. Maybe all the ominous omens and frosty feet were over with for the day.

Just as the wedding party stepped out the front door, they

were intercepted by a wild-eyed Hillary running down from the church with a pink umbrella flailing behind him.

"Hold on, hold on!" he called. "We need to delay." He was out of breath as he ushered them back into the lobby. "Small issue in the church. We're ironing it out."

Of course Audrey had jinxed it by daring to get excited.

"What issue?" Vivien asked sharply.

"It's a little indelicate," Hillary said, shifting uncomfortably.

"What has happened?" Audrey asked.

"We just need ten more minutes to get everything squared away."

"Hillary," Audrey said sharply. "What is it?"

"I hope it's not Josh?" Clara asked.

"One of the ushers, Ben, had a seafood platter for lunch, and let's just say there was a bit of a stomach issue that's occurred mid-ushering. Someone had to drive back to the B and B for some new trousers."

"Did I not warn people about eating seafood?" Vivien said, throwing her hands in the air dramatically. "Did Josh eat seafood? Tell me Josh didn't eat seafood."

Hillary cleared his throat. "He said he had some crab, but not the prawns. We think it's the prawns that were the issue. Josh was fine five minutes ago."

"Well, that's something, at least," said Brian, giving Audrey a reassuring smile.

"Did I not make the no-seafood policy abundantly clear?" Vivien sighed.

"You did. I got several e-mails," said Miranda.

"I had bad shrimp in Me-hi-co once," said Lawrence. "I've not been able to look at the ocean since. Just the smell of salty air makes my bowels brace."

"Anyway," said Hillary, pacing up and down the lobby, "we're an usher down. We've opened the doors and windows, just to air things out, which I think is wise in the circumstances. Plus, the side chapel is a little damp, so we're moving a few people and squeezing everyone into the main section."

"Well, how long is that going to take?" asked Vivien.

This was all beginning to feel like a terrible French farce.

"I have some perfume in my bag, if that's helpful?" offered Miranda.

"That would be great. We're still letting in a few stragglers who got delayed on the A303, so I think we should just give it five minutes." Hillary paused. "Worryingly, Mark did eat the prawns at lunch, so we're all waiting for him to blow, though he claims to have the gut constitution of an alcoholic ox. I've come to fetch some hot, sugary tea for Reverend Daniels—he was looking a little overwrought by all the drama."

"I'll need to go up there," said Vivien. "Didn't I say? You get what you pay for with these ushers."

"We're not paying them, they're Josh's friends," said Audrey.

"My point exactly," said Vivien. She picked up a lilac umbrella and marched out into the rain, heading up the hill toward the church.

"Wait!" said Miranda, scrabbling around for a perfume spray and handing it to Vivien. "You might need this."

"If anyone can put things right, Vivien can," said Brian, giving Audrey's arm a reassuring squeeze.

Audrey sat down on the stairs. She wasn't sure she would remember this day as the happiest day of her life, but it was certainly beginning to feel like the longest.

35

Three Years Before I Do

಄

*A*t seven a.m. one Friday morning, three weeks after they started dating, Josh turned up at the Tooting house with a shovel in his backpack. He and Audrey were at that stage of mutual besottedness where everything the other did seemed full of untainted wonder.

"I've come to move the tree," he told Audrey, who was bleary-eyed and still wearing pajamas.

"In the middle of the night?" she asked, self-consciously wiping sleep dust from her eyes.

"Not a morning person?"

"No, definitely not a morning person."

"Duly noted," he said, kissing her on the cheek and then striding down the hall toward the kitchen door. "You can go back to bed if you like."

She wasn't going to go back to bed. Not when Josh and Josh's biceps would be doing manual labor in the garden. She made him coffee and watched as he dug a fresh hole in the sunnier side of the garden. When he finished, he wrote "Audrey" on the trunk in chalk.

"Does this count as one of my hundred and sixty trees?" she asked.

"Why, because I did all the digging?" he asked, wiping sweat from his brow.

"No, because we only moved it, we didn't plant it."

"It wasn't going to thrive if we didn't." Josh paused. "Shall we count it as half?"

Audrey nodded, satisfied.

As they drank coffee together in the garden, admiring her half tree, Audrey reflected on the last few weeks with Josh. He was so straightforward, she found it slightly disconcerting. There were no games, no telephone cat and mouse. When things went too well, it made Audrey nervous. She thought there had to be a catch. It had been three weeks, and they hadn't done much more than kiss. Every time he touched her, it was like he'd turned on a fire inside her, but then he'd say good night, and there was nothing left to burn. Now that he was coming over, digging stuff up with his shirt off, it felt almost cruel.

Josh put down his coffee cup and looked at his watch.

"I'd better go, or I'll be late for work. I'm seeing you later?"

Audrey nodded. "I promise I will look less revolting."

"You could not look revolting if you tried," he said, and then he kissed her properly, and suddenly she felt very awake and very aware she hadn't brushed her teeth yet.

⁓⁓⁓

Later that evening, they met up for beer and tacos on Greek Street. When the bar got crowded, Josh suggested they go back to his place in King's Cross. It was the first time he'd proposed it. Josh, it turned out, lived in exactly the kind of place Audrey had imagined him living in. It was minimalist and utilitarian; there were no pictures on the wall, no dirty dishes in the sink, and a neatly ordered bookcase of biographies and reference books lined one wall of the living room. A tablet stood on a stand in the kitchen, next to a notebook full of handwritten notes.

"What's this?" she asked.

Josh closed the book and put the kettle on. "I'm doing an online cookery course on Thursday nights."

"You've taken more notes than I took the whole time I was at uni." Audrey laughed, trying to read the notebook, but Josh picked it up.

"It's how I digest information. I like to follow instructions, write stuff down."

"Let me see," she said, reaching for it, but he held the book above his head.

"You'll think I'm a massive geek."

"I already think you're a massive geek."

She leaned in to kiss him, and as soon as she did, the outside world melted away. His arms curled around her, and their bodies took over. The recipe notes fell to the floor. "So, do you want me to sleep on the couch tonight?" she asked, putting both hands around his lower back, pressing his body against hers.

"I don't want you to sleep on the couch," he said, his voice shifting to a lower tone.

"You have more self-control than I do."

"I don't," he said, kissing her neck, pressing his hands around her waist, and lifting her up onto the table behind them, slowly running a hand up her thigh. She let out an involuntary moan.

"I asked you up on our first date," she said, her voice breathy and ragged as he started gently moving his thumb up and down across the soft, silky fabric of her underwear. "You turned me down."

"And I haven't been able to think about much else since," he said, his breath hot against her ear.

"But you wanted to wait?"

"Because I want all of you, not just your body," he whispered in her ear, leaving a trail of kisses down her neck as his thumb hooked over the top of her underwear.

"What makes you think you've got all of me now?" she said in a sly whisper, her hand clasping on to his back.

His hand stilled, and she rocked into him.

"Oh no, don't stop, you've got me, you've definitely got me."

He carried her into the bedroom and they made love for the first time, on his perfectly made bed. It wasn't like anything Audrey had experienced before. It was slow, sensuous. It didn't feel as though Josh was "racing to finish," as some of Audrey's previous experiences had. He genuinely wanted to please her, held her eye contact in a way that gave Audrey goose bumps but also made her fearful, though she didn't know why. If sex before had felt like a tennis game, a friendly back-and-forth that ended in a draw, with Josh it didn't feel like a game at all, and Audrey didn't know if she was ready to feel everything she was feeling. This couldn't last. This was the kind of sex that made you get too attached, that forged intimacy, that made things so much worse when they ended.

He lent her a T-shirt to sleep in and let her choose which side of the bed she wanted. She had never had a "side of the bed" before. In the night, when she couldn't sleep, she wandered through to the living room and found a map of Britain on his desk. It had all the trees he had planted marked and numbered. Her heart filled with him. When she finally slept and woke, she found him, wearing only boxers and thick-rimmed glasses, presenting her with tray of food—a bowl of strawberries, a croissant spread with jam, and a steaming cup of coffee.

"Nice glasses," she said, taking the tray from him.

"I usually wear contacts," he said self-consciously.

"I like them, very Clark Kent. This looks delicious, thank you. Are you not having any?" Audrey sat up in bed and was about to pick up the croissant when she noticed something flash across Josh's face.

"I'm good, I made it for you. Fuel for your day."

Audrey paused and looked around at the meticulously clean room, everything perfectly ordered, then down at the buttery, sticky croissant.

"You don't want me to eat this in your bed, do you? I'll get crumbs on your sheets."

He sat on the bed and leaned forward to kiss her, pulling her lower lip gently into his mouth.

"I'm trying not to be the guy who worries about crumbs on his sheets." Audrey got up with the tray and started walking with it through to the kitchen. "Honestly, I don't mind. The romantic breakfast-in-bed gesture doesn't work so well if you don't have it in bed," he said, following her down the corridor.

"You're allowed to be the guy who worries about getting crumbs on his sheets, Josh. I won't love you any less."

The words stuck in her throat.

"I mean, not literally," she said, correcting herself. "Um, I'm just going to use the bathroom now."

She stood in the bathroom, still holding the tray of breakfast, and glared at herself in the mirror. *You're going to freak him out if you start telling him you love him after three weeks.*

Outside the bathroom, Josh was waiting for her in the corridor.

"Hey," she said awkwardly. Oh great, now it was awkward. She'd made it awkward, and now he was going to ask her to leave and he wouldn't call her again and this would be over—

"Hey," he said with a smile. "I just wanted to say, I won't love you any less for getting crumbs on my sheets, or for anything you might say or do . . ." He looked into the bathroom. "Except maybe leaving the tap running."

She smiled up at him, her shoulders relaxed, and then he ran a hand up inside the T-shirt she was wearing, and the tray of food was soon abandoned in favor of more pressing needs.

36

Ten Minutes Before I Do

$\mathcal{O}\!\!\!\sim$

$\mathcal{B}$rian got a call from Vivien to confirm that the church smelled acceptable. They were good to go. Outside the church, Paul hovered beneath an umbrella by the porch. He looked uncharacteristically stressed.

"All okay?" Audrey asked.

"It is now," Paul said, shaking his head. "Ben is traumatized, though." Then he looked across at Miranda. "You all look lovely, by the way."

"Thanks," said Audrey.

"I'll head in, then. Good luck," said Lawrence, patting Audrey's arm and then striding off to take his position in the church.

"You've got this. You ready?" asked Clara.

Audrey nodded; she felt as ready as she'd ever be.

The string quartet started to play Wagner's "Bridal Chorus." As she walked down the aisle with Brian, all their friends and family turned to watch and smile. Sian snapped photos of her from the front of the church. Audrey breathed in and out, gazing ahead, trying not to focus on all the eyes that were on her. Then Josh turned around, and his smile was like a light-house in the sea of people. His face conjured a feeling of home, of happy memories, of the place her heart felt safe. *How could she have doubted this?* But then she heard a baby cry, and it drew her eye to the side, and the person her eyes landed upon in the crowd was Fred. He was staring at her with such a soulful look, as though watching her walk to the gallows. She looked back to the front, hoping to catch Josh's eye, but he had turned to look at the quartet. Instead, Audrey shifted her gaze down to the bunch of roses in her hand, taking refuge in the details of the petals, squeezing the bouquet so tight that she could feel the individual stems beneath the ribbon.

"By the way," Brian whispered to her, his arm linked in hers. "Your mother gave me a letter I think she meant for you—a letter from your father, to read on your wedding day. Remind me to give it to you after the service. It really is lovely."

Brian. Vivien was having an affair with Brian. As she reached the halfway mark, Brian let go of her arm and handed her over to Lawrence, who shuffled out of the pew to take her arm. Audrey felt the blood drain from her face.

"Nearly there," said Lawrence, squeezing her arm tight. Audrey wanted to throw up. She shouldn't have eaten all those wedding chocolates with Miranda and Clara. Finally, they reached the altar, and Lawrence deposited her next to Josh and the reverend.

"Dearly beloved, we are gathered here today, in the sight of God and those witnesses here present, to join this man and this woman in holy matrimony."

Josh leaned forward and whispered, "Wow."

She took in his perfectly cut suit, his freshly shaven face and earnest smile. If only it could be just the two of them, if they could get off this stage, take off their costumes, pull down the curtain on everyone else. If only she could get the thought of her mother and Brian out of her head—the heartache and drama that would inevitably follow. As the reverend kept talking, Audrey's eyes darted back to the congregation. She saw Josh's friend Harriet looking at her with glassy eyes.

"Firstly, I am required to ask anyone present who knows of a reason why these persons may not be lawfully married to declare it now, or forever hold your peace."

Audrey felt her heart stop. Her whole body tensed, in that way it does when you drop a wineglass and you watch, helpless, as it falls to the floor, waiting for the smashing sound. But no one spoke. Not Fred, not Granny Parker, not Harriet. No one was going to stop this, no one was going to intervene. *Did she feel disappointment or relief?*

"Always a relief when no one says anything." The reverend leaned forward, and Audrey noticed he was sweating, far more than the temperature of the damp church called for. "The vows you are about to make are to be made in the presence of God, who is judge of all and knows all the secrets of our hearts. Therefore, if either of you knows of a reason why you may not lawfully marry, you must declare it now." The reverend's face had gone ghostly pale. Josh and Audrey both said nothing.

"Josh, do you take this woman to be your wedded wife? Do you promise to love her, comfort her, honor her, and keep her, in sickness and in health and forsaking all others, so long as you both shall live?"

"I do," Josh said, firmly, decisively, his eyes on Audrey.

"And do you . . ." The reverend looked to Audrey but then stopped talking, pausing as though he had forgotten her name.

"Audrey," she whispered, imagining he'd had a mind blank. Reverend Daniels shook his head.

"Do you, Audrey . . . ," he tried again.

Another pause elicited a titter of amusement from the congregation.

"Take this man . . . ," Josh prompted under his breath, but then frowned when he looked from Audrey to the reverend and saw the color of his face. Something was wrong, something was very wrong.

"She does!" someone heckled from the back. "Course she bloody does!"

But whoever it was could not see what was happening at the front, because the reverend lurched forward, staggering toward Audrey. She leaped back in panic, colliding with the front pew, stumbling in her heels, and falling sideways onto the cold stone aisle, not quite saving her head from the impact as her hands reached for the ground.

37

Six Years Before I Do

ᶜ∽ᵔ

*A*udrey ran all the way from the gallery to Baker Street station. She was an hour early to meet Fred, but she didn't want to go anywhere else. What had just happened with Benedict had left the day feeling sordid and spoiled. The day before had been one of the best days of her life; she'd felt transcendent, as though in meeting Fred, the wonder of life had briefly come into focus. Now the focus had shifted again, and the world looked murky and blurred.

Audrey raked over the details of the morning in her mind. Had she been wrong to feel threatened? Had Benedict actually grabbed her from behind in the dark as she bent to fetch the peaches, or had she just been scared that he would? She honestly couldn't remember. She knew he had held her body in front of the mirror in a way she hadn't liked. Would she say anything to Vivien? What details could she even vocalize?

She wiped her eyes. Fred would come, and this morning would be forgotten. She thought of the bandstand, the dancing, that feeling of flying. Then she closed her eyes and a rush of other thoughts crowded in. She would need to move out of her home. Her relationship with her mother was sure to change. She would no longer be able to climb into Vivien's bed with two cups of tea on a Sunday morning. She would have no nightly companion to listen to the shipping forecast with.

Don't think about it now. Fred would come, and everything would be better. But one o'clock came and went, and no Fred. A teenage girl and her friend took photos in the booth. Whirr, click, the sound of the machine. Audrey couldn't sit any longer; she started pacing. *Why wasn't he here? He said he would be here.*

Had she imagined him into existence? It had been so real. She pulled the photos of them kissing out of her wallet. She turned over the photos to find his number, but the digits were lost in a dark smear of ink. A seven and a six, maybe a four, but the rest beyond deciphering. It was now twenty past one. Audrey was still without a phone; the rice trick had not worked. She walked to the pay phone on the street and called home. Her mother picked up after three rings.

"Darling, I'm so pleased to hear you had such a successful morning with Benedict. He got back in such a jolly mood—said you were a perfectly eager student."

Eager? Audrey clenched her jaw. "Has anyone called for me?" she asked.

"Called for you?"

"I was supposed to meet someone today, and they're late. I gave them the home number."

"Not that I know of. Let me ask Benedict." She heard her conferring with him in the background. "Who is it? Is it a boy?" she asked Audrey, a mischievous note in her voice. "Benedict, have you intercepted any messages from a suitor for Audrey?"

"Never mind. Just make sure you take a number down if anyone calls." She hung up. She would wait. He would come. She was sure of it.

⁓⁓⁓

She waited for three hours. She knew it didn't make sense, but the lightness of yesterday felt somehow blackened by this morning. Everything felt inexplicably connected. When she finally got home, her mother was waiting alone in the kitchen, a grin like a Cheshire cat on her face. It was only five o'clock, but Audrey poured herself a glass of wine.

"Finally, there you are," Vivien said, clapping her hands together. "Benedict was so happy you took such an interest in his work. I can't tell you how pleased I am that you two are finally getting along." Vivien's eyes were bright with excitement. Audrey took a long swig of red wine, tilting her head into an almost imperceptible nod. "Now, I have two things I need to ask you. Firstly, will you be my maid of honor?"

Audrey looked at her mother's hopeful face and managed another nod. Vivien clapped in excitement. "Oh, won't we have fun planning our outfits, darling, you know I *live* for weddings," she said without a hint of irony. "And secondly, perhaps more exciting, he wanted to ask you himself, but I simply can't wait to tell you." Vivien leaned forward in her chair, clasping her hands together. "Benedict wants you to sit for him. Can you believe it? He wants to make a sculpture of you, as an engagement present for me."

"No, thank you," Audrey said. She clenched her jaw, feeling disappointment turn to anger.

"'No, thank you'?" Vivien laughed. "Audrey, do you know what an honor that is, to be asked to sit for Benedict Van Vuuren? You'd be immortalized. An artist of his caliber—"

"Shouldn't you be sitting for him?" Audrey felt herself bristle.

"It takes him a year to create a sculpture, minimum. *Time and Rain* took two; this isn't some whimsical vanity project, he only uses models in whom he sees himself creating something worthy of his time. He sees that in *you*."

"And do these models all happen to be girls thirty years younger than him?" she said under her breath.

Vivien's face fell, and a dark veil drew behind her eyes. "What is that supposed to mean?" she asked, her voice now a stark whisper.

"Nothing." Audrey downed her drink. "I just don't want to do it. Don't ask me again."

"What is wrong with you? Is it such a chore for you to be civil to the man I love?" She let out a slow, wearied sigh. "Do you not see how much your spiteful aversion to him pains me?"

Audrey narrowed her eyes at her mother and tapped her empty wineglass.

"Maybe Benedict is right, I have spoiled you," Vivien said.

And then something in Audrey broke—the combination of these fierce words from her mother, the crushing disappointment of Fred's not showing, and the shame and indignity of the morning. Tears began to fall down her cheeks.

"Oh, Audrey, what is the matter?" Vivien asked, her voice all soft sympathy now.

"Don't marry him, *please* don't marry him."

"What's happened?" Vivien asked, but Audrey shook her head until she repeated more firmly, "What's happened?"

"I can't bear him, and I can't be alone with him," Audrey said, her words barely audible.

"Why?" Vivien asked nervously.

Audrey took a deep breath, and then she said, "Because he's

always touching me, he touched me in the gallery in a way I didn't like. I asked him not to." Audrey's face reddened. "I found him watching me in the shower once, just standing there, in the doorway of my room." The relief of saying something flooded out of her in fresh tears.

After what seemed like a long pause, Vivien said, "Why didn't you tell me this before?" Her voice was strained.

Audrey just shook her head. Was it because each incident had been too small, too undefinable, that it was more of a feeling than one specific event?

"I didn't want to upset you. I thought maybe if I moved out . . ."

They hugged for a while in silence, then Vivien shuffled in her chair and said quietly, "And it definitely can't have been a misunderstanding? He has a tactile manner, his boundaries are . . . It couldn't have been a mistake?"

"No. No mistake," Audrey said; then, after a pause: "You don't believe me?"

Vivien looked up, locking eyes with her daughter, and there was a steeliness in her face now.

"I believe you. I would always believe you."

38

One Minute After I Didn't

~⁓~

 ast night, during her bath, Audrey had googled "things that can go wrong on your wedding day." After the dramas of the rehearsal dinner, she thought it best to be prepared for every eventuality. The list she'd found featured problems such as "guests deciding to go vegetarian for the day," "speeches going on too long," and "forgetting to download your wedding playlist." Nothing she had read mentioned the possibility of dead bats falling from the ceiling, the man who might be your soul mate unexpectedly turning up, an usher getting food poisoning, finding out your mother is having an affair with your ex-stepfather *as* he walks you down the aisle, or the reverend practically dropping dead *during* the service.

After the vicar and Audrey went down, Josh leaped forward, reaching out a hand to her first.

"Are you okay?"

She nodded dumbly, and he quickly turned his attention to Reverend Daniels, rolling him into the recovery position in the aisle.

"Any doctors? Samar!" Josh yelled, his voice commanding.

Josh's school friend Samar ran down the aisle to help. The church hummed with a wave of sound as people shuffled to see what had happened, Debbie's shrill cries of panic escalating above the rest.

"Call an ambulance." Josh's eyes darted up to Paul.

Audrey could see she was in the way, so she got to her feet, kicked off her shoes, and tucked them into a pew near the altar. *Was this really happening?* Audrey looked up and caught Granny Parker's eye. Had Audrey caused this?

"Oh God, oh God." Miranda was covering her mouth, staring down at the scene on the floor, and then Audrey felt a hand on her arm, guiding her away from the throng of bodies who were crowded around, trying to help.

"Are you all right?" Fred asked as he led her to the empty side chapel. Audrey turned to see Clara and Miranda following behind.

"Audrey, your head," Clara said with a grimace. "I can't believe that just happened. That was worse than *The Graduate*."

"Is he okay?" was all Audrey could say.

"I'm going to get you ice, a bandage, some tissues. Will you wait here?" Clara asked Audrey, and then sprinted off out of the church.

"Can you see what's happening?" Audrey asked Fred, trying to stand up so she could see. "He's dead, isn't he?"

"I'll go and find out," Miranda said, patting Audrey's hand and heading back toward the front of the church, where Josh was asking everyone to stand back and give Samar space.

Audrey found herself alone with Fred once again. With a stab of guilt, she wondered if this had been the answer to some unconscious prayer, and the thought made her feel physically sick. She needed to get out of this church, to breathe fresh air.

"Don't try to stand. That was a hard knock, just take a

minute," Fred said, then he paused, as though fighting back the urge to say something. He reached for her wrists and pressed a thumb to each pulse point. It was strangely comforting, and she let him do it. It was as though he was channeling some calming energy into her, and she felt her heartbeat become less frenetic. *If this was fate intervening, fate had a dark sense of humor.*

"He's not dead," Miranda said, coming back toward them. Fred dropped her wrists. "Paul says he's breathing." Miranda burst into tears, fanning a hand in front of her face. "I'm sorry, but can you imagine if he died during their wedding?"

Fred stood up to comfort Miranda, and Audrey took the opportunity to slip away, down the side chapel, back through the open church door.

જ઼

Ten minutes later, Paul found her sitting in the woods.

"Here you are," he said, sitting down beside her. He'd taken his tie off and was absentmindedly threading it between his fingers. "They've taken the reverend to the hospital. He was conscious, and the paramedics sounded optimistic."

"Good," Audrey said, reaching out to take Paul's hand, squeezing it in relief.

"They're all back there debating what to do. Josh is looking for you."

"I just needed a moment," Audrey said.

"You two haven't had the best luck today, have you?" Paul gave a wry smile. "People aren't sure if you're married or not."

"I didn't say 'I do,' so I don't think we are, no," she said quietly. They sat in silence for a moment, then Audrey asked, "Do you believe in soul mates, Paul?"

"Soul mates, hmmm." He seemed to contemplate the

question for a moment. "I read this article that said if you be-lieve in soul mates, you're less likely to be happy, you're more likely to get divorced."

"Really? How come?" Audrey asked, intrigued.

"Something to do with the fact that if you believe every-thing is destined, then when things get hard, you're more likely to pull the rip cord. There's a sense of, 'I shouldn't have to com-promise on anything, because if it's meant to be, it's meant to be.'" Paul shrugged. "People who don't believe in that stuff work harder; they know going the distance will require effort. Love might be easy, but relationships can be hard."

"Why did you break up with Miranda?"

Paul frowned; he looked thrown by the question. "Why does anyone break up?" he said.

"That's not an answer. People break up for a million differ-ent reasons. I always thought you guys were so good together. I didn't want to pry at the time because I was friends with both of you, but I'm still not clear what went wrong."

"Are you asking me difficult questions because you don't want to face everyone back at the church yet?"

"Maybe," said Audrey.

"Fair enough." Paul hung his head in his hands. "Miranda and I were great together, you're right, but . . . I don't know, she kept making these big assumptions about our future. She'd say, 'When we live together,' or 'When we have kids.' It bothered me. I wasn't there yet, you know?" Paul leaned back against the tree, put down his tie, and started fiddling with a stray stick, picking the bark off it. "We were watching TV, some bride show, and she said, 'When you propose, I definitely want you to get down on one knee.' She caught me in the wrong mood, and I just lost it. I said, 'I'll propose however the hell I like, and why would you even assume I will?' I overreacted. I didn't know how to take it back, without saying I *was* going to propose one day." Paul exhaled. "The stupid thing is, if she hadn't kept going on about it, I probably would have. And now she's here, with her ridiculously good-looking hipster boyfriend, and I want to shake him, I want to take him by the shoulders and say, 'Do you know what you've got there? You lucky fucker.'" Paul pinched his forehead. "It's my own fault. Miranda told everyone we broke up because I was a 'commitment-phobe,' which pissed me off. I've never been scared to commit, not with her. I just wanted to do it in my own time, in my own way."

"It's not serious, between her and Fred," Audrey said, shuffling up beside him and reaching out to link Paul's arm in hers. "I think she misses you."

"You think?" Paul's eyes darted to her face, as though he was anxious to see if there was truth in what she was saying.

"If her getting ahead of herself was the only reason you broke up, then that's crazy. You made each other happy."

"What am I supposed to do? Get down on one knee?"

"Just talk to her. Tell her you miss her too."

"Why are we talking about this now?" said Paul, getting to his feet and then helping Audrey up. "Classic Audrey, trying to divert attention away from herself by making other people look bad. You used to do it all the time when we lived together."

"I did not!" Audrey said, gently punching him on the shoulder.

"You did. Whenever you felt too drunk, you'd always top up everyone else's glasses to even out the average level of drunkenness in the room."

"I didn't think anyone noticed that I did that." Audrey bit back a smile as they walked away from the trees, toward the church.

"Well, I noticed, and it's not going to work here, Lavery.

You can't kill everyone else to make the reverend look less dead."

Audrey hugged herself into Paul's shoulder, grateful that he had been the one to find her.

꒰৹৹৹৹৹꒱

$\mathcal{O}$utside the church, the rain had finally stopped; the sun was beating down on the churchyard. Guests were milling about on the grass, talking in anxious, hushed voices. Baskets of confetti—dried roses from Debbie's garden that had taken her all year to prepare—sat on the porch, untouched. Josh had been pacing but rushed over when he saw her.

"Audrey, where did you go? How's your head?"

"Fine, I just needed some air." He pulled her into a hug and kissed her forehead. "The poor reverend."

"I know, I feel terrible."

Audrey felt a rush of nausea, as though a backlog of bad karma was laying claim to her insides.

"We have to decide what to do," Josh said. "The verger says he could call in a replacement reverend from town to finish the service. We could postpone the ceremony, get married after our honeymoon. Or we delay until Reverend Daniels is well enough to marry us. Either way, there's food waiting at the hall. People are cold and hungry."

"We should call a backup reverend," said Debbie, joining in their conversation. "You can't have a wedding without a wedding."

"I don't know, it feels disrespectful somehow, to replace Reverend Daniels," said Audrey.

"I agree." Josh nodded. "I think we have a ceremony at a later date, even if it means doing it on a random Monday in a few weeks' time."

"A *random* Monday," Debbie repeated in horror.

"Dad followed the ambulance to the hospital. We thought someone should go with him until his wife gets there. Clara's gone back to the hall to let the caterers know why the timeline's a little off."

Audrey nodded, relieved that Josh was being decisive. He had always been good in a crisis. He reached out a hand and tilted her chin up to his. "I know this feels like the worst thing that could have happened, but at least he's okay and in good hands. There was a moment there where I really thought—" Josh shook his head, not wanting to finish the sentence. "I'm glad Samar was here."

Everyone walked down the road to the hall together, Audrey and Josh side by side. Miranda retrieved Audrey's shoes from the church, but her feet were now dirty; she would stain the white silk lining if she put them on. So she carried them in one hand, hitched up her dress with the other, and walked barefoot on the tarmac.

As she walked, one thought tapped away at the inside of Audrey's head. She had been granted a reprieve. Now, what was she going to do with it?

39

Two and a Half Years Before I Do

⟡

"*I*'ve highlighted the program, so we know what we want to see on each stage and when," said Josh.

"Who brings a highlighter pen to a music festival?" laughed Jay as they lay on the grass beside their tents.

"Um, have you met Josh?" said Clara.

Josh had also brought a blow-up mattress, a camping stove, a waterproof money belt, and flannel pajamas. Jay had pretty much brought the clothes he was wearing.

"I'm always up for a highlighted agenda," said Audrey, hugging Josh's arm in hers.

Clara had been given free tickets for the weekend festival through work. She had proposed it as a "bonding experience" for the four of them. In reality, the only people she wanted to bond were Josh and Jay. The two men had met many times before, and they were civil to each other, but they'd never formed a particular friendship. Clara and Audrey were desperate for their husband and boyfriend to be as close as they were. They could go on holidays together, double-date, and hang out all the time—if only these men would become friends.

One spanner in the plan was that two friends of Jay's, Amadeus and Sadie, had tagged along at the last minute. All Audrey knew about them was that they lived on a houseboat and ran an organic fennel tea company. She wasn't sure their presence was going to help the Josh/Jay bonding project.

"Let's just chill," said Amadeus, flicking his long auburn dreadlocks over one shoulder, then he held out his hand to Sadie, who was dancing around him in a long cotton skirt lined with bells.

Clara and Audrey went to find the loos. When they came back, they found Jay and Josh locked in a heated conversation about the monarchy.

"But surely you at least respect the Queen—everything she's done for this country?" Josh was saying.

"No." Jay shook his head. "You can't pick and choose, they've all got to go. We live in a democratic society, there's no role for a monarchy in the twenty-first century."

"This sounds heavy," Clara said, leaning to put her arms around Jay's neck.

"Josh here's a fucking monarchist," said Amadeus.

"I just said I respect the Queen," Josh said, a muscle pulsing in his jaw.

"That makes you a monarchist," said Jay with a smirk. "Do you sing the national anthem before bed?"

Josh looked to Audrey and Clara for support.

"Ignore him, Josh, he's winding you up," said Clara.

"Shall we go see some music?" Audrey suggested.

They didn't see many of the bands that night. Jay distributed hash brownies that were so strong, they inhibited everyone's ability to stand. Josh didn't partake, claiming they had random drug testing at his work. Audrey couldn't imagine him stoned; she didn't think she'd ever really seen him drunk.

"Vampire Weekend are on the main stage in five minutes, we can still make it if we go now," Josh said, clearly frustrated by the group's indolence.

"Don't you think that cloud looks like a puppy fighting a squid, holding a watermelon?" said Sadie, giggling.

"Oh wow, it so does." Clara sighed, her head flopping backward as she looked up, dreamy eyed.

"I'll come with you," Audrey said, struggling to her feet. Her head was spinning, and all she could think about was finding the cheesy chips van they'd passed earlier.

"It's fine," said Josh, helping Audrey to sit back down. "You stay with your friends, I'll just see you back at the tent."

Audrey lost all sense of time after that. The sun went down, and the stars came out, and stoned stargazing turned out to be almost as fun as regular stargazing. When she and the others finally made it back to their tents, she found Josh tucked into their double sleeping bag on the blow-up mattress, wearing his flannel pajamas. He had bought her a large bottle of water and a carton of cheesy chips, which he'd laid neatly by her side of the bed. She snuggled in beside him and loved him for being there.

Over the course of the weekend, it became clear that Josh and Jay were never going to be great friends, a source of acute disappointment for Audrey and Clara. It was like trying to get Batman to be friends with the Joker, or Kim Kardashian with Taylor Swift. It just wasn't going to happen.

On Sunday, as they were about to leave, the atmosphere grew taut as Jay announced he was going to abandon his tent in the field.

"You can't just leave it here," Josh said.

"Our tickets cover the cost of people collecting up rubbish at the end. They recycle everything," said Jay, clearly too hung-over to have this conversation, let alone pack up a tent.

"I don't think that's true, and you still shouldn't leave your shit for other people to clear up."

Josh was usually so polite and amenable; Audrey could see this was the culmination of a weekend of biting his tongue. Audrey and Clara ended up dismantling Jay's tent as the two men argued.

On the car ride home, they stopped at a gas station and Audrey nipped into the garage to pay. Josh followed her in, venting as he paced back and forth in the deli aisle.

"He is just the worst kind of liberal bullshitter. He says he's voting for the Greens, then in the same sentence complains about the cost of the airfare to get to Burning Man!"

Audrey tried to be sympathetic. She knew Jay had plenty of opinions that couldn't be examined too closely, but he didn't take himself too seriously, and his heart was usually in the right place.

"Look, that's just Jay. Sure, he's not always right, but he's good fun and . . . and he's married to my best friend."

Josh sighed, rubbing his face with the palms of his hands. "I'm sorry, I know he's your friend. It's just that the world is full of people like him, people who think they have all the answers after scrolling through one article on their phone."

"I know." Audrey leaned in to kiss him. "Come on, it's only two hours back to London, and then it will be just you and me again."

Their relationship felt so easy when it was just the two of them, and Audrey relished the newfound joy of simply having someone to share her life with. She loved weekends spent at his place. They would cook together; Josh always followed a recipe, while she improvised with whatever ingredients she could find in the cupboard. She hung framed prints of her most colorful photos to brighten up his empty white walls. She loved evenings spent lying on the sofa watching rom-coms, while Josh rubbed her feet and pretended to read *The Economist* rather than watch the film. Together, they wallowed in their glorious little universe of two. But when they were out in the world together, around other people, Audrey sometimes wondered if they weren't pieces from two different puzzles. Perhaps they didn't quite fit.

And it was no easier for Audrey with Josh's friends. One Saturday morning a few weeks after the disastrous music festival, Josh invited her to join him on one of his reforesting expeditions. Audrey had no idea what she should wear to plant trees. It was a damp day, and she knew she might get cold, so she wore the warmest things she owned—salopettes and a ski jacket.

"Are we reforesting the Alps?" Josh asked her with a quizzical smile.

"I didn't want to be cold. Do I look ridiculous? Shall I change?"

"No, you look perfect," he said, hugging her into him. "Just looking at you makes me want fondue."

They met up with the other volunteers at a community park in Finchley. The plan was to plant out a whole bank of saplings. Everyone seemed friendly enough, but there wasn't much opportunity for chitchat. It was hard work, really hard work, and Audrey only managed to dig one hole in the time it took everyone else to dig five. Her hands hurt, her toes were cold, and she concluded pretty quickly that this wasn't her idea of fun.

When she finally had a hole big enough to plant a small tree, Josh took a photo of her standing next to it and wrote her name on the support stake. As soon as Josh was out of earshot, a woman called Sharla said under her breath, "Got the Instagram shot, then."

Sharla clearly had no idea, because Audrey wasn't even on Instagram, and if she had been, there was no way she would have been posting pictures of herself looking like a drowned rat, planting trees in a muddy field. After attempting a little more digging, Audrey offered to nip to a nearby coffee shop to buy everyone a coffee. She soon sensed this was not the thing to do, as everyone politely declined and pulled out their eco-friendly thermoses.

The lowest point of the day came when Audrey discovered the toilet facilities consisted of a Portaloo and some hand sanitizer. White salopettes and a muddy Portaloo were not a good combination. Maybe she would leave the tree planting to Josh. You didn't need to enjoy the same hobbies as your boyfriend, did you?

⁂

Audrey didn't gel with Josh's Cambridge friends either. They all had impressive jobs—lawyers or doctors or CEOs for some tech start-up. They talked about politics and macroeconomics, and in truth, Audrey found their erudite conversations intimidating. There was always a pause when she said that she didn't have a degree, or when she told them she was currently working in a gallery or a pub or as a dog walker. The pause was barely discernible, quickly plastered over with an overenthusiastic smile, but Audrey was keenly aware that it was there.

At one dinner party, when the topic of "what she did" came up, Josh's friend Harriet asked, "Why did you drop out of uni, then? I'd have thought with a famous playwright for a father you'd be top of the class."

"I'm not sure it works like that," Audrey said with a tight smile.

"Audrey's one of the smartest people I know," said Josh, which garnered a raised eyebrow from Harriet. Audrey loved him for defending her but was annoyed he felt he had to. Did it matter if she wasn't as academic as his friends? And if it didn't matter, then why did she feel so intimidated?

"Audrey knows everything there is to know about space," Josh said.

"Aw, Tree Boy and Space Girl, sweet," Harriet said, shooting Audrey a grimace masquerading as a smile.

"What's the most interesting thing you know about space?" asked Greg, another of their college friends.

"I think some of the most interesting stuff is what we don't know," said Audrey. "Like whether our universe is the only one." Everyone paused eating to listen to her. She went on, nervously, "If our universe goes on forever, or if there are multiple different universes, then there could be an infinite number of planetary possibilities. There will be worlds just like ours, where every conceivable reality plays out an infinite number of times. Somewhere out there, identical versions of us might be at an almost identical dinner, except we're all speaking Danish."

"Oh, I love that idea," said Dee.

"Those kinds of theories are closer to religion than science, it's all completely speculative," said Greg, who worked in biotechnology.

"Sounds like Everett's many-worlds theory, which we covered in first-year philosophy," said Harriet, stifling a yawn.

"I think it's a fascinating question," said Josh loyally. "If there are parallel universes, with infinite possibilities, I'm glad we'll never know about them. I'm very happy in this one." He reached out a hand to stroke Audrey's arm.

"What about the universe where you've got a slightly bigger cock?" Ben laughed, throwing a potato across the table at Josh, which made everyone, bar Audrey, laugh.

Later in the meal, Audrey excused herself to go to the loo. In the hall, she overheard Harriet whispering to her friend Ester as they shared a cigarette on the front step.

"I miss Kelly. She was so fun at things like this," whispered Ester.

"I just can't see her appeal. She must be great in bed," said Harriet.

"If it's that, I'm sure he'll get bored of her soon." Ester sighed. "Then he'll realize the perfect person was right under his nose all along." Harriet cut her off with a loud "Shhh" as they heard movement inside the house.

Rather than going back upstairs to the dinner table, Audrey found herself walking down, toward the back door and out into the small garden behind Ben and Dee's flat. It was a warm, clear night, and the grass beneath her feet felt dry. She lay down on the ground and looked up at the moon, visually mapping the constellations she could see. There was something so comforting in the familiarity of those shapes in the sky. She wondered what an alternate version of her was doing out there. Was she lying on similar grass, looking up, just as she was now? Had alternate Audrey found her calling in life? Was she studying astronomy? Was she dating Josh?

Audrey lost all sense of how much time had passed, until she saw Josh, standing over her, looking down in complete bemusement.

"What are you doing out here?" he asked.

"Oh, sorry," she said.

"You've been gone half an hour. You missed dessert."

"Oops."

He shook his head in incomprehension as he reached out a hand to help her up.

They went inside and said their good-byes.

In the cab home, Josh was uncharacteristically quiet. He usually made a point of chatting to taxi drivers.

"I lost track of time," Audrey muttered, reluctant to tell him about the conversation she'd overheard between his friends.

"Do you know how strange that looked, when Dee glanced out the window and saw you lying in the garden?"

"You do strange things in front of my friends too, you know," she said defensively.

"What have I ever done that's strange?"

Audrey racked her brain for an example. "You alphabetize your cookbooks."

"What?" Josh flung out his arms, and Audrey noticed the cabdriver give them an amused look in the rearview mirror.

"You do!" Audrey said, interpreting the gesture as denial.

"It helps me find what I'm looking for, and that's not something I do *in front* of your friends."

"Well, I told my friends about it, and they think it's strange. They also think it's strange you buy special deionized ironing water, and that you have a swiper to clean the shower after you've used it."

"Okay, Audrey." Josh shook his head and pulled a hand through his hair.

They sat in silence again, until the cabdriver said, "I use that deionized water for ironing. It extends the life span of the iron."

"Thank you!" said Josh, and then he and Audrey caught each other's eye and couldn't help smiling.

"I'm sorry I embarrassed you in front of your friends," she said, suddenly contrite.

"You could never embarrass me." He sighed. "I was just worried about you."

"I had a headache. It came on suddenly and it was painful to talk to people, I just needed some quiet," she said.

"Why didn't you just tell me that?" His eyes were all concern, and he reached for her hand. She shrugged. She didn't want to admit to the insecurities that some of his friends brought out in her. She didn't want to listen to the nagging concern that their little universe for two would not be enough.

Forty-Five Minutes After I Didn't

⌒

When they got back to Millward Hall, Audrey went straight upstairs to their room. She wanted to wash her feet. Josh followed, sat on the bed, and watched as she rinsed her toes in the bath, then dabbed concealer on her bruised temple and tried to fix her wind-whipped hair.

"You really do look incredible," Josh said, and she smiled back at him in the reflection of the bathroom mirror. "I know today has been the mother of all disasters, but can we try to make the best of it?"

"Do you think we're soul mates?" she asked, meeting his eye in the mirror.

"What?" He shook his head, bemused. "You know I don't believe in that stuff."

"I didn't know that, no."

"Do you?" he asked, eyes narrowed in concern.

"Honestly, I don't know." Audrey paused and squeezed the edge of the sink. "Have you had any doubts at all about today, about getting married?"

He frowned, stood up, and came to stand behind her in the

bathroom mirror. She tensed. She had a thing about people standing behind her in mirrors.

"Not one. Why? Have you?"

Audrey took a breath; pushed her hands against the top of her rib cage, as though to steady herself; then turned around, preferring to speak face-to-face.

"Yes." She looked him straight in the eye. This was her opportunity to be honest. "Sometimes, I worry we're too different—you're sensible, I'm flighty; you're tidy, I'm messy; you're an early bird, I'm a night owl; you have your whole life planned out and I'm working it out as I go along. We don't know who we're going to be in the future. What if we change, and we end up wanting different things?"

"Audrey, there's a reason those vows say 'in sickness and in health, through good times and bad,' because I'm here for all of it, whatever happens, you know that." He bent down to kiss her. "And whatever changes in our lives, it's not going to change how I feel about you."

She looked up into his eyes and saw everything she loved about this man, his sincerity, his kindness, his calm confidence, but she forced herself to keep talking.

"It's my fault the reverend had a heart attack."

Josh let out a disbelieving laugh. "Audrey, you do come out with the strangest things sometimes."

"Did you know my mum is sleeping with Brian? It's like she's been through all the available men and now she's circling back around. What if there's part of me that's like her? What if it's in my genes?"

"You are nothing like your mother," Josh said firmly, his warm eyes drawing her in like a beacon. "Look, I know watching Vivien go through it so many times, it's probably hard to believe love can last forever, but it can, if you want it to." Josh looked serious for a moment, his eyebrows drawn into a low frown. Audrey nodded, wanting his words to be true. "I know it's a lot, Reverend Daniels collapsing during the service. It's understandable you're shaken up, but trust me, it's all going to be fine." She nodded, and he pulled her into a hug. She relaxed against his chest, listening to his strong, even heartbeat. "Can we go downstairs and celebrate being *almost* married now?" Then he kissed her on the lips, and she felt that warm familiar glow that had always been there.

41

Six Years Before I Do

⌒⌒

"*W*hat happened?" Hillary asked when she arrived on his doorstep with an overnight bag. "Have you and Vivien had a falling-out?"

Once Audrey had confided in her mother about Benedict, Vivien asked if she would go and stay with a friend for the night so she could speak to him alone. Audrey had opened Pandora's box, and now there would be no closing it.

"I don't want to talk about it," she told Hillary.

"Trouble in paradise with the great Benedicté? Or has your mother lost out on a role to Helen Mirren again? No, don't tell me, Emma Thompson?"

Audrey didn't want to tell Hillary what had happened, because she feared being interrogated. He would not shy away from wanting to know *exactly* what Benedict had done. What if he told her she had overreacted?

"Can we just watch *Gilmore Girls* and eat Chipsticks?" she asked as Hillary took the bag from her shoulder.

"That bad, is it?" Hillary walked through to his kitchen and

Audrey followed. "You know I keep Chipsticks in my cupboard now, just in case you come over."

⋘⋙

She went back to the photo booth the next day, hoping that yesterday had been some cosmic blip and Fred had simply gotten the day wrong. She tried calling combinations of numbers with sevens, fours, and fives. None of them worked. It crossed her mind briefly that maybe the number he had given her hadn't been real, that he had smeared the ink on purpose before handing it over. But why would he have done that? It didn't make sense.

After Hillary had left for the theater that evening, the doorbell to his flat rang. Audrey answered it to find Benedict, his hair and clothes disheveled, his face full of shadows.

"I molested you?" he asked in bewilderment.

"How did you know I was here?" she said, every muscle in her body going rigid.

"How many friends do you have?"

"I don't think you should be here," she said, trying to shut the door, but he jammed his foot between the door and the frame.

"When *exactly* did I molest you? I'd love to know."

Her cheeks burned. She read in his face a man who felt genuinely wronged. "I didn't use that word, I . . . you were inappropriate—"

"When?" He shook his head in complete disbelief. "Are you confused, insane, or just making this up to be spiteful? I had to look you in the eye, because I genuinely needed to know which it was." Audrey tried to shut the door again, but he was too strong, and he pushed his way through into the hallway. "I didn't think even you could stoop so low, to make up these lies, just to get your mother's attention."

He closed the door behind him and then turned back to look at her. Her heart pumped with blood and fear.

"Girls like you are a disgrace. You see perversion where there is none, you distort and tangle innocent things. What is the world coming to, when a man cannot even compliment a woman's body without being perceived as some kind of monster?" He threw his hands in the air. "You need serious psychiatric help, you know that? I knew you were delusional, with your aspirations of mathematical grandeur, but I didn't know you were certifiably deranged."

"Mathematical grandeur?" Audrey echoed weakly, and he turned on her with a new ferocity in his eyes.

"How many more unfinished courses do you expect your mother to pay for?" He paused, a sneer on his thick pink lips. "I know your tutor is happy to take your mother's money, but he's already warned her that you haven't a hope of getting the grade you need in this exam." He lowered his face to hers and she felt the spittle on her cheek as he talked. "Vivien has indulged your every whim. It's lucky your father's not here to witness what a talentless, deceitful waste of space his daughter turned out to be."

She knew he was trying to hurt her, that it wasn't necessarily true, but the words cut into her like a hot knife. Her body physically reacted, folding into itself, and the air started ringing, as though her ears were trying to block out his words. As she cowered, she closed her eyes, and only when there was silence did she dare open them again. She saw Benedict leaning against the opposite wall, his fury spent. When he spoke again, his voice was more measured.

"I love her, you know, I really love her." He sighed. "But you win, she's called it off."

He stood looking at her for a moment, and then his voice shifted from mournful back to angry. "I hope one day you love someone, maybe even plan to marry them, and someone comes along and takes it from you. *Quod severis metes*—'As you sow, so shall you reap.'"

"Just leave me alone," she cried. "Please, just leave me alone."

And finally, he did.

ᴖᴐᴏᴖᴐᴖᴏ

*W*hen Audrey returned to her mother's house, she found all the light had left Vivien. She had shadows beneath both eyes, and her hair looked greasy and limp. One of her neighbors, Garth, was there, sitting with Vivien in the kitchen. Audrey wondered, cruelly, if her mother had ever navigated a crisis without calling on a man for help.

"I'm going to head off," said Garth, standing up and giving Vivien a hug. "I'm here if you need me."

Once Garth had gone, Vivien said, "We'll both need to go and stay at the club. I am giving him a few days to move his work out of the studio."

"Can we talk about what happened? What Benedict—" Audrey started weakly. Maybe it wasn't too late to clarify the ambiguity she felt.

"I never want to hear that man's name again," Vivien said.

"Okay, but I just—"

"It's done. We don't need to talk about it any further."

Audrey stayed silent. She saw the misery in her mother's eyes, and it crushed her to know she was the person who had caused it. She had taken every man her mother had ever loved away from her.

Over the next few days, she watched Vivien retreat into herself, getting quieter, paler, thinner. She noticed her mother could hardly look her in the eye. That day in the gallery played out over and over in her mind, especially at night. The more she thought about it, the more she doubted herself. She found herself wishing Benedict *had* grabbed her, that he'd done something indisputable. The feeling that she might have been wrong, that she had overreacted, was almost unbearable.

When the morning of the math exam came, she hadn't slept for two nights in a row. She was so wired, she nearly got herself run over getting to the exam venue. As she sat at the narrow wooden desk, looking around at the other students, her palms began to sweat. When the proctor told them to begin, she turned over the exam paper, and her eyes swam as she flicked through the pages. She couldn't see one question that she could answer. Her hands began to shake as she reached for her bottle of water on the desk, hoping it might combat the growing wave of nausea threatening to envelop her. She closed her eyes and just tried to breathe.

Sometime later, she sat up, managed to collect herself enough to focus. She worked her way through the first section, breaking each question down into its component parts, but her mind felt muddled, like she was thinking through sludge, and before she was even a quarter of the way through the paper, her time was up. She walked out of the exam hall in tears. She did not turn up to the next exam. She gave up the idea of studying astronomy at university. She had tried and failed at too many things. Some burning fire of self-belief had been extinguished.

42

Ninety Minutes After I Didn't

⁓

"'The wedding that never was' or 'the wedding with no "I do,"' which sounds better for my speech?" Hillary asked, putting an arm around Audrey as she and Josh came down to the lobby full of wedding guests.

Audrey shrugged. "Do you think it's appropriate to do any kind of speech?"

"I'm not wasting a perfectly good speech. I'll take out the toast to the bride and groom and raise a glass to the good health of Reverend Daniels."

"That's a good idea," Audrey said, leaning into him.

"This isn't some voodoo shit you made happen to get out of the wedding, is it?" Hillary whispered in her ear. Audrey looked up and gave him a tight smile. "Come on, have some champagne, Mrs. almost-Parker."

"Do you think we should be drinking champagne?"

"What, you think we should be substituting it with cheap prosecco in a show of self-flagellation?" Hillary rolled his eyes but then saw in her face she was serious. "Fine, why don't I do my speech now, just to warm up the crowd?"

He pulled over a chair, climbed onto it, then clapped his hands together to get the attention of the gathered guests.

"Ladies and gentlemen, as you all know, our dear reverend has been whisked away to the hospital, but I have an update from Josh's father that he's stable and most upset he didn't get through the 'I dos.' Truth be told, it was probably the sight of Audrey in that slinky number that did him in. I did warn her, 'Audrey—that dress is far too sexy; the reverend is going to have a heart attack.' Did she listen? She did not."

Audrey's face glowed with embarrassment, and a nervous laugh went around the crowd.

"'I do' or no 'I do,' I don't think the reverend would want his dicky ticker putting a damper on things. For those who might not know me, I used to be Audrey's nanny, or 'nactor,' as Vivien called us. I was twenty-five when I met an eight-year-old Audrey. I had zero interest in children, zero idea how to look after one, but also a bank balance of . . . zero. Vivien clearly saw something in me that resembled competence, and there began what would become one of the most important relationships in my life. It still is. Audrey, I know if Richard had been here to see you on your wedding day, or non-wedding day, as the case may be"—Hillary paused to grimace but then smiled fondly down at Audrey—"he would have been so proud of you, proud of the man you chose."

He said it softly, as though that last line was meant only for her. She'd thought Hillary's speech was going to be full of jokes and silly anecdotes; she had not prepared herself for sincerity. He took a sip of his drink and then went on, louder now.

"So, on to the things I was told not to talk about: Audrey's illustrious career, who Vivien is planning to marry next, and bets on whether one of the bridesmaids is secretly pregnant." He laughed at his own joke, but Audrey watched her mother's face across the room turn milky white. Then Clara mouthed, "Am I?" to her, as though unbeknownst to her sleep-deprived brain, she might secretly be pregnant. Audrey shook her head, reassuring her that she wasn't.

"Seriously, though," Hillary went on, "today is a celebration of Audrey and Josh and their life together. The vows can wait, but alas, the food and festivities cannot. So, let's raise a glass to Audrey and Josh. Married or unmarried, don't they make a gorgeous pair?"

The congregation cheered. It was still too wet for the reception to take place in the garden, so drinks and canapés were served in the morning room and the lobby of the hall. Waiters circulated with champagne flutes, and people's unease about the tone of the celebration dissipated. Hillary had succeeded in warming everyone up to the idea of a party. Josh emerged from the crowd and wrapped an arm around Audrey's waist. The feel of his arm and his warm Josh-like smell was so blissfully reassuring. *Everything was going to be fine.*

"To no more bad omens, you said they came in threes," she said to Josh, touching her glass to his.

"Hurdles," he said. Of course Josh would see hurdles rather than omens. Josh, who saw the best in everything, including her.

They circulated among the crowd, and for the first time, Audrey registered that all her friends were here—friends from school and university, friends from traveling, from the café, the bar, and the theater, all the stops in life that Audrey had made, picking up friends along the way. She had been so caught up in her family, in Fred, in the drama of the day, she had not anticipated the simple pleasure of seeing all her friends in one place.

"Oh, Audrey, you look divine," cried Traci, an American friend she had worked with at the gallery. She reached out her arms to pull Audrey into a hug. "I nearly died for you during the service, my sweet girl, I nearly died. How's your head?"

"Jeez, what happened to your neck?" her school friend Marumi asked, shuffling forward to join the conversation. "The service, Audrey, I felt like I was in an episode of *Hollyoaks*. The drama! I was so stressed for you."

"What would you have done if he'd died? Can you imagine?" said Hester, a friend from her geography course days.

"Are you married then, or not?"

"Where's your dress from?"

"You look so thin, bitch. Jealous."

"What table am I at? Are we still having dinner? I'm starving. Please can I not be next to that boring bald guy I met at Josh's birthday party, what's his name? Did I remember to tell you I'm veggie now?"

"Josh looks completely scrummy, by the way. You really hit the jackpot, Auds."

"And look at your mum. I hope I look as good as she does when I'm her age. Is it weird if I ask for a photo with her? My dad's a huge fan."

They were her friends, they were being kind and enthusiastic, but the barrage of questions felt slightly overwhelming. Audrey moved through the crowd, politely thanking everyone for coming, fielding congratulations and commiserations. Friends of Vivien's, her godparents, all Josh's extended family— everyone wanted a piece of her.

As she worked her way around the room, engaging everyone briefly but no one properly, she made sure to avoid Fred, darting out of his eyeline whenever he came into view. She successfully navigated this little dance until she saw someone in the crowd she really did want to speak to: Brian.

"Do you have my letter?" she asked, pulling him into a corner where no one else would hear.

"Ah yes." Brian reached into his jacket pocket, pulled out an envelope, and handed it to her. Audrey tucked it safely into her clutch. "I don't know why Vivien gave it to me—"

"You're seeing her again," Audrey said sharply, and watched his face freeze in horror. "Why?"

Brian let out a sigh and then briefly closed his eyes. "I never stopped loving your mother, Audrey," he said slowly.

"What about Lawrence?"

"It's a mess. I know."

It was time to sit down for dinner. She could not think about this now. Audrey would file it away in a mental drawer, though she was running out of mental drawers to hide unpleasant thoughts in. She weaved her way through the crowd to get to the top table. Josh was to be on her right and Hillary on her left, but when she reached the round table, she saw the place card on her left had "Fred" scrawled in lilac ink. No one had known Miranda was going to bring a plus-one when the seating plan had been printed.

"I thought you might not get a chance to speak to him otherwise," Miranda said, nodding to the place card. "Trust me, you guys are so similar, I think you'll really get on."

Audrey noticed that Miranda had moved herself next to Paul. What was it with people thinking they would mess with the seating plan? If she protested, it might only make things more awkward. Just as she'd started to feel reassured that everything was going to be fine, that the worst of the day was over, the seating plan from hell had been thrown into the mix.

She found her gaze flitting around the room, stopping on all the men she knew—friends of hers, friends of Josh's, partners of their friends. Could she have found herself marrying any one of these men if just a few twists of fate's wheel had been different? Was there some guiding force pulling her toward the right person, or was it just a giant game of chess with a billion different outcomes? If Clara hadn't found the house share with Paul on Craigslist, if she hadn't been taking photos in Covent Garden that day or been sitting next to Josh at Dee's wedding, would her life have been completely different?

If it was purely down to chance, if there were a million forks in the road, then of all the ways her life could have played out, was this the best outcome? Could the human heart handle the idea that it could have loved another just as well? So many ideas of romantic love are spun around the belief that there is just one perfect person, that the journey to find them is beyond our control, that it is destined—but what if it is merely a lottery? Her mental spiral stalled as Fred pulled out the chair next to her. She tried to set her face to a neutral expression but felt her eyelid twitch with the pressure of hiding what she was feeling.

An artfully presented salmon terrine was laid in front of her, but Audrey felt sick at the idea of eating.

43

Thirteen Months Before I Do

⟡

"*I* can't eat another thing," Audrey said.

"No dessert, *gracias*," Josh said to the waiter. They were in a beachside café in Ibiza, enjoying a long lunch of seafood paella and fruity sangria. The waiter nodded and presented them with two shots of *hierbas*, on the house.

"I'm not sure about aniseed-flavored alcohol," Josh said.

"Well, you won't know until you've tried it," she said, downing hers, nudging him with her foot to do the same.

Before meeting Audrey, Josh had planned his holidays like he planned his life—rigorously. He would book time off between projects at work, so as not to inconvenience his colleagues. He'd research all the deals, read all the reviews, and then make an informed decision about where to stay and what to do. He often returned to the same places because he liked knowing what to expect. He always wrote a Tripadvisor review for everywhere he stayed. Audrey, on the other hand, had a slightly more whimsical approach to holidays. She would narrow it down to a continent, depending on how far she could afford to travel, and then stick a pin in a map. She wouldn't make any plans or book anything except the first two nights' accommodation. This approach had resulted in some complete disasters, and some unforgettable adventures.

This week they were in Ibiza, somewhere neither of them had ever been before. It had been Audrey's turn to choose their summer holiday, so she had closed her eyes and stuck a pin in the map of Europe. Technically, the pin had landed in the Mediterranean Sea, but she'd decided this island was the closest landmass. She had planned everything her way, i.e., planned nothing, and Josh was trying to be okay with her unstructured approach.

"Didn't I tell you we'd find somewhere to eat?" she said, reaching for his hand across the table. "Sometimes, winging it lets you find the real gems, the places that aren't in the guidebook."

Josh looked tense but valiantly made no comment about the fact that they'd had to try two other restaurants before finding this one, and that they'd had to wait forty minutes for a table.

After lunch and another round of aniseedy alcohol (which Josh decided he did like after all), they took a stroll along Cala d'Hort beach, the majestic tower of Es Vedrà jutting out of the sea ahead of them. The sun was warm on their faces, and the soft sound of the sea lapped hypnotically at the shore. Audrey felt her stomach gurgle. She probably shouldn't have had a large coffee *and* two shots of *hierbas*. She was about to suggest they go back so she could find the bathroom when Josh dropped a few steps behind her. When she turned around, she found him down on one knee in the sand.

"Audrey Lavery," Josh said, pulling a ring box from his pocket, "you make me laugh like nobody else. You push me to try new things, to visit new places. You've shaken up my world in the best possible way. When you look up at the night sky, I know you're always searching for the North Star. Well, Audrey, you are my constant, my immovable Polaris. Whatever else shifts or moves around us, my feelings for you will not change. I love you, Audrey, body and soul, and I'm asking you to marry me."

Wow. She should have seen it coming, but she hadn't.

He opened the ring box, and a vintage emerald-and-gold engagement ring sparkled in the sunlight. Audrey was momentarily dumbstruck. *Josh was proposing?* Josh, who believed in "pinning his colors to the mast," wanted to pin his colors to hers? She didn't think they were anywhere close to this; they'd never even discussed it. But my God, that was one hell of a proposal—"my immovable Polaris." Who could say no to that?

As she looked down at Josh in the sand, at his warm, kind, handsome face, her surprise was replaced by something else— an overwhelming urge to say yes, which she did, with barely a moment's hesitation. They both laughed in heady exhilaration as he slid the ring onto her finger. She noted briefly that it was not the sort of ring she would have chosen for herself but then chastised herself for the thought, because it was undeniably beautiful.

"Yes?" Josh asked, sounding almost as surprised as she had felt a moment ago.

"Yes! Of course yes!" she cried.

She had just enough time to kiss him before she needed to run off down the beach, calling behind her, "I'm sorry, I'm not running away, I just really need the loo!"

❧

That evening they went out to dinner to celebrate. Josh had booked a table at Priah, a trendy hotel on the west coast of the island. It was the place to be seen, with a Michelin-starred chef, a spectacular view of the sea, and a garden famous for containing almost every shade of bougainvillea in existence.

"I had to book this three months ago," Josh told her.

"You broke my 'no planning' rule," she said with a friendly frown. "We're supposed to be doing this holiday the Audrey way, remember?"

"I know, I'm sorry. When you taste the food, you'll forgive me."

"What would you have done if I'd said no?" Audrey asked.

"We'd be having a delicious commiseration dinner." Josh put his arm around her waist and leaned in to kiss her. She was wearing a new midnight-blue silk dress, with her hair pinned up, while Josh wore a crisp white shirt and chinos. She noticed a few people turn to look at them as they walked in.

"I should have said no, made you sweat, like they did in the old days."

"Would you rather I'd have worn breeches and done my, 'Miss Lavery, you must allow me to tell you how ardently I admire and love you'?" Josh said in a husky voice.

"Don't do the Darcy," Audrey said. "You know what that does to me."

They were taken to the best table, right at the edge of the terrace, overlooking the sea. The manager sent over a bottle of champagne—Josh must have called ahead.

"You know, I wasn't sure what you were going to say," Josh said, sounding serious now. "I remember a conversation we had over coffee, before we got together. You said you didn't know why anyone got married."

"Well, what did I know? I hadn't fallen in love with you yet." She said it flippantly, but it was true.

"And you're sure you like the ring?"

"I love it," she said.

"I wasn't sure. I deliberated for days."

Damn. Too late to retract.

"Ooh, great menu," she said, looking at the thick folder in front of her. "Tempura chili oyster, kohlrabi scallops, squid risotto—this is literally heaven."

"I knew you'd love it." Josh reached for her hand.

"Can we bottle this moment? Before we look at the prices." She made a comical grimace.

"Don't think about it. It's not every day you get engaged."

"I'm just going to nip to the ladies' before we choose," she said, leaning in to kiss him as she stood up. As she walked away from the table, she felt a warm glow as though experiencing some internal hug. Did she deserve to be this happy? *Had she ever imagined she'd be coming back from this holiday engaged?* As she looked around at the incredible setting, she had to concede that Josh's "planning approach" had some benefits.

The quickest way to the ladies' was along the garden walkway, framed by a pergola covered in bright red bougainvillea. She turned to look further into the garden, and that's when she saw it, down by the carp pond, a sculpture she recognized—a huge golden flower made of petals that looked like breasts. The sight of it sent a physical jolt of pain into her gut. Her eyes darted around in panic, as though Benedict might actually be there, her body unable to separate him from his work.

Audrey clutched her stomach and hurried to the hotel lobby, following the signs to the loos. Logically, she knew Benedict wasn't there. It was only his sculpture, the exact sculpture he had shown her in his gallery all those years before—*Bloom*. As she sat in a cubicle, her heart racing, she felt the beginnings of a panic attack—her palms grew sweaty, the lights were too bright, the taps too loud.

She stumbled out of the toilets, her head spinning. Looking out at the packed restaurant and the busy terrace beyond, the challenge of walking past all these people and back to her table felt insurmountable. All she could hear was Benedict's voice in her mind, reminding her that karma would come for her in the end, that the universe had not forgotten what she had done, the lives she had ruined. She turned, walked back along the corridor leading away from the restaurant, and went out the front door. She made her way around the side of the building and found a quiet, empty patio. She found a chair and sat with her head between her knees and tried to breathe.

Thoughts piled in, one on top of another. *Wasn't it strange that Benedict's sculpture was here, on the very night she was celebrating her engagement?* It felt like some prophetic warning. *Quod severis metes*—"As you sow, so shall you reap." *Why had she said yes? Weren't they happy as they were? Why was Josh asking her now? She didn't even know who she was yet, what if she changed and Josh didn't like who she became? What if there was someone better out there for Josh, someone kinder, more intelligent, less selfish? What if Audrey never managed to unstick whatever it was that was stuck inside her? What if she was just like her mother?* She closed her eyes, furious with her chaotic mind for sucking all the light out of this perfect day, like some monstrous black hole.

She sat up in the chair and tipped her head back to look up at the sky, her breath ragged as she searched for stability in her beloved stars.

44

Three Hours After I Didn't

❧

"**S**o where do you live in London?" Audrey asked Fred, grasping for the safety of small talk. She had to say something, or people would notice and think it strange.

On the opposite side of the round table, Clara took her seat between Lawrence and Hillary. She had deposited the twins in a bedroom with her mother and was nipping out at tactical moments to check on them. As Clara arrived at the table, Audrey saw in her friend's unblinking gaze the full horror of the seating arrangement sandwich she'd found herself in.

"I live in Muswell Hill," Fred replied, his body tilted toward her. She remembered so much of what they had spoken about that day, but she knew so little about the basic details of his life. Audrey glanced up at him and saw the familiar faint scar by his eyebrow, the wild blond hair, the quizzical look in his green eyes. She breathed in the intoxicating smell of his skin. He really hadn't changed at all.

"Josh mentioned you restore old things?" Audrey said.

"Yes, I run a small museum in North London, the Museum of Obsolescence. I collect and restore all sorts of technology that's now fallen out of use—floppy disk drives, typewriters, photo booths. I like to rescue things that might otherwise be destroyed, the casualties of progress. You should come and visit."

"It sounds intriguing." Audrey paused. "We actually hired a vintage booth for tonight."

"I love those old machines. They always make me think of you."

"Shhh," she hushed him. "Don't."

Audrey's eyes darted around the faces at their table as she checked that no one was listening. Hillary reached across Fred to top up her champagne glass. He seemed uncharacteristically relaxed about having been demoted from his place beside her. Vivien was sitting between Brian and Lawrence, which now did not feel like an accidental seating arrangement. On Josh's right, Miranda leaned a cheek on her fist and gazed doe-eyed up at Paul, who was amusing her and Josh by doing a puppet show with the bread rolls. *Was everyone at this table lusting after someone they hadn't come with?*

"So, Audrey, do you think the universe is trying to tell you not to marry Josh?" Jay called across the table, giving Josh a wink to let him know he was joking.

"Hello to you too, Jay," said Audrey, feeling herself blush. "And no, I think the universe has got better things to do. Like making sure your hair stays perfectly vertical at the front." They made playful faces at each other.

"Jayson, how's your coffee business going?" Vivien asked, and people went back to their individual conversations.

Fred turned to her and asked, "How are you feeling? Is your head okay?"

"Fine," she said with a wry smile.

"Do you believe in things happening for a reason?" he

asked quietly, and she didn't reply. *How was she supposed to get through this conversation?* "Because I think I do. And last night I didn't want to say anything, to make things harder for you, but now, with the wedding not happening, I have to say, I feel like I was meant to come here, meant to find you. I don't think you were supposed to get married today. You don't have to go through with this just because you said yes."

"So, books?" Audrey asked loudly. "Read anything good lately?"

"Audrey . . ."

"What are you two sounding so serious about?" Josh asked, leaning into their conversation as he tore a bread roll in two.

"Books," said Audrey.

"Love. Life. Destiny. The eternal, unending, and ultimately futile search for meaning in this fragile plane of existence," said Fred.

Josh laughed, reaching behind Audrey to pat Fred on the back. "I can see why Miranda thought you two would get on."

Audrey wanted to shrink to the size of the bride figurine on top of the cake, wrap herself in a lilac napkin, and hide inside it for the rest of the day. Preferably with a miniature bottle of champagne and a few giant crumbs of wedding cake to keep her going.

Josh turned to the waiter, who was offering him wine, and Audrey glanced back at Fred, who was observing her with soulful eyes.

"I didn't tell you the whole story last night, about that day I didn't come."

"Okay, is this book fiction or nonfiction?" Audrey asked, trying desperately to get him back onto the safer topic of books.

"Nonfiction," he said, bowing his head slightly, taking

her cue. "It's the story of a guy who had this one amazing afternoon with an incredible girl. He should have said something at the time, but he was seeing someone. Technically he was not free, and he didn't want to see her again until he was. He was cycling to break up with his girlfriend the morning after they met, and that's when he got knocked off his bike." He paused. "He should have tried harder to call straightaway, but his girlfriend came to look after him at the hospital, and he couldn't break up with her then, it felt too cruel."

Audrey was listening, but also checking to see that Josh was not. Luckily, he was now engaged in conversation with Brian across the table.

"He was seeing someone, and he didn't think to mention it once that whole afternoon?" she said quietly.

"I know it's no excuse, but she was the Photo Booth Girl. She'd held a place in his imagination for so long, and he felt this immediate connection with her. He didn't plan to deceive anyone."

"You said the number he had didn't work. Did it smudge?"

Fred looked perplexed by the question. "No, he called and got through, but the person he spoke to said he had the wrong number, that no one by that name lived there. He tried it several times."

"The person he spoke to. Does he remember anything about them?"

Fred thought for a moment, trying to recall. "It was a man, with a South African accent. He remembers because it was a distinctive voice, and the man got angry the third time he tried the number."

Fred *had* called. He had spoken to Benedict, probably on the day Benedict was packing his things to leave. Audrey's skin prickled with cold at the thought. Of course he wouldn't have taken a message. *The cruelty of karma.*

"Well, I don't feel like I need to read the book now you've told me the whole plot," Audrey said, feeling her throat tighten. If she had not said anything to her mother, if she had gotten Fred's message, would she be sitting here now?

45

Ten Months Before I Do

⌒∽

"*Y*ou'll need to decide where you want to sit, what we want to eat and drink. There's the guest list, caterers, florists, venue, music. There's a lot to think about in a wedding, Audrey. I have fifteen tabs on this Excel document alone," said Josh. "I also have a hundred other non-wedding-related jobs. One of us needs to write to the council and tell them they put us in the wrong council tax band."

"Okay," said Audrey, then paused.

"I'll do that then, shall I?" Josh asked, a note of resignation in his tone.

Audrey nodded. They were sitting at the kitchen table in their flat, going through Josh's to-do list. They had moved in together a few months after getting engaged. Josh's flat felt too small for them both, so they'd taken on a new lease on a two-bedroom place in Kennington in South London. Audrey had been excited to create a grown-up home, to choose soft furnishings, to have stationery printed (people still did that, right?), to say good-bye to student living and a fridge where Paul still insisted on labeling his cheese.

"Wedding list," Josh said, scrolling down the list on his phone. "Are we happy going with the place your mother suggested?"

"Sure," Audrey said, pouring herself a glass of wine.

"Did you want me to confirm those caterers, or were you and Vivien going to meet a few more options while I'm away?" Josh tapped his pen on the table and then the washing machine made a loud beeping noise. He jumped up to transfer a load of clothes from the washer to the dryer. "We're out of the anti-color-run paper. Can you add it to the online order? The tab is open on my laptop."

This was what cohabiting looked like. This was the happily-ever-after great romances were written about.

Audrey had known Josh was organized, that he liked to be on top of things, but sharing a flat with him had illuminated a whole new world of Joshisms. Josh got up at six, even though he didn't need to leave the house until seven thirty. He liked time to "collect himself" in the mornings, to go for a run and then read the newspaper over a leisurely breakfast. Audrey prided herself on being able to get from bed to shower and out of the front door in seven minutes flat. Josh owned seasonal duvets—four tog for summer, ten for winter. Audrey had only ever owned one duvet, and before dating Josh she'd had no idea what a tog rating even was. Josh put salt in the dishwasher at regular intervals. He had a to-do list on his phone full of tasks, like "update contents insurance." Audrey had a to-do list in her head, which often got muddled and rarely got done.

"Shall we go to the pub?" Audrey suggested when Josh had finished loading the dryer.

"Why?"

"Because this might be more fun in the pub."

"It's a Monday night. We need to make some decisions on this stuff. I don't have any time on the weekend, and I'm rammed all week." Josh looked tense.

"I know, you're right." Audrey sighed.

"Look, why don't we work on the invitation list?" he said, coming to sit beside her and opening yet another tab on his Excel sheet. "I've made a list of my friends and family in this column, and then a list of yours here. I've highlighted the definites in green, and the orange are maybes."

"Ugh, why is Ester green? You're hardly friends with her anymore."

"She was in Pembroke with me, I can't invite some of the college gang and not the others. They come as a group."

"She hates me, she wanted you to marry Harriet."

"Why would I marry Harriet?"

"Because she's been in love with you since university."

"Don't be ridiculous."

"You're so blind. It's very obvious." Audrey took another swig of wine, warming to the topic. "Have you noticed, whenever she takes a group photo, she *always* posts the one where I have my eyes closed or I'm looking in the wrong direction?"

"How malicious of her," Josh said, nodding in mock sympathy. "Are you saying we can't invite Harriet now? Harriet's a good friend of mine."

"Who wants to sleep with you."

"Are you jealous of Harriet?"

"No, it's fine." Audrey shrugged. "Maybe I'll invite Handsy Hamish."

"If you're going to start inviting every random guy you've kissed at a party, then we'll need to find a bigger venue."

"Ouch."

Audrey closed the laptop. She knew she was being petulant.

You couldn't be with someone like Josh and get jealous every time another woman looked at him.

Josh closed his eyes and then said, "I'm sorry, that was unnecessary. Why don't you just work on your own list before vetoing mine?"

"Fine," she said.

"Okay, I'm going to take all these boxes to the tip. If I don't leave now, I won't get a parking space on the street when I get back," he said, reopening the laptop. "Just type in all the people you want to invite."

Once Josh and their huge pile of cardboard boxes had gone, Audrey walked over to the window and called Clara.

"Is it just me, or is planning a wedding not that fun?"

"It's not just you. It's the first test of married life—can you make it through the tedium and the spreadsheets. Wait, isn't this level of admin the kind of thing Josh lives for?"

"He's crazy busy with this new job and, you know, bleaching the shower grouting," she said in a low moan.

"I don't know why you say that like it's a bad thing," said Clara. "I'd swap a domesticated clean freak for a man-child any day of the week."

"I know, but sometimes, being with Josh makes me feel like *I'm* the man-child," Audrey mused. "I thought living together would be a bit more . . . I don't know . . . ripping each other's clothes off at the door, staying in bed all weekend with the Sunday papers."

"So, you're not having enough sex?"

"Oh no, we are, and it's great, it's just we have sex and then talk about the online shopping order or whether our wineglasses can go in the dishwasher. I miss the part where we go on exciting mini-breaks and talk about how much we love each other."

Clara laughed. "Being in love doesn't eradicate life's admin—it is not a panacea. Wait until you're pregnant, it's like being in a rom-com directed by M. Night Shyamalan. Everything Jay says pisses me off at the moment. All I can think about is when I'm next going to eat or pee."

"I know, you're right," Audrey said, her eyes finding the familiar line of Orion's belt in the sky.

"Speaking of which, my peanut-sized bladder calls. Chat tomorrow?"

"Sure. Good luck."

"You too."

When Josh got back from the recycling center, he looked over Audrey's shoulder and said with a sigh, "How have you only added four names? I am leaving for Sweden on Wednesday, there's a lot of pressure on me at work. I can't do everything for the wedding too."

She noticed how stressed he looked, the worry lines that had appeared beside his eyes. She felt horribly selfish.

"I'm sorry." She stood up and pulled him into a hug. "I know you've got a lot on your plate. Leave all the wedding stuff to me, I will sort it."

"Really?"

"Yes, I'll ask my mum for help, you know how she loves a wedding."

"Thank you," said Josh, kissing her on the forehead. "Right, I need to iron a shirt for tomorrow."

As he left the room, Audrey reopened the online shopping order and filled in the rest of the food they would need for the week.

Josh called from the bedroom, "Audrey, have you been eating food in bed again?"

"No," she yelled back.

"Why are there crumbs everywhere, then? We only changed these sheets two days ago."

Audrey made a face at the door. *How did he know?* That man had laser crumb vision.

As she opened her wallet to find her card to pay, her fingers stopped on the strip of photographs buried in the inside pocket. The four pictures of Fred, saying "I will find you," and the two of them kissing. She had almost forgotten they were there. She should throw them away. She was living with her fiancé; it wasn't appropriate to carry around a photo of her kissing another man.

But something made her pause on these photos, the what-ifs dancing through her mind. Would she have been doing online shopping orders and spreadsheets with Fred? Or would they have been backpacking around darkest Peru, perhaps living out of a van in Mexico? Was marriage really the beginning of the adventure, or was it the end? She remembered what Fred had said to her that day: *"Sometimes life feels like a hamster wheel . . . Sometimes you just need to jump off the wheel."* Audrey could hear Josh whistling a tune from *Winnie the Pooh* as he ironed in the next room. Sometimes she found his whistling habit endearing, other times she found it intensely annoying. Today, it was the latter. Her gaze lingered on the image of her twenty-two-year-old self. She looked so confident, so assured, so full of fire. What had happened to that girl? Where did she go?

Audrey didn't need to throw the photos away. She would just take them out of her wallet and put them in a shoebox somewhere—a memento of another life, a reminder of the person she was before. As soon as Josh finished ironing in the bedroom, she would find somewhere more appropriate to put them. But then she started sorting out the next load of washing and forgot to do any such thing.

46

Four Hours After I Didn't

⤜⤏

"*T*ime's up, Fred. You've been monopolizing my wife-to-be long enough," Josh said, leaning into their conversation.

"Sorry," Fred said, a red flush rising up his neck.

"I'm joking, monopolize away." Josh reached out around Audrey to slap Fred on the back again. "I'm going to say a few words. I know you hate being the center of attention, Auds, so I'll keep it short." He stood up and tapped his glass.

Audrey's palms began to sweat, and her ears began to ring; she suddenly had a pounding, fierce headache. She looked down at the wedding menu in front of her and felt it was an exam paper she didn't know the answers to. Time distorted, and phrases danced into her consciousness like a wind-whipped storm of words.

"I was planning to start my speech with the traditional 'My wife and I . . . ,' which usually gets a round of applause, but that might not be applicable just yet, so I'm going to start with, my Audrey and I . . ."

"You don't have to go through with this just because you said yes."

". . . When we're together, I feel like the windows of the world have been thrown open and all the stale air let out . . ."

"When you fall in love, you'll understand."

"Quod severis metes—*'As you sow, so shall you reap.'*"

"You fill my life with color, and I can't wait to be married to you, however long it takes for us to say 'I do.'"

"Sometimes you just need to jump off the wheel."

Audrey was drowning in the sea of words. As she looked around the room at jubilant faces, she felt as though she was in some surreal hall of mirrors; people's features appeared stretched and distorted, and it made her feel woozy and off balance. She could feel the heat of Josh's body on one side of her, smell the oaky aftershave Fred was wearing on the other. As soon as she sensed Josh's speech was over, she leaned in to hug him, held steady through the applause, and then excused herself from the table, lurching out of her seat.

She walked up to the cake at the far side of the room, blocking people's view with her body as she removed the bride figurine from the top and buried it in her palm. Out in the corridor, beyond the loos, she found a quiet space to inspect the figurine. She held it up to her face and asked the bride, "Did you jump, earlier, when you fell off the cake?" The bride refused to answer, her mouth painted stubbornly closed. "You jumped, didn't you. Why? What is *wrong* with you?"

Still the bride refused to answer, and in anger, Audrey used a nail to pick off the paint on the figurine's face, so now she had no expression at all. She then popped the faceless bride on top of a door frame, alone, punishment for being so uncooperative.

As she stood glaring at the faceless bride, she heard the band strike up a tune back in the Grand Suite. It was not the song they'd planned for their first dance; it was "Singin' in the Rain," the song she and Fred had danced to at the band-stand. "You're kidding me," Audrey said to the figurine. She could feel her sanity teetering on some edge. "No, I am not going to answer you, call of the void, not today."

She picked the bride back up, walked further down the corridor, and entered the Grand Suite through a narrow conservatory at the far end of the dance floor. It was separated from the main room by a wall of dark blue glass. In the conservatory stood the photo booth. It was just like the one in Baker Street all those years before, hired from the same company, perhaps even the very same one. Was it disloyal that she had wanted one at their wedding? She told herself it was not just something she associated with Fred; the photo booth was where her love of photography had begun—it had shaped her whole career path, her ambition to become a photographer.

In the relative quiet of the conservatory, with the band still playing, she stroked the illuminated panel of the booth. She sat down on the stool inside; the money slot now asked for tokens rather than pounds, and there was a pile on the ledge, waiting to be used by wedding guests. She pressed one into the narrow slot and saw her face in the booth's mirror. She thought she looked terrible. Unhinged.

Then the curtain drew back, and there was Fred, of course.

"You're here," he said with a huge grin.

"I am here," she said, looking up at him. His piercing green eyes focused on hers, full of questions, full of hope. His head tilted to one side, his wild blond hair nudging the doorway of the booth. She didn't get up from the stool. She wanted to stay here, in the place synonymous with good things, with innocence, with the time before she'd felt wretched and guilty and directionless. Fred dropped to his knees, so he was looking up at her. He reached out and took her hand.

"The band is playing our song, and here you are in our booth."

She sat, blinking down at him.

"I think everything that's happened today is a cosmic red thread, leading me to you. I'm not going to pressure you at all. I just need you to know, I still feel it too."

Audrey stood up, suddenly claustrophobic in the booth with him blocking her exit. Fred must have read her standing up as an acceptance, as her running into his arms, because he stood too and pulled her toward him, pressing his lips firmly to hers.

With her head swimming, the shock of his firm kiss and confident arms, Audrey found herself momentarily a passenger in his embrace, her mind not quick enough to register what was happening, not quick enough to stop it.

"Audrey?"

Audrey pulled her lips away, but Fred's arms stayed where they were as they both turned their heads to see Josh standing in the doorway of the conservatory, a horrified expression on his face.

47

Thirteen Months Before I Do

ᐤ

*A*udrey didn't know how much time had passed before she noticed Josh standing over her. Panic attacks tended to distort her sense of time. She was still sitting in the courtyard at Priah, looking up at the Ibizan night sky, when Josh found her.

"Here you are," he said calmly. "Can I join you?"

She nodded silently, gearing herself up to explain something that she couldn't.

"I . . . Josh, I'm sorry, I . . . I had a panic attack."

"You don't need to explain," he said gently. "Can I do anything?" Audrey shook her head. He sat down beside her. "If you need to sit and look at the sky, you can sit for as long as you need to. I just hope that sometimes, you will let me come and sit beside you." He reached for her hand and squeezed it. Being able to sit with someone and not have all the answers, that was love.

By the time they left the courtyard, their table had been given to someone else. They bought chips from a roadside stall and walked down to an empty beach to eat them.

"I'm sorry about the restaurant," Audrey said.

291

"It's fine. I think these chips are just as good as the kohlrabi scallops and squid risotto. Maybe better, more potatoey." She smiled at this, at his unwavering ability to see the best in every situation. He put his hand over hers. "Do you want to talk about it?" She shook her head. She didn't. "I hope it's nothing I said?"

"No, God no. Just something in the restaurant reminded me of someone and . . . my brain makes these silly, irrational connections."

"My brain does that too sometimes," he said.

"It does?" Audrey asked in surprise.

"Yes. Like when I see Chipsticks in the supermarket, it makes me smile because I think of you. I can't walk past a coffee bar menu now without wondering which weird fruit-based coffee you would order if you were with me. Whenever I see stars, I want to know what constellations you would be pointing out. My mind has been Audreyed."

Audrey felt something melt inside her.

"That's the most romantic thing anyone's ever said to me." She leaned over to kiss him.

"Really? With all those romantic films you watch, I feel like there's a high bar for romantic declarations—I've been led to believe all the great love stories must end with a dance routine on a Greek island. I wasn't sure musings about Chipsticks were going to cut it."

"Well, your musings were definitely better than Andrew Lincoln holding up all those signs in *Love Actually*," she said with a smirk, because she knew Josh hated that scene.

"I don't know who could find that amount of wasted paper romantic," Josh said, his tone completely serious.

"Not me." Audrey bit back a grin.

Josh sighed, put an arm around her shoulder, and pulled

her toward him. "I don't think we need a dance number or a fancy meal to celebrate getting engaged. All I need is you, me, five euros for chips, and the promise of a lifetime of this."

It was right there, eating chips in the sand, that Audrey knew for sure, she had no doubts: she wanted to marry this man.

48

Four and a Half Hours After I Didn't

❧

"Audrey?" Josh said again.

Audrey tried to speak but found the words gelatinous in her mouth.

"It's not what you think," she said.

"What the hell should I think?" he said, eyes wide in dismay.

Fred let go of Audrey and took a step toward Josh, holding out a hand, as though to prevent Josh from getting any closer.

"You should just tell him," said Fred, turning back toward Audrey.

"Tell me what?" Josh said, his forehead pinched into a deep-set frown. "Audrey?"

"No, Fred," Audrey said firmly, but Fred turned away from her. Audrey clenched her hands into fists, steeling herself for what Fred might be about to say. She had that feeling again, of everything happening in slow motion.

"Audrey's not supposed to be with you, she's supposed to be with me."

Josh laughed a chesty, disbelieving laugh. "Why are you

kissing Miranda's boyfriend?" His voice took on an edge as shock and disbelief turned into something sharper, angrier, the reality of what he had just witnessed beginning to sink in. The look on his face cut right through Audrey. It was amazing, the clarity that came from witnessing the loss of something you thought you could bear to lose.

"That's not true." Audrey shook her head, the taste of Fred's unwanted kiss still on her lips.

"She doesn't want to hurt you," Fred said with a sigh, laying a hand on Audrey's arm, which she shook off.

Audrey swallowed, the words not coming, her head spinning, the bruise on her temple throbbing with renewed pain. Maybe she'd banged her head harder than she thought when she'd hit the stone floor of the church; all her thought patterns felt jumbled and confused.

"Audrey?" Josh asked again, his eyes pleading with her to somehow explain all this away. "What's going on? Do you know him?"

"Yes, we met years ago. It threw me slightly, him showing up last night, it . . . it brought back a lot of things from that time in my life . . ."

A flash of fear sparked in Josh's eyes. "Is this what you were talking about upstairs, about having doubts?"

Audrey shook her head. "No, he just kissed me. It took me by surprise. It's not what I want."

"From where I was standing, you really looked like you were kissing him." Josh's voice broke as he spoke. His face crumpled with anger and pain, impossible to hide. Audrey had never seen this expression on his face before, every small muscle a turmoil of contorted feeling. "Why did you keep this a secret?" Josh's eyes were tearing up now. "We told each other everything about our pasts, everyone we were with before."

"It was only one day." She stepped toward him, but he stepped back. Looking up into his face, the hurt in his eyes, Audrey felt as though her heart was being slowly crushed by a steamroller. *How had she let this happen? What madness had overtaken her?*

"But you kept my photo in your wallet all this time," Fred said beneath his breath.

Josh must have seen something in her face then, because his jaw tensed, and his eyes turned a steely shade of gray.

"Where's your wallet?"

"Josh, please, this isn't—" Isn't what? *What could she say in her defense?*

"Where is it? In our room? In your bag, on our wedding bed?"

Without waiting for a response, he turned, striding out of the conservatory, back across the dance floor, through the dining room full of guests. Audrey hitched up her dress and ran after him, calling his name.

"Josh! Wait!" she called, desperate for him to stop, ignoring the room full of wedding guests.

"Audrey!" Fred called, and in that moment, she hated him. She hated him for being there now, hated him for not being there all those years before, hated him for speaking for her now. Mainly she hated him for hurting Josh. But she only had herself to blame, because she had not listened to what her heart had been telling her all along.

Guests had gathered on the dance floor, waiting to see the first dance, now that the band had warmed up. Instead, they all watched as the bride chased the groom across the hall. Audrey noticed Granny Parker chatting with Hillary. Clara was swaying from side to side holding baby Lily on her hip, her arm around Jay, who was holding Bea. She had a look of such joy in her eyes, but then as her gaze shifted to Audrey, it turned to concern.

Josh was already at the stairs, he was too quick for her in her heels, and when they got to their suite, he had already found her handbag and was tipping its contents out onto the bed.

"It doesn't mean anything, it's just a memory." She was crying now, reaching for her bag, trying to get to it before he could, but he had her wallet and tore through it, searching every compartment, holding it out of her reach above his head. Then he held the two photo strips in his hands, and she sank back onto the bed, any hope of retrieving them gone. Fred and Audrey kissing, Fred and Audrey happy. Fred and Audrey, soul mates.

He shook his head, closed his eyes, as Audrey sobbed, "Josh, I love you—"

"But you kept this," he said, hurt juddering his words. "All these years. Why?"

"It was a moment in time. It meant something to me then. The person I used to be."

"So he's right."

She couldn't lie anymore, not now. "There was a time I did think about him," she conceded. "But it was a fantasy, it was never real."

Only as she said it did she realize how true this was. Fred had always been a what-if, a symbol of everything that might have been—what if she hadn't failed her math exam, what if she'd never gone to the gallery with Benedict, what if she hadn't ruined her mother's relationship for a third time. Josh looked down at the strip of photos, then threw them onto the bed, raking both hands through his hair. "Well, you can have your fantasy, Audrey, I'm done. Do you think you're an easy person to love? You're not. But I did, unreservedly, every minute of every day, and now I see you never felt that way about me. I sensed deep down you were holding something back."

"Josh, no. You're wrong. I did, I do, I do love you!" Audrey cried.

But Josh wasn't listening. He'd already picked up his suitcase, which stood on the floor, waiting to be unpacked, and stormed out the door.

⟳

*A*udrey pulled off her dress; it was restricting her ability to move, to run, and she needed to go after him. As she stood in her underwear, looking for something to put on, she almost didn't notice that Fred was standing in the hallway.

"Audrey, I'm sorry—" Fred started talking, and Audrey looked up at him, wearing only her underpants and bra. She strode into the hall and spoke right into his face.

"How dare you walk into my life like this and tear it all down? I said no! Last night I said no, today I said no, I didn't choose you, I chose Josh."

"You kissed me back," he said firmly.

She screamed up at the ceiling, a guttural, animal cry, just as Hillary, Clara, and Vivien came up the stairs into the corridor. She screamed again, kicking the wall, as her audience looked on, wide-eyed.

"Right," said Clara, stepping forward and steering a half-naked Audrey back into the bedroom. She looked around the room for some clothes. "Let's get dressed, shall we, take this down a notch? This is all feeling a little Kardashian."

"I don't want to calm down!" Audrey screamed.

"Darling, are you quite well? Everyone can hear you. Why are you in your underwear? Where is Josh going?" Vivien asked.

Audrey looked out the window and saw Josh getting into his car.

"Hillary, Josh is leaving. Please, please stop him."

Hillary did as he was asked, running back down the corridor, and they heard the thud of his feet thundering down the stairs.

"Why are *you* here?" Vivien asked Fred, looking back and forth between him and Audrey, her eyes snagging on Audrey's bra and underpants.

"I'll give you some space, shall I?" Fred said to Audrey, his eyes pleading for some kind of reassurance.

She picked up the kettle from the side table and threw it at the wall.

"Okay, and scene. Do I need to call a doctor?" Vivien asked. "Have you taken something?"

"You need to go," Clara told Fred, but he had already turned to leave.

"Audrey," Vivien said firmly. "A little decorum, please."

Audrey ran to the window to see Hillary run out into the driveway, but he was too late. Josh's car, which had "Just Married" written on the back and cans trailing from the back bumper, was already driving away. Then all the fight left her. Her rage evaporated, and she sank to the floor, knowing, deep down, that she had no one to blame but herself.

Why had she been dwelling on Benedict today, on Fred, on Vivien? Why had she let her mind filter her relationship with Josh and show it to her through a distorted, doubting lens? She knew that was not the whole picture, that she had left out so much of the story.

49

Two and a Half Years Before I Do

c⁓

"*Y*ou know you just turned north?" Audrey said as Josh turned his car the wrong way onto the motorway.

"Damn," Josh said, drumming his hand against the wheel. "I'd hoped you weren't going to notice that."

"Why, where are we going?"

They'd driven to Yorkshire for the weekend to meet Josh's parents and the formidable Granny Parker. Now they were supposed to be driving home to London.

"I wanted it to be a surprise, but I need the GPS to get me there."

Audrey leaned forward in the passenger seat. "Are we running off to Gretna Green?" she asked conspiratorially.

"Do you want to run off to Gretna Green?" he asked, glancing across to the passenger seat.

"We've established your family would never approve of a marriage, since I'm not from Yorkshire, so I think Gretna Green is our only option."

Clearly, she was joking. It had been six months; they were hardly about to elope. It was going well between them, disconcertingly well, but Audrey hadn't even said "I love you" yet. Josh had said it to her. They'd been walking hand in hand across the Millennium Bridge one evening. They'd stopped in the middle to watch the sky reflected in the Thames, and Josh had turned to her and said, "I love you, Audrey." She had said, "Thank you." *Thank you?* What was wrong with her?

She loved him too, of course she did. She'd never been in a relationship that made her feel this way, as though the lights on the stage of her life had finally been turned on and she was no longer stumbling around in the dark. Her initial attraction to Josh had been a slow burn; so too had the depth of her affection. The first bloom of infatuation had grown roots, as she got to know him, as she came to trust that he wasn't going anywhere. His guileless affection made her feel secure and valued; it was helping her challenge some ingrained feeling of unlovability. So why couldn't she tell him all this?

"We're not driving to Gretna Green, but my parents loved you, so don't worry on that count," Josh said, thrusting his arm forward to change gears. "I've already had four texts from my mum, all telling me how charming she thought you were."

"Well, Granny Parker did not find me charming."

"Granny Parker doesn't find anyone or anything charming."

"Don't keep me in suspense, then, where are we going?"

"It's an early birthday present," Josh said, and she could see in his face he was pleased with whatever it was he had organized. "We're going to one of the darkest places in Europe," he said mysteriously.

"To murder me?" She laughed, changing the radio station again.

"No, though if you keep changing the station, I might. You're always saying there's too much light pollution in London, that it's not great for seeing the stars. So we're going to stay in a dark-sky park, nowhere near any cities or towns. There's no light pollution, so you'll be able to see your stars properly."

"Are you joking?" Audrey asked, grabbing his arm in excitement, then quickly letting go, since they were currently traveling at seventy miles per hour on the motorway.

"No." He laughed.

"Eeee!" Audrey squealed, but then her face fell. "But I don't have my telescope."

"Don't worry, I think there's one there," he said.

~~~

They drove deep into the Northumberland countryside, through the dark spruce forest of Kielder, skirting around a huge reservoir, then winding their way gradually up the Black Fell. Looking at the landscape around them, Audrey felt that Josh had found her spiritual home. Above them was a pristine sky, and as the light began to dim, she could sense what a clean view of the stars it would offer them. They drove out onto a high clearing of land and ahead of them was a strange, boxlike wooden structure.

"What's this? Is this where we're staying?" Audrey asked.

"It's an observatory," said Josh. "I booked us a private sky tour with one of the guides."

Audrey stared in wonder at the huge open shutters of the building. *An observatory, all the way out here?* Josh's eyes sparked with pleasure at her reaction.

They were welcomed in by Phileas, a retired astronomer and volunteer. He explained a little about the dark-sky park and then showed them up to the telescope. For the next few hours, Audrey found herself in her personal heaven. She had visited the Royal Observatory in Greenwich many times, but always as part of a tour group. Here, they had the place to themselves. As she put her eye to the lens of the huge telescope, the sight left her momentarily speechless. The fog of light, which normally dulled her view, was gone. It helped that tonight's sky was cloudless, with a new moon, and the heavens were a blanket of ebony dotted with the brightest diamonds of light. To Audrey, it felt like putting on glasses for the first time; now she could see everything as it was supposed to be seen.

"Do you want me to tell you what you're looking at?" Phileas asked.

"Oh, there's Altair." Audrey sighed. "And Alpheratz . . . and, oh, I can see the rings of Saturn so clearly!" It soon became apparent that Audrey didn't need telling anything.

"Oh, Josh, you have to see this, the Milky Way is so unbelievably vivid," she said, and she didn't even need the telescope to show him. "Look, this band of light, you see that glow across the sky? That's the combined light of four hundred billion stars, and these dark patches are cosmic dust; that's the edge of the galaxy we're living in."

Audrey looked up at the sky, but when she turned back to Josh, she saw that he was watching her.

"You're supposed to be looking at the sky, not at me," she said.

"Are you happy?" he asked, his eyes brimming with fondness.

"Yes, Josh, this is incredible. Can we live here?" She leaned in to kiss him, feeling the welcome heat of his lips in the cool air of the observatory.

"Come and see Andromeda, Audrey, she's clear as anything tonight," said Phileas, beckoning her back to the telescope.

"What's Andromeda?" Josh asked, a hand caressing her back as she leaned over the lens to look.

"Another galaxy," Phileas explained.

"That's going to collide with ours," said Audrey.

"Really?" Josh said with a note of concern.

"But not for another four billion years, so you don't need to worry."

"Audrey, do you want a job here?" Phileas laughed.

They spent three hours looking out at the universe, and Audrey and Phileas were soon having conversations that Josh had a hard time keeping up with. As Josh tried to stifle a yawn, Phileas finally said, "I'm sorry, Audrey, I was meant to close an hour ago, we should really let Josh get to his bed." They both looked at Josh, who quickly tried to appear more alert. "I can't tell you how much I've enjoyed talking to a fellow enthusiast." Phileas shook her hand. Something about the astronomer reminded Audrey of her father, and she didn't want to leave, she didn't want him to stop talking. Her dad would have loved this place.

⤳✦⤳

*J*osh had booked them two nights in a remote cabin in the woods. As he opened the door, they found a large futon bed in the middle of the room, draped in cozy sheepskin rugs, and floor-level lanterns. Best of all, above them was a glass ceiling, revealing the entire pristine, star-speckled sky.

"It's a stargazing pod," Josh explained.

"I am not going to sleep," Audrey said, jumping onto the bed. "How will we sleep when there's all this to look at?"

"I feel the same whenever I'm in a bed with you," said Josh, lowering himself down beside her, kissing her neck as he unbuttoned her blouse.

"Josh, this is the most incredible, thoughtful present, I . . . I love you."

And it felt so natural, she didn't even brace herself to say it. She loved him. She loved that he was trying to plant a thousand trees to make the world a better place. She loved how considerate he was to strangers. She loved how self-conscious he was when he wore his glasses, how his top lip started to sweat when he got embarrassed. She loved how oblivious he was to the attention he got from other women. She loved how he had a list on his phone of every book he'd ever read. She loved that he unknowingly whistled *Winnie the Pooh* songs to himself when he ironed. She loved the way he held her, as though she was something precious, and she loved the way his broad, firm body felt against hers.

"I love you too," he said. "More than you can know."

After they made love, Audrey lay in his arms and pointed out all the constellations they could see. She told him the stories she knew, many that her father had told her.

"Isn't it strange to think that every human who's ever lived has looked up at this same sky, and that all these stars will still be here long after every one of us is gone? My dad used to tell me we're all made of stardust—that's where the atoms in our bodies originally came from." She paused, feeling overwhelmed by a strange cocktail of emotions. "This has been the best night of my life."

"Me too," he said.

They fell asleep with their bodies entwined, Audrey's head on his chest as she listened to the steady beat of his heart.

50

Five Hours After I Didn't

⤨

*A*udrey felt as though she'd woken up from a dream and arrived in a nightmare.

"I don't understand what has happened. Why did Josh leave?" Vivien asked as Clara tried to pull a gray shirtdress over Audrey's limp body. "Do *you* know what this is all about?" Vivien asked Clara.

Audrey looked up at Clara, then gave a small nod of the head, allowing her friend to explain.

"Fred is someone from Audrey's past. Him showing up out of the blue at the wedding just got Audrey a little confused, and then with the reverend, and everything else going wrong— well, it's been a stressful day for everyone."

That was one way of putting it.

"It's all my fault," Audrey said. "I've made a mess of everything. Benedict told me this would happen, he said, 'I hope one day you love someone, maybe even plan to marry them, and someone comes along and ruins it for you.' Look, someone has, it was me." Audrey slowly pulled her knees to her chest.

Vivien exhaled, a long breathy exhale, then she sat down on the bed.

"Clara, would you leave us, please?" she said.

Clara looked between the two women, seemingly indecisive about whether she should go. "I'll be outside if you need me," she said, squeezing Audrey's shoulder.

Once they were alone, Vivien said, "What on earth has Benedict got to do with Josh leaving?"

"You asked if I was sure about Benedict, and I wasn't." She kept her eyes on the floor, unable to look up at her mother. "What if I was wrong? What if I ruined your happiness on a gut feeling?"

"Audrey, he was not a good man."

Audrey took a huge gulp of air, as though loading a gun, readying it to fire.

"I don't even know what happened anymore, I just felt uncomfortable around him. He did touch me in his gallery, but . . . not explicitly, he was looking for a light switch, it *could* have been an accident." She rubbed her hands against her face, against her lips, trying to pull the words out. How many times had she raked over the events of that morning in her mind? "Just because I didn't like it, maybe that didn't make it wrong. You were so happy and then he left, and I stole that from you, and then I couldn't be around you, couldn't stand to see how broken you were because of me."

Still, she didn't dare look up. She didn't want to see the disappointment, the anger, at this admission. When she finally dared to look at her mother, she saw that Vivien was crying.

"And you've felt like this, all these years, that it was your words alone that made me throw him out?"

She nodded then, before starting to sob. "I've felt so guilty, every day since he left. Some days it's so heavy, I think it's going to pull me under."

"Then this is all my fault," Vivien said quietly.

Audrey looked up at her from the floor, feeling tears run down her cheek.

"I had no idea you felt bad about it. When you said what you did about Benedict, I . . . I'd already had my doubts. It was a feeling I had not let myself dwell upon—I was too besotted." She paused, knitting and unknitting her hands in her lap. "I didn't want to listen."

"But you listened to me?"

She shook her head. "When you were staying at Hillary's, I asked my friend Warwick to come around. He knows about computers." Vivien started biting one of her nails, a habit she abhorred. "He helped me access Benedict's laptop. I had this instinct that he was hiding something there, the way he closed it whenever I walked into the room."

Audrey's eyes were pinned on her mother's face now; she had no clue what she might be about to say. "There were photos, in a file, of women. Lots of women, posing for him. Some women I had met, his 'protégées' from the studio."

"Posing for his art?" Audrey asked, hearing her naivety as soon as she said it.

"No, Audrey, not for his art." Vivien winced, clearly pained by the memory. "They were in a file marked 'Tax Returns,' and they were"—she blushed—"explicit. All date stamped, taken in the time we'd been together."

Audrey took a moment to digest this. Vivien pressed her knuckles into her other hand. "I should have told you, but I was ashamed."

"Why? What did you have to be ashamed of?"

"Because I loved him," Vivien sobbed, her face finally

breaking. "Because I loved him, even then, when I could see what he was. I still wanted him, my body wanted him. What kind of monster does that make me?"

Audrey got up from the floor now and went to sit on the bed next to her mother. She put an arm around her shoulders. "It doesn't make you a monster."

"I thought you already knew what he was. To tell you about the photos, the indignity of it, I couldn't bear it." Vivien pressed her hands over her eyes. "I have always gotten love wrong, haven't I?"

"You haven't." Audrey leaned her head against her mother's shoulder.

"Brian was the best of them, I see that now. I risked every-thing because a man flattered me and ran his hand down my shoulder blade in the mirror of a gallery."

This detail twisted something in Audrey's stomach.

"And now you're seeing Brian again," Audrey said.

"No, I—" She shook her head.

"You gave me the wrong letter—the one you meant for him."

Vivien hung her head. "I had forgotten that was in my bag." She sighed. "It wasn't something I planned. We ran into each other in Florence last month. It can't go anywhere, I know. I can't go through another divorce," Vivien said, fighting to keep her voice even.

"Maybe you need to stop marrying people then?" Audrey said, and suddenly they were both laughing. Audrey felt the release of it, like a glacier melting into a pool of warm water. It was not even especially funny, but the laughter was infectious and soon they could not stop. When they finally caught their breath, Audrey said, "I miss this. I miss how we used to be together."

"So do I." Vivien's face flinched, as though the memory

alone was enough to cause her pain. "You left when I needed you."

"I couldn't deal with seeing you so sad; I thought you blamed me. And then when I failed my exam, another failure, there was nothing for me to stay for."

"Losing you that summer was so much worse than losing Benedict. I realized how I had come to rely on you; I suppose I tried to stop being so needy after that." Vivien ruffled Audrey's hair with a hand.

"You shut me out. I thought you hated me."

"Oh, Audrey, I could never hate you. I love you more than my life." She made a "tsk" noise and then she hugged Audrey, a proper tight hug.

"Can I ask you something else, and please be honest?" Audrey asked, and Vivien nodded. "Did you think I was going to fail that math exam? Did you think I was deluded, ever thinking I could study astronomy?"

Vivien paused, weighing the question for a moment.

"I'm not surprised you failed on that occasion, no. It was a lot to ask of yourself, going back to a subject you hadn't studied in years, trying to cram it all in so quickly. Your tutor said it would have been ambitious for anyone." She paused, squeezing Audrey's hand. "But you've always been as bright as a button, darling. If you'd given yourself a proper amount of time, I'm sure you would have breezed through it. I never understood why you gave up on it, why you didn't retake it. I have made a conscious effort not to judge your career choices, the way my parents judged mine. I always felt you had a calling, though"— she pointed up—"coming from up there."

Audrey leaned into her mother and blinked back a tear. "Oh God, I've ruined everything," she said, her voice a whisper. "I think I've misread a lot of what happened back then. I wasn't honest with Josh. I had cold feet about getting married and making a mess of it."

"Like me, you mean," Vivien said ruefully.

"I'm not blaming you. This was my fault."

"I don't think bad judgment is hereditary," Vivien said, hugging Audrey close. "Besides, I never saw myself in you. You are just like your father, and he was loyal as a St. Bernard. So, what are you going to do?"

Audrey wiped her eyes and stood up.

"I'm going to wash my face. I'm going to get dressed. Then I'm going to go after Josh and win him back."

"That's my girl," said Vivien. "Nothing's over until you stop fighting for it."

51

Six Hours After I Didn't

❧

*C*lara was the only one sober enough to drive Audrey up to London. They assumed that was where Josh had gone. As soon as he heard the plan, Hillary insisted on coming too, claiming his drama training made him an expert in conflict resolution. As the car raced up the now empty A303, and Hillary fiddled with the radio station and handed out sugared almonds, Audrey might have mistaken this car ride for a fun road trip with her friends. But then her state of misery and remorse reminded her that this was no such thing.

"You know who you are?" Hillary asked, turning around to look at Audrey, squished into the backseat of Clara's car.

"Who?"

"You're Scarlett O'Hara."

"What? Why?" asked Audrey.

"Yes! You're so right, she is," said Clara, slapping the steering wheel with a palm.

"What are you talking about?" Audrey shuffled forward and pushed her head between the seats.

"*Gone with the Wind*," Hillary said, and Audrey nodded. "Remember how Scarlett is obsessed with Ashley the whole way through—he's her perfect guy, 'Ashley, Ashley, Ashley.'" Hillary affected a breathy, high-pitched voice. "And then sexy Rhett Butler rescues her, and she marries him despite thinking her heart belongs to Ashley. At the end, she finally realizes it was Rhett she loved all along, but he 'Frankly, my dear, I don't give a damn's her, and she's left right about where you are now."

Audrey scowled. "Firstly, Scarlett O'Hara is horribly selfish, so if you're saying I'm like her, then cheers. Secondly, if Josh is Rhett, are you telling me it's too late, that he's 'Frankly, my dear, I don't give a damn'ed me?"

"No, no, he's not saying that," said Clara, rubbing her earlobe between her thumb and forefinger. "Anyway, I think they get back together in the sequel."

"It's a problematic film," Hillary said, pursing his lips. "Clark Gable—I still would, though, wouldn't you? I once dated an actor who looked exactly like a short Clark Gable, he had the tiniest—"

"Okay! Can we get back to talking about *me* and *my* situation?" Audrey said.

"That is *exactly* what Scarlett O'Hara would say," said Hillary.

"Have you tried calling him?" Clara asked.

"Who, the guy who looks like Clark Gable?" Hillary asked, frowning in confusion.

"No! Josh!" said Clara.

"Yes, it's going straight to voicemail," said Audrey.

"Text?"

"No reply."

Just as she was looking at her phone, willing it to ring, a

message pinged through. Clara and Hillary both audibly inhaled.

"It's from Brian," Audrey said, unable to hide her disappointment. "He wants to know what I'd like done with the cake. Should the guests be eating it?"

They had left Brian and Vivien in charge of the abandoned wedding reception.

"Well, I can't imagine they should be bathing in it or smearing it over their clothes," Hillary said drily.

"He means do we want to keep it, save it for next time," Audrey said, rereading the message.

"Well, that's setting yourself a target—can you win Josh back before the vanilla sponge expires?"

As Audrey debated what to reply, her phone lit up with the name she wanted to see—Josh.

"There's a message from Josh," she said, her hand wavering as she opened it.

"And . . . ?" Clara asked, both hands tight on the wheel.

Audrey read the message aloud.

Please don't try to call. I am too angry and upset to speak to you right now. I'm staying at an airport hotel tonight and going to go to Ibiza in the morning. The honeymoon is nonrefundable, and I have the fundraising meeting with the Almond Project out there this week, so I need to go. You'll have the flat to yourself this week. We can talk when I'm back.

Audrey stared at the words, rereading them, willing them to be different. He sounded so cold.

"He's going on your honeymoon, without you?" Clara said. She sounded horrified.

"I wouldn't want to waste a five-star hotel in Ibiza either," said Hillary. "I mean, if you're going to be heartbroken, you may as well be heartbroken surrounded by luxury and sunshine."

"He's got a meeting out there with this tree charity he's on the board of. Oh, I don't want him to be heartbroken." Audrey felt as though her heart was being compressed in a vise. "Poor Josh."

Another text pinged through, and Audrey immediately looked back at her phone.

"Is it him again?" asked Clara.

"No. Brian's asking what I want done about the wedding presents. Oh hell, what do I want done about the wedding presents?" Audrey wailed.

"Let me deal with Brian. Cakes and crises are my forte," said Hillary, reaching back to pat Audrey on the knee.

When they arrived back at the Kennington flat, Hillary and Clara both insisted on staying the night. It was eleven o'clock now, and they didn't want Audrey to be alone. Clara went to call Jay, whom they had left behind at Millward Hall, to check he'd gotten the girls to bed without her. Hillary riffled through Audrey's cupboards, found some crisps, and then wrapped himself in a blanket on the sofa next to Audrey.

"I feel like I went a little bit mad back there," Audrey said. "It was like the wedding version of *The Shining*."

"Don't be too hard on yourself," said Hillary, putting an arm around her shoulders. "Getting married is scary at the best of times. I find it hard to commit to what I want to eat for lunch each day, let alone a lifetime of sex with only one person. Add in a few omens and heart attacks and ghosts of boyfriends past, and honestly, Audrey, it's a wonder that things went as well as they did."

"How did *anything* go well?" Audrey asked.

"Well, we're all alive to tell the tale, and everyone looked fabulous. I don't think anything's unfixable."

Audrey reached for a handful of crisps. "I think Fred was this fantasy embodiment of the perfect guy, but I never really knew him. Him showing up this weekend just reminded me of the person I was at twenty-two, when I thought I knew who I was, what I wanted. It reminded me how stuck I've been. Maybe I'm not sorted enough to get married."

"Bullshit," said Hillary, making a single clap with his hands, just as Clara came back through from the spare room.

"Excuse me?"

"I call bullshit on what you are saying. I don't like this narrative that's crept into books and films. This idea that you are not worthy of love until you have your life sorted out, that you need to be sure in your career, completely mentally stable, and happy before you can be loved. I fucking love you, whether you're a work in progress or a finished article. So should Josh, and so should *you*." Audrey had rarely seen Hillary so animated. "Do you really want to live in a world where only the sorted people get to be in love?"

"I agree," said Clara. "Do you think I'm a finished article, do you think Jay is? Everyone's just winging it, working life out as we go along."

"Weren't you saying how difficult it's been between you lately?" Audrey said with a frown. "I feel like if you and Jay find marriage tough, what hope does anyone else have?"

"Of course it's tough. I haven't slept for months, my hormones are all over the place, but I wouldn't be without Jay, not really, not for a minute." She paused. "I'm sorry if I made you think that I wasn't happy. I wasn't being fair on him earlier, he's been amazing this weekend, really stepped up with the girls.

He even suggested he could do more flexible hours when I go back to work. It's made me feel like we're a proper team again."

"Oh, thank goodness." Audrey pulled Clara down onto the sofa, so she could hug a friend in each arm. "So, you don't think I need to have a career epiphany and start going to therapy?"

"Hopefully you will do both those things, but they shouldn't be a precursor to being lovable." Hillary narrowed his eyes at her. "Even if you're always a bit indecisive and selfish, even if you change jobs as often as you change your underwear, we don't care."

Audrey felt herself tear up. "I think that's one of the nicest things anyone has ever said to me." She wiped away a tear. "Where have you put my brutally sarcastic friend?"

"Occasionally he needs a day off. Seriously, though, you should tell Josh what happened with Benedict and your mother, give him a chance to understand."

"I feel pathetic that I let that man get to me. People out there have actually been abused, have been physically hurt, and I—well, I don't think I ever felt entitled to be as upset about it as I was."

"If it upset you, you're entitled to be upset," Hillary said firmly.

"A hundred percent," said Clara.

She leaned over to Hillary to close the circle in a full group hug.

"I still can't believe Josh is going on our honeymoon without me," Audrey said softly.

"Don't look so defeated. What would Scarlett O'Hara do?" asked Hillary.

"Cry? Steal? Make herself a dress out of the curtains?"

"She would get herself on a plane to Ibiza, and she wouldn't take no for an answer," said Hillary triumphantly.

"You really think I should just turn up at the airport and insist on going too?"

"Your name is on the ticket," he replied with a shrug. "Today may have been a disaster, Audrey, but tomorrow? Tomorrow is another day."

52

Twenty Hours After I Didn't

∽

"I'm sorry, I'm afraid this ticket has been reallocated," said the woman at the airline desk.

"What do you mean, reallocated?" Audrey asked.

"I mean the cardholder who purchased the tickets has paid to reallocate the seat to a different passenger name."

Josh was taking someone else on their honeymoon?

"Who's he taking? Who's it been reallocated to?" she asked, tapping her finger against the desk.

"I can't give you that information, I'm afraid, since you are not the cardholder." The woman gave Audrey a sympathetic look. "I do have space on the flight, if you'd like to purchase a new ticket?"

Audrey bought a new ticket on a credit card and tried not to think about the expense.

Walking toward security, she kept her eyes peeled for Josh. Who would he be taking? Paul? Paul would surely have given her a heads-up first. Miranda had to be the most likely candidate. Miranda was probably not her biggest fan right now, what with Audrey kissing her date and breaking her brother's heart, all in the same evening. If there was anyone who was going to help broker a reconciliation, she didn't think it was going to be Miranda. What if it was Harriet? What if she'd somehow muscled her way in and offered herself up as a shoulder to cry on?

Hillary and Clara had both volunteered to come with her and lend moral support, but as much as Audrey had been grateful for all their help yesterday, this was something she needed to do on her own.

She didn't see Josh at the gate, and it was only when she was sitting on the plane that her confidence in her plan began to wobble. Mainly because the plan had only been thought through as far as "get on the plane to Ibiza." She literally hadn't thought beyond that. Not having a plan was usually her raison d'être, but in this situation, she felt a plan was probably required.

First, she needed to check that Josh was actually on this plane, that he hadn't changed his mind about going. So, as soon as the flight attendant said "boarding complete," she jumped out of her seat to go and peep through the curtain into business class. Audrey only got halfway up the aisle before she was ushered back with a firm smile by a female flight attendant.

"If you could take your seat please now, miss."

Audrey shuffled back to her seat, feeling foolish. The redheaded man next to her turned to her with a panicked expression.

"Were you trying to get off the plane? Are you scared of flying? Do you think there's something wrong with this plane?"

"No, not at all. I'm so sorry," she said, and then realized she'd grabbed his arm rather than the seat rest. "I'm fine with flying, I doubt there's anything wrong with the plane. I'm just a little on edge—long story."

"I'm Clive," said the man, offering her his hand. He had bright red hair, freckly skin, and a warm, paunchy face. "I am afraid of flying, so sorry if I get a little jittery when we take off." Looking again at Clive, she saw his brow was beading with sweat. "I get worried about the engine noises."

The airplane made a noise and Clive flinched.

"I'm sorry. You'll be fine, I think statistically you're more likely to die at a water park or something."

"Really?" Clive looked hopeful.

"Maybe it was a boating accident or a car crash? I'm not helping, am I? Is there anything I can do?" Audrey asked.

"Your long story might be a welcome distraction."

That's how Audrey ended up telling a man she'd just met about the events of the last forty-eight hours. She told him all about Fred, about the bad-omen bat and the reverend having a heart attack. She told him about the bride jumping off the cake and the band playing "Singin' in the Rain" and Fred kissing her in the photo booth in front of Josh. She explained that her almost-husband was sitting up in business class with someone else, she didn't know who, and she'd bought a new ticket to try and win him back.

As Clive became more and more absorbed by her story, he started to look more relaxed about the engine noises, and by the end he appeared perfectly serene.

"Well, Audrey, as I'm hearing it, you know what you want now," said Clive, patting her hand gently on the armrest. "I think the key to seeking forgiveness is giving up on the hope that the past could have been any different. You have to accept what has been in order to become."

Audrey did a double take. Was she sitting next to the male Oprah?

"Excuse me. I couldn't help but overhear all that," said the middle-aged women on Clive's left. "But this is the most outlandish story I've ever heard."

Clive and Audrey both turned to the woman.

"No one has that much bad luck on one wedding day."

"Well, it all happened." Audrey shrugged. "I guess it does sound kind of crazy now that I'm saying it out loud."

"Go and see if he's up there. We need to know how this ends," said the woman. "I'm Elena, by the way."

"Audrey," said Audrey.

"Clive," said Clive.

After peering around to ensure the flight attendant was nowhere in sight, Audrey scuttled back up the aisle, weaving through passengers waiting for the toilets. When she finally got to the curtain and peeped through, she saw Josh immediately. She would have recognized his thick head of hair anywhere. *Yes! He was on the plane!* She couldn't see who was sitting next to him, though.

"Miss, I'm afraid you can't go through there." The same flight attendant yanked the curtain closed and furnished her with another hard stare.

"Oh, I know, I'm just looking for someone," Audrey said, attempting her most disarming smile. "My fiancé is up there, I'm surprising him. He doesn't know I'm here." Both of those statements were true. The woman's face instantly transformed. "I wanted to make a grand gesture," Audrey went on. "Maybe you'd let me use the PA system so I could let him know I'm here?" Audrey conjured an image of declaring to the whole plane how sorry she was. Maybe she could sing a song like Adam Sandler did in *The Wedding Singer*. She had nothing prepared, but she could probably make something up on the spot.

"No one uses the PA system," said the flight attendant sharply, as though Audrey had just asked if she could man the controls of the plane and fly a loop-the-loop. Then she tilted her head to a sympathetic angle. "Look, if you wanted to nip in there, just to say hello, I'll make an exception, just this once."

"Thank you so much," Audrey said, slipping through the class divide.

Josh was sitting with his eyes closed, listening to headphones. He looked exhausted, and in the chair next to him was—

"Granny Parker? You brought Granny Parker?" Audrey said, causing Josh to open his eyes and remove his headphones.

"Audrey?"

Audrey noticed that all the other passengers were now looking at her, and she crouched down to be less conspicuous. "You brought Granny Parker on our honeymoon?"

Josh sighed. "She has a lung condition. Her doctor said a holiday in the sun could do her good." On cue, Granny Parker coughed weakly.

"Look, I'm so sorry about everything. Yesterday was completely insane. I don't want to make excuses, but please, can we talk?" Audrey said, ignoring Granny Parker and focusing on Josh. "That can't be how we leave things—you running off to the airport without me."

"Me running off?" Josh said, shaking his head in bemusement. "Me *running off* is not the reason you're not here beside me. You having another man's photo in your wallet all this time and then kissing this guy on *our* wedding day is the reason." He spoke calmly, quietly, but he was clearly still furious.

Granny Parker tutted and shook her head. Audrey was suddenly very aware of every ear in business class now tuned in to their conversation.

"I knew it wouldn't end well, as soon as we hit traffic on the way out of London. I felt it in my knuckles," muttered Granny Parker.

"Please, Josh . . ."

"And then the one thing I asked of you—to give me some space—and you couldn't even do that, Audrey."

"I didn't want you going away thinking I was in love with someone else! I'm not. I swear I'm not, I can explain—"

"Is this woman bothering you, sir?" The flight attendant was back and standing over Audrey, frowning as she realized this was not the romantic reunion she had been promised.

"She is," said Granny Parker stoutly. "She is bothering us."

"Josh?" Audrey pleaded.

"I am going to have to ask you to go back to your seat, miss," said the flight attendant.

"Josh, please," Audrey tried again, but he wouldn't meet her eye. He looked so miserable. All Audrey wanted to do was reach out and hug him, but now the flight attendant was taking her arm and physically frog-marching her back to her seat. She could feel the eyes of disapproval from the other passengers, as though she had broken some code of conduct by daring to step on the wrong side of the blue curtain.

"Shame on you," muttered a woman two rows behind Josh.

"Your fiancé?" the flight attendant asked, her sarcasm clear.

"He is, he was. It's just a misunderstanding," Audrey said, but then they were through the curtain and the attendant drew it firmly closed behind her.

As she sat back down in her seat, a girl in the row behind leaned forward and asked, "So, who's he here with?" Audrey turned around in bemusement to see who was asking her this. The girl was in her twenties; she had platinum-blond hair and several lip piercings. "I'm Keeley, I overheard the whole story. I'm kind of invested now."

"His grandmother," Audrey said, too deflated to even care that half the plane had overheard her story.

"Wow," said Elena. "I wouldn't have called that. I thought it would have been the sister for sure."

"I thought it was going to be the best man," said someone two rows behind Keeley. *Exactly how far back had her story gone?* She turned around, and Keeley said, "We're all together, all the way back to row eighteen. We were taking bets on who it might be."

"All of you?" Audrey turned to look at the group of people behind her, and some of them waved.

"We're all dancers. We work the clubs," said a woman with short blue hair next to Keeley.

"You and Josh should come down to Pacha if you patch things up," Keeley suggested brightly. "I can get you on the guest list."

"Maybe Josh needs some cooling-off time? Perhaps the plane isn't the best location for this conversation," said Clive thoughtfully.

"Excuse me," came a voice from the plane corridor. It was a man in a leather jacket queuing to use the bathroom between business class and economy. "I couldn't help but overhear, and I'm afraid I'm Team Josh on this one."

"Wait, what? Who are you?" Audrey asked.

"Oliver Bevan. I'm sitting up there in business and I over-heard your little speech, we all did. Have you told your friends back here that you kissed someone else on your wedding day?"

"She didn't kiss someone else, this other bloke kissed her," shouted some random man five rows back. "Get your facts straight, Oliver Bevan."

"Doesn't sound like she stopped the kiss, though, did she?" said the flight attendant, who had now joined in the conversation.

Audrey buried her head in her hands, and Clive gave her a gentle pat on the shoulder.

"I think you should just leave the poor man alone," said a woman with gray hair, wearing dark orange lipstick, who had poked her head through the curtain.

"Team Audrey! Team Audrey!" Keeley's group started chanting.

This was going to be a long flight.

53

Twenty-Five Hours After I Didn't

osh was pacing, waiting for Audrey in arrivals. Granny Parker was sitting in one of the plastic chairs, nose deep in yet another Jilly Cooper novel. This woman was a fast reader.

"What is going on?" Josh asked, his brow knitted in confusion. "Why were people chanting 'Team Audrey' at me at the bag carousel?"

"People get weirdly emotionally invested on planes. Look, can we go somewhere and talk, just the two of us, please, Josh?"

"I don't want to have a big conversation right now, and I don't want the whole plane knowing my affairs," Josh said, holding up a hand. "I just needed to check you have somewhere to stay, that you haven't followed me here on one of your whims, when it's peak season and everywhere will be booked up."

That's exactly what she had done.

"No, I've figured it out," she lied, hoping she could make it true.

Josh looked skeptical but then hit a palm against his forehead, as though angry at himself for still worrying about her admin concerns when he was furious with her.

"I'm sorry I came, when you asked me to give you space, but I want to explain. Maybe in a few days, when you've had a chance to—"

"To what? Get over it? This isn't like you losing your mobile for the fiftieth time or locking yourself out of the flat again, Audrey. You can't fix this just because you feel bad." His eyes began to well up and a muscle pulsed by his jaw.

Audrey got her wallet out of her handbag and riffled through it, pulling out the only two photos she now kept inside. One she'd taken of him in Covent Garden, when he was still Bad Jeans Josh; the other was of them both at the bar at Ben and Dee's wedding, caught midlaugh over drink parasols.

"Look, I always had you in my wallet too. I know I shouldn't have kept the ones of Fred, but they were just a memory of who I used to be. You have to believe me, I didn't initiate that kiss at the wedding. I don't want him, I want you," Audrey pleaded.

"The thing is, I've been thinking about it all night, and whether you kissed him back or not, I don't think that's even the relevant part. Yes, our wedding was a disaster, but if we'd been a real team, if you'd been excited to marry me, you would have rolled with the punches. I didn't see anything that happened yesterday as a 'bad omen' or a sign that I shouldn't be marrying you." Granny Parker coughed loudly into her book behind them. "But it made you doubt everything. Life is going to bring falling bats, heart attacks, probably even temptation from other people. If we can't weather these things on our wedding day, what hope do we have for the next fifty years?" He paused, his eyes wide and full of sadness. "You know what I always admired about my parents' marriage? They're a great team. They've faced their share of challenges, but they were always in it together. I think I realized last night that I love you— God, I love you, Audrey—but we're not a team. I don't know if we ever have been." He took a deep breath and looked at her with such a defeated look that she didn't know how to respond. Then he turned back to Granny Parker, picked up their bags, and walked out of the airport.

Audrey felt herself physically deflate. She'd been so anxious to talk to Josh, to explain, but now that she'd spoken to him, she felt even worse. *What if this wasn't fixable?*

꙰꙰꙰

$\mathcal{A}$s usual, Josh was right. There seemed to be no hotels on the island with any availability. After scrolling through online booking portals for a good half hour, she finally found somewhere called Foamtopia that had a few single rooms available.

Audrey followed the GPS on her rental car to an ugly highrise hotel in San Antonio, on the west side of the island. It soon became clear why Foamtopia had availability. In the lobby, women walked around in bikinis and high heels, and a team of cleaners were sponging down the bar floor in preparation for something ominously named "Foam O'clock."

This was a far cry from the Mirador Agroturismo, where she was supposed to be staying. The Mirador had an on-site goat farm, a meditation yurt, an olive press, and a hot-stone spa. Audrey took a wild guess that Foamtopia had none of those things.

"Would you like Foam dollars?" the receptionist asked in perfect English.

"What are Foam dollars?"

"Cash gets damp, so we offer Foam dollars to use at the bar."

"I won't be attending the foam party," Audrey said.

"Oh, you can't stay at Foamtopia and not come to the foam party," said the receptionist cheerfully while handing over a complimentary waterproof lanyard pouch. "Best foam party in Ibiza."

Things didn't look any better once she'd lugged her case upstairs. Her room resembled a walk-in cupboard, with white bars on the window, and there was a waterproof cover on the mattress that made a crunching sound when she sat down. There were no carpets in the room, only porous blue matting, which made Audrey wonder if the foam was going to start coming out of her bedroom ceiling.

Lying on her bed, she turned on her phone for the first time since last night. She had hundreds of messages from friends, asking why she and Josh had left the party so early. Others seemed oblivious to how the wedding had ended; Traci had sent a photo of herself dancing in just her bra and skirt, with the message "Great wedding! Have a fab honeymoon!" No one seemed to know the real story.

Audrey didn't reply to anyone; she didn't know what to say. She just sent messages to Vivien, Hillary, and Clara saying she'd arrived safely in Ibiza and that she'd found somewhere to stay. None of them needed to know it was a foam-proof cell on the eighth floor of a tower block.

In her inbox, she found an e-mail from Miranda.

Dear Audrey,

You and Josh both have your phones off, so I'm sending this in the hope that you might be picking up e-mails. I don't know what happened yesterday, Fred was acting erratically after you left but he wouldn't say why. We got the train back to London this morning and that's when he told me about how you two met six years ago and—dated? Connected? I'm not sure what you'd call it. You can imagine how strange I felt, especially hearing it from him rather than you.

I don't know what to think, Audrey. Clearly you and Josh had an argument and then left, without saying anything to anyone. Did you argue about Fred? Or the wedding? Are you in Ibiza together now?

Look, if I played any part in this, I am so sorry. I should never have brought a man I hardly knew to your wedding. Honestly, the way Fred was talking about you—about how "fate had intervened"—he sounded like a bit of a lunatic. I can't believe any of his feelings were reciprocated. Surely Josh knows that?

While we were on the train back to London, midconversation, Fred noticed that his watch had stopped at almost the exact moment he checked the time. The train had just pulled into a station, and there was a poster that said "Time to Leave" hanging outside, and you know what he did? He got off the train, right there, at Bridgwater. He messaged me later to apologize, but he felt the watch and the poster were telling him to get off the train. Seriously, who does that?

On a more positive note, I did as you suggested and talked to Paul at the wedding. We are going for coffee next week. Whatever it was you said to him, thank you. It would be nice to be friends with him again if nothing else.

I hope you can sort out this misunderstanding with Josh and then come back and get married properly. Let me know what I can do, if anything.

Oh, and sorry for crying on you yesterday, I just got my period today, so that explains a lot.

Love from Miranda

This e-mail from Miranda cemented something Audrey already knew—Fred was not the man for her; he was certainly not her "soul mate." On that day six years ago, he had swept her off her feet; she had been awed by him, his buzz of energy, bright as the Dog Star. It was the first time she had really fallen for someone, and it had left its mark. But what she knew about Fred had been a few dots in the sky; she had filled in the rest of the picture. Clearly, he was whimsical, impulsive, maybe a little selfish. He had not even been single that day they met. Her fantasy had obscured reality.

Audrey wanted to call Miranda, to hear a friendly voice, to say how pleased she was about Paul. But she also wanted to work things out for herself first, not involve anyone else. What she needed was to think of a grand gesture, a show of how much she loved Josh and how much of a team player she could be.

She googled "Big romantic gestures to win him back" and found a helpful list. Josh loved lists; maybe she would find the answer here.

Romantic gestures to show him you care:

1. *Cook his favorite meal.*
2. *Tag him in a funny meme you think he will like.*
3. *Plan a romantic vacation.*
4. *Cuddle him in bed.*
5. *Pre-cool or pre-heat his car for him, so it's the perfect temperature when he gets in.*

Who invented the Internet? These were all terrible ideas. Maybe a grand gesture wasn't the way to go. Maybe she just needed to be honest. She needed to make him see that she was a team player (even if she was one of the crap players who spent most of the game on the bench). And if that didn't work, then she could think about getting an "I heart Josh" tattoo and maybe sending him some funny memes.

$\mathcal{U}$nsurprisingly, Foamtopia turned out not to be the best place for a restorative night's sleep. Not only was Audrey's single bed the width of an ironing board, but the foam party downstairs went on until the small hours of the morning. Every time she thought the pounding bass through the floor had stopped, a few seconds later, it started up again. At two a.m., she gave up trying to sleep and went to lie on the beach. The stars were out, the same stars she'd seen on Friday night from the garden of Millward Hall. They shone just the same, completely oblivious to the fact that her whole world had combusted like a supernova.

Her father's letter was still in her bag. After the drama of yesterday, she had held off opening it. She wanted to be in the right frame of mind, to savor reading these final words from her father, because there would be no more. Now, lying alone in the sand beneath the crescent moon, it felt like the right time. She pulled the creased letter from her handbag and opened it, bracing herself for another mistake, another letter meant for someone else. But it wasn't.

Darling Audrey,
I will always think of you as my little girl, but one day I imagine you will grow up. One day you will be a

woman; you might even get married and feel that I should have been there. As I sit at my desk, writing the closing scenes of my life's work, I realize this future imagined day is the one I will be most sad to miss.

So, I am writing you something for that day. Firstly, to say I am sorry not to be there. I am sorry that my absence might add a somber note to a happy day. I am sorry I will not meet the person you have chosen to spend your life with. When I imagine this person, I hope they are kind, I hope they are selfless, I hope they are happy to build you up and watch you shine, because, trust me, some people won't do that, however much they profess to love you. I hope loving them makes you see the world as a brighter place and gives your heart a safe harbor in which to thrive. My main advice for you, my darling, is never give up on love. Never. Give. Up.

You are the best story I ever began, Audrey—and I trust you to write the middle and the end. Remember, we are all simply atoms of stardust, you need only look up to find me.

All my love, Dad

It was as though he knew the exact words she needed to hear. Audrey wiped away a tear. "Thanks, Dad," she said aloud to the sky.

54

Two Days After I Didn't

❦

*A*udrey woke up the next morning full of fresh resolve. Her night alone had allowed her time to pull her thoughts into focus, to work out what she wanted to say. She threw on a sundress and picked up the keys to her rental car.

As she drove across the island toward Josh's hotel, Audrey reflected on some of the clarity she'd gained last night on the beach. She knew that in any relationship there would be conversations about council tax and arguments about who left crumbs in the bed. There would be friends the other person didn't love as much as you did, hobbies you didn't share, and that was okay—that was real life, not just the highlights reel. Love couldn't be all dancing around bandstands or throwing yourself off Ferris wheels—frankly, that would be exhausting. Perhaps love was not about finding a jigsaw piece to fit you or a mirror to reflect you, it was simply about finding another human being who made your heart sing. Why did it all seem *so* obvious to her now? Would she be too late to convince Josh she knew all this?

Never. Give. Up.

The Mirador Agroturismo was an exclusive boutique hotel on the east side of the island, near Cala Llonga. The sprawling villa was all square white walls, dark wooden shutters, and tasteful wicker furniture. As she walked up the pebble pathway, under a trellis of pink bougainvillea, Audrey tried not to feel sorry for herself that she wasn't staying there. The hotel looked just like it did on the website. Neat palm trees lined a pale blue, kidney-shaped pool. There were artfully placed wooden sun loungers with plush taupe cushions, and at the far end of the pool, two white four-poster beds with billowing linen drapes. It looked like the set of a music video, or somewhere Gwyneth Paltrow's de-stressing therapist might come to de-stress.

To the left of the pool was a polished wooden bar. To the right, a cobbled patio framing an old olive press, and around the corner she could just make out the goat field and massage yurt. She remembered looking over Josh's shoulder when he found this place. It had been his turn to choose their holiday, so everything had been planned to perfection. She even knew which room they'd booked and recognized the Juliet balcony of the honeymoon suite, overlooking the patio.

Well, if it was good enough for Romeo, it was good enough for her. Surely there was something romantic about proclaiming your love from beneath a balcony? The hotel looked practically deserted, with only a uniformed barman behind the bar and one elderly man in swimming trunks, facedown on a sun lounger. It was siesta time, everyone was probably asleep, which worked in Audrey's favor—she didn't need an audience for this.

Standing below the balcony, she called up, "Josh! Josh!"

What would she do if he wasn't here? She called his name again, just as a figure opened the door to the balcony. Audrey couldn't see his face, with the sun shining right into her eyes.

"Josh, it's me! I just want to say one thing, and then I promise I'll leave you alone for the rest of the week," she called up to the balcony, shading her eyes with a hand. "When I met you, I don't think I was looking for love, but you showed me how amazing it can be. You ground me, in the best possible way. That guy, Fred, might have been a long-ago what-if, but, Josh, you are my 'what is.' I'm so sorry that I hurt you. And you know, I don't think love is destined, I think you choose who's worth fighting for, and, Josh, I choose you. I'd choose you every time. I just hope you can forgive me for ever giving you a reason to doubt that."

"Audrey?" A figure stepped out of the shadows, and Audrey saw that it wasn't Josh standing at the balcony. It was Granny Parker.

"Oh hi, Granny Parker." Audrey felt her shoulders slump in disappointment, her chest redden, and her brow start to sweat. "Is Josh there? That was kind of meant for him."

"That depends." Granny Parker adjusted the hotel robe she was wearing. "Is there more to this speech of yours?"

"Um, no. That was pretty much it," Audrey said, offended. She thought that had been a pretty good speech. People were coming out of the hotel now, populating the bar and pool area. Some guests eyed her with idle curiosity as she stood calling up to the balcony. Before she could think of what to say next, a voice by the pool squealed, "Audrey!"

It was Keeley, the girl from the plane. She was wearing a huge straw sun hat and a bright blue shoulderless playsuit. "Oh my God, it *is* you! Jenny, look, it's Audrey from the plane— Team Audrey!" The whole group of dancers from the plane was here. *Was everyone staying in the lap of luxury but her?*

"Is Josh here? Are you trying to get back with him?" cried Keeley. "Oh my God, are you staying here?"

Audrey opened her mouth to reply, but then Granny Parker gave an indiscreet cough.

"Sorry, I'm kind of in the middle of something here," she explained to Keeley, nodding toward the balcony.

One of the managers from the hotel had come out of the reception building and was now walking briskly toward Audrey.

"Don't worry, she's with me," Granny Parker called down. "She's come to deliver a romantic speech."

"Well, I've kind of done the speech, I don't have much more to say," Audrey said, wiping her brow with the back of her hand. Romantic declarations really should be appreciated for quality, not quantity.

"I bet it's going to be dead romantic," said one of Keeley's friends, clapping her hands in excitement.

Audrey looked back and forth between the group by the pool, the confused hotel manager, and Granny Parker. Keeley and her friends had shifted their loungers in her direction, ready for whatever performance they thought they were about to witness.

"If you want to be romantic, you should sing it," offered an elegant Spanish woman who had now joined the crowd of onlookers.

"Definitely do a song," said Keeley, clapping. "Everyone loves a song."

Audrey felt the flush of embarrassment creep across every inch of her skin. "I don't have anything prepared . . . ," she muttered, but the crowd of guests were now all watching her, waiting expectantly.

"I'd like to hear a song," said Granny Parker brightly. "I'm sure Josh would too."

Audrey thought back to the conversation she'd had with

Josh about romantic gestures. Hadn't he once joked that all the great love stories end with a dance routine? Fine, if this was what it took to get Josh to come out here—a public, musical declaration, in front of all these people—then so be it. Audrey closed her eyes and was trying to think where to start when Keeley cried, "Wait!"

Audrey snapped her head left, to see Keeley having a quick word with the barman. He turned on a music system and a backing beat started to play on outdoor speakers. It gave Audrey something to work with, and she started to sing, freestyling as best she could.

> "Oh, Josh, you are the only man for me,
> I love you more than all the stars I see.
> Josh, you're so great with my mum,
> And you're really good at making me . . . laugh."

Audrey trailed off as she took in the crowd, who were looking on in bemusement. She was quickly losing confidence in this idea, and in her ability to make up appropriate lyrics on the spot. Keeley must have sensed she needed support, because she clapped her hands at her friends and then four of them rushed in to start dancing encouragingly behind Audrey.

Looking up, Audrey could see the shadow of a figure in the room behind Granny Parker. Josh was up there; she needed to keep singing.

> "Josh, I love that you moved a tree for me,
> And every morning you bring me tea.
> I'll try and stop getting crumbs on our bedding,
> I'm just so sorry that I ruined our wedding!"

Her pitch had gotten steadily higher as she'd gone on. Audrey was many things, but she was not a good singer. Behind her, the backing dancers had started trying to help her out by singing a refrain of "Josh, Josh, forgive her, Josh, Josh," and snapping their fingers as they danced.

Audrey glanced over at Keeley, who was nodding along appreciatively and filming the whole spectacle on her phone. Looking behind her, she could see the backing dancers were excellent. Maybe this really was going to work. Who wouldn't be won over by a live, improvised musical number outside their hotel room? Audrey joined in with the dancers' refrain of "Josh, Josh, forgive her, Josh, Josh," and even attempted a little twirl. Then there was a loud bang and pink glitter rained down from the sky.

Audrey turned to see a girl next to Keeley holding what looked like a glitter cannon.

"Liz! We needed that for tonight," cried Keeley.

"Sorry, it felt like a glitter cannon moment," said Liz. "I always carry one in my bag for emergencies."

Audrey had run out of words; she also had glitter in her mouth and her nostrils. The backing dancers stopped singing, and they all looked up and waited for Granny Parker, or indeed Josh, to say something.

"Well, that was impressive," Granny Parker declared at last. "But I'm afraid Josh isn't here."

The figure beside her stepped forward, and Audrey could see that it was a man dressed in the hotel's burgundy uniform. "Me and Samuel from housekeeping thoroughly enjoyed it, though."

Audrey sighed. All that glitter and embarrassment for nothing. The crowd of hotel guests by the pool were all staring, and Keeley was still filming on her phone.

"Please don't post that anywhere, Keeley," she said, hanging her head in disappointment.

"Wait there, I'm coming down," called Granny Parker.

Audrey shuffled over to find a table by the pool bar, smiling awkwardly at all the people who had witnessed her failed performance. When Granny Parker arrived, she was wearing huge black sunglasses, a giant sun hat, and a hotel robe. She took a seat imperiously opposite Audrey.

"So, Josh isn't here. Will he be back soon?" Audrey asked, anxious to know where he had gone.

"They don't have places like this in Yorkshire, you know." Granny Parker was not in any kind of hurry to put Audrey out of her misery. "You ask for anything here and they bring it to you. They even found me a Yorkshire tea bag last night, I feel like the queen of Sheba."

"Yes, it's a nice place. And Josh is . . . ?"

"He slept on the sofa bed last night but then decided he didn't want to stay here. He's given me the room."

"So where is he now?" Audrey tried to hide her irritation that this information hadn't been imparted to her ten minutes ago, before the song and the backing dancers and the glitter cannon.

"The tree people he's meeting with on Friday told him about a new farm they might invest in. He volunteered to do a recce, take some photos, meet the owners. They've offered to put him up for a few nights while he's there."

Audrey felt crushed. Here she was, thinking of nothing but Josh, and meanwhile he was getting on with his life without her. He was using their failed honeymoon as a chance to do something useful. Granny Parker must have noticed her face fall, because she said, "Don't worry, he's still mardy and miserable. He hasn't forgotten he's heartbroken."

The older woman let out a long exhale. "Listen to me, Audrey. All I heard in that speech and that song of yours was what you want. Maybe it's time you asked yourself what Josh might want. Why does he need *you*? How do you make *him* happy?" She paused. "Love and marriage, it's a two-way street. You need more than a showy performance; you need to ask yourself what it is you bring to the party."

Audrey sat back in her chair and nodded slowly. Granny Parker was right. All this time, she'd been wondering if Josh was her one true love and had not stopped to think about whether she was his.

"You're right. I've been self-involved and selfish."

"Well, everyone's capable of change." Granny Parker paused.

Audrey nodded, grateful for her softer tone.

"And I'll say your heavy soul looks a little lighter than it did before. He still loves you. Where there's love, there's hope. Have you got the Yorkshire soil I gave you?" Audrey nodded. "Then dig deep, and I'm sure you'll think of something."

With that, she tapped a sharp finger against Audrey's chest, and Audrey felt the seed of an idea planted.

55

Four Days After I Didn't

❧

*A*udrey was sunburned, her hands were blistered, and her back was killing her. It had been a grueling couple of days, but her bones sang with the warmth of purpose. The work had given her clarity; the work had given her time to think. She had persuaded Granny Parker to contrive a way to bring Josh to the almond farm today; the rest would be up to her.

As Audrey sat waiting under one of the blossoming trees, she saw Josh and his grandmother walking up from the car park toward her. Her heart beat hard in her chest. She had planned everything this time. She knew exactly what she wanted to say, but she still didn't know if it would be enough. Even from a distance, she could see in Josh's face that he had softened, though there was a sadness in his gait and the roll of his shoulders. When he saw her, he hesitated, just for a moment. She saw his shoulders lift and then fall as though he was taking a deep breath.

As they came closer to where she was sitting, Audrey stood up, but Josh was the first to speak. "Granny Parker told me she wanted to see the farm. I see she had ulterior motives."

"If you want me to go—" said Audrey.

"It's okay," said Josh.

Granny Parker patted Josh on the arm. "I'll go read my book in the car. Just reached a juicy bit, so take your time."

Josh gave a single nod. He was wearing a white linen shirt and blue shorts and had caught the sun on his face. They fell into step beside each other walking through the grove of trees. "Your skin looks red. How long have you been waiting out here in the heat?" he asked.

"I'm fine, just a little warm. Do you still have your meeting with the owner, Leon, tomorrow?" Audrey asked.

"Yes, he's going to be happy. With the funds we've raised, we're hoping to be able to support buying and replanting several more groves. They're such an important part of the island's history."

"That's wonderful." She paused, unsure how to begin.

"Look, I'm sorry I wasn't ready to talk before, at the wedding or at the airport," Josh said. "I was worried I would say something I might later regret."

"You don't need to apologize." Audrey took a breath. "Look, I know I might not be able to fix what I broke, but there are things I want to tell you. They're not the reason things went wrong on Saturday, they're things I should have shared with you before."

Josh nodded silently, and they carried on walking up the gentle slope of the almond grove. That's where she told him. She told him about Benedict, about her day with Fred and the next day when he didn't come; she told him about her relationship with her mother and how it had changed after Benedict came into their lives. She told him about the panic attack she'd had in the math exam, how it had dented her confidence to pursue anything academic. She explained that keeping those photos had been more about preserving an image of who she had been before any of that happened. Josh walked beside her and listened. Gradually, the space between them narrowed until they were side by side, their arms almost touching.

"I'm sorry that happened to you, that he came between you and your mother, that he made you doubt yourself."

"I don't want to blame anyone else. Everyone hits road bumps in life; maybe I didn't navigate mine too well."

At the top of the low-walled field, they came to a row of saplings freshly planted in newly dug red earth. Josh pointed them out. "These are all new trees. They must have had a fresh wave of volunteers."

"I planted them," she said.

"What, all of them?" He raised his eyebrows.

"Yes. That's why I'm sunburned and sweaty. Turns out I'm still terrible at digging." She bent down beside one of the saplings and showed him the label she had tied around one of the branches. "I wanted to show you that I am on our team." On the label she had written: "Josh and Audrey." "These aren't your trees, or my trees, they're our trees."

Josh smiled, and the relief of seeing him smile again made her heart sing.

"Audrey, this must have taken you all morning."

"It took me two days," she said, slightly indignantly.

"Two days?" His eyes grew wide in disbelief.

"Yes, I was here all yesterday and the day before too. This was my big romantic gesture." She frowned. "What? I'm a slow digger!"

They fell into step again, walking along the row of trees Audrey had planted. His hand lightly brushed hers, and she tingled with nerves. "I know I've been selfish, not just about the wedding. I think I've taken you for granted, all the things you bring to my life, your generosity, your kindness, how straightforward you are. But I hope there are things I bring to your life too. I think I push you to try new things, even if it's only a berry-flavored latte or asking for what you want at work. You used to live in a flat with empty white walls and now our home is full of color."

"Yes, you do all those things," he said, his voice warm with affection now.

"So yes, I have my head in the stars and you have your roots firmly anchored in the ground, but I think that's why we work. And I still might not have found my calling in life, I might not be able to make up my mind about what flowers I want in a church or what I want to eat for dinner, but I know I want to spend my life with you. It's the only thing I've ever been certain of."

Josh reached out and took her hand. "Don't think that you having a midwedding life crisis would be enough to stop me from loving you."

"You still love me?" she repeated, and he nodded. Audrey jumped up and down in the field, which made Josh smile.

"It doesn't mean you're off the hook entirely, I just—" Josh frowned. "I hate that Benedict made you doubt yourself, and that you didn't tell me any of this stuff before."

"I know, I should have . . ." She paused, overjoyed to see the sparkle back in his eyes. "Was it the trees that swung it? Was it worth the blisters?" She looked up at him hopefully.

"You had me before the trees," he said. "You had me way before the trees."

"So, you *do* pay attention during rom-coms." She shook her head.

"Sometimes." He grinned.

"I didn't even need to do all this digging, then?"

"No. But I'm glad you did."

And then Josh leaned in to kiss her, and Audrey felt that maybe this was the beginning and not the end.

56

Two Weeks After I Didn't

❧

To: audreylavery@gmail.com
From: themuseumofobsolescence@home.com
Subject: An apology

Dear Audrey,

Sorry for jumping into your inbox. I know you probably don't want to hear from me. I managed to track down your e-mail address from Miranda, but I promise I won't contact you again, unless you ask me to.

Firstly, I'm sorry everything got so heated at the wedding. You made your choice and I respect that. I strongly believe in fate guiding us to what we need, and I couldn't believe fate hadn't led me to that wedding for you, but clearly, I misread the signs.

I told you about my Museum of Obsolescence, the objects I collect with no use in the modern day. Their time has passed, and they are now a part of history. Perhaps the people we were in that photo booth now belong in my museum.

I recently learned that Millward Hall sits on two converging ley lines. There's a concentration of ancient, primordial energy there—which might explain why things got so intense. I don't know if you believe in these things, but I do.

On the way home from Somerset, I got off the train at Bridgwater; I just sensed that I should. I walked cross-country, all the way to the Glastonbury stone circle. There is so much energy around those stones, it was like being in a vortex. It's hard to explain if you haven't experienced it.

Why am I telling you all this? Well, I remember you telling me about multiverse theory when we met—how, if there is an infinite number of universes, then there is an infinite number of ways our lives will have played out. Somewhere out there, every life you might have led will be happening. When I was lying down in the middle of the stone circle, I had this vision of another world, where we didn't lose each other's numbers, where I didn't get knocked off my bike, where Photo Booth Boy and Photo Booth Girl were both at Baker Street to meet each other that Sunday six years ago. It was so clear, Audrey, this glimpse. I just wanted you to know that alternate us, we were happy. You were a vet and made mini ceramic dogs in your free time, if that detail is of any interest.

So, no regrets about this reality, have a great life, and maybe I'll catch you in the next one.

All my positive cosmic energy,

Fred

To: themuseumofobsolescence@home.com
From: audreylavery@gmail.com
Subject: Re: An apology
    Dear Fred,
    Thanks for your e-mail, and for your apology,
I appreciate it. I don't think I am Photo Booth Girl
anymore, but if she's happy somewhere, then I'm
glad. For me, I think maybe that initial spark, that
first meeting, could be written in the stars, but it is
only the first page—the rest of the story we have to
write for ourselves.
    Best wishes and good-bye,
    Audrey

꙳

Clara: Did you know there's a video of you on TikTok, down on one knee, singing some terrible song to Josh?!? Search #proposalfails

Audrey: Oh no, bloody Keeley! How do I take it down?

Clara: Er you can't. It's gone viral. People are doing electro remixes of your song (attached). "Josh, Josh, forgive her, Josh, Josh," is now a meme. Jay says to tell you that singing is definitely not your calling. I think it's sweet. Where did you get the glitter cannon?

Josh: Having the strangest day. People keep singing this weird song at me.

Josh: Someone just sent me the video. 😱

Audrey: I was going to tell you about that . . . 😖 Didn't you say all the great love stories end in a dance routine?

57

Six Months After I Didn't

❧

*I*t was a small wedding. Just close family and a few best friends. Audrey hadn't wanted to go back to Millward Hall; the church was too big, the acoustics too intimidating, the place too full of bad memories and converging ley lines (apparently). Reverend Daniels had made a full recovery and wished them both well, wherever they decided to get married.

They ended up choosing a tiny church in Sussex, where Audrey's father's family were originally from. It was in fact one of the smallest chapels in the UK and only had room for twenty people. As soon as Audrey stepped inside, she knew this was the place. She and Josh had planned every detail between them this time—just twenty guests, wildflowers, Spanish tapas, and a playlist of songs with a decent speaker. There wasn't a salmon terrine or a lilac napkin in sight.

When she'd finally unpacked her bag from the first wedding, Audrey had found the bride figurine with the face scraped off wrapped up in her crumpled wedding dress. Carefully, she repainted an enormous smile. No one could find the groom from the original cake, so Audrey bought a new one. She searched online through hundreds of figurines until she found one that looked like Josh. The wedding cake was a chocolate mocha gâteau. Audrey chose it herself. The little bride and groom stood together shin-deep in chocolate ganache. They looked incredibly happy—this little bride wasn't jumping anywhere.

Vivien accompanied her daughter in the car to the church and held her hand as they walked up the churchyard path. Vivien had separated from Lawrence and was now seeing Brian again. They were taking things slowly, but Audrey hadn't seen her mother this buoyant in years. She was laughing more, stressing less. She and Audrey had fallen into a new routine of spending Sunday afternoons together, just the two of them, the way they used to.

"Your dress is perfect. You look so much like yourself, darling."

"Thank you, so do you," said Audrey.

"No allergies today?"

Audrey checked her arms. "None."

This time, she had chosen a long-sleeved, forties-style, ivory evening gown with a slit up the front. She had found it in a vintage store and chosen it for no other reason than that she felt fabulous wearing it. She didn't need to wear her mother's old dress to feel close to her.

Before Vivien went to take her seat in the church, she pulled Audrey into a hug. There was no rigidity in her frame, no urge to pull away; they just held each other tight for a moment. As she embraced her mother, Audrey looked down at her gold and emerald engagement ring. It might not have been the exact style she would have picked for herself, but now she wouldn't change it for anything. Josh had chosen it for her; that made her love it.

Audrey had decided to walk herself down the aisle this time, and she would not walk at a funeral pace, she would stride toward the altar, confident in where she was headed. She and Josh had chosen every word of the service, every reading and poem, including a passage from Josh's favorite book—*The Hidden Life of Trees*. "Starman" by David Bowie played them out of the church, in honor of Audrey's dad. It all felt so personal, the perfect way to commit to a life together of their own making.

For the reception, they'd found an idyllic venue in the woods, just a ten-minute drive from the church. It was perfect for a small winter gathering. There was a cabin with an open fire, a long trestle table, trees hung with fairy lights, and a firepit surrounded by a circle of cushions and fake-fur rugs. Audrey had set the table herself; it was laden with tapas dishes and decorated with holly, ivy, and red candles. She had decorated each place setting with a hand-drawn map of a constellation and a brown paper bag with an acorn inside. They wanted their guests to plant the acorns somewhere special to them. There was no seating plan; it would be a moveable feast, so that everyone got a chance to talk.

Halfway through the meal, Hillary came to sit between Audrey and Clara.

"What did you tell everyone who didn't get invited to Wedding Take Two, then?" he asked.

"That we couldn't afford to do another one that size. Which is true," said Audrey.

"I don't have to get you two gifts, do I?" Hillary asked, and Audrey shook her head. "Good, because I haven't even gotten you one yet. Oh, I have some exciting news to share. I've been cast as the lead role in the musical version of *The Road* by Cormac McCarthy."

"They're making that into a musical? Wow, that's huge, well done!" said Audrey.

"Thank you. It's incredible, and the best part is that the role doesn't rely on my boyish good looks. It's postapocalyptic, so they want me to be filthy and hideous and close to death. It's a serious, weighty part. My agent says it's going to open so many doors for me."

"Well, I'm happy for you. I can't really envisage that book as a musical, but I'm sure they know what they're doing."

"They're pitching it as *Matilda* meets *The Walking Dead*. It's going to be bigger than *Hamilton*," said Hillary.

"While we're sharing, I have some news too," Clara said. "I'm pregnant. Again."

Audrey turned to her friend and froze, not sure how to react.

"What? Why are you making that face?" Clara asked, frowning at Audrey.

"Wow, no, that's great—if you're happy about it. I just thought having three under two might be, well, suboptimal."

"I'm thrilled." Clara grinned. "I mean yes, it's exhausting, and probably the hardest job I've ever done, but I can't wait to have another one."

"Well, I'm thrilled too then. Congratulations."

"Work is going to kill me. I've only been back five minutes. Plus, I just got that promotion." Clara grimaced.

Jay came over to join them and put his arm around Clara. "She told you? We'll have enough for a band soon." He beamed with a wink.

"It's wonderful news," said Audrey.

"So, I can't believe you actually married Bad Jeans Josh. I guess we're condemned to hang out with the sanctimonious prick forever now, are we?" Jay grinned.

"You are," Audrey said, ruffling Jay's perfectly coiffed hair.

"I better go have a beer with him then. Wind him up about how shit wind farms are. You want him to be all riled up before tonight," Jay said, winking again and then kissing his wife full on the lips.

At the far end of the table, Miranda and Paul were kissing like teenagers. "I think those guys might out-cute you and Josh if you're not careful," said Clara.

"Isn't it great? They're tying the knot in Yorkshire next summer, in Granny Parker's local church. They're having Yorkshire everything, even Yorkshire wine. Paul is competing with me to become the favorite grandchild-in-law, but honestly, he can have that one."

After the food had been cleared away, they all danced around the firepit to the playlist Audrey and Josh had chosen. They didn't do a first dance; they wanted everyone dancing together. Vivien shimmied over to talk to Audrey.

"Are you enjoying yourself, darling?" she asked.

"Immensely," Audrey said. "I know this is only the second wedding I've had, but it's definitely my favorite."

"I have a little news. I didn't want to tell you earlier, I thought it might be somewhat crass to talk divorce just before the service." Vivien pursed her lips in excitement and pulled Audrey to the edge of the dancing circle, away from the music.

"Lawrence has agreed, then?" Audrey asked.

"He won't contest it, especially since he's now shacked up with that Mexican dental assistant in Parsons Green. But that's by the by. The thing is, this new divorce lawyer I've hired, Stephanie—quite the character, makes her own cheese— anyway, she's done a little digging and she suspects my first marriage, to Kosmo in Greece, might not have been properly annulled. The paperwork was missing a signature or some such. Anyway, long story short, if the marriage was never annulled, then technically, none of my other weddings were legal. Stephanie thinks if we track down Kosmo, fill in the missing paperwork, get the annulment completed, then it will be as if I've never been married at all. Isn't that the funniest thing?"

Audrey frowned. It didn't sound all that funny to her. "So you were never married to Dad?"

"No, none of them. Brian thinks it's all most amusing. If Brian and I were to get married next summer, it would be as though it were my first *real* wedding. Say you'll be my matron of honor, darling? We'll have such fun dress shopping and cake tasting. I really do feel in my element planning a wedding. It brings out the best in me."

Audrey gave a noncommittal smile. She wasn't sure if she agreed, but they could have that conversation another time.

～✵～

*A*fter dinner and dancing and a few too many revelations from guests, Josh and Audrey wrapped up warm and took a stroll through the woods, just the two of them. They headed away from the party through to a woodland clearing lit by tiki lights. The moon was high in the sky and the air sharp and clear. Audrey hugged her white fluffy coat around her shoulders, and they had their first dance in silence, just the two of them.

"What's that smell?" Josh asked, leaning into her neck.

"The perfume Miranda made me as a wedding present. It's called Jodrey."

"Not sure about the name, but it smells good. Are you excited about next week?" Josh asked.

"I can't wait," she whispered into his shoulder. They were planning an extended honeymoon. They were going to spend two months in Kielder Forest while Audrey did an Introduction to Astrophotography course at the observatory. Then they were going traveling for a month. Josh had suggested they do it "Audrey style"—stick a pin in a map and see where they ended up.

"I feel like astrophotography is going to be your thing," Josh said into her hair as they slow-danced in the clearing. "What you were meant to do."

"Maybe. I don't know if anything is meant to be, certainly when it comes to love. There could be a million versions of us out there in the multiverse where none of this worked out. Aren't we lucky that we get to live in the world where it did?"

"I'll send back the matching 'soul mate' bracelets I had made as a wedding present then, shall I?" Josh asked, a smile playing on his lips.

"You didn't?" she asked, a flicker of doubt in her eyes.

"No, I didn't. I did get you something, though."

Josh pulled a small velvet bag from his jacket pocket and emptied something into his palm. It was a silver bracelet with a tiny silver acorn charm.

"I love it," she said, holding out her wrist for him to fasten it to.

"I got it for you because I think love is a seed. We choose to plant it, nurture it, and at the end of our lives, if we end up with a glorious old oak tree, with huge branches and plenty of shade, then that's on us, not the cosmos."

"Well, I choose you, James."

"I choose you, Amy. Do you think we got it right this time?" Josh asked, kissing the top of her head and looking back at the small wedding party dancing beside the firepit.

"I do," said Audrey. "I really do."

Epilogue

Fifty Years After I Do

୧ଚ୍ଚ

New Scientist Magazine

Dame Audrey Parker, world-renowned astrophotographer, has been awarded a Lifetime Achievement Award for Services to Science. Parker came to fame when she utilized the Hadron Pale space telescope to capture images of uncharted regions of deep space. Her legacy of photographs, specifically of the Andromeda Galaxy, are groundbreaking in the level of detail they reveal about previously unknown planets and star clusters.

Parker once famously described herself as a "late bloomer." She did not embark on a career in astronomy or astrophotography until her thirties. When asked the secret to her extraordinary success, she often credits her supportive family. While collecting her award at the Royal Observatory last week, she said, "I have always loved to look up. Astronomy helps us understand where we are from and where we are going. It teaches us humility. As my life has progressed, I have been privileged to see further and further out into space, capturing images of many millions of stars. As yet, not one has outshone the love of my life, my guiding light, my husband."

Acknowledgments

This novel was such a jigsaw puzzle to write. As soon as I started thinking about Audrey's story, I knew it was going to be as much about Audrey's past as it was about the wedding day itself—an unpacking of all the emotional baggage she'd been carrying up to this point. As such, the novel naturally evolved to have numerous timelines and became the most complicated edit I've ever done. On more than one occasion, I found myself sitting at my desk with various chapter Post-it notes all over the floor, swearing to myself, "I'm never writing a book with multiple timelines EVER again!" For steering me through this complicated edit, I must thank my editors, Kate Dresser at Putnam and Kim Atkins at Hodder. They both did an amazing job of helping me pull all the strands together to find the heart of Audrey's story.

A huge thank-you to Naz Jahanshahi at Kielder Observatory for fact-checking some of the astronomy references in the book. I am hugely grateful for your time and expertise. I must caveat that any errors or mistakes are entirely my own. I knew nothing about astronomy when I started writing this book, and now find myself looking for the Northern Star whenever the stars are out, so thank you, Audrey, for teaching me something new. Thank you to Reverend Paul White for answering my questions on what would *really* happen if the vicar had a heart attack during a wedding service. Again, I have taken some artistic license here, so any errors are mine, but I appreciate you taking the time to discuss it with the archdeacon!

A few more thank-yous—Traci O'Dea, my brilliant friend and literary sounding board, whom I trust implicitly with a first draft. Bizzy Brooks, who invented the trademarked Sausage Fandango dinners. Alex McGurk, who furnished me with the "nactors" idea after telling me stories from her own childhood. Clare Wallace, my ever-supportive agent, and the phenomenal rights team at Darley Anderson. The Bookstagram community, who have been so supportive of my work, and who have created a little corner of the Internet that still manages to feel kind and uplifting. To all the authors I know online, too many to list here, but who I regard as the most wonderful colleagues. I wish a women's fiction staff room existed in real life and we could spend our tea breaks together.

Finally, to my husband, Tim, to whom this book is dedicated. While Tim is certainly not Josh, he does share a few of his characteristics—he uses deionized water to iron his shirts, he writes a Tripadvisor review after every holiday, and he is *very* good at Excel spreadsheets. I think that behind many creative people there is often a lovely, patient person helping them with their tax return and giving them the space they need to write, paint, think, create, whatever it may be. Tim, I want to thank you for supporting me in everything I do. You are truly the yin to my yang.

Most important, thank you to you, my readers. Thank you for reading, for discussing, for sharing my books—genuinely, where would I be without you. I hope I shall see you again, in the next acknowledgments.

Before I Do

Sophie Cousens

Discussion Guide

PUTNAM
— EST. 1838 —

Discussion Guide

1. From falling church-hanging bats to flying cake ornaments, Audrey experiences a few "bad omens" during her wedding weekend. Out of all the fiascos that occur, which one would be the most disastrous for you, and how would you go about remedying the situation? How would you differentiate a bad omen from a triggering event in this story?

2. Audrey has many interests, hobbies, and jobs, from photography to astronomy to dog walking. Discuss what each interest says about her and what they have in common. How much of Audrey's identity and self-esteem is affected by how she makes a living?

3. When Audrey feels anxious, or feels a panic attack coming on, she often finds comfort in the night sky. What do you think it is about the stars and astronomy that she finds comforting?

4. Audrey feels swept off her feet when she first meets Fred. What do you think Fred sees in Audrey, and how does it contrast with what Josh sees in Audrey?

5. Vivien has been married five times and engaged six. How do you think Vivien's experience of love and marriage might have affected Audrey's outlook on love and her anxiety about her own wedding day?

6. On p. 255, Cousens writes, "She didn't want to listen to the nagging concern that their little universe for two would not be enough." Audrey struggles with the idea that Josh is delightfully different yet may be too different from her. At what point do differences become incompatibility? Do you think opposites attract?

7. If you were Clara, and Audrey were your best friend, what advice would you give about her Josh-versus-Fred dilemma? What experiences of your own would you draw from to help Audrey make the "right" decision, if there is one?

8. Despite the love Vivien and Audrey have for each other, personal obstacles cause mother and daughter to grow apart. Why do you think this distance is so difficult to reconcile, on both ends?

9. Sarcasm, teasing, and banter mark many of Audrey's interactions, both romantic and platonic. Using an example from the book, discuss whether you think quips and jests can foster a sense of intimacy, and why.

10. Audrey depends on her friends Hillary, Clara, and Paul as found family; though they try to support her on her big day, how do her friends' dramas and anxieties contribute to her own doubts and concerns?

11. How did the events of the weekend six years before the wedding influence the trajectory of Audrey's life? Which had more life-changing significance—meeting Fred, or the morning in the gallery with Benedict and the ensuing fallout?

12. Hiding spots, secret meetings, and intrusive thoughts all heighten Audrey's wedding angst. Do you agree with how Audrey handled herself throughout the wedding weekend? What would you have done in the same circumstances?

13. Cousens illustrates the complexities of many kinds of relationships in *Before I Do*. Which characters' dating story did you find the most romantic? Why?

14. How does *Before I Do* illustrate the essence of love alongside the role of fate versus choice? Do you think we choose who to love, or that fate chooses for us?

About the Author

Sophie Cousens worked as a TV producer in London for more than twelve years and now lives with her family on the island of Jersey, one of the Channel Islands, located off the north coast of France. She balances her writing career with taking care of her two small children, and longs for the day when she might have a dachshund and a writing shed of her own. She is the author of *This Time Next Year* and *Just Haven't Met You Yet*.

Putnam/US team

Kate Dresser—Editor

Shina Patel—Marketer

Kristen Bianco—Publicist

Tarini Sipahimalani—Editorial assistant

Sanny Chiu—Jacket designer

Anthony Ramondo—Art director

Sally Kim—Publisher

Ashley McClay—Marketing director

Alexis Welby—Publicity director

Emily Mileham—Senior managing editor

Maija Baldauf—Managing editor

Hannah Dragone—Production manager

Erica Rose—Production editor

Tiffany Estreicher—Design director

Elke Sigal—Interior designer